**The Fatal Series by Marie Force**

**Now available in ebook**

**Suggested reading order**

**And stay tuned for *Fatal Frenzy*, the next book
in the Fatal Series from Marie Force**

**Coming in ebook Fall 2015
Available in print Spring 2016**

## Praise for the Fatal Series
## by *New York Times* bestselling author Marie Force

"Sam is a fun, strong character about whom readers will want to know more. Her relationship with Nick is spicy and realistic. The mystery is well constructed and forms a solid base around which all the other events revolve."

—*Library Journal* on *Fatal Jeopardy*

"The romance, the mystery, the ongoing story lines...everything about these books has me sitting on the edge of my seat and begging for more. I am anxiously awaiting the next in the series. I give *Fatal Deception* an A."

—*TheBookPushers.com*

"The suspense is thick, the passion between Nick and Sam just keeps getting hotter and hotter."

—*Guilty Pleasures Book Reviews* on *Fatal Deception*

"Force pushes the boundaries by deftly using political issues like immigration to create an intricate mystery."

—*RT Book Reviews* on *Fatal Consequences* (4 stars)

"Force's skill is also evident in the way that she develops the characters, from the murdered and mutilated senator to the detective and chief of staff who are trying to solve the case. The heroine, Sam, is especially complex and her secrets add depth to this mystery... This novel is *The O.C.* does D.C., and you just can't get enough."

—*RT Book Reviews* on *Fatal Affair* (4.5 stars)

# MARIE FORCE

# FATAL
*jeopardy*

**Book Seven of the Fatal Series**

**BONUS CONTENT INCLUDED**

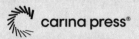

carina press®

If you purchased this book without a cover you should be aware
that this book is stolen property. It was reported as "unsold and
destroyed" to the publisher, and neither the author nor the
publisher has received any payment for this "stripped book."

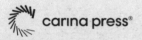

carina press®

ISBN-13: 978-0-373-00272-6

Fatal Jeopardy

Copyright © 2014 by HTJB, Inc.

Cover Image: Randy Santos

Recycling programs
for this product may
not exist in your area.

All rights reserved. Except for use in any review, the reproduction or
utilization of this work in whole or in part in any form by any electronic,
mechanical or other means, now known or hereinafter invented, including
xerography, photocopying and recording, or in any information storage
or retrieval system, is forbidden without the written permission of the
publisher, Harlequin Enterprises Limited, 225 Duncan Mill Road,
Don Mills, Ontario M3B 3K9, Canada.

This is a work of fiction. Names, characters, places and incidents are
either the product of the author's imagination or are used fictitiously,
and any resemblance to actual persons, living or dead, business
establishments, events or locales is entirely coincidental.

This edition published by arrangement with Harlequin Books S.A.

® and TM are trademarks of the publisher. Trademarks indicated with
® are registered in the United States Patent and Trademark Office, the
Canadian Intellectual Property Office and in other countries.

www.CarinaPress.com

**Printed in U.S.A.**

For Dan, Emily & Jake, who make my world go round.

# FATAL JEOPARDY

## Book Seven of the Fatal Series

# ONE

THE GAME WHIZZED by so quickly Sam could barely keep up. Next to her, Scotty bounced with excitement as they watched Nick fly around on the ice with skill and stamina that astounded her. Although she shouldn't be surprised he was so good. Not only had he played hockey for years when he was younger but he regularly demonstrated his stamina in other important ways.

Chuckling at her own joke, Sam tried to keep her eyes on his white helmet and green jersey with number 22 on the back. With the campaign over and the election won, he had time now to rejoin the men's league he'd played in before his life took an unexpected turn almost a year ago.

That's when his best friend and boss, Senator John O'Connor, had been murdered. From that awful tragedy had come two interesting things—their relationship and his ascendancy into the Senate, where he now held the seat from Virginia in his own right after a resounding win in the election.

"He's so good," Scotty said, dazzled by Nick's skill on the ice. "I'll never be that good."

Sam hooked her arm around the twelve-year-old she and Nick were adopting out of state custody in Virginia and brought him close enough to drop a kiss on the top of his head. "Sure you will. Keep working hard and do what Nick tells you, and you'll be up to speed in no time."

"I don't know," Scotty said hesitantly, his eyes fixed on Nick. "All the other kids are way better than me."

That's because they'd been skating and playing hockey for as long as they could walk, while Scotty had been well cared for but without the frills and extras most kids took for granted. "I have faith in you, and in Nick. If you guys keep practicing as much as you have been lately, you'll catch up."

Nick had spared no expense in outfitting Scotty with top-of-the-line hockey skates and all the required protective equipment. Sam had joked that the hockey bag was bigger than the kid, but Nick had assured her it was no bigger than anyone else's. Hockey, she was learning, took a tremendous amount of time, equipment and money—not to mention the warmest coat she owned whenever she ventured into the ice rink.

"I hope you're right," Scotty said.

"I'm always right."

That drew an expected snort of laughter from the boy. "And totally full of yourself."

Sam tightened her arm around him into a headlock that made him laugh even harder.

They froze when Nick was checked—hard—into the boards and went down in a boneless pile on the ice.

Sam gasped and would've left the stands to get closer to him, but Scotty held her back.

"Don't. He wouldn't want you to make a thing of it in front of the guys."

When had he gotten so wise about such things? With her eyes riveted to the ice, she waited breathlessly for any sign of movement from her husband. All she could think about was her dad and the egregious gunshot injury he'd suffered nearly three years ago, which had left him a quadriplegic.

The coach and several other players huddled around Nick, making it impossible for Sam to see what was happening. One of the other wives sent her a sympathetic glance that set her nerves even further on edge. "Come on, come on," she whispered. "Get up."

Scotty's hand curled around her arm, and Sam wasn't sure if he was giving comfort or taking it.

After what seemed like an hour had passed, the other players and coaches moved back and one of them helped Nick to his feet. Everyone in the stands applauded as he made his way—slowly—to the bench. It was killing her not to know what he'd hurt or whether it was serious, but at least she could breathe again watching him glide over the ice with coaches on either side of him.

He was moving, and that's what mattered.

Sam blew out a deep breath. "Well, that was fun. When can we do this again?"

"Don't be such a worrywart, Sam. Guys get banged up playing hockey. We don't want to be treated like babies."

"Is that right?"

"Nick will probably be mad that he got checked out of the game, so I wouldn't say anything about it if I were you."

"Now I'm taking marriage advice from a twelve-year-old?"

"Soon-to-be thirteen-year-old," he replied with the engaging grin she and Nick had loved from the start.

"Ahhh, so I've heard. I suppose I have to get a cake or something, huh?"

He rolled his eyes at her. "Mrs. L got me an ice cream

cake every year," he said of his former guardian at the state home. "That's my favorite."

"I can't compete with Mrs. L. I'm sure to mess this up in some important way. You know that, right?"

"You don't have to compete with anyone. You and Nick have given me everything. I don't need an ice cream cake."

The kid was too damned much. Sam put both arms around him. Her usual rules of public displays of affection absolutely did not apply to the son she loved beyond reason. "You've given us so much more than we could ever give you."

"Doubtful," he said in the dry tone she'd come to anticipate.

Sam kept an arm around him until the game came to an end and she could go check on Nick—without making a fuss, of course. She wouldn't want to be accused of hovering or any other unsavory "girl" thing.

They waited for him outside the locker room with several of the other spouses and family members. He was one of the last to come out, his hair damp with sweat, his face red from exertion and pinched with pain. It was all she could do not to run to him, but she heeded Scotty's advice and hung back until he joined them.

"Awesome game," Scotty said, beaming up at Nick. "You're so good! You've never skated like that when we practice."

His smile more of a grimace, Nick mussed Scotty's hair. "Because that's about you, not me." He glanced at Sam, who could tell with one look he was in pain and trying hard to hide it from them. "Who's up for pizza?"

"Me!" Scotty said. "But can I get a hot chocolate first?"

"Sure, you can." Sam handed him a five-dollar bill

and watched him run toward the concession stand. A couple of months ago he never would've asked them for anything. They'd been working on that, trying to get him to act like other kids who were constantly asking their parents for money and other things. Scotty would never be like other kids, but Sam took the request for hot chocolate as a good sign that he was beginning to get the message that what was theirs was also his.

She glanced up at Nick. "What'd you hurt?"

"Smacked the rib I broke last winter and got the wind knocked out of me."

Sam winced. "The same rib that took forever to heal?"

"That'd be the one."

"We should hit the ER on the way home."

"No need. It's just a bruise."

Sam gave him her best cop stare. "What would you say if it were me telling you it was 'just a bruise'?"

To his credit, he had the good sense to squirm under her glare. "I, um…"

"We'll drop Scotty at Dad and Celia's on the way to the ER."

"After the pizza. I'm starving."

Scotty rejoined them, carrying a steaming cup of hot chocolate with a huge dollop of whipped cream on top. "Looks like someone is having dessert before dinner," Sam said.

Scotty handed over the change without being prompted. "Don't worry. I'll still eat a ton of pizza." With his free hand, he reached for Nick's hockey bag and started toward the door, the bag rolling behind him. Over his shoulder, he said, "I'll get this, but only cuz you're injured."

"Thanks, buddy." Leaning in close to Sam, Nick said,

"I make him take care of and carry his own equipment. Never too soon to learn that lesson."

As they made their way through the crowded rink, Sam noticed people watching them with a mix of curiosity and envy. The curiosity stemmed from the high-profile lives they led. The envy came from the women, who took extra-long looks at Nick. He was even hotter than usual with his cheeks red from the cold and the workout and his hair mussed from the helmet.

Feeling possessive of what was hers, Sam curled her hand around his arm, and then smiled with satisfaction when he raised his arm, put it around her and brought her in tight against his uninjured side. She knew a rare moment of complete contentment with her husband's arm around her, their son walking in front of them and a full week off to spend together before they confronted the looming reality of her dad's surgery.

*Let them all look,* she thought as a group of women stopped talking to watch him go by, one of them actually having the nerve to lick her lips. *He's all mine.* The funny thing was, if you could call it funny, he didn't even notice the women checking him out. His gaze was fixed firmly on Scotty, watching over the boy as always.

Snuggled up to him, Sam could tell he was favoring his left side, which meant he was probably more injured than he was letting on. She withdrew her phone from her jacket pocket, looked for their friend Harry's phone number in her contacts and put through the call before Nick noticed.

"Hi there," Sam said when Harry answered. "Am I getting you at a bad time?"

"Not at all. What's up?"

"Your buddy Nick took a hard hit to the left side during a hockey game just now, in the same neighborhood as the earlier rib fracture. I was wondering if you might be able to meet us at the ER in about ninety minutes or so."

"Why the delay?"

"I'm told I have to feed him first."

Nick scowled playfully down at her, but she could see the pain reflected in his hazel eyes.

"Tell him to be careful," Harry said. "I doubt he wants to go through another collapsed lung."

"No chance of that," Nick said, speaking toward the phone so Harry could hear him.

"See you in an hour and a half," Harry said.

"Thanks, Harry."

"No problem. You two are enough on your own to keep me in business."

"Hardy har-har." Harry was still laughing when she closed the phone and stashed it in her pocket. "Always a comedian, that one."

When they reached Nick's black BMW, he held the passenger door for her.

"No way, buster. You're not driving. Get in."

"I'll remember this the next time you have blood streaming down your face and tell me you're fine and don't need a doctor." This was said as he moved gingerly into the car.

Scotty snorted behind his hand and got into the backseat after stashing Nick's hockey bag and stick in the trunk.

"I heard that," Sam said to Scotty when she got into the driver's seat. She loved driving Nick's car. It was like a vacation from her basic, boring department car. When she punched the accelerator in his car, things happened.

They went for pizza at the same place Nick had taken

her when they first got together during the O'Connor investigation. As soon as they were seated, he reached for
her hand under the table and winked at her, reminding
her of the night they'd held hands under the cover of the
tablecloth when their relationship was still the best-kept
secret in Washington.

Back then, being seen holding hands with him in public would've put her career in jeopardy. Now she could
touch him and kiss him and sleep with him and live with
him and be with him any time she wanted. How far they'd
come in eleven months. He glanced at her, and she knew
he was also thinking of the first time they'd come here
together and how much had changed since then.

He gave her hand a squeeze that had her leaning her
head on his shoulder, proud to make a public declara-
tion of her love for him—as long as there were no cops
in sight. Her PDA rules when it came to her colleagues
were still quite stringent.

After Scotty and Nick polished off a large and a small
pizza while Sam stuck to salad, they dropped Scotty at
her dad's house, three doors down from their place on
Ninth Street.

"We're apt to be a while at the ER," Sam said, "so
we'll see you in the morning. Okay?"

"That's fine," Scotty said. "Abby and Ethan are sleeping over too. We'll have fun."

"Enjoy the cousin time, buddy," Nick said.

"Hope your ribs are okay, Nick. Will you guys text
me and let me know what Harry says?"

"We sure will," Nick said. "It's nothing like the last
time, so nothing to worry about."

"Okay."

Sam watched Scotty scamper up the ramp and into

Skip and Celia's house, where he was a daily visitor. Scotty and her dad had become fast friends and could talk for hours about everything and nothing. Sam loved watching the two of them together, and she adored Scotty even more for making Skip an important part of his new life.

"The boy is becoming very comfortable in his new world," Nick said as Sam pulled away from the curb and headed for the George Washington University Hospital on 23rd Street, where she was a frequent flyer.

"I was just thinking the same thing as I watched him go busting into Skip's place like he owns the joint."

"I love that."

"So do I," Sam said. "What's the latest from Andy on the adoption? I'll be happy when it's signed, sealed and delivered."

"I will too. I expect to talk to him early this week about a few things, and that's number one on my list."

"He's been a huge help to Gonzo on the custody situation with Alex. I can't believe that's going to court on Thanksgiving week, of all times. I sure hope it goes his way. I don't even want to think about the alternative."

"I'm sure it'll be fine," Nick said. "The fact that he's had custody all this time has to count for something."

"I hope so." Baby Alex had come into Detective Tommy "Gonzo" Gonzales's life last winter when a woman from Gonzo's past let him know he'd fathered a child. Now the child's mother was back in the picture, her drug problem rehabbed and her scumbag boyfriend out of the picture. Sam would never let on to Gonzo that she was worried about the baby's mom getting custody after all the effort she'd put into changing her life.

At the hospital's Emergency entrance, Nick insisted

he was capable of walking in with her and didn't need to be dropped off.

"I'm going to remember all of this the next time I'm the one who's injured. You're a terrible patient."

"Like you have any room to talk about being a terrible patient," he said with a scoff. "I'm totally fine. You're totally overreacting, and this is me humoring you. You might want to try it sometime. It's really good for marital tranquility."

"If you weren't already injured I might be tempted to punch you for using the H word. No one *humors* me."

"If that's what you want to believe, my love, have at it."

Sam was still scowling at him when they entered the ER through automatic doors that swept them into the madhouse that was the waiting room. She was doubly glad she'd called ahead when she saw Harry waiting for them at the check-in desk.

As he waved them in, she saw Nick hesitate. No doubt he was considering how it would look to the scores of people waiting their turn when they walked right in, which was yet another downside to being recognized everywhere they went.

"Glad to see you guys," Harry said jovially—and loudly. "I've got those forms you need in my office. Right this way."

"Very smooth, Dr. Flynn," Sam said with a smile for their good friend.

"Extremely smooth," Nick added. "Thank you."

"I know how our resident politician thinks," Harry said as he escorted them into an exam room. "Now let's see the boo-boo so we can all go home."

With a roll of his eyes for his friend, Nick took off

his coat and reached for the hem of his long-sleeved polo shirt.

Judging by the way he moved, Sam could tell he was in real pain, and when he revealed his chest, she could see why. She gasped at the angry purple bruises already decorating his left side. "Holy shit! I never would've taken you for pizza if I'd seen that!"

"It's fine, babe. It looks worse than it feels. I swear." Harry leaned in for a closer look, then gently pressed against Nick's side, drawing a sharp intake of air from him. "It's going to require an X-ray to make sure nothing's broken. I'll get that going. Be right back."

When they were alone, Sam said, "Just for the record, you totally downplayed this, and you won't do that again. Got me?"

He smiled and reached for her from his perch on the exam table. "Come here."

"I don't want to. I'm mad at you."

"Samantha... I need you."

"Oh, now, don't do that! I'm trying to be extremely pissed with you."

"Please?"

Staring at the handsome face she loved more than life itself, she stepped into his outstretched arms.

"That's much better," he said.

"Why are you comforting me when you're the one who's hurt?"

"Because I know from lots and lots and *lots* of experience that it's harder to see the one you love get hurt than it is to be hurt yourself."

Sam released a dramatic sigh. "You do that on purpose, don't you?"

"Do what?"

"Say things to make me all fluttery when I want to be so mad with you."

His quiet chuckle made her smile as she made herself comfortable in his arms—her favorite place to be. "Do you two *ever* give it a rest?" Harry asked when he returned to find them wrapped up in each other.

"As infrequently as we possibly can," Nick said. "We're on vacation this week, so leave us alone."

"I'll be happy to leave you alone as soon as I get some film on those ribs." A nurse came into the room, pushing a wheelchair.

Nick groaned in protest. "I don't need that."

"Hospital policy," Sam and Harry said in stereo.

"She ought to know," Harry said, pointing his thumb at Sam.

They cajoled Nick into the wheelchair, and Harry got them in and out of X-ray in record time. By the time he returned to the wheelchair for the ride back to the ER, Nick was sweating and obviously breathing through the pain of being twisted and turned on the table.

"Worse than advertised," Sam declared.

"No, it isn't."

"Yes, it is."

"Now, children, don't bicker," Harry said. "The proof is in the films." Back in the exam room, he popped the X-rays into a light box and took a close-up look at Nick's ribs. "I don't see any sign of a fracture this time around." He pointed to a shaded area. "That's where the earlier break was, but it's healed up nicely. I declare this latest injury a bad bruise and order you to take it easy for the next week. I'll prescribe something for the pain."

"Taking it easy is very doable," Nick said with a smug smile for Sam. "That's the plan for this week anyway."

"Excellent." Harry shut off the light box. "I'd recommend staying off the ice for a couple of weeks too. It might be time to admit you aren't as young as you used to be."

"Hey! I'm not even thirty-seven yet!"

"Soon enough, my friend." To Sam, Harry said, "Keep him quiet for the next week to ten days."

"There goes my all-sex-all-the-time plan for the vacation," she said with a pout that made both men laugh.

"You can do all the work, babe."

"On that note," Harry said, signing a form and handing it to Sam along with a prescription for pain meds, "you're released. Call me if anything starts to seriously hurt, and don't delay for pizza or anything else. Got me?"

"Yes, sir," Nick said. "Let's get together with the boys this week. It's been too long."

"I'd love to."

"Thanks for coming in special for us," Sam said.

Harry kissed her cheek on the way by. "Anything for you guys."

Sam helped Nick back into his shirt and coat and took hold of his hand on the way to the car. She held the door for him and waited until he was settled to go around to the driver's side.

"I hate to say I told you so, babe, but…"

Sam glanced at him. "In this case, I don't mind being wrong. We've had enough serious injuries over the last year to last us a lifetime. I'm fine with a bad bruise, and I'll be sure to kiss it better every chance I get this week."

"Is that right?"

"Uh-huh."

"That almost makes getting hurt worth it. I'm picturing a lot of time on my back watching you do what you do best."

"You have such a dirty mind, Senator," she said with a laugh.

"You inspire me. Speaking of inspiration, the boy is at Skip's tonight, so we can be loud like the old days."

"There'll be none of that tonight. You're injured."

"Yes, there will. Harry said I'm fine."

"He said you have to take it easy."

"I will take it easy. I'll let you have your wicked way with me."

The "argument" continued at the pharmacy while they waited for his prescription to be filled. At home, Sam parked at the curb outside their house and held the passenger door for him. As they walked up the ramp to their house they stopped short at the sight of a bundle on the stoop.

"What the hell?" Sam said.

Nick used the flashlight app on his smartphone to shine some light on the area. The "bundle" let out a moan, making them startle. "Is that blood?"

Sam dropped to her knees and leaned in for a closer look. She pushed dark hair back off the face and cried out in dismay when she recognized the girl underneath all the blood and bruises. "Oh my God! It's Brooke!"

# TWO

"CALL NINE-ONE-ONE." SAM lifted the thin sheet that covered her niece and discovered she was naked underneath. "Holy shit," she whispered as Brooke shivered uncontrollably, and Sam tried to identify the source of the blood using only her hands to guide her. When she couldn't find any sign of an open wound upon a quick check of the areas she could reach without moving her, Sam whipped off her own coat and put it over her niece, who smelled of booze and vomit.

"Brooke, it's Auntie Sam. Can you hear me? Say something." In the background, Sam was aware of Nick calling for an ambulance and a follow-up call to Harry, telling him to get back to the hospital ASAP.

"It's Sam's niece," she heard him say over the roar of her own heart, which seemed to be beating in her ears. "We found her bloody and unconscious on our front stoop when we got home."

"Will you turn on the porch light and get some blankets?" Sam said when Nick ended the call with Harry. "I have to call Tracy." Sam's mind was racing almost as fast as her heart was pounding. In the span of minutes, she came up with what felt like a million questions.

"Can we move her inside?"

"No. We shouldn't move her until the paramedics get here. What's taking so long?"

"I'll get the blankets and call Tracy. What should I tell her?"

"That Brooke is here and not feeling well. Tell her to meet us at the GW ER."

The porch light came on, and Sam winced at the sight of Brooke's bruised and swollen face. "God, what happened to you, and where the hell are the paramedics?" In the distance she finally heard the sound of sirens getting closer. "Hang in there, honey."

Nick came out with a couple of blankets. "Tracy's freaking out. She wanted to come here, but I told her to go to the hospital. Mike is with her, and he's going to drive."

Sam nodded and helped him cover Brooke with the blankets.

"Where's all the blood coming from?" Nick asked.

"I can't tell, and I'm afraid to move her." Sam pulled her cell phone from her pocket and realized her hands were shaking when she couldn't make them cooperate to call her partner.

Nick took the phone from her. "Who do you want?"

"Freddie."

Nick put through the call and handed the phone to her.

"We're on vacation," Freddie said with a sleepy-sounding groan.

"I need you."

"What's wrong?" he asked, immediately on alert. Sam quickly filled him in on what was going on.

"I need someone to canvas my neighborhood to see if we can figure out how she got here. And I need someone who isn't going to blab all over town that my niece was found naked and bleeding on my doorstep. I need *you, Freddie.*"

"I'm coming. Of course I'm coming. I'll get Gonzo too. If there's anything to find, we'll find it."

"Keep it between us for now. I'll pay you out of my own pocket if need be."

"For you, we'd do it for nothing, and you know it."

"Thank you," she said, her voice breaking on the words.

"I'll be in touch."

Nick put his arm around Sam. "She's alive, and that's all that matters. We'll figure out the rest."

Sam gave herself one second to appreciate the comfort only he could provide. Then the ambulance arrived in a flash of color and noise, followed by a fire truck that lit up Ninth Street.

"Stay with her," Sam said to Nick as she went down to the sidewalk to stop the patrolman who'd arrived with the ambulance from going up the ramp. "I've got this."

"Oh, Lieutenant Holland. I didn't recognize you in the dark. Are you sure everything is okay?"

"I'm sure. You can take off and file a not-needed report."

"Oh, um, okay."

"What've you got, Lieutenant?" the lead paramedic asked as he rushed up the ramp with Sam, who shot a glance over her shoulder to make sure the patrolman was heeding her orders.

Sam recognized the paramedic and gave him all the information she had at the moment. "She's my niece," she said quietly. "If you could use all the discretion you have at your disposal, I'd consider myself in your debt."

"Yes, ma'am. I understand, but you're going to have to back up and let us get to her."

"Come on, babe." Nick took Sam's hand and drew her back from Brooke. "Let them take care of her."

"Sam! Nick! What's going on?" Sam's stepmother, Celia, came rushing up the ramp Nick had had built to allow Sam's dad to come visit in his wheelchair.

Sam left Nick's embrace to meet her stepmother halfway up the ramp and led her back down to the sidewalk. "It's Brooke."

"What? What's she doing here? I thought she was in school in Virginia."

"I did too. I don't know anything yet beyond the fact that we found her here, wrapped in only a sheet with blood all over her."

"Oh, God. Is she going to be all right? Have you talked to Tracy?"

"Yes, she's meeting us at the hospital. Scotty said Abby and Ethan are at your house," Sam said of Tracy's younger children. "Will you keep them until we know more?"

"Yes, of course. I'll keep all of them. Scotty too."

"Thanks, Celia."

The paramedics came down the ramp with Brooke on a gurney. Nick followed them and met Sam on the sidewalk. "They said we can ride with her."

Thinking of his injury, she said, "You don't have to—"

"Don't finish that thought, Samantha. She's my niece too. Let's go."

"I'll be here with the kids," Celia said. "Let us know as soon as you hear anything."

"We will," Nick said for both of them.

Sam and Nick got into the back of the ambulance and sat on the cot on the other side from where two paramedics were assessing Brooke's condition.

"Can't figure out where all this blood is coming from," one of them said.

"Might not be hers," the other one said. To Sam, he said, "Does she do drugs?"

"No!" But as the word burst forth from her lips, Sam realized she honestly didn't know if Brooke did drugs. Her niece had become someone totally unrecognizable in the last year, and her parents had recently sent her to a special school in Virginia, hoping to separate her from the friends who'd been a bad influence on her. "At least I don't think so."

"She's definitely on something."

Sam felt like she was coming out of her skin. The idea of her sweet baby Brooke willingly taking drugs was something she couldn't bear to wrap her head around.

Nick's hand on her leg provided a much-needed slice of calm as Sam watched the paramedics work to stabilize Brooke.

"What're you giving her?" Sam asked as they started an IV.

"Narcan. It'll offset the effects of whatever she's on. If it was an opiate, it'll work. If it wasn't, it won't, which will tell us more about what she might've taken."

"I thought she was in Virginia," Nick said quietly as he watched the paramedics insert a needle into Brooke's hand. She never stirred.

"So did I. Trace was going tomorrow to pick her up for Thanksgiving, which is why Dad and Celia had the kids. She and Mike were leaving early in the morning."

"So what's Brooke doing in the District tonight, and where do the people at the school you all paid so much money to send her think she is right now?"

"That's a very good question," Sam said. "And one

I'll be tackling the minute we know she's okay. I'd also love to know how she ended up at our place."

"Me too." His gaze was fixed on Brooke. "This is the stuff that scares the shit out of me as a parent."

"Yeah." As she stared at Brooke's bruised and blood-ied face, Sam tried to imagine her adorable Scotty as a surly seventeen-year-old who took drugs and ran away from school. In her wildest dreams, she couldn't see Scotty becoming that kid. But then again, she never would've expected it of Brooke either.

Well, that wasn't entirely true. Brooke had been born with a bit of a chip on her shoulder, and had been a source of constant strain in Tracy's family. Brooke's biological father had hit the road the minute he learned Tracy was pregnant, and they'd never heard from him again. Maybe knowing one of her parents hadn't wanted anything to do with her was responsible for the chip.

Tracy's husband, Mike, had come along when Brooke was a toddler and had raised the girl as his own along with Abby and Ethan, the children he and Tracy had to-gether. Mike had recently laid down an ultimatum where Brooke was concerned... He no longer wanted Abby and Ethan living in the same home as their wild and uncon-trollable older sister.

Sam had given them the money to send Brooke to the strict boarding school in Virginia, which had been somewhat of a last-resort measure. They'd pinned their hopes—and a lot of money—on the school's track record of turning around troubled girls.

Sam blew out a deep breath as a staggering array of questions cycled through her mind.

They arrived at the hospital, and the paramedics whisked Brooke inside. Sam and Nick followed behind them. She wasn't surprised to find her other sister, Angela, waiting with Tracy and Mike. When Tracy tried to follow Brooke into the exam room, the nurses stopped her and asked her to wait outside.

Sam wrapped an arm around her older sister.

"I don't understand," Tracy said between sobs. "What's she even doing here?"

"That's what I'd like to know too," Sam said.

"I'm going to call the school," Mike said.

"Do me a favor and hold off on that," Sam said. "I'd like to attack this entire situation the same way I would an investigation. I'd rather they not be tipped off before I can approach them as a cop."

Mike thought about that for a second and then nodded. "Okay."

"Let's focus on Brooke right now and whatever she needs," Sam said. "I promise I'll get to the bottom of what went on tonight as soon as we know she's going to be all right."

A nurse appeared then with forms for Tracy to sign that gave consent for treatment and provided insurance information.

While Tracy and Mike dealt with the forms, Angela approached Sam. "What. The. Hell."

"I don't know. I just don't know."

"How'd she get to your house?"

"I don't know that either."

Angela, who'd given birth to her second child, a girl named Ella, a few months ago, shuddered. "What has she gotten herself into?"

"The paramedics said she was definitely on something."

"God… Poor Tracy. This'll kill her. After all she's done for that kid…"

Nick came up behind Sam and rested his hands on her shoulders.

"You should be off your feet," she said.

"What's wrong with you?" Angela asked her brother-in-law.

"He took a hard hit in a hockey game earlier," Sam said. "We've already been here once tonight."

"I'm fine," Nick said. "Don't worry about me."

"I am worried about you, and you need to sit."

"I'm sitting," Nick said, easing into a chair. "Happy?" Sam nodded. "Now stay there."

A doctor came through the double doors looking for Brooke's parents.

Tracy gestured Sam and Angela over to her. "This is my sister, Sam Holland, and my other sister, Angela Radcliffe."

The doctor nodded to Sam. "I thought I recognized you."

"We don't understand how any of this could've happened," Tracy said, her eyes welling with new tears. "Brooke was supposed to be at school in Virginia."

"I can't answer those questions," the doctor said, "but the tox screen came back positive for methamphetamines. We're waiting for more info from the lab. Based on her lack of consciousness, we suspect it's some form of Molly, but we also think there might've been GHB involved too."

"The date rape drug," Sam said, her heart sinking at that news. If she'd been given GHB, Brooke would have very little memory of what'd happened to her.

"Right. We've also inserted an NG tube to administer

active charcoal, which will neutralize the effect of the methamphetamines. We've inserted a Foley catheter to monitor her urine output, as well. Our biggest concern at the moment is hyperthermia, or potential heat stroke."

Mike kept an arm around Tracy as they absorbed each bit of information. "*Heat* stroke?" he asked.

"It's a side effect of the drug, which raised her core body temperature to nearly 105 degrees. We're working to cool her and lower her temperature, internally via chilled saline as well as externally with ice packs. She was briefly conscious and extremely paranoid about what we were doing to her, where she was and why she was naked. But she couldn't tell us what she took or what happened."

"What about the blood that was all over her?" Sam asked.

"We suspect most of it isn't hers. We've been unable to find any open wound that would account for that much blood. However… We're going to do a rape exam as there's indication of sexual activity."

Only Mike's arm around Tracy kept her from collapsing at that news.

"What kind of indication?" Sam asked, fighting through her own need for hysteria.

"When one of the nurses was putting in the catheter she noticed bruising. Upon further examination, we confirmed vaginal bruising, tearing and fluid consistent with intense sexual activity. Only she can say for certain whether it was an assault, but chances are she won't remember due to the GHB."

Tracy broke down into heartbroken sobs while Sam fought a violent battle to keep from doing the same.

"I'll be back to talk to you when we know more."

"When can we see her?" Angela asked.

"As soon as we get her stabilized and do the rape kit."

"Our family doctor, Harry Flynn, is on his way to consult," Sam said.

"Of course," the doctor said. "No problem. We'll keep you informed."

Sam's cell phone rang, and she checked the caller ID where Freddie's name was lit up. "What've you got?"

"Nothing on the canvas, but we just heard Dispatch call Carlucci and Dominguez to a homicide up on Mac-Arthur Boulevard Northwest. From what we heard, someone went sick on a bunch of teenagers with a knife."

The news struck Sam in a pang of fear that landed right below her heart.

"What do you want us to do? Continue the canvas or help them out?"

Sam's brain refused to process the staggering array of implications that came with this news.

"Get up there and see what they've got. I can't leave here, so keep me posted."

"Will do."

"Freddie."

"Yeah?"

"Do you think... I mean, this thing with Brooke... Is it related?"

"We have no way to know that, Sam, so don't go there. Not yet."

"You're right. Okay, call me as soon as you know anything."

"I will."

The line went dead and she stashed the phone in her pocket and took a seat next to Nick.

"What was that about?"

"Homicide on MacArthur Boulevard. A bunch of teenagers were attacked with what looks to be a knife." Nick's eyes widened as the implications hit him too.

"Oh, Jesus. Do you think it's related?"

"I don't know, but… It would be an awfully big coincidence if it wasn't." Saying the words out loud filled Sam with an overwhelming sense of foreboding—and fear.

FREDDIE AND GONZO arrived at the scene on MacArthur Boulevard and had to park on the next street over due to the emergency vehicles blocking the street. Flashing their badges to the Patrol officer guarding the yellow crime scene tape, they ducked under it and made for the front door of a fancy brick townhouse in an exclusive development.

"Nice place," Freddie muttered.

"No kidding. Outta my price range."

Inside, Dominguez and Carlucci were working a grisly scene in the basement family room. There were six bodies, all of them naked and most of them murdered while in the midst of a sex act. They were in pairs in three different areas of the big room.

"What the…" Gonzo's voice trailed off midsentence. "Is this what kids are doing for fun these days?"

"That's what we said too," Dani Carlucci replied. She was tall, blonde and stacked, not that Freddie noticed such things. No sir, not when he had the incredibly gorgeous Elin at home in his bed. Dani's partner, Gigi Dominguez, was a shrimp next to her Amazon-like partner, but every bit as gorgeous with dark hair and olive-toned skin.

"What've we got so far?" Gonzo asked. He'd recently been promoted to detective sergeant, which made him the ranking officer on the scene.

Carlucci consulted her notebook. "The home is owned by William and Marissa Springer. According to the maid, who is upstairs with Patrol, the parents are at their home in Aspen this weekend. The maid confirmed their seventeen-year-old son, Hugo, is among the victims." Carlucci pointed to a young man with dark hair and a trim, muscular build who'd been repeatedly stabbed in the back while having intercourse with a female victim, who was dead under him on one of the sofas.

"We found drug paraphernalia and all kinds of booze," Carlucci continued, gesturing to a pool table that was covered with bottles and pipes and pills. Clothes and cups and bottles were also all over the floor and furniture. "We think they were all so out of it and caught up in the sex that they never saw the attack coming."

"What I want to know," Freddie said, "is how you can kill this many people, with a knife, and not have the others hear the first ones being killed."

"They were high and drunk and getting laid and not paying attention," Dominguez said bluntly. "Plus the maid said most of the lights were off and the music was blasting when she got home, so whatever happened occurred mostly in the dark."

"Any sign of forced entry?" Gonzo asked.

"Not that we could see at any of the doors, and all the first-floor windows are locked," Carlucci replied.

"So it could've been someone who was at the party," Freddie said, his heart heavy with the task that lay ahead of notifying parents. Dealing with victims' families was one of the most difficult parts of a difficult job, especially when young people were involved.

"We called Dr. McNamara in on this one and requested she bring help," Carlucci said of the District's chief medical examiner, who usually relied on deputies to cover for her on weekends. "And Crime Scene is on the way."

"The owners of the home have been notified?" Gonzo asked.

"Yes, the maid gave us their number, and we called them," Dominguez said. "It was horrible."

"Wonder what they were thinking leaving their seventeen-year-old son home alone," Freddie said.

"Apparently, they didn't. He was supposed to be at the home of one of his friends." Carlucci consulted her notes. "Michael Chastain. Based on the description of Chastain that we were given by the Springers, we believe that's him there." She pointed to a blond boy who'd suffered multiple stab wounds to the chest and neck. It appeared that a dark-haired girl had been performing fellatio on him when they were killed.

The senselessness of it all weighed on Freddie, as it often did. Adult homicides were hard enough to handle, but when kids were involved, it became that much more excruciating.

Dr. McNamara arrived a couple of minutes later with her top deputy, Dr. Byron Tomlinson. As Lindsey took in the gruesome scene her green eyes filled with tears. "Oh my God."

"Holy shit," Tomlinson added.

While Carlucci and Dominguez brought the MEs up to speed, Gonzo pulled Freddie aside. "I'm thinking the sitch with the LT's niece has to be related."

"You read my mind."

"You don't think her niece went crazy with a knife, do you?"

"I don't know Brooke all that well," Freddie said, "but I'd be shocked to think she was capable of such a thing."

"If she was hopped up on drugs, anything is possible." Gonzo glanced at Freddie. "We'd be crossing all kinds of lines if we keep quiet about the possible connection."

"I know, but that's what we're going to do, right?"

"For as long as we can. If they turn up evidence that she was here, it's out of our hands."

The implications for Sam and her family weren't lost on Freddie and weighed heavily on him as he went through the motions of working the crime scene.

WHILE THEY WAITED for more news from the doctors overseeing Brooke's care, Sam sat with Tracy, who continued to sob uncontrollably.

"I knew something like this was going to happen," Tracy said. "This is why I sent her away. I just don't understand what she's doing here."

"That's the first thing I'm going to find out," Sam said. "What's the name of the headmaster at the school?"

"Gideon Young. He's been so nice to us and so accommodating with weekly reports on how she's doing."

"Do you have the main number for the school?" Tracy retrieved her phone from her coat pocket and found the number.

Sam wrote it down. "I'll call there shortly. I also need to know the names of her friends here in DC. We talked once about a girl you didn't like. I can't remember her name."

"Hoda," Tracy said disdainfully. "I don't know her last name. According to Brooke, she's just Hoda, like Pink or Cher."

"And this kid is seventeen?"

"Or eighteen. She was at Wilson with Brooke."

"I'll check with the school to get more info about her. Is there anyone else I should be looking at who might know where she was tonight?"

"It's embarrassing to admit that I don't know a lot of her other friends. When things between us began to go bad, she kept her friends away from us because she knew we wouldn't approve."

"I'll figure this out, Trace. I promise."

Harry emerged from the treatment area through double doors. "They're ready to do the rape exam, and since she's a minor, they need a parent or parents' designate in there for that."

"I can't," Tracy said as tears rolled down her cheeks. "I can't hold it together, and that's what she needs."

"I'll do it," Sam said, glancing at her brother-in-law, who nodded in agreement. Her stomach knotted with fear and nerves as she remembered holding the hand of her detective and friend Jeannie McBride through a rape exam after a vicious assault earlier in the year.

"Are you sure?" Tracy asked.

"I got it, Trace. Try to calm down. When she wakes up, she's going to need you."

"I know." Tracy wiped the tears from her face. "You're right."

Mike put his arm around his wife, who turned into his embrace.

Sam stood and wiped sweaty palms on her jeans. Nick came over to her. "Are you sure about this, babe?"

"Hell, no, but I'd like to make sure it gets done right."

"Harry's in there and can make sure it gets done right. They can designate him as easily as they designated you."

Sam shook her head. "She needs her family with her right now."

"Harry said she's totally out of it."

"What if she comes out of it in the middle of a rape exam? She needs someone there with her."

Her cell phone chimed with a text from Freddie. Six dead teens, all of them naked and stabbed while having sex. Drug stuff and booze all over the place. Two vics ID'd: Hugo Springer, son of home owners William and Marissa Springer, and Michael Chastain. More to come.

Sam's entire body went cold with fear for her niece as she read and reread the text.

"What is it?" Nick asked. She showed him the text.

"Jesus. You don't think… Brooke…"

Sam blew out a deep breath. "I don't know what to think right now. William Springer is a lawyer. He's always defending the scumbags I arrest, and now his kid is dead, and my niece is in the hospital."

"Babe, listen to me. I know you feel like you have to do this for Tracy and for Brooke, but you don't. As much as you love her, she's not your kid, and I hate to see you put yourself through such an ordeal."

Sam wanted to snap at him, but the concern she saw on his face had her biting back a nasty retort. "Tracy does *everything* for me. She always has. This is something I can do for her. Look at her. She's hysterical. She can't handle it."

"But what about you? What about the toll it'll take on you?"

"I can deal with it," Sam said with more confidence than she felt. "I appreciate your concern, but I need to do this."

Harry returned to the waiting room. "Sam? Are you coming?"

She squeezed Nick's arm and followed Harry through the doors to the corridor that led to the exam rooms where she'd spent far too much time in the last year. Sam, who despised needles and all things medical, discovered a totally different set of frazzled nerves was involved when someone she loved was lying in one of the beds.

Brooke's face had been wiped clean of blood, which made it easier to see how bruised her left cheek and lips were. At first glance, it looked to Sam as if someone had punched her. The skin that wasn't black or blue was as white as the bed linens with only her freckles standing out in stark relief. A trail of grayish drool stained her mouth and chin.

"Was the sheet she was wrapped in bagged?" Sam asked.

"This is MPD Lieutenant Holland," Harry said to the medical professionals tending to Brooke. "She's the patient's aunt."

One of the nurses gestured to a paper bag that sat on a metal table off to the side of Brooke's bed.

"Thank you," Sam said, eying the evidence bag with trepidation. What would the lab uncover about Brooke's involvement, if any, in what happened tonight on Mac-Arthur Boulevard? Whose blood had been all over her? What would she do if her investigation placed the blame for mass homicide on her own niece? *No*, she thought, dismissing that notion the second it registered. *That couldn't happen.*

"Any word on the tox screen?" Sam asked the doctor in charge.

"She's hopped up on Molly," the doctor said, "with a

side of GHB and vodka, or so we think from the smell. Her BAC was 0.16."

*Molly,* Sam thought, as she desperately tried to remember the details of the briefing they'd had at work recently about the drug that was running rampant among young people, even resulting in several deaths. MDMA, she recalled, the main chemical found in Ecstasy.

As the nurses prepped Brooke for the rape exam, Sam moved to the head of the bed where she could be close by if Brooke needed her but still able to watch what the nurses were doing.

"We're going to begin by photographing her injuries and scraping under her fingernails," the nurse in charge of the exam explained to Sam. "We'll clip the nails to preserve them as evidence. We'll swab her mouth and use a special light to check for semen and swab any samples. Hair samples will be taken so we have a baseline for her DNA, and we'll comb her hair and pubic regions for any stray hairs. We'll do an internal exam to check for injuries and take fluid samples from the vaginal and anal areas. If you have any questions, please feel free to ask at any time."

Sam nodded in acknowledgement as she braced herself for what she knew would be hours of painstaking work to collect evidence. It had been the right thing to keep Tracy away from this, but that didn't make it easy for her to watch.

Fortunately, Brooke was still unconscious as two nurses settled her feet in stirrups and raised the sheet to expose her genitals for photographs of her injuries.

Sam flinched with every flash. She knew from having been through this once before that the exam could be every bit as invasive as the attack itself. They turned

Brooke over and photographed her from all angles until Sam wanted to scream that they certainly had enough photos. But she held her tongue and let the experts do their jobs. After nearly thirteen years as a cop, Sam was painfully aware that an entire case could come down to a single eyelash or fiber.

Brooke remained still through it all, so still that Sam had to watch the rise and fall of her niece's chest to ensure she was breathing. However, when the nurse inserted the speculum, Brooke came to, screaming and thrashing.

Sam took hold of her shoulders as Harry and one of the nurses each took an arm and a leg. "It's okay, Brooke. It's Auntie Sam. I'm here and the doctors and nurses are trying to help you."

Her entire body convulsed with twitchy movements and violent trembling. "It *hurts!* Make them stop! What're they *doing?*"

The ER doctor asked for Ativan, which was administered through the IV.

"Brooke, honey, you have to relax and try to be still," Sam said, using all her strength to restrain her niece while trying not to add to her injuries. "You've been assaulted, and we need evidence—"

"*No!*" Brooke screamed at the top of her lungs, straining mightily against the hands that held her in place. "*Don't touch me!*" Between outbursts, she was grinding her teeth and licking her lips frantically.

"The Ativan will kick in momentarily," the doctor said. "Let's wait for it."

While they waited, Brooke continued to scream and sob and struggle and grind her teeth as Sam tried to soothe her.

Sam used her sleeve to wipe away the tears that

blinded her as she tried to provide comfort to the girl. "It's okay," Sam said, smoothing the hair back from Brooke's sweaty brow as she caught Harry's gaze.

He nodded, silently encouraging her to keep talking to Brooke.

"You're okay." She was so damned relieved that Brooke was awake and talking that she could handle the screaming and the crying if need be, even if every scream and every tear broke her heart.

"Sam, make them stop," Brooke said between sobs. "They're hurting me."

"They aren't the ones who hurt you, honey, but what they're doing will help us to find out who did. It's really important, or I wouldn't ask you to go through it. Is it okay if they finish?"

Brooke looked up at Sam with wild eyes, but she bit her lip and nodded as tears slid from the corners of her eyes.

Sam watched as the nurse practitioner worked quickly but efficiently, taking swabs and samples and cataloging Brooke's injuries.

Brooke screamed again when the speculum was removed, and Sam caught a glimpse of blood smeared on the plastic instrument.

Wrung out emotionally, Sam pressed her lips to Brooke's forehead. "The worst part is over, honey."

"She's going to need some sutures," the doctor said, debunking Sam's theory that the worst was over.

"*No*," Brooke said, tears streaming down her face. "Don't let them touch me there again, Sam. Make them stop!"

"Can we sedate her for that?" Sam asked.

"Yes."

"It's okay, Brooke. You won't be awake for it. It'll be over before you know it."

She looked up at Sam again with big, frightened eyes. "Why is this happening to me, Sam?"

"I was hoping you might be able to tell me why."

# THREE

IT WAS AFTER three in the morning by the time Brooke was transferred from the emergency department to a room in the Intensive Care Unit. Sam had stayed by her side throughout the entire ordeal, including when she was sedated for the procedure to stitch the wounds in her vagina. Thankful for the sedation that had knocked the girl out, Sam dropped into a chair next to the bed and texted Tracy to let her know what room they were in.

While she waited for the others to arrive, Sam took a moment to collect herself after hours of hell. Her hands were trembling, her legs and back were aching and her legendary cop cool had been shot straight to hell. Everything was different when crime and violence struck close to home. Someone had had very rough sex with Brooke, but whether she'd been a victim or a willing participant remained to be seen.

Harry had kept Brooke's parents informed throughout the evening, so when Tracy, Mike, Angela and Nick came into the room a few minutes later, Sam was spared from having to take them through the whole thing again.

Nick came right over to her while the others surrounded Brooke.

Sam stood, stepped into his welcoming embrace and let him lead her into the hallway.

He kissed the top of her head and held on tight, which

went a long way toward addressing the trembling that had besieged her.

"How are the ribs?" she asked.

"Fine. I'm far more concerned about you."

"I'm better now that she's sedated and settled in a room."

"We could hear her screaming from the waiting room."

"It was pretty brutal in there. She came to in the middle of the rape exam, freaking out over what they were doing to her. As far as I know, that was her first pelvic exam. Hopefully, she won't remember it tomorrow."

"The press has picked up on the MacArthur murders."

"Shit." Sam ran her fingers through her hair, attempting to comb some order into it after the long night. "So we've already lost control of the story, and we haven't even begun to dig into what happened there."

"Luckily, it's not your problem this time around." She kept her voice down in an attempt to keep their conversation private from the nurses who eyed them with recognition and interest as they walked past.

"What do you mean?"

"You're on vacation."

"Um, my vacation was canceled the minute I found my niece naked and bloody on my front porch. And it was definitely canceled the second we learned of six teenage murder victims in my city."

"There's no reason your team can't handle this case without you."

"There's every reason they aren't going to handle it without me. Do you have any idea how hot this case is going to get with six dead kids strung out on drugs, stabbed while having sex in the basement of a prominent lawyer's house?"

"What if we'd left tonight to go to France or Italy or somewhere else?"

"I'd be on my way back."

He dropped his arms from her shoulders and took a step back from her, his displeasure obvious.

"What do you want me to say? This is my *job*. She's my *niece*. I have to know what happened to her. I have to know for her and for Tracy, and I have to protect her from whatever this investigation may uncover."

"It doesn't have to be you, Sam."

She blew out a deep breath that was equal parts exhaustion and disbelief. "Have you *met* me?"

"What the hell kind of question is that?" he asked, no longer making an effort to keep his voice down.

"A direct one. If you knew me at all, and I usually think you know me better than anyone, you wouldn't question my need to run this case."

"I do question it. Everyone needs a break, even you. *We* need a break. I'm so freaking sick of the treadmill we live on. I want off for *one* goddamned week, and I want my wife with me. We had *plans*."

"You're married to a goddamned Homicide detective, Nick. You know the drill. How in the world do you expect me to take a step back from this of all cases?"

"I expect you to keep your plans with me."

"I can't believe you're doing this. I never would've expected this from you."

"Sam, come on," he said imploringly. "We've had the year from hell with nonstop work and insanity. We've been in a car wreck, lost a baby, nearly got blown up in our own house, had numerous injuries—some of them serious—lost several of our close friends, been stalked by the media, ran a campaign, got married and adopted a son. How am I out of line to desperately need a week completely off with my family after all of that?"

"You're not out of line." When he recited the list, she couldn't exactly argue with his logic. "But there's no way I can relax and enjoy a vacation with six dead kids on my conscience and a niece who's been drugged and sexually assaulted lying in the hospital when who knows what has been done to her. I'll go crazy if I can't work this case."

"You do what you've gotta do. I'm going home to our son. Tell Tracy and Mike I'll help Celia take care of Abby and Ethan for as long as they need me."

Sam took hold of his arm, rocked by the rare disagreement. "Nick, come on. Don't leave mad. Please?" He kissed her forehead and then her lips. "I'm not mad. I'm fed up. I've been living for this time with you, and I need it, babe. I really need it. But I guess it's not going to happen. I'll see you when I see you."

Sam watched, incredulous, as he walked away from her without telling her he loved her or asking her to be careful or any of the things he usually said to her. She could tell by the way he walked that he was in pain, and the set of his shoulders indicated he was angry, too, despite his claims to the contrary.

Awesome. That was just what she needed right now. She took a deep breath and went into the room to speak to her sisters and brother-in-law. "I'm going in to work to try to figure out what went on last night. Will you call me when she wakes up?"

"We will," Tracy said, her gaze fixed on Brooke as she stroked the girl's long dark hair.

"She didn't say anything about what happened?" Angela asked.

Sam shook her head. "She was too agitated and out

of it for most of the time I was with her. She had a few lucid moments, but for the most part, she couldn't process what had happened, and I didn't give her more information than she needed."

Mike came over to hug Sam. "Thank you so much for being in there with her."

"Sure, no problem." Sam tried not to think about the huge problem this case was already causing between her and Nick. "Nick said to tell you he'll help Celia with Abby and Ethan for as long as you need him."

"That's great. Thank you."

"I'm going to see if I can start to make some sense of all of this."

"Will you let us know what you find out?"

"Yes, of course." She eyed Brooke in the bed, pale and sick and changed forever by the events of the previous evening. "Do the names Hugo Springer or Michael Chastain mean anything to you?"

Mike shook his head. "Should they?"

"They're two of the kids who were found dead in the Springer home last night."

"What's that got to do with Brooke?"

"I don't know yet. Maybe nothing. Maybe something."

"Sam...what aren't you saying?"

"She was naked, stoned, bruised, possibly raped and had blood all over her that wasn't hers. An hour later, six other kids roughly her age are found stabbed to death in a local home. All of them naked, stoned, bloody and killed while having sex. I'd love to think there was absolutely no connection between these two events, but..."

His already pale face lost all remaining color. "How can they not be connected?" he asked in little more than a whisper.

"Exactly."

"What does this mean for Brooke?"

"I wish I could say. Let me do my job and get some answers for all of us."

"I feel like I'm coming out of my skin. I don't know what to do. Tracy… She's a wreck, and I want to comfort her, but I'm so damned mad with Brooke. I've been mad with her for such a long time, sometimes I forget that I used to love her more than just about anything." Mike's voice caught on a sob. He covered his eyes with his hands. "I feel like a monster for even saying that out loud, but what she's done to our family…"

Sam put her arms around the brother-in-law who'd been like a big brother to her for fifteen years. "You're not a monster. You're human, and she's been a huge pain in the ass by anyone's standards. We've all seen it over the last year or two."

"I thought this school was the answer to our prayers."

"I thought so, too, and you can bet I'm going to find out what happened there." Sam stepped back from him. "The best thing you can do right now is be here with Tracy and help her through this. Brooke is going to feel like death when she comes to, and it'll be a long road for her. They're both going to need you."

Mike nodded, wiped his eyes and ran a hand over his close-cropped dark blond hair, which had begun to go gray in the last year. "Nick seemed pissed earlier. Out of sorts. Not at all himself. Is everything okay?"

"It will be." Sam hoped she was right about that. They didn't have much experience with being at serious odds with each other. "He's hurting from the hit to the ribs. Between that and everything with Brooke… We're all out of sorts. I'll be back as soon as I can. Keep me posted on how she's doing."

"We will."

Sam hugged both her sisters and promised to be back soon.

"Find out what happened, Sam," Tracy said with new tears in her ravaged eyes. "Please find out what happened to my baby."

"I will." Sam was in the elevator when she remembered she didn't have a car. Normally, she would've called Nick for a ride, but since he was furious with her at the moment, she called Freddie. "Hey, where are you?"

"Still at MacArthur."

"Can you take a break to pick me up at GW? I'd like to take a look at the scene."

"Yeah, I can do that."

"I'll be at the ER entrance."

"See you in a few."

As Sam paced back and forth in the waiting room, she ignored the curious stares directed her way by the handful of people sitting in chairs, waiting to be seen. She focused on the television, where special coverage of the MacArthur murders was the lead story.

"Police are being tight-lipped about what transpired inside the MacArthur Boulevard townhome of prominent Washington attorney William Springer, his wife, Marissa, and their son Hugo, who is rumored to be among the victims found murdered in the home around midnight. According to information obtained from police communications, at least six individuals are believed dead inside the home. Mr. Springer and his wife reportedly were in Aspen, where they own a second home, and are on their way back to the District at this time." They showed a photo of the lawyer Sam had faced off against many times in court. "Mr. Springer's biography on his company's website lists Hugo as the youngest of his five children. The other four no longer reside at home."

If the news outlets were relying upon Springer's website and bio to fill airtime, her people had done a good job of keeping a lid on the details. Staring at the TV, she watched Freddie come out of the house. The second he stepped under the crime scene tape, he was mobbed by reporters. He ignored them all and kept his head down as he headed for his car. They gave chase but didn't catch him.

"That's the way," Sam said softly. "Don't give them anything until we're ready to."

"What's going on?" a voice behind her asked.

Sam turned to face Harry. "Homicide on MacArthur Boulevard. Six teenagers."

"Oh, Christ. How?"

"Stabbed while drunk, high and in the midst of having sex."

His eyes widened with comprehension. "You don't think…"

"I don't know. I don't know anything. But I'm going to find out."

"I'm sure you will."

"What's being done with the evidence collected from Brooke?"

"It's awaiting pickup."

"I could take it. I'm heading to HQ now."

"I don't recommend that, Sam. If there're any chain-of-custody issues, it could be a problem for you."

"Yes, you're right, and I know better. I'm not going

to lie to you. I'm a little freaked out by where this investigation might lead."

"With good reason."

"Is that supposed to be comforting?"

"Sorry. I don't mean to add to your worries."

Sam blew out a deep breath. "You didn't. I'm all over the place right now."

He squeezed her shoulder affectionately. "It was tough in there. I could barely stand to watch that, so I can only imagine how it was for you. Go easy on yourself. Contrary to press reports, you're not superwoman."

"Don't tell anyone. You'll ruin my image."

"Your secret is safe with me."

"Thanks for coming tonight. Both times."

"No problem. Is that your ride?"

Sam looked out the glass doors to see Freddie's rattle-trap Mustang sitting outside. "Yep."

"Good luck with the case."

"Thanks. I'm going to need all the luck I can get. I'll see you." Sam went out through the double doors into the chilly pre-dawn, zipping her coat as she made her way to Freddie's car.

Freddie leaned over to open the door for her. It made a creaking noise as it opened.

"Is this tin can roadworthy?"

"Fit as a fiddle." He glanced over at her as he put the car into drive. "How is she?"

"Not so good. She was high on Molly of all things, sexually assaulted or abused or roughed up or something that required stitches."

Freddie winced. "Holy crap. Is she awake? Could she tell you anything?"

"She was awake for the rape exam, but I couldn't really grill her then. They sedated her for the stitches, thank God. I'll go back to talk to her later when she's awake. Did you guys get anything at all from the canvas of my neighbors before you got called to MacArthur?"

"Nothing useful. No one saw or heard anything. We didn't bother your dad and Celia, though. We figured they'd let us know if they saw anything."

"Why do I have the sick feeling this entire thing is going to lead right back to my niece, who wasn't even supposed to be here?" As she spoke, Sam pounded her fist against the car door, expelling hours of frustration and agony.

"Um, it's not outside the realm of possibility that the door could fall right off if you keep that up."

"Goddamn it, Freddie. What the fuck was she thinking? Leaving school? Taking drugs?"

"I can't begin to know." The fact that he didn't take her to task for using the Lord's name in vain or swearing told her he understood how upsetting this was for her. "But we'll figure it out."

"I'm sorry about the vacation."

"It's not your fault."

"Nick is pissed with me."

"How come?"

"He's mad about the vacation getting messed up by another case."

Freddie gave her a side-eye look. "And he gets that your niece is possibly tied up in that case?"

"Yeah, he knows. He's still pissed."

"Elin's not too thrilled either, but it's what we do. It's who we are."

"That's right, and if he can't see that then he doesn't know me at all."

"Yes, he does, Sam. He knows you as well as anyone. You can't blame the guy for wanting a break from the madness."

"I don't blame him, but how can he ask me to choose between him and Brooke? I'd always choose him. But this… This is different."

"It's personal."

"Right."

They arrived at MacArthur Boulevard just as the sun began to rise over the capital city. The area was still surrounded by emergency vehicles, two medical examiner's trucks and hoards of media. Satellite trucks lined the street, which was completely impassable. They had to park more than a block from the scene.

"What a fucking circus," Sam said as she pulled her phone out of her pocket and called her mentor and boss, Captain Malone.

"I thought you were on vacation," Malone said when he picked up the call.

"Murder has a way of screwing up plans."

"I was over there earlier. Unreal."

"So I've heard. I'm about to experience it firsthand. Patrol has completely lost control of the area, however. Can you get someone over here to kick them in the ass?"

"Sure thing. So you're going to take this one?"

The argument with Nick was still fresh in her mind as she walked with Freddie toward the yellow crime scene tape. Take Brooke out of the equation and she would've been fine with handing the case over to Gonzo to run. But with a possible connection to her family, Sam wasn't leaving anything to chance. "Yeah, I'm on it." *Tell him about Brooke.* Sam's conscience picked a hell of a time to rear its ugly head. *You have to tell him. Not yet I don't. Yes, you do.*

"It's going to be a hot one with the Springer kid involved. Keep me posted."

"Will do." Sam stashed her phone in her coat pocket just as a bloodcurdling scream came from the crowd of people gathered outside the tape. She tipped her head at Freddie, and they changed course toward the screamer, who was being restrained by Patrol officers.

"What've we got?" Sam asked one of them.

"A Mrs. Chastain. Has reason to believe her son, Michael, is among the victims."

"Please come with us, Mrs. Chastain," Sam said, taking the woman by the arm and guiding her under the tape. "I'm Lieutenant Holland. This is my partner, Detective Cruz." To Freddie, she said, "Where can we take her to get her away from the cameras?"

"The next-door neighbors have been great about letting us use their living room."

"My Michael," she said between hiccupping sobs as Sam led her up the concrete stairs to the neighbors' townhouse. A woman greeted them at the door, her eyes sad and sympathetic as she wordlessly led them to a comfortable seating area. "He didn't come home last night, and he always calls if he's going to stay with one of his friends. He always calls. And then I saw on the news that something had happened at Hugo's house. The reporters... They said there're dead kids in there.

That's not true, is it?" She clutched Sam's arm. "Tell me it's not true."

In that moment, Sam hated her job with every fiber of her being—not only because she had to decimate the woman currently clinging to her, but also because of the way it managed to screw up her own life on a regular basis. But right now, Mrs. Chastain's needs trumped her own and they would until Sam could get answers for her and every one of the parents who'd be receiving unimaginable news on this sunny morning.

"I'm sorry to have to tell you it is true."

The other woman's wails would stay with Sam long after she closed the book on this case. She kept her arm around Mrs. Chastain as she guided her to a sofa. "Please no. Not my Michael. He always calls. He's a good boy."

"We haven't positively identified the victims yet," Sam said, although her words were little comfort to a mother who knew the grim truth even if Sam couldn't yet confirm her worst fears. "When was the last time you heard from Michael?"

"Around ten. He called to say he was staying with Hugo."

"Did you know Hugo's parents were out of town?"

"No! I had no idea. I never would've allowed him to come here if I'd known that."

"From what we were able to ascertain from the Springers' maid," Freddie said, "Hugo told his parents he'd be staying with you and your son while they were away."

"I never heard from Marissa about that," she said, wiping tears off her face.

"And would you have?" Sam asked. "Normally?"

She nodded. "Hugo has stayed with us before when his parents were away. That's not unusual. But Marissa wouldn't leave town without talking to me first. I don't understand." She looked up at Sam with heartbreak in her eyes. "How could this have happened?"

Sam wasn't about to tell a grieving mother that her

teenage son had pulled one of the oldest tricks in the book to get a night alone with his friends.

"The maid, Edna, she's been with the Springers for years. She would know my Michael. Did she say he was here? That he was…"

Sam glanced at Freddie, who nodded.

"I'm afraid Michael was among the victims the maid was able to identify. We were coming to tell you this morning."

Mrs. Chastain broke down again, and Sam did her best to offer comfort to the grieving mother.

"We're so sorry," Sam said. "We'd like to figure out what happened here, and to do that we could use your help. I know this is so intrusive at such an awful time."

"I'll tell you what I can."

"Where does Michael go to school?" Sam asked, using the present tense intentionally. She'd learned from experience that family members who'd just been informed of a loved one's death weren't ready yet to refer to them in the past tense.

"Wilson. He's a senior this year and planning to go to college. He's a good boy. He's never been in any trouble."

"And where does Hugo go to school?"

"Sidwell Friends."

The prestigious Quaker day school on Wisconsin Avenue was well known in the capital region.

"How do Michael and Hugo know each other?"

"They were our next-door neighbors in Friendship Heights until Bill's career took off. They moved here and sent Hugo to private school, but the boys have remained close friends. Even more so since they're both driving now and can see each other any time they want."

"Do either of them have girlfriends?"

She shook her head. "They both date a lot, but they joke about not tying themselves down. They're too young for that." Her face crumpled when she seemed to realize neither of them would ever get any older or fall in love or have a chance to give a committed relationship a try.

"There were three boys and three girls," Freddie said. "Do you know who the others might've been?"

When it appeared to dawn on her that other young people she probably knew had been murdered, Mrs. Chastain shook her head. "Six of them. Good Lord. Who would do such a thing?"

"That's what we'd like to know too," Sam said. "Can you give us an idea of who might've been with Michael and Hugo?"

"Todd Brantley was another of their close friends."

"What does he look like?"

"He's tall and very muscular with brown hair and eyes. He's captain of the football and hockey teams at Wilson."

Sam looked up at Freddie, who shook his head. "Oh, thank goodness."

"The girls… Any ideas of who they might be?"

"No. I teased Michael and his friends that they changed girls more often than they changed their underwear."

Looking exhausted and unusually pale, Gonzo stepped into the house looking for them. "Dr. McNamara is ready to begin transport, Lieutenant," he said, eying the woman sitting next to Sam on the sofa.

"Mrs. Chastain, I'd like to have you taken home until we have more information for you. Is there someone you could call?"

"I… I can call my neighbor. She'll come."

"Detective Cruz will stay with you until she arrives.

We'll need your address and phone number so we can get back in touch when we know more."

"Thank you for your kindness, Lieutenant. I've read about you and your husband. You seem like good people."

"Thank you." Sam never knew how to take comments like that when on the job. If she had her druthers, no one would know who she was married to. "I'll be back in touch as soon as I know more."

She followed Gonzo next door and down the stairs to view the crime scene before the bodies were removed. "Holy Christ," she whispered as she took in the bloody carnage, the chaos, the drugs, the booze, the utter waste that was being systematically recorded and bagged by Crime Scene detectives.

The thought of Brooke in the middle of something like this… Had she been here? If so, who had gotten her out before she could be killed too? And how close had she come to being murdered?

"Thought you were on vacation," Lindsey McNamara said to Sam.

"I did too. Do me a favor and hold off for a short time on removing bodies. The mother of one of the vics is next door, and she doesn't need to see that. Malone is sending over additional Patrol officers to move the press back too."

"Gotcha. I've got plenty still to do here anyway. There're three more in the back bedroom."

"*More?*" Sam said with a gasp.

"Back here," Gonzo said grimly, leading Sam to a bedroom where another couple had been stabbed, possibly mid-coitus. The young man was sprawled on top of a female victim whose throat had been slashed, their bloodied bodies twisted together grotesquely.

Based on the description of Todd Brantley, she decided that he was the male victim. "So there're eight all together?"

"Nine." He pointed to another naked girl on the floor at the foot of the bed.

"And the rest of the house has been checked?"

"Yes, the incident appears to have been confined to the basement."

"Do you have any gloves?"

Gonzo pulled a set of latex gloves from his coat pocket and handed them to her.

After Sam gloved up she went around to the other side of the bed, stepping over the body of the ninth victim as she went. She raised the comforter and took note of the fact that there was only one white sheet on the bed—the fitted one that covered the mattress. The flat sheet was missing, and the comforter was hanging off the bed as if someone had pulled hard on it.

She told herself that none of this meant the sheet from this bed had been the one wrapped around Brooke. All she knew for sure after her inspection was that there wasn't a second sheet on the bed.

"What do we have in the way of identification for the victims?" she asked Gonzo, who had watched her inspection of the bed without comment.

"Crime Scene has found several wallets and cell phones." He gestured to the pool table where evidence bags were accumulating.

Her heart pounding with fear and dread, Sam went to the pool table and took a look at the bags. Would she recognize a purse, wallet or phone that belonged to her niece? Probably not. Like most girls her age, Brooke had all kinds of bags and phone cases and other such accessories.

"Have you kept a list of victims' names and addresses?"

Gonzo handed her a notebook with a list of nine names and nine addresses.

Sam scanned the list, relieved not to see any names she recognized. "Good work. Where are we with notifications?"

"Carlucci and Dominguez are handling that."

"What does it say about me as their lieutenant that my first thought upon hearing that is, thank God I don't have to do it?"

"Their sergeant had the same thought. What does it say about both of us?"

"That we've been there and done that often enough that we don't mind letting someone else do it this time."

"I hate this shit all the time, but when it's kids…"

"It's so much worse."

"How's Brooke?"

"Not great." Sam kept her voice down. "She's in the ICU."

"God, Sam. What the hell happened?"

"I don't know, but she was hopped up on Molly, GHB and booze. And she'd had rough sex with at least one guy." The idea that there could've been more than one was something Sam didn't want to allow into her racing mind. She zeroed in on the body Lindsey was bagging—a naked female, maybe sixteen or seventeen, with dark hair and skin. Several vicious blows to the neck had ended the life of the exceptionally beautiful girl. "Have you found anything to indicate that Brooke was here?"

"No, but if she was, it'll turn up in the DNA."

"I don't know what to do, Gonzo. Do I tell Malone I

think she might've been here and bring her into it before we know anything, or do I wait until we know more?"

"You have to tell them now. If you wait and it turns out she was here, it'll look like you were trying to protect her by keeping it quiet."

"I don't want to tell them. I don't want to bring that down on her if it's not necessary."

"I know, but if you don't..."

"I could do her more harm than good."

"Not to mention what you could do to your own career. It's a sucky situation no matter how you look at it."

"Don't you have to be in court this morning?"

"Not for another couple of hours." He shook his head, his face set in a grim expression. "I look at these kids, doing drugs, drinking, having sex... I think, what if that's my kid someday? What if I give him everything I've got and something like this happens to him?"

"It won't, Gonzo. You're going to raise him better than these kids were raised. He's going to make good choices."

"Brooke was raised right."

"Yes, but she's always been a tough one. While this whole incident is totally shocking to all of us and way beyond anything we could've imagined her getting into, the trouble itself isn't entirely unexpected."

Freddie came down the stairs into the basement. "Mrs. Chastain is on her way home, and we've got other company." He gestured to Captain Malone and Chief Farnsworth, who were behind him.

"Who can report on what we have so far?" Farnsworth asked. Even though his voice was gruff, Sam could see he was as affected by the scene as the rest of them had been.

"I can, sir," Gonzo said. "We received a nine-one-one call from the maid, a Ms. Edna Chan, at eleven forty-five. She'd returned home from a social gathering to loud music coming from the basement. She went downstairs, turned on the lights and saw Hugo Springer, son of the home owners, William and Marissa Springer, dead of multiple stab wounds. With him were five other young adults—two males and three females. Upon further inspection of the basement and a full search of the upper floors of the house, it was determined that three more victims were in a basement bedroom—one male and two females. In addition to the bodies, drug paraphernalia, including pills and several pipes, and numerous bottles of liquor and beer were found.

"The home owner, William Springer, was with his wife in Aspen for a long weekend. Detectives Carlucci and Dominguez contacted them, and they are in transit home. They believed their son was staying at the home of Michael Chastain, who is another victim."

"I've spoken with Chastain's mother," Sam said. "She was told her son was spending the night here, but was unaware the Springers were out of town."

"So we've got two teenage boys who apparently played the parents to score some adult-free time to party and screw," Farnsworth said. "Where did they think the live-in maid would be?"

"Ms. Chan had planned to visit her sister's family in New Jersey for the holiday week, but the trip was canceled at the last minute because her sister's children contracted the stomach flu," Gonzo said.

"And Mrs. Springer never checked with Mrs. Chastain to make sure it was okay for her son to stay there while she was out of town?" Malone asked.

"Apparently, it was a rare oversight," Sam said, "but the two families have been friends for years, so it's possible Hugo convinced his mom that he'd talked to Michael's mom, and it was fine with her if he spent the weekend with them. We'll know more when the Springers get home."

"Bill Springer is going to raise holy hell and dig into every corner of this investigation," Farnsworth said. "I want every I dotted and T crossed."

"Yes, sir," Gonzo said. "Carlucci and Dominguez are handling the notifications of the other parents."

"I don't envy them that task," Farnsworth said. To Malone, he added, "Let's arrange for some counselors at HQ later if anyone needs to talk it out."

Malone nodded in agreement.

"Anything else?" Farnsworth asked. When no one replied, he said, "I want to be kept aware of every development as it happens."

Gonzo sent a look of inquiry to Sam.

She cleared her throat. "There is one other thing."

"What's that?"

"I believe it's possible my niece, Brooke Hogan, was here at some point last night."

The chief's eyes widened with shock. "Tracy's Brooke?"

"Yes."

"Why do you say that?" Malone asked.

Sam went through the whole thing, from the moment she and Nick arrived home until she left Brooke at the ICU to come to the crime scene.

"Is she going to be okay?" Farnsworth asked.

"Yes, they expect her to be fine—eventually."

The chief expelled a deep breath before he addressed her directly. "Lieutenant, due to the potential for conflict of interest, I'm removing you from command of this scene and putting Detective Sergeant Gonzales in charge."

"But, sir—"

"No ifs, ands or buts about it," Farnsworth said. "If it turns out your niece was either a victim or a perpetrator here, you will need to be far, *far* away from it. You are to have absolutely nothing at all to do with the investigation. Do I make myself clear?"

"Yes. Sir." Sam wished she could take back the last ten minutes of her life. She should've kept her damned mouth shut. Most of the time, she was able to cajole the man she used to call Uncle Joe into letting her do things her way, but that wasn't going to happen this time.

"Go home to your family, and give Tracy my love."

"I will, sir. Thank you."

"I, um… I'm fine with leading the investigation," Gonzo said with a hesitant glance at Sam, "but I'm due in court at nine for a hearing about Alex's custody."

"I'll cover for you until you get back," Freddie said. "First shift will be arriving soon, and we'll stay on it."

"I'll stay too," Malone said.

"Good, then it's all resolved," Farnsworth said. "Sergeant, good luck at the hearing. I hope you know we're all pulling for you."

"Thank you, sir."

"Lieutenant," the chief said. "May I offer you a ride home?"

# FOUR

AFTER THE FIGHT with Sam, Nick was awake all night. He'd walked away from her without telling her he loved her or making sure she was careful on the job—two things he always said to her because he wanted them to be his last words to her should his worst fears ever come to pass.

He was superstitious that way. He never wanted her to wonder where she stood with him, so leaving those things unsaid as she plunged into yet another case didn't sit well with him. Although he didn't regret making an issue out of the way she'd totally blown off their long-planned and much-needed vacation.

And then he remembered they'd also invited both their families and many friends to have Thanksgiving dinner at their house. How would they pull that off with their assistant, Shelby, out of town visiting her own family, and Sam working like crazy once again? It would all fall to him—a thought that only further exhausted him. Sam liked to joke that he made it look easy to keep multiple balls in the air at all times, but even he got tired of juggling after months of endless obligation.

The campaign had kicked his ass, and he still didn't feel like he'd completely recovered from that, which was why he'd probably had no business playing hockey last night.

At six in the morning, he gave up on sleeping and got

up to take a shower. Moving slowly due to the impressive pain in his side that was reminiscent of the injury last winter, he went downstairs to the kitchen for a pain pill that he chased with coffee.

He was sitting at the kitchen table, attempting to read the morning paper two hours later, when his phone beeped with a text. Hoping against hope that it might be from Sam, he smiled when he saw Scotty's name on the screen.

*Are you up? Can I come home?*

*Sure, buddy. Come on over. Make sure you tell Skip or Celia you're leaving and say thanks for the sleepover.*

*I will.*

Nick knew he didn't need to remind Scotty to be polite. Mrs. Littlefield, his former guardian at the state home in Virginia, had instilled beautiful manners in the boy, which was one of the first things Nick had noticed about him when they met last winter. He went to the front door to watch for his son. So much had changed for all of them since that fortuitous meeting. As he watched Scotty come down the ramp from Skip's house and walk the short distance on the sidewalk to the ramp that led to their home, Nick's heart was filled with love.

"How're you feeling?" Scotty asked as he came up the ramp.

"Sore but okay. Nothing's broken."

"Good."

Nick had come to know the boy so well that he couldn't help but notice his usual exuberance was dampened this morning. "Everything okay?" he asked as he closed the door and pointed to the closet, expecting Scotty to hang his coat where it belonged, rather than toss it on the sofa the way Sam would have.

Scotty hung up his coat and shut the closet door. He turned to Nick, seeming hesitant.

"Scotty? What's wrong?"

"You always tell me I can talk to you about anything, right?"

"Of course you can. Come sit." Nick sat carefully on the sofa and patted the seat next to him. "What's on your mind?"

"Last night, after you guys left, I was really worried that you were hurt worse than you said."

"I wasn't. I told you that."

"Still. I was worried."

"I'm sorry, buddy. I hate that you were upset about it."

"I kept looking out to see if your car was back yet, and I saw someone out here. They went up the ramp with something white and then they ran down the ramp and got in a car that was waiting for them."

Nick's heart nearly stopped beating when he realized Scotty had witnessed Brooke being delivered to their house.

"And then this morning, I woke up really early, and there was nothing to do, so I went on the computer. Celia lets us use the computer in the office. I knew she wouldn't care. I went on Facebook and Instagram, and I saw… I saw…"

"What? What did you see?"

Scotty glanced at Nick, seeming embarrassed and afraid at the same time. "Brooke."

Nick's stomach dropped. "What about her?"

"She… She was naked, and there were guys. Doing stuff."

Nick closed his eyes as he absorbed the blow. "Oh,

no." He took a deep breath that caused him considerable pain. "Show me."

"Do I have to?"

"Log me in to your accounts. I'll take it from there." Scotty got up and went to the room Sam and Nick used as an office and sat at the computer to log in to his accounts. "The stuff I saw was on Brooke's page." Leaning over his shoulder, Nick said, "How do I find that?"

"Here." Scotty clicked on the links and opened the pages, which Nick immediately minimized when he caught the gist with a quick glance at what was there. "What's going on, Nick? I thought she was at school until today. That's why Abby and Ethan stayed over last night. Because their parents are leaving this morning to go get Brooke for Thanksgiving."

Nick stood up straight as Scotty turned in the desk chair to face him. A fierce internal debate ran through Nick's mind as he tried to figure out what he should tell Scotty about what happened last night. The boy was almost thirteen and incredibly perceptive. He'd also witnessed a potential crime, and the implications of that hit Nick like a punch to the gut.

"I'm going to tell you the truth, okay?"

Scotty swallowed hard and nodded, his eyes wide with what might've been fear.

Nick explained about how they'd come home to find Brooke wrapped in a sheet at their front door and the long night they'd spent with her at the hospital.

"Why would she do drugs? She knows better than that."

"I don't know, buddy. Everyone is really upset about that and the fact that she was badly injured, but there's more. A bunch of teens were stabbed to death in a basement last night, and it's possible Brooke might've been there at some point. She had blood all over her that wasn't hers. No one really knows what happened. The police are trying to figure it out."

"Is that where Sam is?"

"Yeah."

"I thought she was supposed to be off this week."

"So did I—and so did she."

"She'll want to know what happened to Brooke."

"Yes."

Scotty looked up at him. "Are you mad with her?"

"If I say yes, I look like a selfish jerk, but I'm disappointed that the vacation isn't going to happen now. I was looking forward to it."

"So was she."

"You're on her side, huh?"

At that, Scotty finally cracked a small smile. "She must be really upset. And Tracy and Mike too."

"Everyone is really upset, and they're going to be more upset when they hear about the pictures online."

"Poor Brooke. No one deserves that."

"You're right. I need to call Sam and tell her about this. Are you okay?"

"I'm upset that Brooke got hurt and everything, but I'm okay."

They went to the kitchen where Nick had left his phone. As he put through a call to Sam and waited for her to pick up, he got out Scotty's favorite box of cereal and put it on the table with a bowl, spoon and milk. He was relieved when the boy showed some enthusiasm for breakfast.

"Hey," Sam said. "What's up?"

Nick filled her in on what Scotty had seen the night

before and the pictures that had cropped up on the social media sites.

"I'm on my way home," she said, surprising him with her lack of response to what he'd told her when he'd expected shock at the very least. "I'll take care of it when I get there."

Was she so absorbed in the homicide case that she hadn't heard what he said about their son being a potential witness? "Oh, okay."

"See you soon," she said before the call ended abruptly. *What the hell?*

SAM TOOK A long last look around at the crime scene, cursing her damned ethics. Where had they gotten her but tossed off the case? "Yes, please," she said in response to the chief's offer of a ride. "I came with Cruz."

"Let's go."

"Talk to the maid," Sam said under her breath to her partner.

"Got it. Will do. And I'll keep you posted too."

Sam nodded and went up the stairs, furious with herself and the situation and Brooke too. Yes, she was pissed with Brooke for whatever she'd gotten herself into, which was now impacting Sam's career. And then it occurred to her that following up with Brooke's school had nothing at all to do with the homicide investigation. She'd look into that angle the minute she was free of the chief.

When they were in his car and driving away from the crime scene, Sam vibrated with tension and an overwhelming sense of impotence at having been yanked off a case that should've been hers.

"I didn't have any choice, and you know that," Farnsworth said. "Your people are very well qualified to handle this case. They've learned from the best." After an uncomfortably long period of silence, he let out a deep sigh. "So you're not speaking to me now? Is that how it's going to be?"

"You didn't have to take me off the case. I said there's a *chance* Brooke was there. Until we prove she was actually there, why can't I be involved?"

"Because there's a chance, Sam. Come on. You know I'm right. I can't risk our case being compromised by a potential personal connection with the lead detective, especially with Bill Springer's kid as one of the vics."

"Ahh, so now we get to the heart of the matter."

"You know I'm doing the right thing. If you weren't emotionally involved, you'd see that too."

"I'm going to look into how Brooke managed to leave school last night and try to track her movements. I'll do it on my own time with my own resources."

"And you'll share whatever you uncover with Sergeant Gonzales."

Since he didn't forbid her from running her own investigation into what had happened to Brooke, she nodded in agreement. "Yes."

"I know you want to be right in the middle of the homicide investigation, but you should take this planned week off and spend time with your family. Tracy will need you, and so will Brooke. And with your dad's surgery early next week, you've got a lot on your plate. Take a break, Lieutenant. We all need one every now and then."

She wondered how he expected her to relax and enjoy a vacation when her niece was lying in the hospital after nearly overdosing on drugs and booze and possibly being sexually assaulted—all while she was supposedly at school out of state.

And then she took the call from Nick about what Scotty had witnessed, and things got impossibly worse. She worked hard to hide her reaction from Farnsworth until she knew more about what Scotty had seen and took a look at the pictures that had shown up online. If she tipped her hand to the chief before she knew more, that part of the investigation would no longer belong to her either.

A surge of nausea caught her by surprise when she imagined her naked, violated teenage niece on display for the world to see. Not to mention the fact that her son could be dragged into the middle of a homicide investigation, which was her worst nightmare come true.

The chief parked at the curb outside her house. "I'm going over to see your dad while I'm here. What does he know about Brooke?"

Drawn out of her own upsetting thoughts, Sam said, "I'm not sure. I haven't seen him yet."

"I'll let him tell me then." He looked over at Sam. "If there's anything I can do for you or your family over the next couple of weeks, you know where I am."

He was speaking to her now as her beloved Uncle Joe. "Yes, I know. Thank you."

"It'll be okay, Sam. It always is."

While she wanted to believe he knew best, she wondered if or when anything would be okay again for her niece or her sister's family.

The chief headed for her dad's house while she dashed up the ramp to home. She found a subdued father and son on the sofa in the family room watching Sports Center.

Nick muted the TV when she came in. Sam sat next to Scotty.

"I guess you want to know what I saw last night," he said as she hugged him.

"First, I want to know if you're okay."

"I'm worried about Brooke, but I'm okay."

"The good news is she's going to survive."

"That is good news."

"Do you feel like telling me what you saw?"

Scotty nodded, and Sam met Nick's concerned gaze over the boy's head. All the anger she had felt toward him since their argument dissolved the second her gaze met his and saw nothing but love and concern coming from him.

"I was wondering if you guys were back from the hospital, so I looked out a couple of times, checking to see if Nick's car was there. I wished I'd gone with you so I'd know what was going on."

Nick laid his hand on the boy's shoulder. "I'm sorry you were worried. I promise I'll always tell you if there's something to really worry about, okay?"

"You're not the one who's usually hurt," he said with a roll of his eyes in Sam's direction.

She poked his ribs, which made them all laugh and eased their tension.

"Anyway," Scotty said, picking up the story, "I looked out for the last time around eleven twenty-five."

"How do you know that was the time?" she asked.

"Because I'd just checked my phone to see if you'd texted me."

"We didn't text because it was late when we left the ER, and we were hoping you were asleep by then," Nick said.

"I was waiting to hear something. When I looked out,

there was a car in the street. The back door was open and two people carried something up the ramp and put it at our house. I couldn't figure out what they were doing, so I watched really closely. One of them was tall, and the other was short. When they came down the ramp, they got in the backseat and the car took off before the door was even closed. I remember thinking that was really dangerous."

Sam's heart beat fast with fear when she realized Scotty might've seen the people who'd committed murder at the Springer house. "Did you see their faces?"

He shook his head. "It was too dark, and I was blinded by the headlights. I could just see dark shapes more than anything."

Sam was actually glad he hadn't seen their faces. She didn't want him any more involved than he had to be. "So the car came down Ninth toward Skip's house?"

"Yeah, it was facing me."

"Could you make out what kind of car it was?"

"I think it was an SUV. Maybe a black one, but I couldn't really tell for sure cuz it was so dark."

"This is really good info, buddy. Thanks for letting us know what you saw."

"Will it help you to find the people who hurt Brooke?"

"I hope so."

"I left the pages up on the computer," Nick said.

"I'm going to check it out." She took a good look at him before she got up. "How're you feeling?"

"Sore, but nothing to worry about."

"Let me see."

"Sam—"

"Show me."

Sighing loudly, he lifted his T-shirt to reveal hideous bruising on his left side.

Sam and Scotty gasped at the sight. "Holy cow," Scotty said. "That's gross!"

"Thanks, pal," Nick said with a laugh he seemed to instantly regret.

Sam shook her head with dismay. "It looks awful."

"The pain pills are helping. Try not to worry about me. You've got enough on your mind."

When she thought about getting up and walking to the office to view pictures of her niece doing God knows what or having God knows what done to her, Sam felt sick all over. But the pictures might provide some much-needed insight into Brooke's whereabouts last night, so she had to look at them. And there was no time like the present.

On leaden legs, she went into the study, sat at Nick's desk and hit the space bar to bring the computer to life. She clicked on the browser, and Brooke's Facebook profile popped up to reveal several pictures of Brooke, naked and altered. They'd been posted by an account called WilsonSeniors, and there was no mistaking it was her, even with her eyes only partially open.

She scrolled down to the next posting, a video, clicked on it and instantly regretted it when she realized someone had actually recorded Brooke having sex. It was obvious that she was so out of it she probably had no idea what was happening to her, which meant she hadn't been a willing participant.

Leaning in closer, Sam recognized the blue plaid comforter under Brooke from the back bedroom at the Springer house. She covered her mouth to hold back a moan at the sight of another naked boy smacking his erect penis on Brooke's face while the first one continued to have his way with her.

"Dude, don't choke her," the first one said between thrusts. His words were slurred, but the fact that he was still able to perform indicated he wasn't as far gone as Brooke was. "She's pretty wasted."

"You don't get to have all the fun. Hurry up, would you?"

Sam got to watch the second boy do her and nearly vomited when a third appeared to take his turn. All the while they slapped her face with open hands and erect penises. Tears rolled down Sam's face unchecked as the horror unfolded before her.

She had the presence of mind to save the video to a flash drive along with the other pictures before she read the hundreds of comments that had been posted. They ranged from "You had a party and didn't invite me?" to "Brooke Hogan has always been a nasty slut" to "I thought Brooke was a lesbo now that she's stuck at an all-girls school" to "I want my turn."

After she'd taken screen-shot copies of everything from the pictures to the comments, she called Tracy.

"Have you heard anything?"

"How is she?"

The sisters spoke over each other.

"She's the same," Tracy said. "Still asleep."

"I need her passwords for her social media accounts." Sam had Brooke's email address, but wouldn't know where to begin to guess her passwords. "Do you know them?"

"I know what they were when she started the accounts. I bet she's changed them."

"What were they?"

"AbbyEthan22."

Sam typed that in and got shot down. "Damn it. That's not it."

"Will you tell me why you want to know?"

"I wish I didn't have to."

Tracy gasped. "Is there stuff posted about her?"

"Yes. Pictures, videos…"

"*No*," Tracy said with a moan.

"If I could get into her account, I might be able to get some more information about who posted this shit."

"Could you take it down altogether?"

"Not without access to the WilsonSeniors account, which is where it came from."

"This is a nightmare. Everyone will know. We have to do something, Sam!"

"I'm doing everything I can, Trace. I got taken off the homicide case because I was forced to tell Uncle Joe that Brooke might've been there."

"You told him that? There's no proof she was there!"

"I'm looking at proof that she was, Trace. I think two of the guys are Hugo Springer and Michael Chastain, who are among our victims at MacArthur Boulevard."

"Oh my God," Tracy said.

"Hey, Sam, it's Mike." This came after some jostling on the other end of the call. "What the hell is going on?" Sam brought him up to date on what had been found online.

"This can't be happening."

"I'm so sorry, Mike. I'm doing all I can from my end, but my hands are somewhat tied because of a possible connection between Brooke and the homicide at Mac-Arthur."

"What *connection* could there be? She was stoned out of her mind! You saw her!"

"She was there, Mike. The video puts her at the scene. I recognize the comforter from the bedroom where three of our victims were found."

"Son of a bitch," he said softly. "This is going to destroy Tracy."

Sam had already had the same thought herself. "I'm doing all I can. I'm trying to figure out Brooke's passwords to get into her accounts."

"I had a conversation with her about that last winter," he said. "I told her to make sure they weren't something stupid like the word 'password.' She lit right up, and we laughed over how I'd guessed that she'd done something stupid. That was before everything kinda blew up on us. We were still laughing together then."

Sam typed in the word "password" and gained entry to Brooke's Facebook account, where she quickly removed the offending posts and disabled the account. She did the same on Twitter and Instagram. "That worked. I took her offline on Facebook, Twitter and Instagram. Do you know if there were any others?"

"Check Vine and Tumblr too."

"Jeez, I've never even heard of those."

"You will before long with a teenager in the house."

"All right, I've deactivated those too. Nothing posted there, thank goodness."

"Thanks, Sam."

"I'm going to figure out who did this, Mike. Have no doubt about that."

"I know you will. I've got to go take care of Tracy. She's beside herself. She so doesn't deserve this after all she's done for Brooke."

"You've both given her everything."

"And this is the thanks we get."

"You're upset right now, and for good reason, but try not to leap to any conclusions until we know more."

"I'm trying."

"Call me when she wakes up. Don't let her talk to anyone before she talks to me."

"Okay."

"I'll be in touch."

Sam closed her outdated flip phone and sat at the desk thinking the whole thing through as a detective rather than a distraught aunt.

"It must be bad if you didn't mess with my desk," Nick said when he came up behind her and rested his hands on her shoulders.

"It's as bad as it gets. There was video of her having sex with three different guys."

He blew out a deep breath. "Was she an active participant?"

"Hardly. She was out of it."

Nick turned the desk chair so she faced him. "What're you doing here rather than out chasing down a murderer?"

"I was taken off the case because of the potential conflict of interest."

He sat on a footstool, and Sam caught his grimace as his body made contact with the furniture. "Because of Brooke."

"Yes."

"But?"

"But what?"

"You said earlier I don't know you at all, but because I actually know you better than anyone, I'm asking what you're planning to do."

That earned him a small smile. "I'm not sure yet. The chief was unusually stern with me when he took me off the case, so I have to be careful."

"I bet it wasn't easy to tell him you might have a conflict."

He knew her too well. "It wasn't."

"But you told him."

"With some encouragement from Gonzo."

"It was the right thing to do, Samantha."

"If my niece gets dragged through the mud, and I'm unable to protect her, will you still think it was the right thing to do?"

"If your niece was somehow involved in the murders—and I doubt she was, based on how out of it she was when we saw her—it wouldn't be your place to protect her. You'd be putting your own career—and neck—on the line, and I'm particularly fond of your neck."

"If I supposedly did the right thing disclosing, why do I feel like total shit about it?"

"Because this awful thing has happened to someone you love, and you're completely powerless to fix it. Welcome to my world."

"It's a sucky feeling."

"Yes, it is."

"Farnsworth took me off the homicide case. He didn't say anything about Brooke's case."

"Which may be wrapped up in the homicide."

"And it may not be."

"So you're going to run your own investigation into what happened to her."

"That's the plan."

"And if it intersects with the homicide?"

"I'll cross that bridge when I get to it."

"You're taking a big chance with your career and your reputation."

"What would you have me do? Turn this over to someone else and hope it gets done right? What if it gets bungled and she ends up charged for a murder she couldn't possibly have committed when she was out of her mind on drugs and booze?"

"If that's the case, how could she be charged?"

"I just watched a video that put her at the scene of a crime in which everyone else who was in the video is now dead. What if we can't find the people who brought her here and Springer tries to pin the whole thing on her because she got out alive? What if he tries to say she was faking being stoned while they raped her, and then she lost her shit afterward and killed the whole lot of them?"

"You really think that's what happened?"

"No. I think she got in way over her head with kids who are far more experienced with the drinking and drugging and sexing scene than she is. I think she took shit her friends gave her, and she drank too much on top of it. I think someone slipped her something extra, and those boys took advantage of the fact that she was out of her mind. I think she's the tenth victim, only she didn't die. Now all I have to do is prove it and figure out who dropped her here and whether they're the killers or if it was someone else entirely."

Sam's phone rang and she saw Mike's name on the caller ID. "What's up?"

"A Detective Ramsey is here from Special Victims. He wants to take a statement from us and from Brooke."

"Let me talk to him."

"My sister-in-law," Sam heard Mike say. "Lieutenant Holland." She thought she heard Ramsey mutter something under his breath, but she didn't catch it. She never had figured out what the SVU detective had up his ass where she was concerned.

"This is Ramsey."

"The victim is my niece. I'm handling it."

"I don't think you are. We got called in on this."

"I'm calling you out of it." Even though she was twenty years younger than the detective, she had two ranks on him, and he knew it. Sam suspected that was the source of his animosity toward her.

"You ready to explain this to the brass?"

"I'll take care of them. You leave my sister and her family alone. Got me?"

"Yes. *Ma'am.*"

The condescension in his voice was hard to miss. "Investigating a crime involving your own family is a conflict of interest."

"Is it? I had no idea. Thanks for the clarification. Now stand down and back off. That's an order."

"You're not my boss."

"I'm a lieutenant. You're a detective. Any questions?"

"Yeah, just one. Where do you get off?"

"At home mostly, although sometimes it happens in a hotel room. Those times are the best."

"Such a cocky bitch. One of these days you'll get what's coming to you, and a lot of people will be glad to see you taken down a peg or two."

"Is that a threat, Detective?"

"No. Just the one thing on my Christmas wish list."

"This conversation is boring me, and you've got somewhere else to be. Give the phone back to my brother-in-law."

"Nice guy," Mike said when he came back on the line.

"Is he gone?"

"Yep. He stormed out of here."

"Good. Let me know if he or anyone else shows up."

"Is what he said true, Sam? Is it a conflict of interest for you to be working on Brooke's case?"

"Hell, yes, it's a conflict, but I'm doing it anyway."

"Maybe you shouldn't. You've worked really hard to get where you are. I'd hate for Brooke to get you in trouble."

"Let me worry about that. You take care of Brooke and Tracy."

"I'm trying. Tracy is inconsolable after hearing Brooke is all over the Internet."

Sam could only imagine how her sister was dealing with that news on top of everything else that had happened. "I gotta go. Keep me posted, and you did the right thing calling me when Ramsey showed up. Don't talk to anyone unless I'm there—and don't let Brooke talk to anyone either."

"We won't, Sam. We're counting on you."

The weight of those expectations sat on her shoulders like fifty-ton weights. "I'm doing everything I can. I'll talk to you later."

Sam ended the call, more agitated than she'd been before, if possible.

"I don't like this," Nick said. "I don't like it one bit."

"I know you don't. I don't like it either. But there's no way in hell I'm going to sit idly by and let a ham-handed asshole like Ramsey run this investigation. That guy hates me. Pinning a murder on my niece would bring him pleasure."

"Why does he hate you?"

"Damned if I know. I have my suspicions that it involves my speedy rise through the ranks while he's been sitting still at detective for at least a decade now."

"That would explain it."

"I'm sure he believes I only got where I am because of my last name."

"Which is completely untrue and unfair."

Sam shrugged. "I don't let it bother me, and you shouldn't either."

"I don't like when people hate you because you're good at your job."

"At least we've got Stahl out of the way for the time being. Although he's fighting the charges and suspension with everything he's got."

"He can't fight the fact that he assaulted you at your own home."

"He can try, but the proof is in the pictures. Anyway, now that it's finally after nine, I need to call the headmaster at Brooke's school and figure out how the hell she managed to get out of there last night."

"What's going to happen with Scotty?"

Sam ran her fingers through her hair, attempting to bring order to it as the long night without sleep began to catch up to her. "I'll report to Gonzo with what he saw, but I'm going to try like hell to keep him out of it. It's actually good news that he couldn't identify the people who dropped her off, even if it makes our job that much harder."

"I agree. I nearly had a heart attack when he told me what he'd seen."

"This is exactly the kind of thing I was afraid of when he came to live with us. I never wanted him wrapped up in my cases. I certainly couldn't have imagined him wrapped up in a case that involves my own niece."

Nick leaned forward to rest his hands on her legs. "If it turns out that Brooke was somehow responsible for what happened at MacArthur, are you going to be able to live with that?"

"She wasn't responsible. I saw her on video with three of the vics, and she was out of her mind before they were killed. As sickening as that video was to watch, it's proof there's no way she could've killed them. She was barely conscious. Someone else did the videotaping, the killing, the posting. We'll figure out who that was."

"I know you've got stuff to do, and I'll let you get to it, but I wanted to say… I'm sorry about before. I shouldn't have made an issue out of the vacation getting screwed up."

"Yes, you should've," she said with a sigh. "We've been looking forward to it, and you're right to be pissed. I'm pissed too. I don't want to be dealing with this right now, but I can't turn my back on Brooke—or Tracy. Especially Tracy."

"I know, babe. Is it okay to be secretly glad the chief bounced you off the homicide case so you have to work from home?" he asked with a hint of the sexy smile Sam loved so much.

"It's okay to be glad I got bounced off the case—this one time." She cupped his face and leaned in to kiss him. Leaning her forehead against his, she said, "I hate fighting with you. It's the worst thing ever."

"Same here. I couldn't sleep when I got home because I was so wound up about how we left things."

"My stomach hurt all night after you left."

"I hate to hear that." He leaned in to kiss her, grimacing when his injured side protested. "I hope you know that even when I'm mad as hell at you, I still love you more than anything."

"I love you just as much—even when you're mad as hell at me."

He kissed her lips, her nose and her forehead. "I'll leave you to it. Let me know what I can do to help."

"Keep an eye on our boy. He saw some upsetting stuff. I want to make sure he's okay."

"I will."

"And take it easy too. You're injured. You should be on the sofa with your feet up and your wife waiting on you hand and foot."

"Now that you mention it…"

"Later, Senator. As soon as I get some answers, I'm all yours."

"I'll be looking forward to later then."

Sam watched him go, enjoying the back view of him, which was awesome even in sweats and a T-shirt. She never got tired of looking at him and hated to see him compensating for the pain on his left side. More than anything, she wished she could focus only on him today when he was injured and trying hard to be stoic about it. He rarely got her undivided attention for a full day, which was why he'd pitched a fit about their vacation getting screwed up. She certainly understood, but there wasn't much she could do about it with so many unanswered questions surrounding her niece.

With getting some answers in mind, she picked up the phone to call Gideon Young at the number her sister had given her. He answered on the first ring.

"Mr. Young, this is Lieutenant Sam Holland with the Metro DC Police Department. My niece, Brooke Hogan, is a student at your school."

"Yes, of course, Lieutenant. What can I do for you?"

"Brooke is currently in the ICU at George Washington University Hospital in the city, suffering from the aftereffects of a drug overdose, alcohol poisoning and sexual assault. I'd like to know how all of that managed to happen when she was supposed to be safely ensconced in your school."

Silence.

"Mr. Young?"

"I, um, I have no idea what to say. I'm in total shock."

"You could say that you'll be thoroughly investigating how this happened."

"Absolutely. Of course. I can assure you I'll be looking into this and will find out exactly what happened."

"I'd also like her room locked until I can get a team down there to deal with her belongings. No one goes in there, you got me?"

"She has a roommate."

"Get the roommate out of there, and don't let anyone touch anything of Brooke's. If her laptop and iPad and other belongings aren't there, I'll hold you personally responsible. Do you understand me?"

"Yes."

"Let me give you my number so you can let me know what you find out." She recited the number and had him read it back to her. "My sister and her husband paid your school a lot of money to keep their daughter safe, and you've utterly failed her—and us. We want answers, and we want them right away, Mr. Young."

"I want answers, too, Lieutenant, and I will get them for you. I'll be in touch."

"I'll be waiting." Sam ended the call feeling pleased that she'd ruined his day. It was the least of what he deserved after Brooke managed to somehow escape from the school that Sam had given Tracy twenty thousand hard-earned dollars to pay for.

Sam placed a call to Lieutenant Archelotta, head of the IT department at HQ.

"Hey, Sam, what's up?"

"I need a favor, Archie."

"You caught that big case up on MacArthur?"

"Not exactly."

"Really? What gives?"

"It's possible my niece might've been there before it went down."

"Oh, shit. No kidding?"

"I wish. Crime Scene will be bringing in the cell phones recovered from the house. I think my niece's is going to be among them." Sam brought him up to date on what'd happened the night before. "I'm trying to figure out how she got to the District when she was supposed to be at school in Virginia. I was wondering if you could do me a courtesy and let me know if you have her phone and if you do, whether you'd dump it for me." He hesitated for a second before he said, "Sure, I can do that— as a courtesy and as long as it's between us." She was asking him to cross lines on her behalf, and they both knew it. As the only other cop Sam had ever dated, they'd crossed lines together before. "You have my word. Let me give you the number." She recited Brooke's cell phone number, remembering the thrill of the young girl receiving her first hot-pink flip phone on her twelfth birthday. The memory came with a stab of pain in her chest for the same girl who now lay bruised and battered in the ICU.

"Got it. I assume you want everything?"

These days they had to specify voice, text, data, video

and music when requesting warrants for phone dumps. "Yes, please."

"I'll let you know as soon as I have anything for you. As you know, smartphones take about eight hours. I assume it's smart?"

"Yes, it is. Thanks, Archie. I appreciate it."

"I hope your niece is okay."

"I hope so too."

Her next order of business was tracking down the principal of Woodrow Wilson High School on a Saturday.

# FIVE

GONZO RUSHED HOME to change before court. His nerves were already raw with the hearing bearing down on him, but the added pressure of running the investigation into the murdered teenagers only added to the weight of the world sitting on his shoulders. While he was pumped to have the opportunity to run his first major investigation, all he could think about was the custody hearing that had been scheduled for a rare Saturday morning session due to the backlog in family court.

As he went through the motions of showering and shaving, he downed a cup of coffee to wake himself up after the sleepless night. He was standing at the bathroom sink running a razor over his face when Christina came in and slipped her arms around him.

"Hey, baby," he said, fortified by the press of her body against his. "Is Alex still sleeping?"

"Uh-huh. He was up around five, but I told him he had to go back to sleep for a while."

"And that actually worked?"

"For once, thank goodness." She let out a big yawn. "I was so not done sleeping yet."

Gonzo rinsed the leftover suds off his face and turned to her, drying his face as he moved. "I know you love him and me, and I know you don't mind being here with him when I'm at work. Just the same, I hope you also know how very much I always appreciate it and never take it for granted."

"Of course I do." She ran her hands up his chest to rest on his shoulders. "How could I not when you tell me all the time?"

He bent his head to kiss her, lingering on the sweet taste of her lips.

"I need to tell you something that might help today." Keeping his arms around her and his lips against her neck, he said, "What's that?"

"I've made a somewhat major decision."

Gonzo raised his head to meet her gaze, afraid he wasn't going to like her somewhat major decision. He lived in perpetual fear of the day she'd wake up and realize she could do a hell of a lot better than him.

"Don't look at me like that. It's nothing bad." She cupped his cheeks, her palms soft against his freshly shaven skin. "I'm going to leave my job to stay home with Alex full-time. For now anyway."

Gonzo shook his head, uncertain that he'd heard her correctly. "You're going to do *what?*"

"Hear me out. This isn't something I decided overnight. I've been thinking about it for a while now."

"I can't let you do this, Christina. Your career is important to you."

"My family is too. I'm not leaving my career permanently. I'm taking a break."

"I don't understand where this is coming from." She took him by the hand and led him to the sofa, where he glanced at the clock on the cable box. He had an hour, and he'd gladly give a few minutes of that time to her.

Sitting next to him, she took his hand and curled her fingers around his. "It's been almost a year since we lost

John. His death woke me up to the fact that life is short, and all that matters in the grand scheme of things are the people I love. I want to be here with Alex. I want to take some time to plan our wedding and maybe have a baby of our own." She looked up at him with a shy smile that slayed him. "I don't want to look back and have regrets. I talked to Nick about it—"

"You talked to Nick? Before you talked to me?"

"My decision is going to simplify your life and complicate his. I thought he had the right to know what I was thinking when I first started thinking it."

"You should've told me," he said, trying not to be irritated that she'd told her boss and friend first.

Raising a saucy brow, she said, "So you could talk me out of it?"

"No, so we could make this decision together."

"I didn't want to stress you out when you had so many other things on your mind. I'm only telling you now because I thought it might help today in court to tell the judge that your fiancée will be devoted fulltime to Alex's care."

"It stresses me out to know you had something this major on your mind and didn't feel like you could talk to me about it."

"So you're bummed because you weren't the first to know? I didn't really expect that reaction."

He stood, unable to contain the energy zinging around inside him. "I'm not bummed. How could I be when you're offering to do such a huge thing for our family?"

She came up behind him, putting her arms around him and refusing to let him put distance between them. "Then what is it?"

"What if you do all this and we lose custody? Have you thought of that?"

"No, I haven't, because we'll get custody. How can we not after all we've done and been to him since he came into our lives?"

"I wish I shared your confidence. I have a very bad feeling about this."

"Tommy, look at me."

Reluctant to show her his turmoil, he turned to her. "It's all going to be fine. I know it is. We're his family, and he'll know his real mother, but the judge isn't going to take him away from you."

"You have no way to know that for sure," he said, even if her assurances bolstered his flagging confidence.

"No, I don't, but the truth is on our side. Don't go in there looking nervous and uncertain. Go in there looking confident that justice will prevail. Alex belongs here with us, and the court will see that too."

"I hope you're right, but just in case, don't quit your job yet."

"I'm doing that no matter what. I need a break. I've worked really hard for years. I've saved a lot of money, and now I want to use that money to relax a bit and enjoy life." He knew she took pride in the fact that she never touched the trust fund from her parents. "The campaign about killed me."

"Nick will be lost without you, honey."

"He'll be fine. Terry is amazing. I'm sure he'll promote him to chief of staff, and Nick told me I can come back any time I want. It's all good."

"Tell me you're really doing this for you and not for me."

"I'm doing it for me—and for us."

Gonzo kissed her forehead and then her lips. "I love you, and I want you to be happy. If this is what you need right now, then I'm all for it."

"Good," she said with a sigh that sounded an awful lot like relief. "I love you, too, and I love our family. I want to be here for Alex and our other kids when they're little. I can pick up the career later. It'll still be there."

"How many other kids are we talking?" he asked with a raised brow, hoping to make her smile, which worked as planned.

"I'll take whatever we're blessed to get."

"So will I. Sometimes I still can't believe you picked me when you could've had anyone."

"Tommy... Why would you say that? You're everything to me. You have no idea how much I love you. Every time you walk out the door to go to work I pray so hard that you'll come home safe." Her eyes filled and she blinked back tears. "Every time."

He wrapped his arms around her and held her tight. She was the best thing to ever happen to him—right up there with the baby son he hadn't known about until he saw him and fell instantly in love with him. The tiny dimple in Alex's chin that was an exact replica of his own had sealed the deal for Gonzo.

His ringing cell phone interrupted their embrace. "I've got to take this. The murders at MacArthur are my case." He glanced at the caller ID, saw Sam's name and took the call. "Hey, what's up?"

"I have a situation."

"Another one?" Gonzo had been shocked to hear that Sam's niece might've been at the house before the murders. She'd done the right thing by coming clean about her potential personal connection, but he knew she hadn't done so easily.

"Several of them, actually. Scotty saw the drop-off at my place last night."

"Oh, shit."

"And Brooke is making the rounds on social media. Photos and video of the party before it went bad." Sam let out a rattling sigh. "I'm between a rock and very hard place on this, Gonzo. I heard what the chief said, and I agree about the conflict of interest, but I can't not be involved."

"So we'll keep you behind the scenes."

"That's what I hoped you'd say. I'm waiting to hear from the headmaster at Brooke's school to figure out how the hell she got out of there last night. I want to know everything that happened from the time she left the school until I found her on my front porch."

"If you focus on that part, you'll take a big load off me. I've got to figure out timelines for nine other kids. Cruz, McBride and Tyrone are working on that now. I called in Archelotta to get him going on the cell phones, and Dominguez and Carlucci are going home for six hours and then coming back. We may need some overtime on this one."

"Malone can authorize it." She hesitated before she added, "I'm afraid this whole thing is going to come down on my niece somehow."

"You said she was totally out of it, right?"

"Yeah, and the video shows she was out of it before some of the vics were dead, but still… Where are her clothes? Where's her cell phone and purse? Probably in that pile of clothes and phones at MacArthur, so you'll have no choice but to look at her, which will make this video that shows her being sexually assaulted by three guys necessary to her case, which will in turn ruin her life. The whole thing makes me sick."

"Let's take it a step at a time. Any idea on the source of the pictures and video?"

"It came from an account called WilsonSeniors. I assume that's Wilson High School seniors, so I'm waiting for a call back from the principal."

"You know your friend Hill might be useful here. He could get us access to the FBI's Cybercrimes Unit. You ought to give him a call."

"Ugh. Wouldn't I owe him a favor then?"

Gonzo laughed, relieved to see a spark of humor from his lieutenant and friend. "If it means shutting down the account and getting that video offline before it goes viral, will you care about owing him one?"

"You're right. I'm calling him now."

"Hang in there, Sam, and keep me posted on what you find out about Brooke."

"One other thing before I let you go. When Brooke comes to… She's mine. No one else talks to her until I do."

"Sam…"

"I mean it, Gonzo. I'd never do anything to fuck up your investigation. You know that. But she's mine."

He couldn't deny he'd feel the same way in her shoes. "And you've got my back when this whole thing blows up in my face?"

"I've always got your back."

And that was exactly why he said, "Do what you've got to do, Lieutenant, and let me know how I can help."

"I've got to take this call from the headmaster. I'll talk to you later—and Gonzo, good luck in court."

She was gone before he could reply.

"Lieutenant Holland."

"This is Gideon Young. I have some information for you."
He cleared his throat, which hadn't needed clearing, so
Sam knew he was nervous about what he had to say. "Ms.
Hogan was checked out at nineteen hundred hours yester-
day by her older sister, Danielle, who produced a driver's
license and a notarized note from your sister, Mrs. Tracy
Hogan, allowing her older daughter to pick up Brooke."

"That would be all well and good *if Brooke had an
older sister!* What kind of rinky-dink operation are you
running down there? My sister and her husband paid
you *twenty thousand dollars* to keep their daughter safe,
and now she's lying in the ICU fighting for her life." She
wasn't exactly fighting for her life anymore, but Young
didn't need to know that.

"With all due respect, Lieutenant—"

"Save your due respect for someone who cares. I want
a description of this so-called older sister, and any security video that might show the pickup."

"You'll need a warrant for the video."

"You'll need a lawyer for the lapse. Maybe if we help
each other out, I'll encourage my sister and brother-in-law
to settle out of court rather than making a public spec-
tacle out of your egregious lack of security."

"Are you threatening me, Lieutenant?"

"What do you think? Send me that video within one
hour. Here's my email address. Are you writing it down?"
She gave him her personal address so it wouldn't go
through the department server. "One hour or get ready
for some very ugly press."

Sam hung up before he could reply to that. She took a

moment to run her fingers through her hair as she contemplated her next move. Willingly calling in the FBI went against everything she believed in, but Gonzo was right. Their Cybercrimes Unit was second to none, and if anyone could track down the origin of those pictures and videos, the Feds could. Since time wasn't on her side, Sam reached for her phone with tremendous reluctance.

Avery answered on the first ring. "Miss me, Lieutenant?" That sweet Southern accent would make a lesser woman swoon. Sam was never so grateful not to be a lesser woman.

"Yeah, like a whore misses the clap when it finally clears up."

Ringing laughter had her holding the phone away from her ear. "What can I do for you this fine day?"

"I need a favor. A personal favor."

His silence was just as loud as the laughter had been. "What's going on, Sam?"

She told him what had happened to Brooke and the murdered teenagers. "I need help tracking down the source of that video, and I need to get it offline before it ruins her life. You guys are the best at the cyber stuff. I need the best."

"You'll have it. I was planning to head home to Charleston for the holiday today, but I can change my plans."

"Avery, no. Don't do that. Surely you have people you can call."

"I'll see to this personally."

Sam leaned her head on her hand. "I have no right to ask this of you."

"We're friends, right? Friends help each other out."

What went unsaid was that he'd expressed an interest

in being much more than friends with her, which was never, ever going to happen. Though they both knew that, his help had been invaluable on the Vasquez case this past summer, and she did consider him a friend as well as a colleague. "Yes."

"Wow, that was the longest pause in the history of long pauses."

"I'm sorry. I have a lot on my mind, and I'm not good at asking for help. I got taken off the case."

"Because of the possible connection to your niece."

"Right."

"So what's your plan?"

Sam smiled, because he thought like she did and knew she'd have a plan. "I'm pursuing the portion that involves Brooke, trying to figure out how she ended up in the ICU when she was supposed to be on lockdown at school in Virginia."

"Why lockdown?"

"The usual reasons. She was nasty and willful and in with the wrong crowd and on track to go very bad. Her parents felt they had no choice."

"Sounds like they're good parents who love their kid."

"They are and they do."

"Then let's make sure all their love and care isn't for naught. Have you requested a warrant for her room at the school yet?"

"Not yet. It was next on my list."

"I'll get you one. Our involvement will help with the jurisdictional shit."

"I'll owe you one."

"Yes, you will."

Sam's mouth fell open in surprise.

His soft chuckle made her realize he was joking. At least she thought so.

"I'll be back in touch shortly."

"Thank you, Avery."

Sam ended the call, put down the phone and rested her head on her hands, her head spinning with so many threads to pull she had enough for fringe.

"Why the hell are you talking to him?"

Sam spun around to find her husband in the doorway looking fierce and furious. He'd picked right up on Agent Hill's interest in her and had made it clear he wanted the agent nowhere near his wife. Unfortunately, their work kept throwing them together and they'd formed a collegial, if often uncomfortably reluctant friendship despite her husband's alpha tendencies.

"I need his help."

"What for?"

"He's got access to cyber-geeks who can get the videos of my niece being raped off the Internet faster than I can with my resources. He can cut through jurisdictional warfare to get me a warrant to search her room at school. I need his help." This was said softly the second time as the adrenaline she'd been running on seemed to leech from her bones all of a sudden. She was so fucking exhausted and had miles to go before she could sleep.

"I don't like you being indebted to him."

"I don't like it either, but I like those videos a whole lot less than I don't like him." The statement didn't even make sense to her, but hopefully he got the gist. And frankly, she wasn't up for fighting with him. She had too many other things to do.

"Your dad is here. He wants an update on Brooke and

the case, and he said Darren Tabor is outside hoping for a word with you."

Sam's exhaustion quadrupled at the news that the pesky *Washington Star* reporter was sniffing around. Of course he was. An ambulance had been called to her house last night. He and others would want to know why. First things first, she thought, as she got up to see her dad.

Nick stopped her progress by putting his arm across the doorway.

Sam looked up at him, unused to being so consistently annoyed by him. "What?"

"When are you going to sleep?"

"Later."

"That's not the right answer."

"It's the only one I've got right now." Careful not to brush against his injured side, she scooted under his arm and went to the living room where her dad was talking to Scotty.

Skip's sharp blue eyes shifted to Sam as she walked into the room with Nick right behind her. Seeing her dad in her house reminded her of how thankful she was for the husband who'd had the foresight to install a ramp at their house so her paralyzed father could come and go as he pleased. That ramp had effectively doubled the number of places Skip could visit whenever he felt like it.

Sam bent to kiss his cheek and squeeze the right hand that retained sensation.

"Hey, baby girl. What's the latest?"

Sam glanced at Scotty, reluctant to speak freely in front of him despite what he'd already seen and heard. "How much do you know?"

"Enough to be sick with worry—and fear for our Brooke."

Upon closer scrutiny, she could see the exhaustion etched into his face and deduced he hadn't slept much the night before. A flash of anger directed at Brooke overtook Sam. With a huge and potentially life-threatening surgery pending, her dad needed all the rest he could get, not sleepless nights worried about a granddaughter gone wild.

"Scotty, will you do me a favor, buddy?" she asked. "Sure."

"Will you make me a coffee? I'm about to fall over. I need a boost."

"No problem." He got up and dashed out of the room. After Nick taught Scotty to make hot chocolate in the Keurig, he'd taken over all the coffee-making duties. They called him their barista.

While they had the room to themselves, Sam gave her dad a quick summary of everything she knew so far about what'd happened the night before and recited her list of unanswered questions. Not wanting to upset him any more, she purposely skimmed over Scotty's potential involvement as well as the part about pictures and videos cropping up on the Internet.

"What else?" Skip asked, eying her shrewdly.

"What makes you think there's more?"

"Because I know you, and you never could lie to me. Not sure why you'd try to start now."

"You're supposed to be resting and relaxing and gearing up for surgery. I don't want to lay a pile of shit at your feet right now."

"You didn't. Brooke did. Tell me the rest."

With tremendous reluctance, she told him how Scotty had witnessed the drop-off at their house and about the photos and videos online.

"Goddamn it," he whispered. "This'll crush poor Tracy. And Mike…"

"They'll get through it," Sam said with more confidence than she felt. How did one get through having their teenage daughter gang-raped and then having the attack broadcast to the world? "If there's any blessing, Brooke was so stoned she won't remember any of it."

"Until she sees the video."

"Hopefully we can make it go away before then, but…"

"But what?"

"The video, along with her tox screen and BAC, proves she was stoned out of her mind before the murders. It might be the only thing that keeps her off the suspect list."

"Jesus."

Scotty came back carefully balancing a steaming cup of coffee presented in her favorite Redskins mug. "Here you go, Sam."

"You're the best. Thanks."

"Did I do the cream and sugar right this time?" Sam took a sip. "Mmm, perfect."

He beamed at her.

She extended her arm to him. "Come sit by me." Careful not to jostle her when she held hot coffee, he sat next to her and allowed her to put her arm around him.

He dropped his head onto her shoulder as Nick watched them, arms crossed and a stormy expression on his face that told her he was still wound up about her call to Agent Hill. *Too bad.* She'd do it again if it meant getting Brooke out of this awful mess.

She turned her focus to Scotty, running her fingers through his silky dark hair that was so much like Nick's they could've been biological father and son. "How you holding up, pal?"

"Okay."

"You want to talk about it?"

He was quiet for a long moment. "Not really."

"You saw some upsetting stuff about your new cousin. It's only natural to have questions."

"I was wondering…"

"You can say it. It's okay."

"Why did she let them do that to her?" This was said with a quiver of his chin that broke Sam's heart. She wanted to go back in time to the night before at the ice rink and bring Scotty to the ER with them. Maybe he wouldn't have seen such upsetting things if he'd slept at home the night before.

"She didn't *let* them, buddy. She was drunk and high, and they took advantage of her."

"Why would they do that?"

"Because they were drunk and high, too, and not thinking properly," Nick said. "Real men take care of women and girls. They don't lose control of themselves and take advantage of a girl who isn't able to say no."

"That's right," Skip said. "And whoever did the videotaping is just as culpable as the other boys."

"What does that word mean?" Scotty asked. "Culpable?"

"Responsible," Sam said. "They could've stopped it, but instead they chose to film it. That makes them just as bad as the others."

As he rested against her, Scotty seemed to be processing everything they'd told him.

"You know you can ask any of us anything whenever you want, right?" Skip said. "Even me. I'll never tell you anything but the truth and neither will your mom and dad."

"My mom and dad," Scotty said with the grin that was much more like him. "That's still so cool to hear."

"It's cool for us too," Sam said, as a sudden rush of emotion had her blinking back tears. She closed her eyes and took a moment to breathe in the scent of his clean hair. "You have no idea how cool."

"We need to get going to hockey practice," Nick said.

"Go ahead and get ready," Sam said, giving Scotty a kiss before she released him.

At the word "hockey" Scotty was up and on the way to the stairs to change.

"You feel like taking him?" Sam asked her husband.

"Yep."

"Okay."

Sam watched him follow Scotty upstairs, wishing with all her heart they could've had that vacation they both needed so badly.

"Looks like trouble in paradise," Skip said.

"Maybe a little. He's annoyed the vacation got messed up, he's injured and now he's mad I asked Hill for help."

"That last one explains it all."

"What's that supposed to mean?"

"That FBI agent looks at you like he wants to kidnap you and steal you away from your happy home."

The comment made Sam's face heat, which infuriated her. "That's his problem, not mine."

"True, but your husband doesn't like it, and I can't say I blame him."

"I need Hill's professional help. He can get to the source of the video and pictures faster than I can. That's my only goal here—that and finding out what the hell

Brooke was doing here when she was supposed to be at that fancy school we paid so much money to send her to."

Skip raised an eyebrow. "I had a feeling you might've footed the bill for that."

Sam waved off the comment. "We were afraid of just this very thing that happened anyway."

"You're walking a very fine line here, baby girl."

"I know that. Uncle Joe took me off the MacArthur case as soon as I told him Brooke might've been there at some point. And now the video proves she was there. Not to mention her clothes and phone will be among the stuff they found at the scene."

"So if Joe took you off the case, what're you doing calling in the Feds?"

"I called my *friend* and asked for a favor."

"A favor you shouldn't be requesting when you're off the case."

"I was taken off the MacArthur case. I wasn't taken off Brooke's case."

"Again, I say fine line. You and I have both seen good cops lose their careers by muddying the difference between ends and means."

He was right, and she knew it, but that didn't change anything. "So you're suggesting I let someone else look into what Brooke was doing in the city last night and potentially link her to the murders of nine other kids? I should take a chance that it's going to be handled properly by everyone involved?"

"You should have faith that the people you trained and mentored are going to handle the case and your niece's involvement with all due care and skill. You should step back and let them do their jobs."

"I can't do that, and you wouldn't either if you were me."

He let out a deep sigh that was followed by a gasp. Sam zeroed in on his face, which was twisted in pain.

"What? What's wrong?"

"Same thing," he said with a grimace.

The bullet lodged in his spine had begun to move in recent weeks, and the first sign of trouble had been the return of painful sensation to some of his limbs. He should've had surgery more than a week ago but was determined to get through Thanksgiving before he went under the knife.

"I hope you're not making things worse by delaying this surgery." Any threat to his health made her stomach ache like a bastard.

He laughed through the pain. "Worse than what?"

"You know what I mean, Dad! Worse than this is dead!"

"Life is a fatal illness, and we're all going to die some-day."

"Maybe so, but I vote to postpone your fatal illness for as long as possible."

"And I love you for that, but you need to prepare your-self for the possibility—"

"Do not finish that sentence. Under any circum-stances."

The half of his face that wasn't paralyzed lifted into an indulgent smile. He was living on borrowed time, and they both knew it, but there was no freaking way they were going to actually talk about that.

Her ringing cell phone took her mind off the stagger-ing array of awful possibilities that could result from a surgery doctors had once told them was too risky to perform. Now, with the bullet on the move, they had no choice. Sam flipped open her phone to take the call. "Holland."

"It's Hill. I've got your warrant."

"Wow, you don't mess around."

"No time for messing around. Pick you up in ten?" Sam glanced at the stairs, wondering how close Nick was to departing. Wouldn't it be perfect if he got to watch her leave with Hill? "Yeah, thanks."

"On my way."

She stashed the phone in her pocket, and her gaze connected with the frosty blue eyes that were just like hers.

"Fine line. In more ways than one."

"You've made your point."

"I don't ever want to have to say I told you so, Sam."

"Then don't. I'm going to do what I've got to do, the same way you would. I'm going to figure out what happened to Brooke, and I'll turn over whatever I find to my team."

"And if you find something critical to the prosecution of the person who murdered those kids? It'll be tainted by your connection to Brooke, and you know that!"

"Which is why Hill will be the one to find whatever we find."

"You're playing with fire."

"Just like you did with the Fitzgerald case? Remember how you looked the other way when you figured out that the son of your dead partner's wife killed his brother, and you swept it under the rug to protect her?" Sam had never seen such unmitigated rage directed at her from her father.

Scotty came bounding down the stairs, full of exuberance, unaware he was walking into a battlefield.

"Scotty, do me a favor and get the doors for me, will you, son?" Skip asked.

"You got it."

Without another word for his daughter, Skip turned his motorized chair and headed for the front door. Watching him go, with Scotty trotting after him to get the door on the other end, Sam decided she was truly batting a thousand today.

# SIX

NICK COULD TELL just by looking at his wife that something was wrong. Hell, what *wasn't* wrong today? But judging by the set of her shoulders and the hands propped on curvy hips she was boiling about something.

"What's the matter, babe?" he asked. Even though they'd butted heads earlier, she was still his babe, still the most important person in his life. Well, tied these days for first with Scotty, but he knew she'd understand that. Scotty was first with both of them. Nick placed his hands on her shoulders where tightness was another sign of trouble.

"I just said something to my dad that I shouldn't have. Now he's furious with me, and for good reason."

"He doesn't have it in him to stay furious at you for long."

"I don't know... He's pretty steamed. Scotty went to walk him home and handle the doors for him."

Nick moved carefully to put his arms around her from behind. His ribs hurt much worse than they had earlier, but knowing he'd have to drive Scotty to hockey practice, he hadn't taken any more pain medication.

Sam rested her hands on top of his. "I need to tell you something that's going to make you really mad."

Nick's entire body went tense as he waited to hear what she'd say.

"I'm going to Brooke's school with Hill. He was able

to get a warrant, and we're going down there to get her laptop and try to figure out what happened last night." He had a million things he could say to that, but in the interest of preserving the fragile détente, he kept them all to himself.

Sam turned to face him. "Say something."

"What's there to say? If I tell you not to go, you'll go anyway. If I tell you this isn't your case, and you're risking everything for a kid who has proven she may not be worth it, you'll go anyway."

"I'm doing it for her whether she's worth it or not, but more I'm doing it for Tracy, who is indeed very worth it."

"If I tell you Hill is an opportunist who'll do anything for some time alone with you, you'll deny that too. So what is it exactly you want me to say?"

Sam stepped back from him, folding her arms and shaking her head. "You just don't get it."

"No, I don't, but that's okay. Apparently it doesn't matter if I get it or not."

Scotty came in the front door, back from helping Skip home. "Ready to go, Nick?"

He tore his gaze off his wife to focus on his son. "Yeah, buddy. I'm ready." Without another word for Sam, he grabbed his phone, keys and coat and headed for the door.

"See you later, Sam," Scotty called as he followed Nick out.

"Have a good practice."

"Thanks."

In the year they'd been together, Nick had never been angrier with her than he was right now. She was defying a direct order from her chief to stay out of the case and gambling her hard-won career for a kid who'd shown absolutely no regard for anyone other than herself.

That's what he'd meant when he questioned whether Brooke was worth it. The words had come out wrong, but the sentiment behind them was dead-on, and she knew it. Brooke had been making trouble in their family for years now, and while he wouldn't wish this latest situation on anyone—least of all Tracy and Mike, who totally didn't deserve it—he wasn't as surprised as he should've been that it had happened in the first place. And if she were being truthful with herself, Sam wasn't either.

"What's wrong?" Scotty asked when they had driven halfway to the rink in rare silence.

"Nothing. Sorry. Just a lot going on today."

"You're mad at Sam. I can tell."

Nick still wasn't used to having a perceptive kid in the middle of his marriage, not that he'd want that perceptive kid anywhere else. "We don't agree about her approach to this situation with Brooke."

"How do you mean?"

"She wants to figure out what happened last night, and I want her to stay out of it."

"She can't do that. It's not how she rolls."

Nick glanced over at the boy, who was in fact exceptionally perceptive. "No," he said with a sigh, "it isn't, but I wish this once she'd roll in another direction."

"Because she could get into trouble for helping Brooke?"

"For one thing."

"And because it's messing up the vacation?"

"For another. Not that I blame Brooke for that. Well, not really. It's just…complicated, and this week was supposed to be relaxing."

"Sam was excited about the vacation too."

"I know." He pulled into the rink parking lot and after driving around a few times, he finally found a spot. The place was always crowded. He turned off the car and looked over at Scotty. "Every married couple hits a bump or two along the way. There's always going to be things we don't agree on, and Sam and I are still figuring out how to fight with someone else in the house—someone we'd never want to upset."

"It's okay. I know what you mean, and at least if you're fighting you won't be kissing all the time." He made gagging and choking noises that had Nick laughing so hard his ribs ached in protest.

"You're hilarious."

"I know, right?"

As he got out of the car and followed the boy and his giant equipment bag into the rink, Nick realized he felt a tiny bit better. He was still upset about everything that'd happened, but for the next couple of hours he would focus totally on his son. He'd deal with his wife later.

RATTLED BY THE way Nick had once again walked away from her without finishing their conversation and without any of the words they always said to each other, Sam stood there staring at the door for a good five minutes after he left. Most of the time when she dug in on an issue, she felt pretty confident she was right. This time, she wasn't so sure.

He'd made good points. Brooke had put herself in a dangerous situation by sneaking out of school to attend a wild party at home. However, no one deserved to be sexually assaulted. With that in mind, Sam gathered her belongings for the two-hour trip to Middleburg, Virginia.

Before she left, she placed a call to Tracy, who answered on the first ring.

"How is she?" Sam asked.

"The same. Still sleeping and out of it."

"That's for the best right now. She's going to be sick and in pain when she wakes up."

"I know. That's what the doctors told us."

"I'm going to the school to see what I can find out. I'll be gone about five hours. I've let it be known that no one is to talk to her without me present, so no one from the MPD should bother you."

"Freddie stopped by a short time ago to check on us, but it was a personal visit, not professional."

Sam expected nothing less from her faithful partner, who was friendly with her entire family. "That was nice of him."

"He'd come from the crime scene and looked like hell."

"It's always worse when kids are involved."

"I can only imagine. I don't know how you do it."

"Are you okay, Trace?"

Tracy released a rattling sigh. "I'm shocked and horrified and…" Her voice broke. "Not as shocked as I should be that something like this finally happened. It's like she was leading up to it for the last couple of years. I know Mike feels the same way, though he'd never say it out loud."

"I'm also not as shocked as I should be that she found a way out of school or came home to attend a party or got high or drank. But what they did to her is on them, not her."

"If she hadn't done what she did, they couldn't have done what they did," Tracy said.

"Maybe not, but it doesn't excuse them, and the fact is that after they raped her, someone killed them and everyone else who was there. Because she had blood all over her, it's highly likely that Brooke and others were there when the killings took place. Either they were the killers or they managed to escape with their lives."

"You don't think she…"

"No, I don't think she had anything to do with murder, Trace. She was stoned out of her mind, and the video proves that."

"God, how could she have done this to herself and to us?"

"She's got a long road ahead of her coming to terms with what happened. If there's a bright side, she won't remember much of it. I've got to go, but keep me posted on what's going on there. I'll come by when I get back."

"Thanks for what you're doing. I'm sure you're out on a ledge on our behalf, and I appreciate it."

"She's alive, and that's all that matters right now. Try not to worry about the rest."

"I'm trying."

"I'll see you soon." Sam ended the call filled with feelings of impotence and rage. Here she was, the best-qualified member of the department, relegated to the sidelines in what promised to be another hot case. Her niece was in the ICU, her sister was riddled with misplaced guilt and her dad and husband were angry with her.

This day could only get better from here, right? Wrong. She opened her front door to find Darren Tabor from the *Washington Star* still staked out on the sidewalk. "What do you want, Darren?"

"I'm wondering what you're doing home when there's been a mass homicide in the city."

"I'm on vacation."

"Nine kids were murdered, and you're on *vacation?* Why do I find that hard to believe?"

Sam shrugged, trying to act nonchalant. The last thing she needed was the pesky reporter catching wind of the fact that her niece had been at the scene at the time of the murders.

"Why was an ambulance here last night? I tried to get the police report, but surprisingly all I found was a 'not-needed' report." His tone dripped with sarcasm, and she had to give him credit. He was, as always, incredibly well informed and thorough.

"Private family matter."

"And the senator's trip to the emergency room?"

Sam scowled at him. "A hockey injury. He's fine."

She glanced up Ninth Street, hoping Hill wouldn't arrive until she'd gotten rid of Darren. "Go away, Darren. There's no story here."

"Oh, Sam," he said, laughing. "There's *always* a story where you're concerned. I can see you're not in one of your rare generous moods today, so I'll be on my way. For now. I just hope you're not covering up something."

"You're watching too much television."

"Before I leave you, here's another interesting thing I heard on the beat… Something about Nelson needing to replace Gooding and your husband being his first choice."

Sam stared at him.

"Ah," Darren continued with a smug grin. "I can see this is as surprising to you as it was to me. So the senator hasn't mentioned this news to you? Word is that Gooding is sick, and it's serious. He's going to step down after Thanksgiving. My source tells me that even though Senator Cappuano turned down the president's offer, he's still Nelson's first—and only choice."

She felt like she'd been electrocuted. Nick had been asked to be *vice president*, and he'd never mentioned that to her? Forcing herself to focus on the crisis of the day, she scoffed at Darren. "The news is so slow you're forced to make stuff up now, huh, Darren?"

"I'm not making this up. I got it directly from the guy who covers the White House for us. He said he heard it from a West Wing staffer. If you don't believe me, ask your husband."

"I gotta go. Have a nice Thanksgiving."

"You too. I'm sure I'll see you before then."

"I'm sure you won't." Walking to the corner, she sent Avery a text asking him to pick her up on the next block. She glanced over her shoulder to make sure Darren wasn't following her, but didn't see any sign of him.

Her mind whirled with the information Darren had given her. Was it true? Had Nelson talked to Nick about being his vice president? If so, why wouldn't Nick have told her that? After all his preaching about being open with each other! She'd changed her entire way of doing business to accommodate his need to know everything. Clearly, he wasn't playing by the same rules.

By the time Avery pulled up to the curb where she waited, she'd gone from shocked to furious. She got in the car and slammed the door.

"Jeez, take it easy on the car, will ya?"

"Sorry."

"Everything okay?"

"Yeah, it's great. Best day of my life." She noticed he wore a casual black jacket with faded jeans. She'd never seen him in anything other than a three-thousand-dollar suit and was taken in once again by his striking good looks. His golden-brown hair matched his equally golden eyes.

Chiseled cheekbones and that accent made for one hell of a handsome package. But since she was married to the best-looking guy she'd ever known, golden boy Hill barely registered a second glance from her. The fact that he'd confessed to having a major crush on her was just another reason to keep her eyes to herself.

"How's your niece?"

"The same. Out of it. Still in ICU."

"I've called in some of our best cyber guys to track down the source of the video and photos."

"Will they be able to get it taken down?"

"That's the goal."

"Thanks. I really appreciate this."

"You must've been feeling pretty desperate to call me," he said with a hint of humor in that dreamy Southern accent.

"Desperate is a good word for how I feel. Brooke, my niece… She's been a handful the last few years. This school was a last resort. And now…" Sam sighed, exhausted and unable to wrap her mind around the implications of what was ahead for Brooke—and her parents.

"I know it seems overwhelming right now, but you'll figure out what needs to be done to protect Brooke."

"I just hope I'll have a career left by the time I get it figured out." Resting her head against the seat, she intended to rest her eyes for a few minutes. She came to, disoriented and unsure of where she was when she saw Avery looking over at her. "Sorry. Long night with no sleep."

"No problem."

"I didn't snore, did I?"

"I'll never tell."

Heat infused her face, which infuriated her. What did she care if he'd heard her snore or not? "So this is the Remington School for Girls," she said, looking for something—anything—she could say that would get his gaze off her.

"In all its stone and ivy-covered glory."

"You got the warrant?"

He patted his chest where the warrant presumably resided in a pocket.

"Let's get this over with." Barely fortified by the two-hour nap, Sam steeled herself to kick some ass when her senses were fuzzy around the edges. She preferred to be at her best when she had to flip the bitch switch, but the fuzziness wouldn't stop her from doing what needed to be done here.

She marched into the school's main entrance like she owned the place, which was her favorite way to walk into an establishment where she had business. Inside she confronted one of her other favorite things—a receptionist, who acted like she hadn't the first clue as to why Sam had come.

"Get your boss out here," Sam said, flashing her badge. "Immediately."

The heavyset older woman got up and walked into another office, closing the door behind her.

"I do so enjoy watching you work, Lieutenant."

"I hate stupid people who pretend they don't know what's going on when Brooke's big escape is all they've talked about since I called this morning."

"You do make a good point."

The woman returned with a tall, skinny, balding guy.

Wearing a gray three-piece suit and gold wire-framed glasses, Gideon Young walked like he had a stick up his ass. The walk told her a lot about what she could expect from him. She flashed her badge, and Hill did the same.

"Lieutenant Holland, MPD."

"Special Agent-in-Charge Hill, FBI."

At the mention of the FBI, Young seemed to deflate a bit. "What does the FBI have to do with this?"

"We have nine murdered teenagers in the city and a tenth in ICU," Hill replied. "That's what the FBI has to do with this."

His complexion visibly drained of all color. "*Murdered?* Who was murdered?"

"That's none of your concern," Sam said. "We'd like to know how Brooke Hogan was able to check herself out of here with bogus documents. We'd like to know why a minor was allowed to leave here without her parents being contacted before she was released into the custody of a sister she doesn't have."

Hill's hand on her arm was the only indication Sam had that she was on the verge of losing her shit with Young. She took a deep breath and shook off Hill. "I would like some answers, Mr. Young, and I'd like them now."

The older woman who'd been watching their exchange with big eyes suddenly broke down in tears. "It's all my fault. She said she was Brooke's sister and provided a notarized note from Brooke's mother that said she was authorized to pick up her sister. I should've called her parents. It's my fault. If you need to arrest anyone, arrest me."

*Oh, for fuck's sake, Sam thought.*

"There, there, Linda," Young said, patting the other woman's arm. "No one blames you."

"Um, I do," Sam said. "My sister does, and her husband does. We all blame you for letting a seventeen-year-old con artist scam you so easily."

As Linda wailed with distress, Young glowered at Sam. "Is that really necessary?"

"Mr. Young, as you are painfully aware—because I have no doubt you've consulted with your legal counsel since we spoke earlier—my sister and her husband have the grounds to bring a gigantic lawsuit against your school. The lawsuit will be so huge, it may put you right out of business. In light of the tremendous liability you're looking at in this situation, I would urge you—and your staff—to fully cooperate with our investigation."

His shoulders sagged at Sam's use of the word "lawsuit." He wore a resigned expression when he said, "What do you need from us?"

"First and foremost, I'd like to know what time Brooke left here."

Linda wiped her wet face. "It was about five thirty, I would say."

Sam made a notation in the notebook she'd pulled from the back pocket of her jeans. "I'd also like a physical description of Brooke's so-called older sister."

"Linda, do you feel up to describing her to the lieutenant?" Young asked his receptionist in a gentle tone that made Sam want to smack him.

Hill nudged Sam's elbow. "Sam, look." He pointed to a camera in the corner above the reception area.

"Never mind, Linda." To Young she said, "I want the video."

"I sent it to you as directed."

"As you can plainly see, I'm not at a computer, so get me somewhere that I can look at it. Now."

Nodding, he picked up a phone, pressed a series of buttons and said, "Please come to the main office right away."

"Anything like this ever happen before?" Sam asked while they waited.

"No!" Young said. "We've built our reputation on helping at-risk girls turn their lives around. Something like this... Well, it could ruin us."

Linda let out another sob at that news.

Sam glared at Young, hoping he'd get the message. "Um, Linda, why don't you take a break in my office and get yourself together."

"Yes, Mr. Young," she said between sobs. "I'll do that. I'm so sorry."

"I know you are."

A young man came into the office through a door in the back. Tall and muscular, he had dark, curly hair and soulful eyes. Sam's first thought was that the students at the all-girl school must drool over him.

"This is Sebastian Ryder, our director of security," Young said.

Sam snorted out a laugh at the guy's soap opera name. "*You're* the director of security?"

Ryder's dreamy poet's eyes narrowed with displeasure. "Who are you?"

She flashed her badge and took great pleasure in saying, "Lieutenant Holland, Metro PD Homicide." Using her thumb, she gestured to Hill. "My associate, FBI Special Agent-in-Charge Hill."

Ryder looked back and forth between them before he settled his gaze on Sam. "What can we do for you?"

"Mr. Young hasn't mentioned the fact that my seventeen-year-old niece was sprung from here last night by someone claiming to be her older sister?"

"I just got here. I don't normally work on Saturdays."

"So you just happened to come by on your day off?"

"Mr. Young called me and said we had a situation he needed my assistance with, but as I just arrived, I haven't yet had a chance to speak with him about it." Sam found it very odd that Young had taken the time to call in his director of security but hadn't seen fit to tell him why. "We'd like to take a look at the video surveillance of the reception area from last night. We have a warrant."

Avery produced the warrant and held it up for their inspection.

Ryder glanced at Young, who nodded. "Sure, right this way." Ryder gestured for them to come around the counter and follow him through the same door he'd come through. They walked down a long corridor that seemed to house offices and ended in a large room filled with screens that showed numerous views of the bucolic campus. Two other young, handsome guys were monitoring the images on what seemed like a quiet day at the school. Only a handful of students were out and about. "Is it always so quiet around here?" Hill asked.

"No," Ryder replied. "Most of our students have already gone home for the holiday. The big rush was yesterday after classes ended for the week."

Which, Sam thought, could explain how Brooke was able to sneak one by an overworked and overwhelmed receptionist. Knowing Brooke, she'd given the timing of her breakout careful consideration.

"The residence halls close for the week at six o'clock tonight," Ryder continued, "and reopen a week from tomorrow at noon. Trent, can you get me the videotape from the reception area from last night?"

"We're interested in seeing what transpired there around five-thirty," Sam said.

"Sure," the man named Trent replied as he got busy on a computer. Images popped up on an oversized screen.

Sam zeroed in on the progression, which Trent fast-forwarded. "Wait. Stop. That's her." Brooke came into the office with a backpack on her shoulder and her dark hair up in a ponytail. She spoke with Linda and then turned as another girl walked into the office. Sam moved closer to the screen to get a better look at the second girl, but she could only see the back of her.

Brooke hugged her and then introduced the other girl to Linda. They produced the paperwork that Linda scanned as she continued to chat with Brooke. Linda handed the papers back to Brooke's friend, and the two girls turned to leave, giving them a clear view of the second girl's face.

"There! Freeze that frame. Can you email that image to us?"

"Yes," Trent said. "Where's it going?"

"Give them your address," Sam said to Avery. "Your phone is smart, and mine isn't."

Avery recited his email address.

When he got to the fbi.gov portion of the address, Trent paused and glanced up to take a closer look at the agent. "Did you say FBI?"

"Yes," Avery said without giving any more information.

"Okay, I sent it."

Avery retrieved his phone, and when a chime indicated the email had arrived, he looked at Sam. "Where do you want to send it?"

"To my sister for an ID."

"What's her number?"

Sam recited it from memory. "Tell her it's me and I need to know who that girl is."

"Done," Avery said a minute later.

"We'd like access to Brooke's room," Sam said. "Right this way," Young replied from behind them.

His voice startled her, but she wasn't surprised he had followed them to the security area. Young and Ryder accompanied them out of the main administration building, across a grassy quadrangle to a brick dormitory called Aldrich Hall. They went up three flights of stairs to room 301.

"Has anyone been in here?" Sam asked.

"No," Young said. "Brooke's roommate left before she did, so the room has been empty since Brooke left." It was the first lucky break she'd gotten all day, Sam thought, as Ryder used a master key to open the door. The distinctive scent of her niece's perfume was the first thing Sam noticed, and it brought tears to her eyes. Fighting them back with everything she had, she stepped into the room and took in the photos taped to the wall. She didn't have to be told which side of the room belonged to Brooke. No Bieber or One Direction pretty boys for her girl, Sam thought. Brooke was all about the edgy, grungy guys, most of whom Sam didn't recognize.

Her unmade bed was covered in a dark purple comforter, and clothes were strewn about on the floor along with several purple towels. On the bed sat the stuffed bear named Norman that Brooke had slept with all her life.

The sight of Norman, battered and well loved, brought more tears to Sam's eyes.

"They aren't allowed to keep their rooms like this," Young said with an air of disapproval.

"I'd think that with Brooke in ICU, due in part to the negligence of your staff, her messiness would be the least of your concerns," Sam said as she approached the desk.

Avery produced evidence bags and gloves from his coat pockets, and they worked together to bag Brooke's laptop and iPad.

Sam sifted through the papers on Brooke's desk, but didn't find anything other than notes from classes. "Your program includes counseling," Sam said to Young. "I'd like to speak to the person who was working with Brooke."

"I'm not sure what good that would do," Young said. "She's bound by doctor-patient confidentiality."

"Agent Hill?" Sam said.

"We have a warrant," he reminded Young.

"That covers therapy?"

"It covers everything. I am nothing if not thorough." Sam absolutely adored the pesky agent in that moment. He was proving to be the ideal partner in this mission. "Get the therapist. Now."

As Young scurried off to get the therapist, Avery's phone dinged.

He glanced at it and handed it to Sam. "Your sister." The message said, Hoda, of course. Was there any doubt?

Hearing that, Sam placed another call to the principal of Wilson High School, who actually answered this time. "Mr. Galbraith?"

"Yes," he said, sounding rushed and frazzled. No

doubt he was aware by now that several of his students had been murdered. "Who's speaking?"

"Lieutenant Holland, MPD."

After a long pause, he said, "I recognize your name."

"I need some information about a student at your school who goes by the name 'Hoda.' Are you familiar with her?"

He let out a sound that might've been a grimace or a laugh. "You could say that. She's that one student every principal has to deal with. Always in some sort of trouble, always denying her involvement, always blaming someone else."

*Sounds a lot like Brooke,* Sam thought. "What's her last name?"

"Danziger."

"And where can we find her?"

"Tell me you don't think she had something to do with what happened to those kids at the Springer house."

"I'm looking into a separate matter at the moment," Sam said.

"Oh, okay." He sounded relieved, and Sam wanted to tell him the relief might be a bit premature. Galbraith gave her the Danzigers' address, which Sam recorded in her notebook.

"We're trying to track down the owner of the Wilson-Seniors account on Facebook and Twitter. Would you have any idea who runs that?"

"I wish I did. We've been trying to figure that out ourselves as the owner or owners aren't shy about voicing their displeasure with the administration. We have our suspicions, but we can't prove anything. These kids are good at hiding out online."

"Can you give me some names to look into?"

"You have to understand, Lieutenant. These are mostly good kids who feel omnipotent when hiding behind an anonymous handle. I'd hate to see their lives ruined over some harmless postings."

"Have you looked at today's harmless postings by any chance?"

"No, I haven't. I've been doing errands with my wife all day. I came home after I got the call about what happened at the Springers' home. Several of the dead are Wilson students. We're heartbroken."

"Take a look at what your harmless seniors have been up to today. I'll wait."

"Well, um, okay…" The sound of rustling in the background was followed by the click of computer keys. "Oh my God," he said softly—so softly she almost didn't hear him. "Is that Brooke Hogan?"

"It is, and she happens to be my niece."

"Oh, Lord. I'm so sorry. And Michael Chastain and Hugo Springer… I can't believe they'd do such a thing. They were both from good homes. I just… I'm sorry, Lieutenant."

"As you can imagine, we're trying very hard to get to the source of those postings."

"I'll make some calls and see if I can help. I'm so sorry this happened. Brooke is a good kid who fell in with the wrong crowd. I was so hoping for the best for her at her new school."

"We all were, but we'll make sure she gets through this. I appreciate any help you can give me, as well as your cooperation with the detectives who'll want to speak with you about the Wilson kids who were murdered."

"Of course. Anything we can do to help."

"Call me if you get anything on the social media account."

"Will do. Please give my best to Brooke and her family."

"I will. Thank you." Sam stashed her phone in her coat pocket. "Nice guy with a tough job," she said to Avery. "I don't think I'd make for a very good high school principal."

Avery busted up laughing. "Really? What makes you say that? Could it be your bluntness? Your lack of political correctness or perhaps your need to always be right?"

Despite the fact that he'd summed her up rather well, Sam scowled at him anyway. "Very funny."

"Dr. Kelison is here," Young said from the doorway. He introduced her to Sam and Avery.

Sam turned to face the woman who didn't look much older than the population she served. She had long, curly reddish-brown hair and brown eyes. "You're a doctor?"

"I am."

"How old are you?"

"Thirty-three."

"Wow, you don't look it."

"So I've been told."

"You worked with my niece, Brooke Hogan?"

"I did."

"Can you tell me anything she might've said to indicate she was planning to bust out of here?"

"It's been my experience that teenagers can be extremely circumspect when it suits them."

"Is that a no?"

"That's a no. Without betraying her confidences, I can tell you Brooke was making progress toward accepting the changes in her life and getting through her senior year successfully. She was anxious to be done with school."

"Did she say anything about her parents or their decision to send her here?"

Kelison shook her head. "I'm not at liberty to discuss that."

"We have a warrant," Sam reminded her.

"We all know that access to private medical information requires a whole other kind of warrant. Without that, I'm not saying anything else." She paused before she added, "I'm very sorry to hear what happened to Brooke. Underneath all the teenage bluster and drama, she's a sweet girl."

"Yes, she is." Sam took a long look around at Brooke's room, wondering if or when her niece would return here, and picked up Norman to bring him to her in the hospital. "Our work here is finished," she said to Avery. "Let's get back to the city."

# SEVEN

AFTER THREE HOURS of delays, Gonzo's skin had begun to feel too tight to contain the nervous energy zinging around inside him. He tugged on the shirt collar that felt like a noose and loosened his tie. When he wasn't obsessing about how the court might rule on their case, he was thinking about the investigation he was supposed to be running in the lieutenant's absence.

He'd been in touch with Cruz, McBride and Tyrone, and had insisted Carlucci and Dominguez follow orders and go home for a few hours of shut-eye. He'd spoken with Lindsey McNamara about the autopsies and Archie about the dump of the cell phones recovered at the scene. Captain Malone was handling the media and Bill Springer, who'd returned to town looking for vengeance on behalf of his son. According to the captain, Springer wasn't interested in talking about how his son had hosted a drug-fueled orgy that had gone bad in his parents' absence. All he wanted to talk about was how his son had ended up dead and what was being done to find the killer.

Gonzo was doing what he could to stay on top of things while he waited with Christina and his lawyer, Andy Simone. Sam's sister Angela had come from the hospital to pick up Alex as they'd planned before everything happened with Brooke. Gonzo had tried to let her off the hook, but Angela wouldn't hear of it. She'd said she was happy to have something else to focus on while they waited for Brooke to wake up.

Angela had taken Alex to her house to play with her son, Jack, and Christina would pick him up after court. Gonzo's gratitude toward Christina and Angela in particular was overwhelming at times. When Alex had landed unexpectedly in his arms last winter, both women had stepped up to help him, and he couldn't have gotten through his first months of fatherhood without them. Christina was with the baby when Gonzo worked nights, and Angela watched him during the day.

The arrangement worked perfectly, and the thought that today's hearing could upend their harmonious life made Gonzo feel sick and sweaty. With his elbows resting on his knees, he let his hands fall between his legs, his head dropping from the weight of his thoughts. If he lost custody of Alex, he'd never get over it. That much he knew for certain.

Christina put her arm around him and leaned her head against his shoulder, her steady presence giving him the strength to get through whatever might happen. "Are you okay?" she whispered.

"The waiting is killing me. I feel like I'm going to explode."

"I do too."

Knowing she felt the pressure as keenly as he did made it easier to bear somehow. Having her there with him made everything easier to bear. He linked his fingers with hers and took comfort in the heat of her skin against his.

"Let's go, guys," Andy said all of a sudden as he got up to head toward the courtroom.

Now that the moment was upon them, Gonzo couldn't

move. A wave of fear bigger and stronger than anything he'd ever experienced threatened to sweep him under.

"It's okay, Tommy," Christina said. "Whatever happens, I'll be right there with you, and we'll get through it together." She squeezed his hand for emphasis. "Come on. Andy is waiting for us."

Still in a fog of fear and apprehension, Gonzo got up and let her lead the way to the courtroom, where Andy held the door for them. Gonzo was startled to see Alex's mother, Lori, for the first time in months. She looked much more like the woman he'd met initially and bore no resemblance to the drug-addicted person she'd been last winter, before a stint in rehab.

Surely the judge would see that too.

Lori stared at him with trepidation in her eyes. Their one-night stand had resulted in one of the best things to ever happen to Gonzo, and he refused to be ashamed of that. But the thought of Lori taking Alex away from him had Gonzo breaking the eye contact.

The court was called to order, presided over by Judge Morton, who'd granted temporary custody to Gonzo last winter. Like then, he gave no indication now of recognizing Gonzo as the detective who'd solved his sister's murder years earlier. The judge was businesslike as he reviewed the findings of the social worker who'd been a regular visitor in Gonzo's home and had obviously spent time with Lori too. Gonzo couldn't bear to listen to the social worker describe the changes Lori had made to accommodate a young child.

Gone was the felon who'd been her boyfriend. She'd been sober for one hundred twenty-nine days and was working the program religiously, attending daily meetings. She held a job as an office manager, and rented a two-bedroom apartment with a bedroom for her son and had arranged for licensed child care should she get custody. To Gonzo, each bit of information about how Lori had turned her life around to make room in it for Alex felt like a nail being hammered into his coffin.

And then it was Andy's turn to talk about the lengths Gonzo and his fiancée had gone to in order to provide a stable, loving home for the child. Gonzo had reluctantly agreed to allow Andy to mention that Christina would be leaving her job to care full-time for Alex as of January. While he'd initially objected to her decision, he was extremely grateful now to have the advantage she'd given him.

Judge Morton asked the social worker a series of questions about Alex and his routine with his father and Ms. Billings. While she gave them glowing reviews, she had good things to say about Lori's efforts, as well.

Listening carefully to each answer, the judge nodded and then shuffled papers around on his desk. The courtroom went completely quiet as everyone waited for him to say something. Finally, he propped his chin on his hands and turned his attention to Lori.

"Ms. Phillips, I want to commend you for the obvious hard work you've done to turn your life around. However, I see no good reason at this juncture to remove Alex from the only home he knows when that home has been both stable and loving."

Lori let out a high-pitched wail of distress that penetrated the fog in Gonzo's brain.

"Counselor, please ask your client to contain her outbursts in my courtroom."

Lori's lawyer leaned over to speak softly to her. Quiet weeping provided a backdrop as the judge continued.

"Detective Gonzales, I'm awarding you full and permanent custody with the provision that Ms. Phillips have regular visitation privileges to be established by the court. We're adjourned."

For a long moment after the judge left the room, Gonzo sat perfectly still, processing the words *full and permanent custody.* He'd won. Alex would remain with him and Christina forever. And then tears were rolling down his cheeks, and he was leaning into Christina's embrace as she cried too.

"This isn't fair!" Lori cried. "I did everything they said I had to do! And it was all for *nothing!*"

"It's not for nothing, Lori," the social worker said. "Because of all your hard work, you'll get to see Alex and be part of his life."

"Only if *he* lets me," she said venomously as she glared at Gonzo. "I never should've called you! You never would've known about him if I hadn't called you!" Gonzo wiped his face and stood to face the mother of his child. "I'm sorry you're upset by what happened here, but I have no desire to keep you from him."

"Save your sympathy," she said, her face twisted with rage as she jerked free of her lawyer's grasp. "This is *not* over, so don't start celebrating too soon."

Though her threat shot a jolt of fear straight to his heart, he gave her the last word. He had what he wanted.

SAM WAS UNABLE to sleep on the ride back to the District as her whirling mind attempted to process what she'd learned so far. Darkness had come early, as it did this time of year when the weather was gray and gloomy and cold.

With two hours to do nothing but sit and think, Sam

made an important decision. She executed it by summoning her entire squad to her house at ten for an update on the MacArthur case. She included Lindsey McNamara on the text, but followed up to her with a note that her attendance would be helpful if she could make it. Sometimes it galled her that everyone didn't answer to her, but alas the medical examiner was one who didn't.

"How's it going with Shelby?" she asked Hill, breaking a long silence.

"Fine."

"That's all? Just fine?"

"Why are you asking me when you already know every detail of every second I've spent with her?"

"That is not true."

"*Right*," he said with a low chuckle. "She hasn't told me *everything*."

"Whatever you say."

"So you like her?"

"Yes, I like her. If I didn't, would I be spending time with her?"

"You can't give me anything of value that I can take back to her?"

"You can tell her I said this—grow up and quit kissing and telling."

"I'm not telling her that, and P.S., she hadn't told me there'd been kissing."

He groaned. "Christ, I walked right into that, didn't I?"

Sam laughed at his dismay. "She's terrific."

"I'm not disagreeing."

"Do you know about the special 'project' she's got going on?"

"If you're referring to her efforts to have a baby, yes, I'm aware."

"What do you think of that?"

"People need to do what they gotta do to be happy. I've got no gripe with it."

"Will you run for the hills if she gets pregnant?"

"What do you take me for, Sam? I'm not going to run for the hills or anywhere else. I've known all along about Operation Baby. I ran into her in an OB office during the Kavanaugh investigation. And besides, we're just hanging out. No one is making lifetime commitments."

"I don't mean to insult you. I'm looking out for my friend."

"Fair enough, but you've got nothing to worry about and neither does she."

The Danzigers lived on a block of well-kept if nondescript townhouses on the line where Friendship Heights and Chevy Chase came together. They got out of the car and took the front narrow walk single file. Sam knocked on the door and waited, hoping something would be easy today.

A woman came to the door, looking as if she might've been sleeping.

Sam flashed her badge as Avery did the same. "Lieutenant Holland, MPD, Special Agent-in-Charge Hill, FBI."

"What's this about?"

"Is your daughter, Hoda, at home?"

"No. Is she in some sort of trouble?"

"We aren't sure. We'd like to speak to her. Can you tell us where we might find her?"

"I'm not really sure. She's out with her friends."

"How old is your daughter, Mrs. Danziger?"

"She just turned eighteen."

"And you don't know where she is?"

"I don't see how that's any of your business. Hoda is very independent. She doesn't need me around her neck all the time."

Sam glanced at Avery to find that he looked as amazed as she felt. "Are you aware that a number of Wilson High School students were murdered last night?"

That bit of information finally seemed to draw a more human response from the woman. "What? Murdered? What're you talking about?"

"May we come in, Mrs. Danziger?" Hill asked.

"Um, yeah. Sure, I guess."

The house was dark except for the TV's glow. A blanket on the sofa indicated where Mrs. Danziger had been before their arrival. She turned on a lamp that cast a faint light over the room. "Sorry for the darkness. I suffer from migraines, and I do better in the dark."

*The metaphor applied to her parenting style too, Sam thought.* "Would you please call Hoda and ask her to come home."

"You said she's not in any trouble."

"Did I say that, Agent Hill? I don't recall saying that."

"I didn't hear you say that, Lieutenant."

Mrs. Danziger's eyes got very big. "You don't think she had anything to do with *murder*, do you?"

"Call her," Sam said.

With trembling hands, Mrs. Danziger picked up her cell phone off the coffee table and made the call. "Hoda, it's Mom. Call me when you get this message."

"Send her a text too," Sam said.

Mrs. Danziger did as directed. "What now?"

"Now we hope she calls you back." They waited thirty minutes in uncomfortable silence, but the phone never rang. Sam put her notebook and a pen on the coffee table.

"Give me her phone number and a list of where she might be. Friends, hangouts, anything you know about her whereabouts. If you have phone numbers for the friends, that would help."

"I don't know much about her friends. She keeps a lot of things to herself."

At that, Sam snapped. "You understand that as her mother it behooves you to know what she's doing and who she's doing it with, right?"

"I don't see how that's any of your business."

"I'll tell you exactly how it's my business. Kids like yours, allowed to run free and do whatever the hell they want whenever they want, are the ones who end up in trouble, Mrs. Danziger. Sometimes they end up in very grave trouble, which leads them to my Homicide squad or worse yet, the morgue. Not to mention, your lovely daughter checked my niece out of a boarding school in Virginia last night, and now my niece is in the ICU at GW, and your daughter is nowhere to be found. *So don't tell me it's none of my business!*"

"Sam." The single word from Avery brought her out of the exhaustion-fueled rage and back to the reality that she was getting nowhere fast with Mrs. Danziger, who was now crying softly.

"I'm so sorry about your niece. I don't know what Hoda was thinking going to Virginia. She knows she's not allowed to leave the city without telling me."

"How did she get to Virginia, Mrs. Danziger?" Avery asked.

Sam was thankful to him for taking over the interview because she was on the verge of ripping the stupid woman's stomach out her mouth and bitch-slapping her with it.

"She…she has a car. It's an old Toyota Camry."

"We need the license plate number and registration information. Can you get that for us?"

"I'll see if I can find it." Probably grateful for anything that took her away from Sam's hateful glare, she got up and bolted from the room.

"Are you okay?" Avery asked in that goddamned accent that made her want to punch him.

She had to remind herself that he was helping her and wasn't part of the problem. "I'm fine."

"You don't seem fine."

"I'm tired, and I'm furious, but I'm fine."

Mrs. Danziger returned with some paperwork and made a wide circle around Sam to hand it to Avery.

He flipped through it quickly, made a couple of notes and handed it back to her with his business card. "When you hear from your daughter, I want you to call me."

"I will."

"I also need a recent photo of her."

"I have some on my phone."

"Can you email one to me that shows her face?"

He dictated his email address to her, and she sent the picture.

"I want to make it clear to you," Sam said as she got up to leave, "that protecting her is not in her best interest—or yours. If you find out where she is—and I urge you to get busy doing that—and you don't tell us you've located her, we *will* charge you for impeding our investigation. Do you understand?"

"Yes," she said meekly.

Sam headed for the door, hoping Hill was right behind her. "Who are these fucking people who let their kids run wild and then act all surprised when their little darlings end up in trouble?"

"Is that a rhetorical question, or am I expected to answer?"

Not appreciating his attempt at humor, she got in the car and slammed the door.

"Where to?" he asked when he got in.

"Can you drop me at GW and then get the computer and iPad to the lab?" Since the MPD relied upon the FBI crime lab, things would happen faster if he made the request.

"Can do."

On the way to the hospital, Sam called HQ and requested an all-points bulletin on Hoda and her car. When they arrived, she turned to Avery. "I really appreciate your help with this, and I'm sorry if it messed up your holiday plans."

"It's no problem. I can go home later in the week." He pulled up to the hospital's main entrance. "Am I invited to the powwow with your squad later?"

"How do you know about that?"

"I can read."

"You can read a text I'm writing while you're driving?"

"One of my many skills."

Sam tried not to think about what Nick would have to say about Agent Hill coming to their house. The last time he'd been there, she'd had to warn Nick to curb the impulse to pee on her to mark his territory. Her husband could barely stand the sight of the guy, let alone tolerate him as a guest in their home. And since she and Nick were getting along so swimmingly at the moment, Hill's attendance ought to go over really well. "Um, sure, you can come if you want to."

"Wow, another really long pause. I'm underwhelmed by your hospitality."

"I don't have to tell you that your presence won't please my husband."

"Forget it. I don't have to go."

"No, it's fine. You've been a huge help today, and we'll take all the help we can get on this one."

"I thought you'd been removed from the case."

"I was."

"*Soooo…*"

"I'm still their commander, and I want to know what's going on."

"It's none of my business, Sam, and you certainly know what you're doing, but I'd hate to see you get screwed over this. You've worked really hard to get where you are, and there're people who'd love to see you taken down a peg."

"Believe me, I know, and I appreciate your concern. But I can't be disengaged. It's just not who I am." She grasped the door handle. "I'll see you at ten?"

"I'll be there."

"Thanks for today, Avery. I mean it. I owe you one."

"No, you don't," he said in a tone filled with resignation.

"Just the same… Thanks." With Norman the bear tucked under her arm, Sam got out of the car and walked through the automatic doors, anxious to see how Brooke was doing. She took the elevator to the ICU and was surprised to see Nick sitting in the waiting room.

"What're you doing here?"

"Same as you, I suppose. Checking on Brooke as well as her parents."

"How is she?"

"The same. They're going to wean her off the sedation tomorrow, and that's when the fun really begins." Sam winced when she considered what Brooke would have to be told about what'd happened to her. But she was extremely anxious to hear what her niece recalled about the night in question. It only took one little tidbit to blow an investigation wide open. "Where's Scotty?"

"Home with Skip and Celia. I stayed with all the kids so they could come over earlier, and then we traded places. I've been keeping Mike company. He just went to get coffee."

Before she could tell him it was good of him to be here, and before she could ask him how he was feeling, her cell phone rang. Sam took the call but only because she saw it was the chief calling.

"Holland."

"Lieutenant, we have a situation."

"As I see it, we have a number of situations at the moment."

"Then let's call this a new one. Bill Springer is making a big stink out of the fact that you're not running the investigation."

For the first time in hours, Sam had reason to smile. "Is he now?"

"I can hear your 'I told you so' coming, so stifle it." Sam laughed at the irritation she heard in his voice.

"I wasn't the one who thought it was a good idea to take me off the investigation."

"You know it was the right thing to do."

"I can prove Brooke didn't kill anyone."

"And how can you do that?"

Sam explained about the video that showed Brooke out of it while being sexually assaulted by three of the murder victims. "Her tox screen and BAC prove she was stoned and drunk."

Farnsworth was quiet as he processed that information. "So the video puts her at the scene, but shows her as a victim rather than a perp."

"Yes." Sam swallowed a knot of fear as she pressed on. "I've also just been to her school to retrieve her laptop, iPad and a few other belongings. I was also able to view the video of the pickup and identified the girl who went in there pretending to be Brooke's older sister."

"And you just breezed in there and they gave you all that access?"

"Um, not exactly."

"Speak, Lieutenant. Immediately."

"I, um, had some help from Agent Hill. He got a warrant so we wouldn't have to deal with the jurisdictional BS."

The chief's deep sigh had Sam holding the phone away from her ear. The grimace she directed at Nick normally would've amused him. Not today. "If and when my head actually explodes, you'll be one hundred fifty percent responsible for it. You know that, right?"

"Yes...sir. Sorry, sir."

"No, you're not, so don't compound it by lying to me." He cleared his throat in a deep rumble that came through the phone line like a roar. "Here's how we're going to play this. You're going to make a statement to the press in the morning that indicates your niece was at the party but we have eliminated her as a suspect in the homicides. You're going to indicate your niece was the victim of a crime that is being handled by another division."

"But—"

"Sam! Shut up and listen to me!"

She literally bit her lip to keep from talking back to him.

"You're going to say the crime involving your niece is under investigation by a separate division of the MPD, and you're to stay far, *far* away from that investigation. Do I make myself clear?"

"I want to be there when she is interviewed."

"No."

"Yes."

"*No!*"

Startled by his actual roar, she forced herself to remain quiet—for now.

"You're walking the finest line in the history of fine lines, Holland, and if you think I won't hesitate to suspend you and take your badge to keep you from crossing that line, you don't know me at all."

"I want Erica Lucas on Brooke's case," Sam said when she had the opportunity. "I don't want Ramsey anywhere near it." She'd had the chance to work with Lucas during a recent investigation that had unearthed a child prostitution ring in the city, and she'd appreciated Lucas's no-nonsense approach as much as her sensitivity. "Ramsey hates my guts."

"What'd you do to him?"

"Hell if I know."

"Fine. I'll request Lucas, but you're to stay out of her way. You got me?"

"Yeah, I got you. I don't think she'll have much of a case. I think all the boys who raped Brooke are dead."

"Let her come to that conclusion without your assistance."

"So I'm back on the Springer case?"

"You're back on it."

"Excellent. We have a meeting at ten tonight, and I'll

bring everyone up to date." As soon as she finished the sentence, she realized she'd said too much.

"Why would you have a meeting tonight for a case I'd expressly removed you from?"

"I was checking in with my squad, sir. Like any good commander would when her squad was in the middle of a hot case that had the potential to be emotionally dev-astating to them." She laid the shit on super-thick hoping it would soothe him.

"Did you hear that sound? It was my head officially exploding."

Sam held back a laugh that would get her in deeper trouble with him. "If it's just the same to you, sir, I think I'll keep Detective Sergeant Gonzales in charge of the Springer investigation, but I'll be close by to keep Mr. Springer off your ass. Is that okay?"

"You're actually asking my permission? This is a ban-ner day indeed. For what it's worth, I agree with your decision regarding Sergeant Gonzales, and I'll be at the briefing tomorrow morning to show the department's support of you both."

"Thank you, sir."

"Get some sleep. Tomorrow will be a long day."

"Yes, sir. I'll see you in the morning." She stashed the phone in her pocket and turned to face her husband. "How're you feeling?"

"Fine."

"Your ribs don't hurt?"

"I didn't say that."

Though she badly wanted to see Brooke and Tracy, she sat in the chair next to him. Under normal circum-stances when he wasn't angry with her, not to mention hurt, she would've crawled into his lap for some much-needed comfort. Something told her his lap wasn't open for business tonight.

"I'm sorry you're upset about everything. I agree that you have good reason to be. We had plans, and my life, my job and my family has once again gotten in the way of that."

"I've been sitting here thinking about how often that happens."

"I'm really sorry. You have no idea how sorry I am."

When he reached for her hand and held it between both of his, Sam felt like she could truly breathe again for the first time since they'd argued earlier. She hadn't forgotten the little tidbit Darren had tossed in her lap, but she was taking things one crisis at a time.

"What I was thinking is that these things always appear to be your fault because your job is twenty-four-seven, and mine isn't as much, and because you have this big amazing family, and I don't. So it's not really fair for me to blame you when your stuff messes up our stuff."

Sighing, she dropped her head onto his shoulder. "It's fair. I blame me too. I know you may not believe it, but I was looking forward to this week as much as you were."

"I believe it, and I'll let you make it up to me as soon as you're able to."

"I've got something I need to talk to you about." His body stiffened, which caused him to gasp in pain. "What?"

"Let's talk about it later, when we're *alone*."

"We're alone right now."

"Not alone enough."

"Sam…"

"Nick…"

"Fine. Have it your way. I don't know why any of us

ever try to get you to do anything other than exactly what you want to do."

The comment made her laugh—hard. "You're finally starting to get a clue. Took you long enough."

"Kiss me."

"Right here?"

"Right here. Right now."

Sam turned toward him and laid her hand on his face, taking a moment to appreciate his absolute adorableness. And yes, that was a word, and yes, it totally suited him. "I love you so much, and I hate when we fight."

He turned his face into her hand to kiss her palm. "I hate it too."

Sam leaned in to kiss him, and as their lips connected, she reveled in the overwhelming rightness she always felt with him. They might often infuriate each other, but they also completed and complemented each other in more ways than she could count.

"I'm going in to see Brooke and Tracy, and then I could use a ride home. Everyone is coming at ten to go over the case."

"So I heard. Is your friend Hill included in everyone?"

"He was a huge help to me today. He cut through miles of red tape to get me into Brooke's dorm room and to get the footage of the pickup last night."

"So that's a yes?"

"That's a yes."

She felt rather than saw him pull back from her at that news. He had such a blind spot where Hill was concerned. "You've got nothing to worry about there. I've told you that before. I just spent five hours alone with him and never once felt the slightest inkling of what I've felt since I sat down next to you."

"That's nice to hear, but let me ask you this. Say the shoe happened to be on the other foot, and a woman I work closely with made it clear she'd be *all* over me if you were out of the picture. How would you like that?"

"I wouldn't, but I'd do my best to understand that it was her problem, not yours and not ours."

"Sure, you would," Nick said with a laugh. "After you removed her liver with your famous rusty steak knife."

"Why, Nick, honey," she said, batting her eyelashes, "you make me sound so violent and unrefined."

"You're both those things, but you're my violent, un-refined wife, and I wouldn't change a thing about you. Well, except for your sloppiness, your willfulness, your stubbornness, your need to mess with my stuff, your—"

Her fingers squeezing his lips ended his recitation. "You made your point." She released his lips to kiss him again. "I'll be back in a few."

"I'll be here waiting for you."

"Good," she said with a smile, relieved to have put their ship back on an even keel after a long day of rough sailing. She still needed to talk to him about what Dar-ren had told her, but she would bring that up later when they were at home and had the ability to air it out thor-oughly. As she walked down the hallway to Brooke's room, she thought about how much time they'd spent in hospitals during their first year together and hoped the second year would be much less eventful.

She stepped into Brooke's room, where a sleeping Tracy held Brooke's hand from the recliner next to the bed. Sam tucked Norman in with Brooke, bent to kiss the girl's forehead and stood upright to look down at her niece. She tried to imagine what Brooke had been thinking when she and her friend Hoda plotted to bust her out of school. Where was she planning to be in the morning when her parents set out to pick her up for the holiday?

Sam would really like to know the answers to these and other questions, but she wasn't going to get any answers tonight, so she left them sleeping and returned to the waiting room, where Mike had joined Nick.

"Hey, Sam, anything new?" Mike asked.

"I brought Norman from the dorm room and tucked him in with Brooke."

The mention of his daughter's beloved stuffed animal reduced Mike to tears. Seeing her big, strapping brother-in-law in such a state broke Sam's heart.

"I can't deal with this," he said softly. "Half of me wants to kill her, and the other half is bargaining with God to get her through this in one piece."

Sam sat on the other side of him and put her arm around his shoulders. "I don't blame you for feeling both those things because I feel them too. You know what I was thinking earlier? Maybe this will be the wakeup call she needs to get her shit together before it's too late."

"Let's hope so, because if this doesn't do it, I don't know what will." To Nick, Mike said, "Thanks for hanging out. I appreciate the company."

"Happy to."

"I'm going back in with them in case Tracy needs me."

"I'll check on the kids when I get home," Sam said. "Maybe they can come stay with us tomorrow for a change of scenery."

"They'd like that. They love being with Scotty."

"And he loves being with them." Sam hugged him. "Hang in there, okay? We've all got your back."

Mike nodded and wiped new tears off his face when he released her.

"We'll see you tomorrow," Nick said when he hugged Mike. "Call if you need anything."

"Thanks."

As they walked to the elevator, Nick put his arm around Sam. "I've always had so much respect for the way he treats Brooke like his own kid, but never more so than I do right now."

"I agree. He's amazing, and he's been that way toward her from the very beginning. Tracy used to say that Brooke picked him as her daddy. They were so close when she was little. This has to be tearing him up inside."

"It is. He was sobbing his head off earlier. I did what I could for him, but it's tough."

"Thanks for being a good friend to him," Sam said. "I like him. I've always liked him."

In the elevator, he leaned against the back wall and turned so he could see her face. "Are we alone enough now for you to tell me your big secret?"

"It's actually not my big secret. It's yours for once."

"Huh?"

He followed her off the elevator and through the lobby to the main door, where they exited into the frigid evening air.

"Damn, it got cold today," Sam said, burrowing deeper into her coat and nearly drooling in anticipation of the heated seats in his BMW.

"Don't change the subject, Samantha."

"You'll have to excuse me for enjoying the fact that for *once* I've got something on you rather than the other way around." Though she made light of the secrecy, she wanted to know why he'd felt the need to keep such an important thing as the president's offer from her.

On any other day when they hadn't spent an entire day arguing, she might've made a bigger issue out of him keeping a big secret from her. Now she was relieved that they had seemed to recover their footing, and she wasn't exactly anxious to start something new with him.

He held the passenger door for her and waited for her to get settled before he walked around the car to get in the driver's side, moving gingerly as he got in.

"Are you okay to drive?"

"I'm fine." Grimacing as he moved, he started the car, cranked the heat and turned to her. "Speak. What's this *thing* you *think* you've got on me?"

"Oh, I know I've got something, and it's good. In fact, it's so good, I get a free pass to keep things from you for a year after this."

"Samantha, you're trying my patience. Will you stop playing games and spit out whatever it is?"

"Do the words 'Mr. Vice President' mean anything to you?"

His face went totally blank, and his mouth opened and then closed.

"*Aha!* So it's true! When did this happen, and why didn't you tell me?"

"How did you hear about it?"

"I asked first."

He kept his gaze fixed on the windshield. In the orangey glow of the parking lot lights, she could see he was tired and in pain. "It came up on the trip to Afghanistan. Gooding has a brain tumor, and he's going to resign. Nelson was looking for a replacement. He mentioned it to me. That's all there was to it."

"That's *all* there was to it? Then why did my source tell me you were—and are—his first and only choice?"

"Who's your source?"

"I'm not divulging."

"Is it someone who has the wherewithal to blab it all over Washington?"

"Perhaps."

"Fabulous."

Sam wanted all the details. "What did you say when Nelson asked you?"

"I told him the truth. It's not a good time for us to make a move like that. We've just brought Scotty into our home, and your job and everything with your dad. We've got enough on our plates."

"Nick, he's basically setting you up to run in four years. Why would you say no to that?"

He gave her that side-eye look that usually meant carnal pleasures were in her immediate future. "You really have to ask?"

*"Because of me?"*

"Samantha, be honest with me and with yourself. You'd hate that life, surrounded by Secret Service all the time, unable to say what you really think about anything, living at the Naval Observatory, unable to work at the job you love. The whole thing would be a nightmare for you."

She squirmed a bit at the accuracy of that last part. "Still… I don't want to be the reason you turn down amazing opportunities. You could be *vice president*, Nick, and maybe even president someday. I mean… Jesus."

He laughed and took her hand. "I have everything I've ever wanted and then some now that I have you and

Scotty and an amazing job and our incredible life. What more could I want that I don't have besides a little more time alone with my gorgeous wife?"

"You could be *vice president*."

"And my wife, who I love more than life itself, would be miserable and unhappy, and I'd never get any time alone with her. No thanks."

"It's not that simple."

He shifted the car into reverse and backed out of the parking space. "It's exactly that simple."

She shook her head. "I'm not done talking about this."

"There's no point in talking about it. I told Nelson I'm not interested."

"That doesn't mean *he* isn't interested. From what I heard, you're still his first choice. And besides, are people allowed to say no to the president?"

"I don't think there's any law against saying no to him."

"There has to be. Look into that for me, will you?"

"Sure, babe. Whatever you want." He squeezed her hand. "So tell me something. When're you planning to sleep?"

"Right after the meeting. Shower and bed."

"Good. That's one less fight we need to have today."

"Mmm." She took advantage of the opportunity to enjoy the comfortable heated seats, the pleasure of his hand holding hers and the appealing scent of him in the car to close her eyes just for a minute.

"Babe." She leaned toward the sound of his voice. "Babe, wake up. We're home."

"I wasn't asleep."

"Sure, you weren't."

Sam forced her eyes to open and stay that way. "I need

to go over to my dad's for a few minutes before the meeting. I want to see Scotty and see if I can kiss and make up with Skippy."

"Good plan. I'll go with you to make sure you don't fall over while you're there."

# EIGHT

SAM AND NICK went up the ramp to her dad's house and stepped inside where Scotty, Abby and Ethan were in their pajamas watching a movie and sharing a bowl of popcorn.

"Sam!" Eight-year-old Abby got up so fast she almost dumped the popcorn, which Scotty caught right before it toppled over.

Sam scooped up her niece and hugged her, breathing in the scent of her flowery shampoo. "Hey, sweet girl." She kissed Abby's cheek. "How goes it?"

"Good, except we're watching *Cars*." She made a face, and her blond curls bobbed. "The boys picked it."

"Next time is your choice, right?"

"Yeah." She burrowed into Sam's neck, and Sam held on a little tighter. "Sam?"

"Uh-huh?"

"Is Brookie going to be okay?"

"Yes, baby. She's going to be fine."

"Ethan said..."

"What did he say?"

"That she was doing drugs and other bad stuff. Is that true?"

"Some of it's true, but I don't want you to worry about her. The doctors are taking really good care of her, and your mom and dad are with her. If she feels better tomorrow, we'll take you and Ethan to see her, okay?"

"Okay."

Sam kissed her cheek and put her down, undone by the little girl's concern for her sister. "How's it going, E?" she asked her nine-year-old nephew.

He never took his eyes off the TV when he said, "Fine."

Sam sat next to Scotty, hooked her arm around his neck and brought him down for a kiss on his forehead. "Hi, buddy."

"Hey. How's Brooke?"

"She's hanging in there. How are you?"

"Good. We're having fun."

"I've got some work people coming over shortly for a meeting. Do you want to sleep at home or stay here?"

"I'll stay here. These guys will fight if I'm not here to referee. Celia said she needs me to keep things under control."

Sam held back a laugh as she looked up to catch Nick doing the same. "Where are they anyway?"

"She's helping Grandpa Skip get ready for bed." Sam kissed him again and ruffled his hair, earning a playful scowl from him. "I'll let you watch your movie, and we'll see you in the morning, okay?"

"Do you have to work tomorrow?"

"Yeah, but I hope I can wrap things up before turkey day."

"I hope so too. I want you to come to my game on Friday."

"I wouldn't miss it unless I absolutely had to."

"I know."

"Love you. Sleep tight."

"Love you too."

Sam reached across him to give Ethan a poke in the ribs that made him giggle.

"Knock it off, Sam."

"Make me."

"Hey!" Scotty said. "How did I get in the middle of this?"

Ethan reached across Scotty to get at Sam, who dodged him with dexterity she shouldn't have had after more than twenty-four hours with hardly any sleep. Relieved that she'd made Ethan laugh, she escaped to the kitchen to wait for a chance to speak with Celia.

"Grab a beer if you want one," Sam said. "I'll take a water."

Nick opened the fridge and got the beverages.

Celia came in a few minutes later and lit up at the sight of them. "Hi, guys." She hugged and kissed them both. "How're things?"

"The same at the hospital, but we're making some headway in figuring out how she ended up there."

"It's all so upsetting. Your father is beside himself."

"Is he still awake?"

"He is, and I'm sure he'd love to see you."

Sam wished she could be so certain, but she steeled herself nonetheless and went into the bedroom in what used to be the dining room. At night he was hooked to a respirator that helped him breathe when he was lying down.

The look he gave her let her know he was still angry with her. He got an awful lot accomplished with those steely blue eyes.

"I shouldn't have said what I did about the Fitzgerald case. It was a low blow."

"Yes, it was."

"I'm sorry."

"Apology reluctantly accepted." His speech was halting as he worked around the respirator.

Sam let out a sigh of relief mixed with a laugh and flopped into the chair by his bed. "I've been fighting with you and Nick today. All I need is a good row with Scotty to make it a perfect trifecta."

"I'm not going lie to you." He took a couple of breaths. "You pissed me off earlier, but I realized…" More breathing. "I'm not pissed at you. I'm pissed at Brooke."

"We all are. Mike put it best. Half of him wants to kill her and the other half is bargaining with God to get her through it with her life intact."

"Yes, exactly," Skip said, his eyes closing. "Tracy was so upset when I was there earlier."

"She was sleeping when I was there."

"Good."

"You should get some sleep too. You can't afford to get run down before the surgery."

"I'm fine. What's the latest?"

Sam took him through her day and what she and Avery had learned in Virginia as well as the frustrating conversation with Hoda's mother.

"Put out an APB for the kid and the car?"

"Already done, and Archie's trying to get a bead on her phone." She told him about her conversation with the chief and how she'd wrangled her way back onto the case. "He told me when his head inevitably explodes it'll be my fault."

Skip smiled as brightly as he was able to with half his face frozen by paralysis. "You drive him crazy."

"I know. It's one of my special gifts. Driving the men in my life crazy."

"And you do it so well. Wish I could be at your meeting."

"I do too, but I'd rather you get some sleep." She stood up and leaned over to kiss his forehead. "Sorry again about the low blow."

"It was low, but it wasn't entirely untrue." She smiled at him. "Love you, old man."

"Who you calling old?"

Her smile widened at the saucy reply. "See you tomorrow."

"Love you too, baby girl."

Having made peace with the other most important man in her life, Sam knew she'd most likely be able to sleep tonight.

"All better?" Celia asked when Sam walked into the kitchen.

She wasn't surprised her stepmother knew about their spat earlier. "All better."

"That's good. He doesn't need another night without sleep."

"That's what I told him too. We've got to run. My work people are coming at ten."

"Have you heard anything about how Tommy made out in court today?" Celia asked.

"Not yet," Sam said, ashamed to realize she'd forgotten all about the important hearing. To Nick she said, "Have you heard from Christina?"

"Not a thing."

"Oh, God," Sam said. "I hope everything is okay."

"We'll find out soon enough," Nick said, rising to leave. "Thanks for the beer I helped myself to, Celia."

Laughing, she said, "Anytime. Our beer is your beer."

They said goodnight to Scotty, Abby and Ethan and

headed out the door. Nick put his arm around Sam and kissed the top of her head. "That, right there, is the up-side to the big family," he said.

"How do you mean?"

"Other than with the O'Connors, I've never felt like I could walk into someone's house and grab a beer the way I do there. It feels like home."

"It makes me so happy to hear you say that, and I know my dad and Celia would be happy to hear it too. We all want you to feel at home with us."

"Well I do, and I love it."

"We love you."

They went up the ramp into their own home, and Sam followed procedure by tossing her coat on the sofa. Nick, being Nick, picked up the coat and hung it in the closet, which Sam thought was pointless. She'd need it again in the morning.

"What time is it?" he asked.

"Nine forty-five."

"Come here."

She curled up next to him on the sofa. "I'm here."

"We've got fifteen minutes to make out before people get here, and I want every minute of it. That's how you can *start* to make it up to me for letting our vacation get ruined."

"Start?"

"Oh, yeah, it's going to take a lot of atonement on your part before I'll be appeased."

Sam moved carefully to straddle his lap, mindful of his bruised ribs. "Atonement and appeasement. Is that what it has come down to?"

He cupped her ass and tugged her closer. "You know it."

"Go easy," she whispered against his lips. "I don't want to hurt you."

"Shut up and kiss me."

She did as she was told, and the second her lips connected with his, the doorbell rang.

"I'm weeping," he said, making sobbing noises as she got off his lap to go answer the door.

"Save it for later, Senator."

"Your atonement allowance just doubled."

Naturally, the first arrival was Avery Hill.

"Tripled," Nick said from the sofa, forcing Sam to hold back a laugh.

"Hey, come in."

"Am I too early?"

"Not at all. Everyone will be here in a minute." She prayed to God that was true, because the last thing she wanted was to spend more than one minute alone with Alpha Dogs 1 and 2 in the same room together. "Can I get you a drink or something?"

"No, thanks. I'm good." He nodded to Nick. "Senator."

"Agent Hill."

Her normally amiable husband offered no handshake or small talk, but rather a steady glare directed at the agent, who stood awkwardly inside the door.

Sam sat next to Nick and would've elbowed him in the ribs if they weren't already injured. "Have a seat, Avery. While we have a minute, there's something I meant to ask you earlier."

Hill sat in an easy chair, but remained perched on the edge of the seat while Nick continued to stare at him. *He* was going to owe *her* some atonement if he kept up the staring nonsense.

"What's that?" Hill asked.

"Next week my dad is having surgery to remove the bullet that's been lodged in his spine for the last three years."

"Wow, why now?"

"The bullet is moving, and they've determined it's riskier to leave it than to remove it." Sam swallowed hard as she tried not to think about the worst possible outcome of the surgery. "Anyway, needless to say, with his shooting still unsolved we're extremely anxious to get ahold of that bullet and run it through the lab. I was hoping you might be able to expedite that for me."

"Absolutely. Whatever I can do."

"Thanks. Things happen faster there when you guys ask than when we ask."

"Speaking of things moving faster, my cyber squad is close to the source of the video and photos. We've isolated the IP address, and now they're working on identifying the physical location."

"That's great. Thank you so much for pushing that through."

"No problem. The lab has the laptop and iPad with orders to expedite."

"Excellent." While she talked with Avery, Sam was acutely aware of Nick sitting next to her and could only imagine what he was thinking as the favors she owed Avery continued to pile up. When the doorbell rang again, she wanted to sing "Hallelujah."

She swung open the door to find Lieutenant Archelotta there, holding a folder under his arm. Fabulous! Now she had one guy who had a crush on her and another she'd actually slept with, both here at the same time in the home she shared with her husband.

"Hi, Archie. Come on in."

"Heard you were rounding up the troops and thought I might be able to help." He handed her the file. "The dump on your niece's phone."

"Thanks. Have a seat. Do you want something to drink?"

"No, thanks."

"You know Agent Hill and my husband, Nick." Archie shook hands with Hill and Nick. "Senator."

"Lieutenant."

Sam was enormously thankful for the fact that she'd never told Nick she'd dated Archie for a while after her divorce from Peter—although their relationship had less to do with dating than it did with sex. Nick really didn't need to know that.

Where in the name of hell was the rest of her team? She dashed off a text to Freddie and Gonzo. Coming?

Ten minutes out, Freddie replied.

Fantastic. Sam took advantage of the uncomfortable silence in her living room to sift through the report Archie had given her. When all the numbers and letters ran together in an unreadable hodgepodge, Sam wanted to wail with frustration. Her dyslexia tended to rear its ugly head when she was tired, and she was as tired right now as she'd been in a long time.

Tuning in to her dismay, Nick took the report from her and flipped through the pages. "Here," he said, pointing. "Text messages between Brooke and Hoda, planning the whole get-out-of-jail scheme."

Without a thought to the two other men in the room with them, Sam said, "Read them to me."

"Davey snuck into his father's office and notarized the note. Do you think it'll work? It'll be busy with people leaving for the holiday. They won't look as closely. Hope you're right. My mom will freak if I'm not here when they come to pick me up. You'll be there."

"So they intended to get her back there that night," Sam said. "How were they hoping to do that when they were drunk and stoned?"

"Maybe they had a designated driver?" Archie asked.

"That might be giving these kids a bit more credit than they deserve," Sam said. "Including my niece."

"Is the brass giving you grief about the connection to your niece?" Archie asked.

"Some, but we've ruled her out as a suspect in the MacArthur murders, and her case is being overseen by SVU."

"That makes sense. I heard Springer was making a stink about you not being on the case. He said he wants the best, and Lieutenant Holland is the best."

"Well, that is true," Sam said, and all three men laughed, which went a long way toward easing the tension.

Freddie and Gonzo arrived a few minutes later, followed shortly by McBride, Tyrone, Arnold, Carlucci and Dominguez. When everyone was settled, Sam brought them up to date on the decision she and the chief had made earlier. "But before we go any further, Gonzo, I'm dying to know what happened in court today."

A smile stretched across his face. "Full and permanent custody."

"I think I speak for all of us when I say we're relieved and thrilled for you and Christina," Sam said sincerely.

"Thank you, LT."

"Chief Farnsworth and I agreed that even though I'll be helping out on the MacArthur case, you'll still be running the show."

"Oh," Gonzo said, sitting up a little straighter. "Okay."

Sam filled them in on what she'd done that day and the information she'd brought back from Brooke's school. When she was finished, she nodded to Gonzo, encouraging him to take over the meeting.

"Let's hear what everyone else has," he said.

The doorbell rang again, and Sam got up to admit Lindsey McNamara and Terry O'Connor.

"Sorry I'm late," Lindsey said. "We were out grabbing some dinner when I got your message."

"I don't have to stay if it's not appropriate," Terry said.

"Come in," Sam said. "It's fine."

When Nick saw his deputy chief of staff, he got up slowly from the sofa to shake Terry's hand. Nick gestured toward the kitchen. "I was just about to get a soda. Can I get you one?"

"I won't say no to that," Terry said as he followed Nick from the room. He seemed as anxious as Nick to relocate away from the room full of cops.

"Cruz," Gonzo said. "What've you got?"

Freddie referred to his notes. "A list of all our victims, to begin with. Hugo Springer, age eighteen, lived in the house. Michael Chastain, age seventeen, and Todd Brantley, age eighteen, both Wilson High School seniors. Kevin Corrigan, age eighteen, graduated from Wilson this year. The girls were Lacey Morrison, age sixteen, Kelsey Lewis, age fifteen, Julia Pelse, age seventeen, Maura McHugh, age seventeen, and Shana Gilford, age sixteen. Lacy, Kelsey and Julia are students at Roosevelt. Maura and Shana went to Sidwell Friends with Hugo Springer. All the parents have been notified, but we've kept the crime scene details from the parents and out of the reports and the press thus far."

"So the parents don't know there were drugs and booze and sex involved," Sam said.

"Right," Freddie replied. "All three of the schools have brought in therapists to help the other students as needed."

"We'll have to meet with the parents at some point to tell them how it went down," Gonzo said.

"Agreed," Sam said. "Perhaps we can bring them in together when we know more." She told the others what Scotty had witnessed the night before when Brooke was brought to their house. "If possible, I'd like to keep him out of the official investigation because he didn't see anything that identified the people who made the drop or the car. However, he was able to put the drop at some time around eleven-forty. He said two people got out of the backseat with Brooke while another waited in the car. The two carried Brooke up the ramp, left her there and ran back to the car, which took off the second they were both inside. So we can assume that in addition to the nine who were killed, at least four other people were at the Springer house, including Brooke and Hoda. I'd like to know if there were more."

"The neighbors told us there were a lot of cars there throughout the night," Jeannie said. "Lots of coming and going."

"Dr. McNamara," Gonzo said. "What've you got on the autopsies?"

"All the victims died from stab wounds and blood loss. We're awaiting the full toxicology results. The lab was completely overwhelmed today, so it's taking a while, but the smell of alcohol was pervasive. We've established time of death for all the victims between eleven and eleven-fifteen."

"So the whole thing went down over the span of fifteen minutes," Gonzo said.

Lindsey nodded in agreement. "All of them had engaged in or were in the process of engaging in some form of sexual activity at the time of death."

"Agent Hill?" Gonzo said. "Anything to add?"

"My cyber team is getting close to isolating the physical location of the IP address from which the photos and video of Brooke Hogan's assault found on Facebook, Twitter and Instagram originated. I'll pass along that information as soon as we have it. We're also processing the laptop and iPad retrieved from Brooke's room at her school in Virginia to see what we can find out about the party planning and other people she may have heard from in reference to the party."

"We appreciate the assist," Gonzo said.

"Happy to help."

"Until we're able to speak to Brooke and track down her friend Hoda, I think we should split up the victims and go back to the parents to try to get some insight on who else might've been at the party," Gonzo said. He went down the list, dividing the victims among the detectives. "Try to get a handle on their other friends with addresses and phone numbers and then follow up to see if you can find anyone else who was there. Ask about boyfriends, girlfriends, exes, anyone who had a beef with one of them. We also need more info about who had easy access to the Springers' house. Arnold and I will take that angle and look into the maid's story to make sure her alibi checks out."

Sam and Freddie were assigned Todd Brantley and Kelsey Lewis. Sam's stomach turned at the thought of knocking on the doors of grieving families in search of information. It had to be done, but she hated doing it and knew the others did too.

"I suggest we keep an eye on social media," Archie said. "These kids love to air it out online. I can put some of my people on monitoring what's being said about the party and the murders. We can also mine the victims' individual accounts for people expressing condolences and making comments on their walls." As he spoke, Archie was typing into his phone, no doubt issuing orders to his IT detectives.

"Excellent," Gonzo said. "I expect that we'll end up with a long list of people to follow up with, so everyone should work their own lists and keep me apprised of anything you uncover." He glanced at Sam. "Anything to add, LT?"

"This is a tough one," Sam said thoughtfully. "If you need help, ask for it. It's not the time to act like it's not getting to you if it is."

"Agreed," Gonzo said. "We all know our cases are much more difficult when there're kids involved, so reach out if you need anything. Let's reconnect tomorrow at sixteen thirty at HQ. Dominguez and Carlucci, stay on the lab overnight and report in to me at zero six hundred. Everyone else go home and get some sleep. We've got another long day ahead of us tomorrow."

EVEN THOUGH HE'D much rather have another beer, Nick poured sodas for himself and Terry, a recovering alcoholic.

"I don't know how they deal with this shit day in and day out," Terry said as he accepted the icy glass from Nick. "It makes what we do look like preschool."

"A lot of times, the Senate feels like an overgrown

preschool," Nick said with a chuckle as he sat at the table with Terry.

"True. Still… Do you ever worry about Sam breaking under the strain of what she sees every day?"

"I worry more about things like stray bullets flying around her."

"Yeah, I suppose that'd be a bigger deal than the emotional fallout."

"That's a concern, too, but she tends to roll with it all pretty well. This one is tougher than most, though. Her niece Brooke was at the party at some point, and turned up here, naked and bloody and wrapped up in a sheet on our doorstep."

"Oh my God. Is she okay?"

"She will be. We hope."

Terry shook his head and blew out a deep breath. "Tracy and Mike seem like nice people."

"They are. They're reeling."

"Not the vacation you've been anticipating, huh?"

"Not hardly. But family is family, and you do what you've got to do."

"Yes, you do." Terry eyed Nick as if there was something else he wanted to say.

"Something on your mind?"

"Just an odd little rumor I heard at the DNC meeting earlier today."

"What kind of rumor?" Nick asked, though he feared he might already know what Terry was going to say.

"Something about you replacing Gooding as VP."

"Who told you that?"

"Is it true?"

"It's true that Nelson asked me. It's not true that it's happening."

Terry stared at him, mouth agape. "Nelson asked you to be VP, and *you turned him down?*"

"Yeah, I turned him down."

"*Why?*"

Laughing, Nick said, "You sound just like your dad did when I told him I said no."

"I can only imagine his reaction. This is Nelson handing you the nomination in four years if you want it. You realize that, don't you?"

"I get it."

"So again I ask, *why?*"

"Think about it, Terry." Nick gestured to the kitchen door, which was the only thing between them and the team of cops in his living room. "You know why."

"Because of Sam. And her job."

"And Scotty, who's only been with us a few months and has made a very smooth transition. Everything would change, and I like things the way they are." He thought of the interrupted vacation. "Most of the time."

"But… It's vice president…*of the United States*."

"I know," Nick said with a smile. "It's just not the right time."

Terry looked like he wanted to cry as he took a drink of his soda.

"Are you going to be okay?" Nick asked him.

Terry dabbed at his eyes dramatically. "In time. Maybe."

"You and your dad," Nick said, laughing. "Cut from the same political cloth. He nearly had an embolism when I told him I turned down Nelson's offer."

"I'm surprised that's all he almost had. From what I heard, Nelson hasn't given up on you yet."

"What's that supposed to mean? I said no."

Terry shrugged. "You're still his first choice. I think

you can expect the White House to play some hardball before he moves on. You might want to talk to Derek and get his take."

Nick's friend Derek Kavanaugh had recently returned to his post as Nelson's deputy chief of staff, months after his wife, Victoria, was murdered. Derek was easing back to work, but he'd certainly have the scoop on Nelson's vice presidential deliberations. "I'll see what he has to say, but I'm not changing my mind."

"What does Sam think of it?"

"She wasn't happy to have heard about it through the grapevine. She won't tell me how she heard it, but I think one of the reporter-stalkers told her."

"You didn't tell her?"

"What was the point in bringing it up? He asked, I said no, thank you, Mr. President, and that was the end of it."

"Hmm."

"What does that mean?"

"I'm just wondering what she had to say about being kept in the dark about your conversation with Mr. President."

"She wasn't pleased that I didn't tell her, but she gets why I said no. Can you imagine her as second lady?"

"Umm…" Terry's lips quivered.

"It's okay to laugh. The thought of it cracks me up too."

They shared a laugh, and Nick was thankful to have something to laugh about after the brutal night and day they'd just endured.

"She'd do it for you, you know."

"Yes," Nick said with a sigh. "She would, and she'd hate every minute of it. That's not what I want for her— or for us. And speaking of choices made with the best interest of family in mind… Christina has let me know she's resigning after Christmas to spend more time with Tommy and Alex."

"She is? For real? Wow, I didn't see that coming."

"Neither did I, but I get it. Kids are only little for a short time, and she wants to be with Alex. I think she'd like to have a baby of her own too. She knows my door is always open to her if she wants to come back to work." He paused, contemplating the man he'd known for twenty years who'd finally become a close friend in the last six months. "Of course her departure leaves me in need of a chief of staff. Are you interested in a promotion?"

"Seriously?"

"Dead seriously."

"I, um…" When his eyes filled, Terry looked away until he had regained his composure. "I'd be honored."

"Thank you."

"No, thank *you*. When I think about where I was a year ago and where I am now… It's overwhelming, and I have you to thank for taking a huge chance on me when you had no good reason to."

"I had every good reason to. I knew this Terry was still in there somewhere, and it's been a pleasure to have him by my side this year."

"I hate that my brother had to die for me to get a clue and get my life together."

"He'd be proud of how far you've come. He used to worry about you a lot."

"He did?"

Nick nodded. "It pained him that he ended up where he was due to your misfortune. He never wanted it in the first place, but he certainly didn't want it at your expense."

"He and I… We weren't as close as we could've been, which is another of my many regrets."

"He'd love the changes you've made," Nick assured him. "As much as the rest of us do. And he'd love to see you so happy with Lindsey."

"I hope so. I miss him. I can't believe it's almost been a year."

"I know. I find that hard to believe too. And what a year it's been. He wouldn't recognize any of us if he came strolling in here right now."

"No kidding, right?" Terry said with a smile. "You married, me sober and in a stable relationship for the first time in my adult life, Christina leaving the rat race to help raise her fiancé's kid. Who are these people, and what have we done with his friends and family?"

"We got a hard reminder that life is short, and we've all grown up as a result. I have to think he'd approve."

"He would. Of course he would. He'd be proud of you, too, and the way you've embraced the office. And he'd be envious of your incredible approval ratings and over-whelming popularity, which is why Nelson is so very, very interested in you as his VP."

"And we're back to that."

"Don't rule it out completely, Nick." Nick insisted his top staffers call him by name when they were alone or in social situations. "Surely there has to be a way for you to take advantage of this opportunity and keep Sam happy too."

"If there is, I haven't figured it out. Do enlighten me."

"Let me give it some thought and do some poking around."

"Just don't give anyone the impression I'm actually thinking about doing it, because I'm not."

"I hear you."

Lindsey came into the kitchen. "Are you ready to go?" she asked Terry.

"Whenever you are."

"I've had more than enough of this day, and tomorrow will be another long one," Lindsey said. "I'm ready for bed."

Terry waggled his brows suggestively, which made Nick laugh. "I'll keep you posted on what I find out."

"Knock yourself out, but you won't change my mind."

"Duly noted." Terry stood and shook Nick's hand. "Thank you. For everything."

"Same to you. We'll see you both on Thursday?"

"Wouldn't miss it."

Sam and Nick walked them out, closed the door, locked it and engaged the security system.

"Alone at last," Nick said as he took his wife's hand and led her upstairs.

"I need a shower."

"So do I. We may as well conserve water and take one together."

Her smile lit up his world the way it always did. "I do so love your conservationist tendencies."

Because he was aching like a bastard, Nick moved slowly as he shed his clothes and enjoyed the view of her doing the same. She started the water and turned to him as he struggled to remove his shirt.

"Let me."

He gave up the fight and let her work the shirt up and over his head.

"Oh, Nick," she said with a sigh. "It's even worse than before."

"I'm okay."

"I wish you'd stop saying that when it's obviously not true."

"I'm fine. See?" He encouraged her to look a little lower to where he sported proof that everything was working the way it was supposed to.

She snorted out a laugh and gently put her arms around him.

Her softness pressed against him never failed to fire him up, and tonight was no exception. The agonizing pain in his side did nothing to detract from the ache of desire.

She took his hand and led him into the shower, where she carefully washed his hair and every other important part of him.

Nick trembled from the feel of her hands on his skin. "Samantha, you're making me crazy."

"I'm only trying to make you clean."

"Sure you are," he said with a laugh. "My turn." He filled his hands with her shampoo and worked it through her long hair.

"I can finish. You should go lie down."

"Stop babying me."

"You baby me when I'm hurt."

"You never let me."

Very gently, she touched his chest, right above where the angry bruises began. "I hate that you're hurting."

"I know you do." He put his arms around her and brought her in close to him. "But I feel much better now than I did fifteen minutes ago."

"You're so easy," she said, as she always did. "Mmm, only with you." If she hadn't needed sleep so badly, he could've stood there all night with his love, under the warm water. "Let's get you to bed."

"Let's get *you* to bed."

"Let's get *us* to bed."

Sam dried his back and shoulders so he wouldn't have to twist around, and then used another towel to get most of the moisture out of her hair. They stood at side-by-side sinks to brush their teeth.

"Let's switch sides in bed so I don't bump you during the night," she said as they went into their bedroom.

Since he wanted her right up against him where she belonged, he agreed.

"This is weird," he said when they were settled under the covers. "I'm left-wifed."

Sam laughed softly in the darkness as she rested her hand flat against his belly. "I'm sorry again the vacation got screwed up."

"It doesn't have to be a total bust. We can still make the most of the time we have together this week."

"Remember when we got married and I told you that even when it appeared otherwise, there would never be a time I wouldn't rather be with you than anywhere else?"

"I vaguely recall that," he said in a teasing tone. He'd never forget a word of what she'd said to him that day. "It's always true. There's nowhere I'd rather be than right here with you, so any time you think I'm choosing my work or my family over you, I'm not."

"I know, babe. I'm sorry if I made you feel bad about doing what you need to do. I'm just kind of selfish where you're concerned, and we get so little time together."

"I'm selfish about our time together too, and I hate how there's always something getting in the way of it." He ran his hand up and down her back. "There's nothing getting in the way of it right now."

"You're injured."

He took hold of her hand and directed it to where he ached for her. "I'm not injured here."

"Nick…"

"*Samantha…*"

"I don't want to hurt you," she said as she took the hint and stroked him.

Barely able to breathe let alone talk with her hand working its magic, he said, "You won't."

She moved carefully to straddle him and bent to kiss him. Her hair rained down upon him and he grasped handfuls to keep her close. "Don't move," she said as she shifted ever so slightly to take him in.

"*Yes*," he whispered, moving his hands to her hips and then up to cup her breasts.

"You're moving."

"Can't help it."

"Tell me if it hurts."

"Nothing hurts, baby. I swear. Well, one thing hurts, but you're taking care of that."

Sam laughed as she moved ever so slowly, so slowly he thought he'd go mad from the need for more. But he kept his promise and let her take the lead.

"I wish you could see how beautiful you are right now," he said. Her hair had gotten long recently, long enough to nearly cover her breasts, which peeked out from behind the damp curls. Parted lips, flushed cheeks and the gentle sway of her hips had him on the verge of release in no time at all. He forced himself to hold on, to give her time to get there too.

Knowing she needed to sleep more than he needed this, he reached between them to coax her.

"You're moving," she said on a gasp.

"Shhh." He kept up the insistent press on the tight bundle of nerves that throbbed under his fingers and reached up with his free hand to bring her down for another kiss.

She moaned against his lips and turned away from the kiss as she reached the peak.

Nick was right behind her, his arms tight around her as he thrust into her, the pain in his side nearly obliterating the pleasure of his release. It had been worth it, he thought as she settled on top of him. Surrounded by the scent of lilac and vanilla, the scent of his Samantha, Nick was content—for now anyway. He'd long ago accepted that if they both lived forever, he'd never get enough of her.

"I shouldn't be lying on top of you."

"Don't you dare move. I love it."

"Mmm, I love you."

"I love you too. Get some sleep, babe."

"Gonna move in a minute."

"Okay."

She fell asleep right where she was, with him still buried deep inside her, right where he most wanted to be.

He brushed the hair back from her face and kissed her forehead. Any pain he might feel from his injuries was nothing compared to the magic he experienced whenever she was in his arms. She was all he needed, all he'd ever need.

# NINE

WHEN SAM'S ALARM went off at six, she woke to discover she'd slept on top of Nick, and his arms were tight around her. She'd once hated sharing a bed with anyone. Things had certainly changed in the last year.

She took a moment to study his beautiful face as he slept, appreciating the rumpled hair, the scruffy jaw and the gorgeous lips that were slightly swollen from their lovemaking the night before. Sam wanted nothing more than to spend the entire day right where she was, but people were counting on her for answers and until she got them, there'd be no time for herself.

Unfortunately, she was too wrapped up in him to extricate without waking him, so she placed a series of kisses on his chin, his cheek and then his lips, lingering until his sexy hazel eyes fluttered open. Rather than release her, though, he only squeezed her tighter.

"Gotta go to work."

"I know."

"Are you okay after I fell asleep all over you?"

"I love having you sleep all over me."

"That doesn't answer the question."

"Maybe this will." He truly surprised her when he reversed their positions, pinned her arms over her head and slid into her. "Any questions?"

"Just one."

"What's that?"

"Can you be quick?"

He laughed as he heeded her request, taking them on a quick but wild ride.

"Holy shit," she said, breathing hard as she came down from the incredible high. "You sure know how to get a girl's blood pumping first thing in the morning." She wanted to curl up to him and go back to sleep, but that wasn't an option. Instead, she gave him a gentle nudge to dislodge him and sat up to comb her fingers through her hair.

Nick ran his finger down the center of her back, making her startle when he delved between her cheeks.

She got up before he could entice her to stay. "No more dirty tricks, Senator. I've got to go." Sam went into the bathroom to shower and wasn't at all surprised when he joined her. "Keep your hands to yourself, mister."

"What fun would that be?"

Sam turned to him and looped her arms around his neck. "How's the pain today?"

"Much better."

"How can that be possible when you let me sleep all over you?"

"You're the cure for what ails me, baby," he said, waggling his brows.

"That's very corny and very cheesy and very beneath you."

"I loved being beneath you all night. We should do that again sometime. Soon."

Sam rolled her eyes at him and reached for the body wash.

He kept her company while she got dressed and went downstairs with her to make her toast and coffee before she left.

At the door, he gave her a lingering goodbye kiss. "Have a good day at the office, dear."

"Maybe we'll get lucky and wrap this one up quickly."

"Maybe so."

"Thanks for last night and this morning. I needed it more than you know."

"I needed it too." He caressed her cheek and kissed her again. "Fighting with you turns my whole world upside down."

"Same here."

"I love you." He adjusted the collar of her coat and tugged the zipper up higher. "Be careful with my wife. She *is* my whole world."

"And she's got many, many good reasons to be careful, especially her smoking hot husband."

He grimaced the way he always did when she commented on his smoking hotness. "Whatever you say."

Laughing, Sam patted his cheek and kissed him one last time before she scooted out the door. All the way to HQ she thought about him and the way they always managed to get back on track no matter how deep their differences. That was one of many things that set her second marriage so far apart from the first miserable one. She had pulled into the parking lot at HQ when she took a call from Tracy.

"Hey, Trace. How is she?"

"We had a rough night. She came out of the sedation screaming from the pain of the stitches, so they sedated her again."

"God, the poor kid. That's got to be awful."

"I swear, Sam, I don't know how she's ever going to get past this."

"She will. We'll all help her. We'll get her the best

therapist we can find, and we'll figure it out one step at a time."

"The good news, if there is any, is that coming down off a Molly high is supposedly a bitch, so the sedation is helping with that too."

"That is good news. How are you holding up?"

"I wish I could be sedated too. That would be very nice right about now."

"Abby and Ethan want to see her."

"Maybe by tomorrow she'll be up for some visitors. They're going to bring her around again later this afternoon. I know you're anxious to speak with her, and Detective Lucas was here last night to check on her too." Sam wasn't surprised to hear that Erica Lucas had gone to check on Brooke, even though she worked the weekday shift. "I asked for her. I've worked with her before, and she's great."

"She was very nice and very respectful, unlike that guy Ramsey who came earlier."

"You won't be seeing him again. Give me a heads-up when she's awake. I'll come right over."

"Thanks, Sam."

"Hang in there. I know it all seems so awful right now, but she's young and strong and it'll be okay. Eventually."

"I hope you're right."

Thoughts of Brooke and the long road she had ahead of her stayed with Sam as she went into HQ through the morgue entrance to avoid the reporters gathered outside the main doors. She needed to know what'd happened overnight before she could update the media as directed by the chief. In the detectives' pit, Carlucci and Dominguez were finishing up their shift.

"Anything new?" Sam asked them.

"Not really," Carlucci said. "We didn't get much from the families we re-interviewed. They're so numb with shock that they aren't able to really give us much of anything to work with."

Both detectives looked exhausted—physically and emotionally.

"Do you need to talk to someone? Either of you?" As expected, both shook their heads.

"There's no shame in it if you need it."

"Thank you, Lieutenant," Dominguez said, "but I need sleep more than I need to air it out."

"Me too," Carlucci said.

"Alright then. If you change your mind, don't hesitate to ask. I'll see you tomorrow morning." Sam went into her office to check her messages and email before Freddie arrived. She took a call from Avery Hill at seven-forty.

"We've got something on the WilsonSeniors account," he said. "I thought you might want to be there when it goes down."

"I definitely do." She wrote down the address in the city's third ward, again in Friendship Heights where the computer's IP address had led investigators.

"The kid's name is Brody Mitchell."

"Thank you so much for this, Avery."

"No problem. I'm also pushing your niece's rape kit and electronics through the lab. We should have more on all of that later today."

"Appreciate it. I'll see you in thirty minutes."

"See you then." Sam sent a text to Gonzo and Freddie, letting them know they had a lead on the Wilson-Seniors source, and were due to meet Hill and his team at the home in thirty minutes.

Both detectives replied that they'd meet her there. Her

next call was to Lieutenant Archelotta. "I was wondering if you'd gotten anywhere with the GPS search for Hoda Danziger's phone. She's the one who busted my niece out of school the other night, and I think it's possible she had something to do with getting Brooke out of the Springers' house and delivering her to mine. Hoda's in the wind, and we need to find her. She might be in danger if she witnessed the murders."

"The phone has been off, but we're watching in case she gets curious and turns it on."

"Thanks, Archie."

As Sam was gathering her belongings to leave, Captain Malone appeared at her door. "How goes it?"

"Good. I think. We've got a lead on the IP where the pictures and videos from the party were posted. We're heading there now with Hill and his team. I'm hoping the kid who lives there will have some insight into who else was at the party."

"And Brooke?"

"About the same. Sedated again after a rough night."

"Lucas was there last night but wasn't able to interview her."

"That's what I heard from Tracy."

Malone's wise gray eyes took a perusing look at her. "You're holding up okay?"

"Yes, sir. Any word on the DNA from our victims?"

"Being processed as we speak."

Sam wanted to know exactly who had violated her niece, especially if one or more of them were still alive.

"Keep me posted," Malone said.

"I will."

Sam stopped in the conference room where Gonzo had set up the murder board. She took a good look at each of the victims, all of them attractive young people with smiles as bright as the futures that had been stolen from them. They'd done something stupid and had paid an awful price.

Looking at each photo, Sam vowed to get justice for them no matter what it took.

"Lieutenant."

Sam turned to face Carlucci. "The chief is looking for you in his office."

"Thanks. I'll see him on the way out." She left the conference room and the pit, cut through the main lobby and headed for the chief's suite.

His administrative assistant waved her right in. Sam knocked on the closed door. "You wanted to see me?"

Another man was in the office with the chief, and when he turned around, Sam recognized him as Bill Springer, the father of one of their vics and the owner of the home where the murders occurred.

"I believe you know Bill Springer," Farnsworth said.

"Yes." Sam nodded to Springer. "I'm sorry for your loss."

Springer was tall, dark-haired and handsome in a rough-around-the-edges sort of way.

"I'd like to know what's being done to find the person who butchered my son and his friends." Despite the confrontational tone, raw brown eyes told the story of a long, sleepless night filled with grief.

"We're in the early stages of our investigation."

"Which is shorthand for you have no clue, right?"

"It's shorthand for we're working the case."

"Someone known to my son came into my home and murdered him and eight other people. And all you've got are snappy comebacks?"

Sam glanced at the chief, hoping he would step in. He

took the hint. "Bill, give us some time to figure this out. Lieutenant Holland always figures it out, which is why you wanted her on your son's case."

"Mr. Springer, while I have you, can you tell me who else had access to your home other than you and your wife, Hugo and your maid?"

Springer seemed surprised by the question. "Our other four children have keys."

"Are they local?"

"Two of them are."

"Their names and addresses?"

"I don't understand why this is relevant."

"Just being thorough," Sam said. "I assume you expect us to be thorough in investigating your son's murder."

Out of the corner of her eye, Sam saw the chief's brows rise in reaction to her comeback. What did Springer expect? He was bitching they weren't doing enough, but when asked about his own family he clammed up?

"My son William Junior is local, as is my daughter Clarissa."

"Their addresses?" Sam asked a second time. She wasn't surprised to hear they both lived in the Georgetown area. "And where were your other two children on Friday night?"

"Connor was with us in Aspen, and Margaret is in Boston with her fiancé for the holiday week."

"You and your wife were due to be away all week?"

He shook his head. "Only until Wednesday evening. I had a conference to attend in Aspen, so my wife came with me to spend some time at the Aspen house. Our son Connor lives there."

"And where did you think Hugo would be during your trip?"

Springer ran a trembling hand over the stubble on his jaw. "He told us he'd cleared it with Michael's mom, and it was okay for him to stay there."

"You didn't follow up with Mrs. Chastain to make sure that was true?"

"He's never lied to us before, Lieutenant," Springer said sharply. "We had no reason to doubt he was telling the truth."

Sam wanted to laugh in the guy's face. Hugo had never lied before? Based on what she'd seen in the Springers' basement on Friday night, she suspected it was more likely he'd never been caught before.

"I know what you're probably thinking," Springer said, his posture losing some of its rigidity. "What seventeen-year-old boy doesn't lie to his parents to suit his own agenda? But Hugo wasn't that kind of boy. He was a good boy." Springer's voice broke on those last words.

Sam wondered what he'd say when he learned that his "good boy" had been involved in the gang rape of her niece. "Can you think of anyone who might've had a beef with Hugo or Michael or Todd or any of the other kids who were killed?"

"I didn't know any of the girls. The boys were popular kids with a lot of friends. I can't imagine anyone would hate them enough to kill them."

Sam handed him her card. "If you think of anything, even the smallest thing, please call me."

"I will. And you'll keep me apprised of the investigation?"

"To the best of my ability."

"Thank you."

"Lieutenant, I need you to brief the media before you head out," Farnsworth said.

"Detective Sergeant Gonzales is technically in charge of the investigation," Sam reminded the chief.

"Why is that?" Springer asked. "I want you in charge."

"I was on vacation when this happened, so Sergeant Gonzales is in charge, and I'm assisting him. The case is in very good hands with him."

"If you say so…"

"Bill, Lieutenant Holland is absolutely right. Sergeant Gonzales is one of our best detectives. You have my word that we'll do everything we can to get justice for your son and the others."

"I suppose that's all I can ask. I'll let you get back to work." Springer shook hands with the chief and with Sam on his way out.

"Nothing quite like a head-in-the-sand parent on a case like this," Sam said.

"I was thinking the same thing."

"I'm trying to imagine a scenario where Scotty tells us he's spending a weekend with a friend while we're out of town, and we don't actually confirm that with the friend's parents. All teenagers lie. Don't they?"

Farnsworth chuckled. "I'll have to take your word for that as I don't have any of my own."

"You were one once," Sam reminded him as they walked to the lobby to deal with the media. "Didn't you ever lie to your parents?"

"Not that I recall." He glanced at her. "Did you?"

"I refuse to answer that on the grounds that you are friends with my dad, and there's no statute of limitations on parental lying."

Farnsworth let out a ringing laugh. "You've always been a handful, Holland."

"Why thank you. I appreciate your kind thoughts."

"Only you would take that as a compliment." He shook his head as he held the door for her to go ahead of him into the madhouse of reporters gathered outside HQ, waiting for an update about the MacArthur murders.

The crowd quieted when Sam approached the podium. "I want to preface my remarks by noting that Detective Sergeant Gonzales is the officer in charge of the MacArthur investigation. I was on leave when the call came in, and as such, he's the ranking officer in charge, and I'm consulting. He's in the field, so I'll be handling this briefing in his stead. I expect that future briefings will come from him. Let me tell you what we know.

"At approximately eleven forty-eight p.m. on Friday Dispatch received a nine-one-one call from the home of William and Marissa Springer on MacArthur Boulevard. The Springers' live-in maid, Ms. Edna Chan, placed the call. She had returned home from an evening out to hear loud music coming from the basement. When she investigated, she discovered the bodies of Hugo Springer and five other young people. Patrol responded and found the bodies of six victims in a basement family room. They requested backup from Homicide and Crime Scene detectives. Upon further inspection, three more bodies were found in a bedroom adjacent to the family room. All the victims had been stabbed multiple times."

"How is it possible that someone can stab nine kids without anyone stopping them or hearing the screams?" Darren Tabor asked.

Sam scowled at the pesky reporter. "We believe the room was dark and music drowned out any sounds that came from the initial victims."

"Were drugs or alcohol a factor?" another reporter asked.

"No comment."

"So they were factors?" the same reporter said.

"No comment. We're working the case with cooperation from the FBI, and we'll update you when we have more."

"Have all the families been notified?"

"Yes, they have."

"Could we get a list of the victims' names and ages?"

"We'll get that for you within the hour. In the interest of full disclosure, I will tell you that a member of my family is believed to have been at the party up to and through the murders. We have evidence that clears her of any involvement in the murders. Another division within the MPD is handling her case. That's all for now."

"If she's been cleared, what case is being handled by the other division?"

"Which member of your family?" Daren Tabor asked.

"Isn't it a conflict of interest for you to work on a case where a family member was involved?"

"Are you covering for your family member, Lieutenant?"

"I said that's all for now," Sam repeated through gritted teeth. Even though she'd expected the questions, she still resented them.

"Is there any truth to the rumor that your husband is in the running to be Nelson's new vice president?"

Sam froze as the question sent a hush through the press corps.

"Up to you if you want to answer or not," Farnsworth said under his breath.

"We don't deal in rumors," Sam said. Before they could pose follow-up questions, Sam followed the chief inside.

"Is that true?" the chief asked when they were in the lobby.

"It's true he's been asked."

"Wow, Sam. That's amazing!"

"Um, yes, I suppose it is, but he's not going to do it."

"Why not? That would all but hand him the Democratic nomination in four years."

"Which is what I said too. However, he doesn't feel the time is right for us as a family to take that step."

"Because you'd probably have to leave the job."

"Among other things." Since the thought of leaving her job to play full-time political wife made Sam feel twitchy and off center and more than a little sick, she couldn't imagine what the reality would be like.

"You know, if his star continues to rise the way it has in the last year you may have to make some tough decisions at some point."

"I prefer not to think about that. I've got enough on my mind with nine dead kids, a niece in the ICU and a father going under the knife next week. Nick said no to Nelson, and that's that."

"He said no to the president. What must that be like?"

"I don't know." Sam wanted out of this conversation immediately. The thought of Nick as vice president of the United States wasn't something she was able to process, so she preferred to exist in her happy world of denial. "I gotta meet Hill. I'm heading out through the morgue."

"Keep me posted on all the goings-on—police, political and personal."

Sam rolled her eyes at him and headed for the corridor that led to the morgue. She ran into Lindsey McNamara, who was coming in as Sam went out. "What's the good word, Doc?"

"Not many good words after a day like yesterday. I didn't sleep too well."

Sam appreciated that Lindsey took such a compassionate interest in all the victims that came through her lab, but she could attest to the awful toll the constant exposure to murder took after a while.

"Terry was very excited about his promotion," Lindsey said. "Nick's faith in him has been so critical to his recovery."

"Oh… Sure. That's great." Sam had no idea what she was talking about. "Terry is very valuable to him. He says that all the time."

"The promotion was a bright spot in an otherwise awful day."

"Things seem to be going really well for you two."

"Very well indeed," Lindsey said with a smile as a faint blush flooded her cheeks. "I'm so glad I took a chance on him. It was the best thing I've ever done."

"I'm happy for you both," Sam said sincerely, even though she still hated the way her world and Nick's continued to overlap. In a perfect world, her professional and personal lives would be entirely separate. Sadly, she didn't live in that perfect world, and she'd never begrudge great people like Lindsey, Terry, Gonzo and Christina their right to be happy just because their happiness sometimes inconvenienced her. "I've got to go. Hit me up when you have DNA results."

"I will."

As she walked to her car, Sam called her husband. "Hey, babe. Miss me already?"

"Naturally, but I'm wondering about a promotion you might've given Terry O'Connor that I heard about from his girlfriend who is so very grateful?"

"Oh... Sorry. We were otherwise occupied last night, and the last thing on my mind was work."

"If you're promoting Terry, what does that mean for Christina?"

"She's decided to take some time off to be with Alex and to hopefully have a baby of her own."

"How is it I haven't heard any of this? You're not slipping into a pattern of keeping things from me, are you, Senator? Because that would most definitely count as a marital double standard."

Nick laughed at her terminology. "I'm not intentionally keeping anything from you, Samantha. To be honest, it didn't occur to me that you'd care about my staff shake-ups."

"Of course I care! They're the people who work closest with you and make sure you're doing all the right stuff and everything." In truth, she had no idea what Christina and Terry did on any given day. "Not to mention they're dating or engaged to people I work with. If it's just the same to you, I'd rather hear about these things from you rather than their significant others."

"You're right, and I'm sorry. I should've told you."

"This is becoming a disturbing pattern. Should I worry that I'm rubbing off on you?"

"Um, I love when you rub off on me."

"Nick! *Gross*. I'm being serious."

"So am I," he said, laughing, "and there's nothing gross about it. But your point is well taken, and I'll do better at keeping you in the loop on my work stuff."

"Just because my work stuff tends to take over our lives doesn't mean I'm not interested in yours."

"I know, babe."

"I got a press question today about the VP thing."

After a long pause, he said, "You did?"

"Yeah, during the briefing about the MacArthur murders."

"And it wasn't Darren?"

"Nope. Someone else from one of the TV stations."

"Shit. What the hell? That's two reporters who've now asked about it."

"I never told you it was Darren who told me."

"I came to my own conclusions. How is it getting out?"

"Is it possible the White House is letting it out because they want you and they want everyone to know it?"

"I suppose."

"Why don't you give Derek a call, and see what he says?"

"I was just thinking the same thing."

"Make sure he and Maeve have plans for Thanksgiving."

"I will. I'll let you know what I find out from him."

"Yes, you will."

"I love when you get all bossy with me, babe. It makes me hot."

"Everything makes you hot."

"Everything with *you* makes me hot."

"I really wish I was on vacation right now. You have no idea how much I wish that."

"I have a slight idea."

"How's our best boy today?"

"He's fine. Playing video games with Ethan, and I'm taking all three of them skating after a while."

"You aren't skating too, are you?"

"Maybe a little. Abby needs some help."

"Be careful. Do you hear me?"

"I hear you. Where are you right now?"

"Heading to the house where the pictures of Brooke were posted online."

"By yourself?"

"No. Gonzo and Freddie are going too. And Hill's team."

"Of course Hill's going."

"Lalala, can't hear you. Gotta go."

"Love you, babe, even when you're being obstinate."

"Why thank you. Love you too."

She ended the call with a smile on her face. Talking to him almost always made her happier than she'd ever been in her life. When she thought about the four miserable years she'd spent with her ex-husband, Peter, that life felt like a million years ago compared to what she had now with Nick. A year ago today, she would've scoffed at the words "soul mate," but now that she'd found hers she wasn't so cynical anymore.

NICK PLACED A call to his close friend Derek Kavanaugh. Derek's friends were glad to see him getting back to some semblance of normal after the tragic loss of his wife, Victoria. When the call went to Derek's voice mail, Nick took a chance and dialed the White House. It wasn't unusual for Derek to be at work on a Sunday, even now that he was a single father to his daughter, Maeve.

After identifying himself to Derek's administrative assistant, Nick was placed on hold, which gave him time to think about the entertaining conversation he'd had with his wife. He hated to admit that she was right about the marital double standard. He was guilty of failing to tell her a few key things recently, and he knew he had to do better lest she slip back into her old pattern of keeping just about everything that had the potential to be even slightly upsetting from him.

In her line of work, upsetting things happened all the time, and he wanted to know about them, not be kept in the dark. It was only fair that he practice what he preached.

"Good morning, Senator," Derek said when he came on the line. His friend resorted to formality when they spoke to each other in a work capacity. In the time they spent together away from work, Nick insisted on first names. "To what do I owe this honor?"

"Mr. Kavanaugh," Nick said with equal formality. "I'm reaching out to you in your official capacity to ask how the media might've caught wind of the fact that your boss recently made me an offer that I turned down."

"Huh, is that right? What're you hearing?"

"It's actually Sam who's been getting the questions from two reporters now—Darren Tabor from the *Star* and a TV reporter this morning during a press conference on the MacArthur murders."

"I'm not aware of any nefarious plots to shame you into accepting the president's offer, if that's what you think is going on."

"I've got to be honest. That's sort of how it's starting to seem to me."

"Fair enough. I'll do some poking around and get right back to you with what I find out."

"Thanks, Derek. Oh, and Sam wants to make sure you and Maeve have plans for the holiday."

"We're going to my parents' house for dinner, but tell her thanks for thinking of us."

"I'll do that. We'll be home all day—or at least I will

and so will Scotty. Can't ever guarantee Sam's presence. If you want to stop by, we'd love to see you both."

"I might take you up on that. I'll see how Maeve is doing after a day of sugar and cousins."

"Sounds good."

"I'll call you back shortly."

"Great, thanks."

Nick kept his phone with him when he went upstairs to change to take the kids to lunch and then to the ice rink. He didn't feel like doing any of it, but he wanted to get the kids out of Skip and Celia's house to give the grandparents a break for a while. And it would do Scotty some good to get more skating practice.

His skating was coming along, but he had a long way to go before he'd be as good as the other kids his age who'd been skating and playing hockey since they were old enough to stand up. Nick was determined to help his son catch up before he got to high school. He wanted Scotty to have the same experience he'd had playing high school hockey. The sense of camaraderie and friendships had lasted a lifetime for him, and he wanted the same for Scotty.

Nick's phone rang and, expecting it to be Derek, he took the call without checking the caller ID.

"Hey, it's me. Your dad." Leo Cappuano's awkward greeting made Nick smile. They'd come a long way toward a genuine relationship in recent years, but they still struggled from time to time.

"Hey, Dad. How's it going?"

"Good, but I got a strange phone call just now from a reporter asking me if it's true you're going to be the next vice president. What's up with that, Nicky?"

Nick groaned. "Oh, jeez. Sorry about that. Who was it? Do you know?"

"I didn't catch his name, but I think it was the CBC station there in the District. Is it true?"

"It's true that I was asked, but I said no."

"Wait a minute… The president of the United States asked you to be his new VP, and you said *no?* Are you *serious?*"

"Yes, I'm serious, and yes, I said no. It's not the right time for me or Sam or Scotty."

"I don't know much about anything, Nicky, but you might not want to be so hasty."

"I appreciate your concern, but think about it. Can you see Sam filling the role of second lady?"

"I absolutely can see it, and I can see both of you in the White House too."

"Your imagination is a little more vivid than mine. She loves her job. It's such a big part of who she is. How do I ask her to give that up so she can support my career?"

"Maybe she doesn't have to give it up," Leo said. "In this day and age, anything is possible. Have you asked the right questions before you assume she'd have to give it up?"

"Well, no, not really. It never occurred to me that it would be feasible for us."

"You should let it occur to you. It's an incredible opportunity, and if that reporter who called me is right, you're the only one Nelson wants."

"I can't even believe we're having this conversation. A year ago, John was still alive. I was his chief of staff. I hadn't seen Sam in six years… Now… Everything is different, and I'm still trying to get used to this life, let alone taking on something even bigger. Scotty has only just come to live with us, and I don't want to disrupt him either."

"Obviously I don't know him as well as you do, but from the time I've spent with him, I can't believe there's anything that kid couldn't roll with. I suspect I'm not telling you anything you don't already know where he's concerned."

"That is true, but I don't know, Dad… This whole thing is almost too much to get my head around. Sometimes I still feel like a fraud because of how I got my job in the first place."

"Anyone who knows you at all knows you'd give it all up to have John back. But since that's not possible, you're coping with it gracefully and professionally, and I'm so damned proud of you."

Nick sucked in a sharp, deep breath at his father's unusually effusive praise. "Thank you. That means a lot to me."

"You don't have any reason to feel like a fraud, Nicky, especially after you won that election fair and square. Have you talked to Graham about it?"

"Briefly. Right after Nelson asked me."

"What did he have to say?"

"There was quite a bit of whimpering when I told him I'd turned down Nelson's offer."

Laughing, Leo said, "I bet there was. He sees big things in your future, son, and so do I. Don't be too quick to say no. Ask all the right questions before you rule it out."

"Thanks for the advice, Dad. I appreciate it."

"Let me know what happens."

"I'll do that. See you Thursday?"

"We're looking forward to it. See you then."

Nick had no sooner hung up with his dad when Derek called him back. "What's the word?" Nick asked when he answered.

"The president would like to see you at the White House at four."

Flabbergasted, Nick was momentarily speechless. "Nick? Can you come at four?"

"Today?"

"Yes," Derek said with a laugh. "Today."

"That's all you got? Come at four? Nothing more than that?"

"That's all I'm permitted to say."

Nick thought about it for a second, and realized that even if he wasn't interested in the VP position, he was still a United States senator. Declining the president's invitation wasn't in his best interest. "Is it okay if I bring Terry?"

"I'm sure that'll be fine."

"We'll be there."

"I'll meet you at the West Wing visitor entrance." Nick sent a text to Sam. Talked to Derek and I've been "invited" to the White House for a 4 pm meeting with Nelson...

What does he want?

Derek wouldn't say.

The plot thickens. What will you say if he asks you again?

My answer hasn't changed.

Maybe you should consider it.

Have you lost your mind since I saw you last?

Power looks hot on you.

LOL. Shut up.

You shut up. Going back to work. Keep me posted.

Will do. Love you, babe. Be careful out there.

Always am.

She made him smile with her witty comebacks, but he had no doubt that power wouldn't look so good on her. She'd chafe against the confines with everything she had, and she'd come to hate him for forcing her into the gilded cage.

No, his answer hadn't changed, and he fully intended to tell President Nelson that when he saw him.

# TEN

SAM ARRIVED AT the address Hill had given her in the city's Northwest corner. He was waiting with Gonzo, Cruz and two other agents whom he introduced to her. "Sorry for the delay," Sam said. "I had to do a dog-and-pony show with the press."

"No problem," Hill said.

"What's the plan?" Sam asked.

"We were just discussing that when you got here," Gonzo said. "We've agreed to overwhelm them with our numbers so they know right away this is a big deal." Freddie handed a bulletproof vest to Sam, and they suited up.

"This is the home of the Mitchell family," Hill said. "They have a seventeen-year-old son named Brody, who was a friend of Hugo Springer's. We believe he's the one we're looking for."

"Who's got the lead?" Sam asked.

"You all do," Hill said. "Your jurisdiction."

She looked at Gonzo. "What's the plan, Sergeant?"

"We'll go in flashing badges and firepower. The goal is to locate Brody, get him to take down the video and photos while we watch and then take him into custody so we can get more information about what he saw at the Springer house and who else was at the party."

"Sounds good," Sam said. "Let's do it."

They approached the Mitchells' front door as a group. The other two agents circled around the house to cover the back door while Sam, Gonzo, Freddie and Hill took the front.

Gonzo made a fist and pounded on the front door. "Metro PD. Open up."

Inside, a dog howled with outrage.

The door swung open and a woman stared at them with big eyes. "What's this about?"

"Detective Sergeant Gonzales, Metro PD. We're looking for Brody Mitchell. Does he live here?"

"Y-yes. Why?"

"Is he home?"

"He's sleeping. What do you want with him?"

"We're going to need you to step aside, ma'am," Gonzo said.

Mrs. Mitchell did as directed, and they moved swiftly into the house. Sam and Freddie took the stairs to the second floor, opening doors until they found a teenage boy asleep in a messy room.

"Wake up, Brody," Sam said. The lump on the bed barely stirred, so she got down close to his ear. "Wake up!"

He came to abruptly, recoiling when he saw cops with guns drawn standing over his bed. "What the hell?" His dark brown hair stood on end, and he hadn't shaved in days. Sam decided he was probably popular with the girls, and she wondered if he, too, had taken a turn with Brooke.

"Are you the douchebag that runs the WilsonSeniors account online?"

"Uhh, I'm not at liberty to discuss that."

Freddie went to the door to call down to the others. "He's up here."

Hoping to get his attention, Sam slipped the safety

off her gun, which made an ominous-sounding clicking noise. "Get up. Now."

He zeroed in on the gun that was pointed at him. "I, uh, I don't have any clothes on."

"Too bad. On your feet. Hands on your head." Moving slowly, he got out of bed and did as directed.

He was tall and lean with muscles in all the right places and sported a hard-on that stuck straight out in front of him.

He flashed a grin that probably made the teenage girls swoon. "Morning wood."

Sam shuddered at the thought of his wood touching her niece. "Shut up and put some pants on."

Brody pulled on a pair of basketball shorts.

"Get on the computer and open the WilsonSeniors account."

"I really can't do that."

"Yes, you really can. The FBI has tracked the IP address for that account to this house, so we know it's you. Now get on the computer and open the account before I lose my patience."

"You don't want that to happen," Freddie said. "She can be a bit trigger-happy when she loses her patience." Brody wisely sighed and moved toward the laptop on a desk strewn with books and papers. He pressed the space bar to bring the computer to life and clicked around until the WilsonSeniors account opened.

"Take down the video and pictures from the party at Hugo Springer's house."

"What the fuck? We were just having some fun."

"Take. Them. Down. *Now*."

He did as he was told while Sam watched carefully to make sure he didn't miss anything.

"Now take them off all the other sites you manage. And if we find that you missed any, we'll be adding to the list of charges you're already facing."

It took more than ten minutes, but Brody systematically went through each social media site and removed the pictures and video.

"Where's your cell phone?" Sam asked.

"Um, on the charger?"

"Hand it over."

"What the hell for?"

"I assume you used it to record that video and take those pictures?"

Brody looked down at the floor, which was littered with sneakers and clothes and takeout coffee cups and other crap.

"What've you done, Brody?" his mother asked from the door. Tears streamed down her face as she stared at her son.

"Nothing, Mom."

"You told me you weren't at the party where Hugo was killed. Was that a lie?"

Brody crossed his arms and stared mulishly at the wall, which was covered with snowboarding posters and pictures of women in skimpy bikinis.

From the doorway, Gonzo nodded to Sam.

"Brody Mitchell, you have the right to remain silent," Sam said as she cuffed him. "Anything you say can and will be used against you in a court of law."

"Wait a minute! I'm under *arrest?* For what?"

"For filming a gang rape, for one thing, and not doing anything to stop it or provide aid to the girl," Gonzo said. "You're also one of the only people who got out of that party alive. Suffice to say we've got a few questions for you."

"He's a minor!" Mrs. Mitchell said. "You can't just haul him out of here like a criminal."

"He may be a minor, but he witnessed a gang rape and did nothing at all to stop it," Gonzo said. "Rather, he filmed it and posted the images to social media, so he faces felony rape and video voyeurism charges. He's also a potential suspect in mass murder."

At that, all of Brody's teenage bravado completely deserted him. "*Mass murder?* I didn't kill anyone! I left before that happened! And I didn't *rape* anyone!"

Sam grabbed him by the arms and headed for the door. "So you say."

"Where are you taking him?" Mrs. Mitchell asked.

"Metro PD headquarters."

"I'll be right there, Brody," his frantic mother called after him. "I'll get you a lawyer, and we'll get you out. Don't say anything to them until your lawyer is there."

"That's extremely bad advice, ma'am," Sam said.

"No, it isn't." Mrs. Mitchell's tears had been replaced by rage. "I know how you people operate. He'll say one wrong thing, and you'll pin the whole thing on him. You're not making my son into a murderer. Don't say anything, Brody."

"I won't, Mom. Hurry up and get me some help." They hauled him out of the house and into Gonzo's car.

"Since he's lawyering up," Sam said to Freddie, "let's stay up here and get the family interviews we were assigned out of the way."

"Sure."

"I've got Brody," Gonzo said. "I'll get him processed and into a room until the lawyer shows up."

"Run a check on the mother too," Sam said, playing a hunch. "She was rather well informed on how we operate. Perhaps she's had some personal experience."

"Good thinking," Gonzo said. "I'll check her out."

Turning to Hill and his agents, Sam said, "Thanks so much for your help with locating the IP. I feel better knowing those images are off the web."

"They may crop up again later," one of the other agents said. "We'll keep a lookout for them."

"I'd appreciate that." She nodded to Freddie and they headed for her car, leaving his parked in front of the Mitchells' house.

"Do you think my precious baby will be safe here?" he asked, with a look back at his car.

"If Mrs. Mitchell eggs it, it'll only be an improvement."

"Very funny."

The banter helped to take their minds off the dreadful task that lay ahead.

"Do you have addresses for the two families?"

"Yeah. The Brantleys live pretty close to here." He directed her to a stately colonial house on a quiet side street. Cars lined the road in front of the home.

Sam parked and stared at the house for a moment. "I hate this."

"I do too. Let's get it over with."

They walked up the sidewalk to the front door of a white house with black shutters and knocked on the door. An older woman answered. Her face was swollen from crying.

Sam showed her badge. "Lieutenant Holland, Detective Cruz, to see Mr. or Mrs. Brantley."

"They aren't seeing anyone right now. Can you come back later?"

"I wish we could, and I'm very sorry to intrude at such a difficult time," Sam said. "But we're investigating a homicide, and time isn't on our side. We'd really like to speak to them."

She hesitated before she stepped aside. "Come in." A hushed silence hung over the interior of the house, which smelled of apples and cinnamon. They were shown to the living room. "Please have a seat. I'll get them."

Sam and Freddie sat next to each other on the sofa, which faced a wall of photos of what had apparently been their only child.

"God," Freddie muttered as he took in the array of photos that spanned from youth through high school football.

When the Brantleys came into the room, Sam stood and introduced herself and Freddie. "We're so sorry for your loss and for disturbing you at such a difficult time."

"I'm Adam Brantley, and this is my wife, Sarah."

He was tall and imposing with gray hair and blue eyes. His wife was tiny next to him. Her dark curly hair was messy and unkempt, and her dark brown eyes unfocused.

When they were settled on opposing sofas, Sam noted the way Adam kept an arm firmly around his wife, as if he was actually holding her up rather than offering comfort.

"We're trying to find out who else might've been at the Springer home on the night in question. If you could tell us about any other close friends of Todd's, including girlfriends, it would be very helpful."

"Most of Todd's close friends were there," Adam said flatly. "They're all dead."

Tears rolled down Sarah's face, but she didn't seem to notice.

"Is there anyone who wasn't there who might've had a beef with Todd or any of the other kids who were killed?"

"I've gone over it and over it in my mind," Adam said. "I can't think of anyone who didn't like them, let alone hated them enough to kill them."

"No one at all?" Sam asked. "No rivals from other high school teams or kids they might've grappled with at the movie theater or someone who was owed money? In my experience, when something like this happens among young people, the motive is almost never proportionate to the crime."

Adam shook his head. "I haven't been able to think of anything that would bring about this kind of result. I assume you're talking to the other parents?"

"All of them. Yes."

Adam fixated on a photo of his handsome son, who was smiling widely. "He was our whole world. We adopted him out of foster care when he was twelve. We'd been unable to have kids of our own, and when he came along, we knew he was meant for us." He fixed his gaze on Sam. "We don't know how to go on without him."

Sarah broke down, wailing in her grief.

Her husband put both arms around her, holding her close as tears wet his face. "I'm sorry we can't do more to help."

Freddie put his business card on the coffee table.

"If you think of anything, no matter how insignificant, please call."

"We will."

Sam couldn't seem to get air to her lungs after hearing Todd had been adopted at twelve. Her feet didn't want to work the way they were supposed to, and she felt like she had traveled outside herself and was watching the scene play out as a spectator rather than a participant.

Tuning in to her distress, Freddie took her arm and steered her toward the front door. He guided her down the stairs and the walk to the sidewalk. "Take a breath."

Sam forced air into her lungs as she combatted an overpowering sense of panic. What if the same thing happened to them someday? The boy she loved like her own, who'd come into their lives so unexpectedly and changed everything...

"Breathe, Sam."

She bent in half, rested her hands on her knees and tried to get air past the enormous lump in her throat. Closing her eyes tight against the burn of tears, she fought for every breath.

"Do you want me to call Nick?"

"No."

"What can I do?"

"Just give me a minute."

He gave her ten minutes and stood by her side until her heart rate slowed and she was able to stand upright.

"Sorry."

"Don't be. The parallels were hard to miss."

"I can't even imagine what they're going through. I can't go there."

"You don't have to. Scotty is fine. He's with Nick, and everything is fine."

"He's lived with us for only a few months and already, if something ever happened to him, I know I'd never survive it. How will they survive it?"

"I don't know, but somehow they will. Somehow they always do, even when it seems impossible."

"Maybe this is why I've been unable to have kids of my own. Because someone up there knows I'm not cut out for this shit."

"Don't think that way, Sam. Who's cut out for what they're going through?"

"Still…" She ran her hands over the hair she'd clipped up for work. "Sorry to freak out. I appreciate you getting me out of there."

"It was no problem. I could tell the part about them adopting Todd hit you hard." He held out his hand. "Want me to drive?"

Since her hands were still trembling, Sam handed over the keys. "Sure. Thanks."

"Another thing to keep in mind," Freddie said when they were on the road, "is that Todd Brantley was participating in illegal activities at the time of his death. I can't see Scotty doing that—ever."

Sam stared out the window, watching the world whiz by. "I bet the Brantleys would've said the same thing about Todd when he was twelve. No one ever thinks it's going to be their kid. Tracy never thought it would be Brooke."

"It's just that Scotty has such a rigid sense of right and wrong. I can't see him ever losing that quality."

"That's true. He's the best person I've ever known. What if we do everything right, and he still goes wrong?"

"With you keeping tabs on him, he'll be too afraid to go wrong. I know I'd be if I were your kid."

Sam couldn't contain the burst of laughter that escaped through her tightly clenched lips.

"You'll keep him on the straight and narrow. I have no doubt about that."

"Thanks. I appreciate you talking me off the ledge. I

feel so bad for those parents. For all of them. No matter what their kids were doing, none of them deserved what happened to them."

"No, they didn't."

Sam reached for her phone and placed a call to Lindsey McNamara. The instant she heard the doctor's voice on the other end of the line, Sam realized she shouldn't be making the call when Gonzo was running the case.

"Sam?" Lindsey asked after a moment of silence. "Sorry. I was calling to see if there's anything new on the DNA, but I totally forgot I'm not in charge of this case. Gonzo is."

Lindsey snorted with laughter. "You'll be glad to know he's one step ahead of you. I just talked to him and gave him what I have."

"Do you have confirmation of who was with Brooke?"

"Yes," Lindsey said softly. "I've consulted with the FBI lab to run the DNA from her rape kit against the DNA from our victims, and we've got three matches with one more profile that wasn't among our victims." Sam fought back the wave of revulsion that made her nauseous when she considered four guys taking turns with Brooke. "I'll bet the fourth guy is our friend Brody Mitchell, who we just took into custody. He's the one who posted the video and photos online. I'm going to request a warrant for his DNA. Can we call you when we get the warrant?"

"I'll be here. I'm really sorry this happened to your niece, Sam."

"So am I. I've got to run. My sister is beeping in. I'll be in touch." Sam pushed the send button to take the call from Tracy. "Hey, what's up?"

"She's awake."

"I'll be right there." Sam closed her phone and looked

over at Freddie. "I hate to ask you to take the other interview by yourself, but Brooke is awake."

"No problem. I'll pick up my car so you can go to the hospital."

"Thanks."

"What did Lindsey say?"

"Four guys. Three of them among the murder victims."

"I'm so sorry, Sam."

She blew out a deep breath. "What'll we tell her about what happened?"

"The truth. If she doesn't hear it from you, she'll hear it from someone who saw the video. It was up just long enough that it probably made the rounds."

"Probably," Sam said as a pervasive sense of dread overtook her. What would become of Brooke once she learned that people had seen her being assaulted? For someone her age, knowing her friends had seen it might be worse than hearing about the actual attack.

"She's got a great family around her," Freddie said. "You'll get her through this." A short time later, he pulled up to his car on the Mitchells' street. "Let me know if I can do anything for you or Tracy."

"Thanks, Freddie. I appreciate that. Keep me posted on what you find out from Kelsey Lewis's parents."

"Will do. See you back at HQ later?"

"I'll be there." Sam got out of the car and went around to get into the driver's seat. On the way to the hospital, she thought about how to handle Brooke. She was one of the few people they'd found who'd been at the party and gotten out alive. Whether she remembered anything that could aid the investigation remained to be seen.

When she walked into Brooke's room a few minutes

later, the teen was hysterical and her mother was attempting to calm her down with the help of a nurse. "Can't we give her something?" Tracy asked as tears fell from her eyes.

"We need to keep her awake," the nurse said. "Doctor's orders."

"There's got to be something we can do for her."

"I'm adjusting her pain meds. Give it time to work."

Undone by the scene she'd come in on, Sam went around to the far side of the bed and put her arm around Tracy, who turned into her embrace.

"I can't handle this," Tracy said.

"Yes, you can."

"It hurts," Brooke wailed between sobs.

"I know, honey," the nurse said. "You should feel better in a few minutes. Try to relax and calm down."

A couple of minutes later, Brooke looked up at Sam with big blue eyes gone glassy with tears, though she was calmer now that the meds had kicked in. "Sam."

"I'm here, honey."

"What happened? Why am I here?"

"I know this is all very upsetting, but I have some questions for you that might help to answer some of yours. Do you feel up to talking?"

Brooke wiped her face and eyes and nodded.

"Do you remember being at a party at Hugo Springer's house?"

Brooke's eyes darted between Sam and her mother.

"Hey, Trace," Sam said. "Why don't you let me take a turn hanging with Brooke? Go get a coffee and call the kids. I'll take over for a while."

Tracy wiped the tears from her face. "Are you sure?"

"Of course. Go on. I'll be here."

"I would like to call Abby and Ethan. Thanks, Sam."

"Sure." Sam had no doubt that it would be harder on Tracy to hear what Brooke remembered than it would be for Brooke to talk about it. Having her mother out of the room might make Brooke more forthcoming too.

"Is it okay if I talk to her about everything?"

Tracy hesitated before she nodded. "Someone has to. It may as well be you." She bent to kiss Brooke's cheek. "I'll be back shortly. Do me a favor—and do yourself a favor—when Sam asks you about what happened the other night, tell her the truth."

Satisfied that Brooke's pain had been successfully managed for the moment, the nurse followed Tracy from the room.

"Thank you," Brooke said in a whisper. "My mom is so upset. I can't deal with it."

"She's worried about you. You've been badly hurt."

"I don't understand. Tell me what happened, will you please? No one will tell me."

"What do you remember? Let's start with that."

"Hoda came to my school," she said tentatively. "I know what we did was wrong, but I asked my parents if I could come home on Friday rather than Saturday because I wanted to see my friends. But they had to work so they couldn't come to get me until Saturday, and I didn't want to miss the party." She sniffed and wiped her eyes and nose with a hand that was still hooked to an IV. Her dark hair swirled about her head like a messy halo and her always-pale complexion was positively translucent after her ordeal, except for the bruises on the left side of her face that were now beginning to yellow.

"When you and Hoda got to the city, where did you go?"

"To Hugo's house. He's a friend of Hoda's."

"What happened then?"

"There were a lot of kids there. Everyone was drinking… And stuff."

"What stuff?"

Brooke shifted to find a more comfortable position and seemed to immediately regret it. "Why does it hurt so bad between my legs?"

"We'll get to that. What other stuff were the kids doing?"

"There were some pills. I think it was Molly. I heard someone saying it was something new and really cool."

"You think but you don't know for sure?"

"I don't know for sure."

"But you took some of it anyway?"

Brooke looked down at her hands, which were fisted around the bedclothes. "I know it was wrong, but everyone was doing it, and I didn't think anything would happen."

Sam held back the desire to snap at her for being so freaking stupid. But since that wouldn't accomplish anything other than alienating her niece, Sam contained herself. "Were you drinking too?"

"Some."

"How much?"

"A couple of drinks."

"Do you know what kind of drinks? Beer, wine, booze?"

"Some kind of liquor, I think. It might've been vodka."

"Do you know where the alcohol and the drugs came from?"

"If I tell you, will Hugo get into trouble? His parents were away, and he wasn't allowed to have anyone over."

Sam sighed when she thought about the many things she had to tell Brooke about what'd happened that night. "No, he won't get into trouble."

"Hugo's brother hooked us up."

"Do you know the brother's name?"

"Billy maybe?"

"Was he at the party?"

"I don't know him, so I can't say for sure."

"Who else was at the party?"

Brooke thought about that for a minute. "Hugo and his best friend, Michael. Their friends Todd, Kevin and Brody, and a bunch of girls I didn't know, and some other guys they went to school with. The only ones I knew before the party were Hoda, Todd, Hugo and Michael."

"What's the last thing you remember about that night?"

She closed her eyes and released a deep breath. "You're going to be mad. Everyone will hate me."

"That's not true. You made mistakes, and we're disappointed you made some bad choices. But most of all we're grateful you're alive."

"Alive? What does that mean?"

"The Molly and the alcohol and the GHB combined to make you really sick, Brooke."

"GHB? What's that? I didn't take anything called that."

"We believe someone gave it to you. Probably in a drink. Do you know what else it's called?"

She shook her head.

"The date rape drug."

Her eyes widened and her mouth fell open as that news plus the pain between her legs added up to horror. "Oh my God. I was *raped?*"

"Yes."

She began to cry in deep racking sobs. "By who?"

Sam remembered what Freddie had said about telling the truth and forced herself to say the words. "There were four of them."

Brooke covered her mouth to muffle the sounds coming from deep inside her.

"Can you tell me what the last thing you remember is?"

She shook her head as tears streamed down her cheeks.

"Brooke, please. It's so important that you tell me what you remember."

With what seemed like tremendous reluctance, Brooke said, "I went into the bedroom with Todd. He was the reason I wanted to go to the party. I met him last summer, and we'd been texting while I was at school. I wanted to see him again so badly."

"Did you have sex with him?"

"Yes," she said softly.

"Was that your first time?"

"No."

Sam worked to keep her expression neutral so Brooke would keep talking.

"It's embarrassing to be talking about this with you."

"I understand, but it's really important you tell me what you remember. Did you leave the bedroom after you were with Todd?"

Brooke tilted her head to the side. "I don't remember leaving the bedroom. Everything is kind of blank after that."

Which meant the GHB had been consumed before she went into the bedroom with Todd and took effect while she was there.

Brooke looked at Sam beseechingly. "You said there were four of them. What happened to me, Sam?"

"I hate to have to tell you this, but someone gave you

GHB, and while you were out of it, Todd's friends took turns with you. That's why you're so sore. You had to have stitches."

"*Down there?*"

"Yes. There was some tearing."

"*Why* would they do that?" she asked so softly Sam could barely hear her. "Todd is my friend. I thought he liked me."

"I wish I had the answers you need, but I don't know why they'd do that."

"Are they in trouble? Did you arrest them?"

Sam's stomach began to hurt when she thought of the other things she still needed to tell Brooke. "No, honey. I didn't arrest them."

"Why not? They *raped* me!"

"Because someone killed them."

"What?"

"Todd, Hugo, Michael, Kevin and five girls were stabbed to death in the Springers' basement."

Brooke began to cry again. "How is that possible? Who would do that? I don't understand. They're *all* dead?"

"I'm afraid so."

She buried her face in her hands. "We were just having fun." Another thought seemed to occur to her, and she looked over at Sam. "Is Hoda dead too?"

"No, she isn't. In fact, I think she might've been the one who got you out of there."

"But you don't know that?"

"We can't find her. No one knows where she is. Do you have any idea where she might be?"

"She's kind of a free spirit, so she could be anywhere."

"If you can tell me anything about who she hung out with or where we might find her, it would really help."

"There's this one guy... Nico. I don't know his last name, but he lives near American University. She really likes him, and I think she hangs with him sometimes."

"Is he a student at AU?"

"No, he works there. I'm not sure what he does."

"In one of her texts to you, Hoda refers to a boy named Davey who took care of the notarizing of the fake note. Who is he?"

"You guys read my texts?"

Sam gave her a withering look. "What do you think? We've spent about thirty-six hours desperately trying to figure out what happened to you the other night. It's safe to say, not much is private anymore."

"I suppose I deserve that."

"So who is he?"

"A friend of Hoda's. His dad is a lawyer."

"What's Davey's last name?"

"Ekland. He goes to Wilson too."

"That helps, honey." After writing down the name, Sam took hold of Brooke's hand. "There's something else I have to tell you, and it's going to be super upsetting."

"More upsetting than hearing the guy I really liked shared me with his friends and then they were all murdered?"

"Possibly."

"I don't know if I can take any more."

"I know this is so awful for you, and everything got way out of control, but I'd rather you hear it from me than from someone else."

Brooke blew out a deep breath and seemed to brace herself. "Okay."

"When the guys took turns with you, someone videotaped it and took pictures. They posted the pictures and videos online."

Brooke's mouth fell open and then snapped shut as new tears slid down her face. She shook her head.

"We tracked down the source and arrested a boy named Brody Mitchell. Do you know him?"

"He was in my class at Wilson. *He* posted that shit?"

"Apparently, he's the brainchild behind the Wilson-Seniors accounts. It's all been taken down, and he's in custody."

"But everyone probably saw it already, right?"

"I don't know about everyone… But it was online for more than twenty-four hours before we were able to isolate the source."

"God. *Oh my God.* So the whole world saw me naked and getting raped by *four different guys?* Oh my God!"

"Technically, three, because the sex with Todd was consensual. I know this is horrifying for you to hear, and it was horrifying for us to realize it had happened to you."

"It's all my fault," she said, weeping bitterly. "If I hadn't left school, this never would've happened."

"That part is true, but the rape is *not* your fault. You were drugged and unable to say no. Those boys took advantage of you, and that was not your fault. I want you to hear me on that, Brooke. No matter what you did or said or took or drank, it was *not* your fault that they raped you."

She looked so young and fragile sitting in the big hospital bed with tears streaming from eyes gone raw from crying. "It was my fault that I was there in the first place. What will people say about me? They'll call me a slut and say I wanted it."

"I'm sure they'll say all kinds of things, but you know the truth. You were drugged and unable to resist them. That much was obvious in the video."

"You saw it too?"

"I did."

"God, what you must think of me. You must hate me for this."

"I could never, ever hate you, and what I saw was a young girl being victimized by boys who were probably drunk and high and out of control."

"They were nice guys," Brooke said in a whisper. "All of them were nice guys. I thought they were anyway."

"Maybe they were until they got the wrong combination of drugs and booze into their systems in a house with no adults present. Things got out of hand."

"It was a pretty wild party. Hugo had gotten all that stuff from his brother, and he was going sick. When I realized how crazy it was getting, I told Hoda we probably ought to leave, but she said there was no way she was leaving. She was my ride. Plus, Todd was there, and I wanted to see him." She looked up at Sam with big, blue heartbroken eyes. "How could he let his friends take turns with me?"

"I don't know, honey, but he was aware enough to have sex with another girl after you. They were killed in the middle of it."

Brooke shook her head at that news. "Todd is really dead. Hugo and Michael, too."

"Yes, I'm sorry."

"It's so hard to believe."

"If you can think of anyone else who was at the party, it would really help us. Other than you, Hoda and Brody, we haven't found anyone else who was there and got out alive. And we can't find Hoda."

"You don't think she's dead, too, do you?"

"No, I think it's more likely she's hiding out until the dust settles."

"Her mom lets her do whatever she wants."

"I've figured that out."

"I always thought she was lucky because her mom left her alone, but now…"

"Now you see why your mom is on you like white on rice all the time."

"Yes," she said softly. "It's because she didn't want something like this to happen to me." A sob hiccupped through her tightly clenched lips. "My life is ruined."

"No, it isn't, Brooke. You've had an awful, horrible thing happen to you, and it'll probably stay with you for the rest of your life. But what you make of yourself going forward is completely up to you. We'll support you all the way, and we'll get you through this. I promise we will."

Brooke held on tight to Sam's hand. "I'm so ashamed."

Sam leaned over the bed to hug the girl as she cried. That's where Tracy found them when she returned. Sam pulled back to let Tracy take over.

"I'm so sorry, Mom." Brooke broke down all over again at the sight of her mother. "I never should've left school or gone to that party, and now everything is ruined and those kids are dead."

"Shhh," Tracy said, running a hand over Brooke's mane of dark hair. "I know it seems so awful now, but everything will be okay in time. You're going to be okay."

Sam was glad to see that Tracy had pulled herself together because Brooke would need the strength of her mom and the rest of their family in the coming weeks and months. Totally drained from her talk with Brooke, Sam tipped her head from side to side, trying to relieve some of the pressure that gathered there in times of stress.

"Nick and the kids are here," Tracy said. "Abby and Ethan wanted to see me, so he brought them over."

"I think I'll go out and say hello if you're going to be here."

"I'll be here."

"Sam?" Brooke said. "What is going to happen to me? I was drinking and I took drugs. Am I going to be arrested?"

"I don't think so, but I'll need you to make a statement to Detective Erica Lucas from the Special Victims Unit. She's going to be following up on your case, and I can't be there when she talks to you because it's a conflict of interest for me as your family member."

"My case? What case? Aren't they all dead?"

"One of them isn't. Erica is a great detective, and she'll be in to see you later today. Is that okay?"

Brooke nodded.

"If you think of anything else you remember from the party, no matter how small or insignificant you think it might be, I want you to call me, okay?"

"I'll think about it, and I'll call you if I think of anything."

Sam pressed a kiss to Brooke's forehead. "You're going to get through this. I promise." She hugged Tracy on the way out, and once she was in the hallway, Sam leaned against the wall, trying to get her emotions under control before she went looking for Nick and the kids.

Nick found her there a few minutes later. To his credit, he didn't say a word. He simply put his arms around her and drew her into his loving embrace, which was exactly what she needed.

With her face pressed to his chest and his heart beating strong under her ear, Sam felt her world right itself again. "Thank you," she said after several quiet minutes.

"Always my pleasure, babe." He smoothed his hand over her back in a gesture that soothed and calmed her.

"It's been one hell of a day so far."

"I heard you were the one who got to tell Brooke what happened."

"Someone had to, and I was able to ask some questions while I was at it."

"And having to tell her all that took another vicious toll on you."

"I'm okay." She smiled up at him. "Better now."

His lopsided grin made her wish they were alone so she could kiss that sexy mouth of his.

"How are you?" she asked.

"Anxious about this meeting with Nelson. I feel a bit like I'm being railroaded into doing something I don't really want to do."

"Maybe you should consider doing it if they want you so badly."

"It's official. You've finally lost your mind."

"Very funny. All I'm saying is don't let me or my career stop you from doing what you want. I'll figure a way around it if it comes to that."

He pulled back from her but kept his hands on her upper arms. "You're serious."

"Of course I am. Our life is all about me and my career so much of the time. If you want this, and you should think long and hard before you say no again, we'll figure it out. Somehow."

"You don't know what you're agreeing to."

"I'm agreeing to support you no matter what you choose to do. I love you so much. There's nothing I wouldn't do to make you happy."

"Samantha…" Right there in the hallway of the busy ICU he laid his lips on hers, and Sam did nothing to stop him. "Just when I think I've got you all figured out, you go and throw me a ringer."

"Gotta keep you on your toes so you don't get bored."

He laughed at that. "No worries there, babe." He gathered her up again, and she took another couple of minutes with him because she needed it so badly. How, she wondered for the thousandth time since they'd reconnected a year ago, had she ever lived without him?

"Hear what they have to say, and then we'll talk about it," she said. "Okay?"

"Okay." He kissed her again.

"The nurses are looking on in envy," she whispered.

"Let them look. I only see you."

"Good thing there're doctors nearby. I may be tempted to swoon."

"I'll catch you."

She looked up at him, so handsome and solid and all hers. "Something else happened today."

"What?" he asked, immediately on guard. The last year had conditioned him to be prepared for anything.

She told him about meeting Todd Brantley's parents and how they'd adopted him out of foster care when he was twelve.

"Oh, man," Nick said. "That must've been tough on you."

She loved that he got it. He always got it. "It was awful. They were so decimated to have lost him. I was a mess after hearing that."

"I'm so sorry."

"What if… What if we do everything right, and he still goes wrong?"

Nick shook his head vehemently. "He won't."

"You can't know that for sure."

"Of course I can't, but I'd bet my life on the straight and narrow for our boy. That's just who he is."

"They're all that way," Sam said, glancing into Brooke's room through the glass wall and relieved to see she was sleeping again. "Until they aren't."

"Scotty is different."

"Freddie said the same thing. That his rigid sense of right and wrong will keep him out of trouble."

"Exactly. That's what I believe too."

"I hope you're both right, because if something like this ever happened to him… I wouldn't be able to take it."

"Yes, you would. You're the strongest person I've ever known."

"Not when it comes to him or my nieces and nephews I'm not. It was all I could do to hold it together in there with Brooke just now. I want to wrap her in gauze and protect her from every awful thing in the world. I'd do it if I could."

"And she knows that. You're already wrapping her in gauze by making sure she has the right people working on her case and by running interference on her behalf. You're doing everything you can—and probably more than you should."

"I just hope it's enough," Sam said with a sigh. "I need to call Detective Lucas and tell her Brooke is no longer under sedation. I'll stay while Erica is in with her, and then I've got to get to HQ to see what's up with the kid who posted the videos."

"Miles to go before you sleep, huh?"

"Looks that way." She glanced up at him. "Good luck at the White House. Let me know the second you're out of the meeting. I'll be on pins and needles waiting to hear."

"You'll be the first person I call."

"I'm so proud of my smoking hot husband, the senator, who has a very important meeting with the president later today."

He rolled his eyes, as she expected him to. "In the meantime, I've got three kids who want to go ice-skating. Think they've spent the ten bucks I gave them to stay in the waiting room with the vending machines?"

"Oh, jeez, you'd better go see how much sugar they've managed to consume."

Leaving her with one last kiss, he headed off to rejoin the kids. Sam watched him go, feeling energized by the stolen piece of time with him. Brooke's nurse approached the room, and Sam straightened to greet her. "Girl, that is one fine, fine, *fine* man you've got there."

Sam laughed at the lusty look on the nurse's face. "Believe me," she said with a wink. "I know."

# ELEVEN

SAM PACED THE hallway while Erica took Brooke's statement about what she remembered about the party. More than an hour after she went into the room, Erica emerged looking less composed than she had going in. "How'd it go?" Sam asked her.

"She has no memory of the assault, which I suppose is a blessing. She's upset about the video, of course."

"She's also worried she's going to be charged because of the drugs and alcohol."

"I'll talk to the ADA and see if we can cut a deal to require drug and alcohol counseling in exchange for no charges."

"I'd consider that a personal favor."

"Throwing the book at her isn't going to teach her anything she hasn't already figured out on her own."

"Your thinking matches mine."

"She may have to testify," Erica said. "Against the guy who got out alive and in the case you're working."

"We'll cross that bridge when we get to it. Thank you, Erica. I appreciate your sensitivity."

"No problem. I'm sorry this happened to your niece."

"So am I." After Erica had walked away, Sam went into Brooke's room.

"She was really nice, Sam," Tracy said.

"Did she say whether I'm in trouble because of the

drugs and stuff?" Brooke asked. Her face was swollen from new tears.

"She said she's going to recommend drug and alcohol counseling in lieu of charges."

"Oh, thank goodness," Tracy said.

"Is it because of you, Sam?" Brooke asked. "Did she do that because of you?"

"Probably in part, but it's also because of you. She said she got the feeling that you'd learned a lot from this episode, and you won't cross paths with the police again."

"I won't," Brooke said, wiping her face with the sheet. "I won't do anything like this again. You can trust me on that."

"We want to be able to trust you, honey," Tracy said. "You have no idea how badly your dad and I want that."

"I'm so sorry," Brooke said. "What if… What if I got pregnant?"

"They gave you something in the ER to prevent that," Sam said. "But you'll need to be retested in a few months for STDs and HIV."

Brooke closed her eyes and shook her head. "I still can't believe they did that to me. I thought they were my friends."

Listening to Brooke, an idea took hold that Sam planned to execute as soon as she left them. "I need to get back to work, but I'll be in tomorrow to check on you." She leaned over to hug and kiss Brooke. "I love you. No matter what happens, that'll never change."

"I love you too. Thank you for helping me. It's probably more than I deserve."

"Don't worry about it, honey."

Tracy followed Sam into the hallway and hugged her. "Thank you so much for everything."

"It's nothing you wouldn't do for me."

"It's way above and beyond, and we both know it."

"We can have this fight another time," Sam said with a teasing smile. "Your daughter needs you, and I've got to get to work." She glanced through the glass at Brooke, who was hugging Norman and staring up at the ceiling, probably trying to process everything she'd learned about what had happened the other night. "I'm going to ask Jeannie to come in and talk to her. It might help for her to talk to someone who's been through it and survived."

"That's a wonderful idea. I hate to say it, but I think this might've been a true wake-up call for her. I hope things will be different from here on out."

"You may still hit some bumps on the road, but she's learned a valuable lesson."

"Let's hope some good came of it."

"I'll check in later."

On the way to work, Sam called Jeannie, hoping it was okay to ask this kind of favor of her colleague and friend, who had been through such a hideous ordeal. "I was wondering if you might have time to go by the hospital and speak to my niece Brooke. She's just found out what happened to her the other night, and needless to say, she's extremely upset. I know it's a lot to ask—"

"Of course I will, Sam. I'd be glad to."

"I hope you know I'm asking this as your friend and not your lieutenant."

"I do know that, and as your friend, I'll do anything I can to help your niece through this awful time."

"Thank you." Sam had been humbled more than once during the last few days by the amazing show of support from her colleagues and friends. "I could use one more favor. Can you get me an address for an Ekland family in the third ward? They have a teenage son named David who we may need to speak to at some point. Goes by Davey. If need be, you can call the principal of Wilson High to get the info. He's been very cooperative. Let me know if you need me to shoot you his number."

"Got it. Will do."

"I'll see you at the meeting."

"I'll be there."

Sam arrived at HQ a few minutes later, pleased to see the usual swarm of reporters down to only a hardy few braving the cold. She ignored them on her way inside.

Gonzo appeared in the doorway to her office. "Got a second?"

"Sure do." Sam took off her coat and settled into her chair. "Come in."

"I wanted to update you on a few things. First, I got the report from the lab on the sheet Brooke was wrapped in. Most of the blood belonged to Todd Brantley. There were smudges that matched the profile for Kelsey Lewis too."

Sam thought about the implications of that. "So Brooke was right there with them when they were killed?"

"It appears that way."

The realization of how close her niece had come to being murdered hit Sam like a fist to the gut, sucking the breath from her lungs. "How did they miss her?"

"It's possible the darkness saved her. Maybe there was some light filtering in from the other room and the killer could only see Todd on top of Kelsey. Or perhaps someone grabbed Brooke and got her out of there while he killed someone else. Or Brooke was already out of the room when Todd and Kelsey were killed, but some-one used the sheet from the bed they were on to wrap up Brooke. We may never know exactly how it all went down."

All of the scenarios Gonzo outlined were plausible. "Where are we with the Mitchell kid?"

"His lawyer just arrived. I was getting ready to go in there. Want to come?"

With her father's lecture about ends justifying means ringing loudly in her mind, Sam shook her head. "I want to, but if there's any chance he's our fourth guy with Brooke, I can't be part of it. You can take Cruz, and I'll watch from observation." It killed her to take a step back, but Sam didn't want to do anything to endanger the prosecution if he was the one guy who'd assaulted Brooke and gotten out alive. "What's the plan?"

"I've got a warrant for his DNA, so I'll be handling that first. Lindsey is on her way to take the sample."

"How much you want to bet he's going to be our fourth perp in Brooke's rape?"

"I'd bet the farm on it, but the proof will be in the DNA. Let's go see what he has to say."

Sam watched from the one-way window that gave her a bird's-eye view of the interrogation room where Brody sat next to a balding man. In the two hours since he'd been arrested, Brody had lost some of his initial swagger and now looked more like a scared kid.

"I'd like to know the charges against my client," the lawyer said.

"We'll get to that. I'm Detective Sergeant Gonzales. This is Detective Cruz, and this interview is being recorded. Our first order of business is a warrant for a DNA sample from your client."

The lawyer looked over the warrant. "For what purpose?"

"To determine what, if any, role he might've played in a sexual assault that occurred at the Springer home during the party—the same assault that he failed to stop while he videotaped it and then posted the footage to the Internet."

Brody's eyes widened and his mouth went slack with what might've been shock. "I don't have to do that, do I?"

"I'm afraid you do," the lawyer said as he perused the warrant Gonzo had produced.

"I never touched her! I watched, but I didn't touch."

"Be quiet, Brody," the lawyer said.

"If that's the case, then your DNA won't be a match," Gonzo said, thrilled by Brody's spontaneous utterance, which could be used against him in court.

A knock on the door preceded Lindsey into the room. "This is Dr. McNamara, and she'll be taking the sample."

Brody looked like he might piss his pants in fear as Lindsey went over the procedure involved with swabbing his inner cheek.

Once she had the sample, Lindsey left the room. "You understand that by failing to intervene on behalf of the girl being assaulted you'll be charged with sexual assault, which is a felony," Gonzo said. "In addition, you're looking at charges of video voyeurism, which became a cyber-porn charge when you posted the video and pictures online."

Brody grew visibly paler as Gonzo rattled off the charges.

"There were three men visible on the video, but we have proof that four men assaulted her," Gonzo continued. "The three that were shown on the video are dead. We're looking for the fourth man. If you weren't involved in the sexual assault, we're willing to entertain lesser charges if you provide us with information that will lead to the arrest and successful prosecution of the fourth man who assaulted her, as well as anything you know about the person or persons who might've murdered the nine young people at the Springers' home."

Brody looked to his lawyer for guidance. "What does all that mean?"

"It means," the lawyer said grimly, "they're willing to consider lesser charges for you if you tell them who the fourth man was and if you help them to figure out who the killer was. Keep in mind, you'd have to testify against them."

Brody blanched. "I'm not doing that. You can't make me tell on the friends I've got left."

"You're a material witness to at least one felony," Gonzo reminded him. "And you're looking at felony charges of your own for failing to provide aid to a girl who was clearly unable to resist her attackers. Your video is all the proof we need to put you away for a long time, especially if we can prove it was taken with your phone. Was it taken with your phone, Brody?"

The boy broke down at that juncture. "We were just having fun with her. I don't get how that's a crime."

"Brody," the lawyer said in a tone thick with warning. "Shut up."

"No! We didn't do anything wrong. She wanted it."

Even from a distance, Sam could see the muscle pulsing with tension in Freddie's jaw as he held back the retort she knew he was dying to make to that audacious statement.

"I can assure you," Gonzo said calmly, "she did not want it, and because she was unable to say so, what you all did to her is a crime. Now, you can either protect yourself or your friends, but you can't have it both ways."

Brody buried his face in his hands, shaking his head over and over. "I don't get how I can be charged with rape when I never touched her."

"Let me tell you how. Say you and I get a big idea to rob a gas station. You drive me there and wait in the car while I go in and do the deed. Say I get trigger-happy while I'm inside the store and the clerk ends up dead. You're as responsible for that clerk's death as I am, even though you were in the car when it happened. He was murdered during a felony that you took part in. Same thing here. The young woman was raped during a felony sexual assault that you took part in by videotaping it and failing to intervene on her behalf." Clearly losing patience with the kid, Gonzo concluded with, "You all got drunk and stoned and did stupid shit that you were doubly stupid enough to videotape. Any remaining questions?"

"We didn't mean for anyone to get hurt," Brody said softly as it seemed to settle in on him that his carefree life as a teenager had ended.

"And yet nine kids are dead and another is lying in ICU after being gang-raped," Gonzo said. "It's safe to say people got hurt. The question that remains is, what're you going to do to make this right?"

"I'd like some time to consult with my client," the lawyer said.

Gonzo and Freddie stood and left the room.

Sam switched off the intercom to the interrogation room and went out to talk to them in the hallway.

"What a freaking idiot," Gonzo said. "How do kids grow up to be this stupid?"

"It's in the genes," Malone said when he joined them.

He handed a piece of paper to Gonzo. "Your hunch was spot-on, Lieutenant. His mother has a record of drug possession and dealing."

"Apple, meet tree," Freddie said. "I couldn't believe when he said they were just having fun with her, and no one got hurt."

"I could tell you were trying not to punch his lights out," Sam said.

"When I think of Brooke in that hospital bed... It was all I could do not to punch him."

"Hopefully, he'll do the right thing," Gonzo said, glancing at the closed door to the interrogation room. "The lawyer gets it, even if Brody doesn't."

"For once, a lawyer might actually come in handy," Cruz said.

Jeannie McBride came down the corridor. "Lieutenant Holland? There's someone here asking for you."

"Who is it?"

Jeannie consulted her notebook. "A couple named Jeff and Pauline Barnes and their son, Tyler."

"Go ahead, LT," Gonzo said. "We've got this." While Sam desperately wanted to hear the next phase of the Mitchell interview, she also wanted to know what the visitors had to say.

Sam walked away, wondering if Brody Mitchell was their fourth man or if the fourth guy was someone they didn't even know about yet. She went out to the lobby, where the Barnes family sat huddled on the small arrangement of sofas outside the Dispatch area. "Mr. and Mrs. Barnes?"

The parents stood quickly. The father all but dragged the son to his feet.

"I'm Lieutenant Holland. You asked to see me?"

"I'm Jeff Barnes. This is my wife, Pauline, and our son, Tyler. He has something he needs to tell you."

"Come in." Since the conference room was being used as their command center, complete with gruesome photos of the murder victims, Sam led them to one of the empty interrogation rooms. "Have a seat." She arranged the chairs on all four sides of the table to keep things friendly and non-confrontational. "Do you mind if I record our conversation?"

"He doesn't mind," Jeff Barnes said on his son's behalf. Pauline looked like she might break down at any second as she stared at her sulky son.

"Tyler?" Sam said. "Do you mind?" He shook his head.

Sam turned on the recording device and recited the date and time. "Lieutenant Holland speaking with Jeff and Pauline Barnes and their son, Tyler. How old are you, Tyler?"

"Seventeen."

"Tell her what you told us," Jeff said to his son, his tone leaving no room for negotiation. The tension between the three of them was palpable.

"I was at the party at Hugo Springer's house," Tyler said as his eyes filled with tears. "Hugo, Michael, Todd and Kevin were friends of mine. Close friends."

"I'm sorry for the loss of your friends."

Tyler nodded and wiped a tear from his cheek. "Can you tell me about the party? What time did you get there?"

"It was after nine. Hugo and Michael had been at it for a while by then, and they were pretty lit."

"I want to say for the record that my son was prohibited from attending that party, but he snuck out of our house and went anyway," Jeff said.

Tyler seemed to shrink under the rage coming from his father.

"Mr. Barnes, I understand you're upset, and with good reason, but if you could please let me talk to Tyler and refrain from commenting for the time being I'd appreciate it."

Tyler seemed shocked that she'd spoken that way to his father and glanced at Jeff to gauge his reaction.

Thankfully, Jeff bit back whatever he had planned to say when he caught the frosty glare she directed his way. His rage wasn't going to make Tyler any more forthcoming, but because he was a minor, she couldn't kick his parents out of the room. After all, they'd come forward willingly, and she wanted to treat them as respectfully as possible.

"You got there at nine," Sam said. "Can you tell me how many other people were there then?"

"Had to be more than thirty."

"You said Hugo and Michael had a bit of a head start. Do you know what they had taken or drank?"

"Hugo had scored a stash of Molly, a case of vodka and some beer."

"Do you know where he got it?"

Tyler glanced at his mother, who nodded in encouragement. "I think he took it from his brother, Billy."

That was the second time Billy Springer's name had come up in the investigation, and Sam made a note of it. "You say he took it. So he did it without Billy's permission?"

"I don't really know."

"Was Billy at the party?"

"I didn't see him there."

"What else did you see?"

Tyler exhaled and looked down at his fingers, which were drumming nervously on the table. "There was a girl…"

Sam swallowed back the urge to yell at him to hurry up and say it. "What girl?"

"She was pretty. Dark hair and pale skin. She hooked up with Brantley, and then he came out and told us we could have a go with her if we wanted to. He said she wouldn't care."

Pauline wept silently as her son spoke.

Sam cleared her throat of the bile that surged upward. "Did you take him up on the offer?"

Tyler shook his head. "Some of the other guys did, but I didn't."

She released a deep breath she hadn't known she was holding until it became apparent that Tyler probably wasn't the fourth man. "Can you tell me who went in there?"

"Most of the guys went. Hugo, Michael, Brody and some other guys I didn't know. I think they went to school with Hugo."

Sam was dismayed to realize so many young men had been in the room when Brooke was attacked, and no one tried to stop it. "Did anyone speak up and say that maybe it wasn't a good idea for all of them to go in there?"

"I had some words about it with Brantley. I told him it wasn't cool to offer her up that way. He told me to shut up and mind my own business. He said I was a pussy because I didn't want to do her. I told him I didn't want his sloppy seconds, and he punched me in the chest. I hate that the last thing I said to him was that he was a douchebag." He swiped at new tears. "He was my friend even if he could be a douchebag at times."

"While you were there, did you take anything or drink anything?"

He glanced nervously at his dad. "I took some Molly, but I didn't drink anything. I don't like vodka or beer."

"And what time did you leave?"

"I think it was around ten-thirty or so. Some other people were leaving, so I went with them to get a ride home."

"Besides the nine victims, can you tell me who else was still there when you left?"

"The chick who'd been with Brantley. I don't remember her name. Her friend who had a weird name. Started with an H."

"Hoda?"

"Yeah, that's it. Some other guys were still there too. I don't know who they were."

"This has been really helpful, Tyler. I appreciate you coming forward."

"That's it?" Tyler asked, wide-eyed and incredulous. "I'm not in trouble?"

"I assume you're in trouble with your parents, but you won't be charged with a crime, if that's what you mean."

Jeff and Pauline sagged with relief.

"I'd recommend you stay away from situations where there's underage drinking and drugs present," Sam said. "Nothing good ever comes from that."

"I know," Tyler said, looking much younger than his seventeen years as tears streamed down his face. "I can't believe what happened there after we left. It's like a bad dream."

It was a nightmare that would stay with the kids who'd

gotten out alive for the rest of their lives. Sam didn't feel the need to share that thought with Tyler, who'd already been through enough. She asked him to write down his name, address and phone number in case she needed to follow up with him. As they were leaving, she shook hands with Tyler and his parents.

"Thanks for coming in. I appreciate it."

"We asked for you because we know you're fair," Pauline said. "I'm glad we did."

"That's nice to hear. Thanks." She walked them out and returned to the interrogation area to see where they were with Brody Mitchell and found Gonzo and Freddie leaning against the wall outside the room, both messing around with their phones while they waited.

"They're still in there?" Sam asked.

"Yep," Gonzo said. "What was that about with the visitors?"

Sam updated them on what she'd learned from Tyler. "I think our next move is to track down Billy Springer and figure out where he was on Friday night. If what Tyler said is true, Hugo helped himself to his brother's stash. Maybe Billy came to his parents' house with vengeance on his mind."

"Christ," Gonzo muttered as Freddie scowled at his derogatory use of the Lord's name. "Can you imagine Bill Springer on that case?"

Sam rolled her eyes. "That'll be fun. How do you want to proceed?"

"Does it *kill* you to ask me that?" Gonzo asked with amusement.

"It causes me physical pain."

The three of them shared a laugh.

"You and Cruz go find Billy Springer," Gonzo said. "I'll get Arnold to help me finish up with Brody."

"Got it," Sam said. "We're on it. I'm also going to follow up with Archie to see if he's been able to track Hoda Danziger's cell phone."

"Sounds good. Keep me posted."

Sam glanced at the closed door to the interrogation room. "You do the same."

"If he's the guy, you'll be the first to know."

"Thanks." As she and Freddie went to the detectives' pit to gather their belongings, it occurred to Sam that knowing for sure who the fourth guy was wouldn't change anything for Brooke. She'd still be injured and broken in ways that might never be fixed.

"Hey, Sam," Archie said as he appeared at her door. "Hoda got curious and fired up her phone, so I've got GPS coordinates on her." He handed her a slip of paper with an address near American University, right where Brooke predicted her friend might be.

"This is great. Thanks so much."

"No problem." He took a closer look at her. "How ya holding up?"

"Pretty good, all things considered."

"And your niece?"

"On the mend."

"Glad to hear it. Let me know if I can do anything else to help."

"I appreciate what you've already done."

"That's what friends are for," he said with a smile as he took his leave.

"What've you got?" Freddie asked when he came to the door wearing one of his signature trench coats. He had white powder on his lips that was indicative of an afternoon snack.

"If you're going to eat doughnuts on the sly, you might want to get rid of the evidence," she said, pointing to her own lip.

"Whoops," he said with an adorable grin as he wiped the powder off his lip.

"Archie found Hoda for us. Let's go there first."

"Want me to text Gonzo and let him know?"

"Yes," Sam said with a smile. "I keep forgetting."

"We made a bet you couldn't do it, so I'm impressed at how well you're doing so far."

"You actually bet against me?" Sam asked her partner as they headed for the parking lot.

"Not technically. No money exchanged hands, but I might've nodded ever so slightly when someone else said they didn't think you couldn't do it."

Sam scowled at him. "I expect better from you."

"No, you don't," he said with a laugh as he nudged her with his elbow. "Come on, admit it. It's funny."

"Hardy. Har. Har."

"I'd think you'd be complimented by the fact that your squad knows you so well."

"Yes, it's very flattering," Sam said in a tone that dripped with sarcasm.

The address Archie had given her was on 47th Street Northwest, a couple of blocks from the American University campus. Upon arrival, they discovered a duplex. "It's the one on the left," Sam said, consulting the paper Archie had given her. She took a look around at the quiet street where nothing seemed to move. Even the leaves on the trees were perfectly still.

"I've got an itchy feeling about this," Freddie said.

"Do you think we should call for backup before we go in there?"

"I'd hate to tip her off, but I've got the same itch." Sam reluctantly called for backup and sat tight until two Patrol officers arrived in a marked squad car. "You two take the back," she said to them as she and Freddie got out of her car and proceeded to the front door, where she rang the bell.

When there was no answer, she opened the storm door and pounded on the inside door. "Metro PD. Open up."

"What do you want?" a male voice asked.

"I want you to open this door before I blow it open."

"We haven't done anything."

"Then you've got nothing to worry about. Open the goddamned door." She and Freddie simultaneously retrieved their weapons and took position on either side of the door.

"Let me see your badges."

They held them up to the peephole and waited until they heard a series of locks disengaging. The door swung open to reveal a man with brown hair in his early twenties. Dark eyes stared back at her in a surly glare.

"Are you Nico?" Sam asked.

He seemed stunned that she knew his name. "Yeah. So?"

"I'm Lieutenant Holland. My partner, Detective Cruz. We're looking for Hoda Danziger. Is she here?"

"I don't know anyone by that name."

"Are you seriously going to stand there and lie to my face?" Sam asked.

He had the good sense to squirm under her glare. "Where is she, Nico?"

Releasing a deep sigh, he stepped aside to admit them.

Sam was about to re-holster her weapon when a click-ing sound had her removing the safety and keying the receiver on the radio attached to her hip.

"Stay right there," a female voice said. "Don't come any farther."

"Hoda, you're making a huge mistake pulling a gun on cops," Sam said.

"What do you want?"

"We'd like to talk to you."

"I have nothing to say."

"I think you do. I think you have a lot to say, and we can do this the easy way or the hard way."

"Hoda," Nico said. "Don't do this. Don't make it worse than it already is."

"How can it get any worse?" she asked, her voice cracking with emotion.

"It can get a lot worse if your finger slips and you shoot a cop," Sam said.

"I don't want to shoot anyone, but I don't want you here."

"If you put down the gun right now and come talk to us, we'll forget you pulled a gun on us."

"No, you won't! Cops say stuff all the time to get people to do what they want them to do, but I don't be-lieve you!" Her gun discharged, and a bullet whizzed by Sam's head. If she hadn't dropped to the right when she did, she'd be dead.

"Take her," she said into her radio from a crouch on the floor.

Upon hearing what was transpiring inside the house, the Patrol officers had entered from the back and appre-hended Hoda.

"No! *Don't touch me!*"

"Clear," one of them said on the radio as they dragged Hoda kicking and screaming out of the bedroom into the living room. The girl was strikingly gorgeous, even with a tearstained face and wild-looking dark hair. With a quick glance, Sam could see how she might've successfully passed as Brooke's sister. She wore a revealing tank top that showed off impressive breasts and a pair of barely there panties that left little to the imagination. Her outfit gave Sam a pretty good idea of how she'd passed the time while hiding out with Nico.

"Lieutenant," a dispatcher said over the crackling radio. "Report."

"Active shooter neutralized," Sam said. "No injuries. Send another car for transport." She slapped cuffs on Nico.

"What'd I do?" he asked as he resisted her.

"Where'd she get the gun?"

"I didn't tell her to shoot at cops!"

"You made sure she was armed, which makes you eligible for attempted murder charges too. How old are you anyway?"

The words "attempted murder" seemed to have sobered him somewhat. "Twenty-four," he mumbled.

"And she's just turned eighteen. Hmmm."

"What does that mean?"

"It means, scumbag, that the U.S. attorney is going to be really interested in whether your relationship with her began when she was still a minor, and how she ended up in possession of a gun. Her mother has been looking for her for days, and all that time she's been here. You could be looking at kidnapping charges." That last part wasn't true, but he didn't need to know that.

"*Kidnapping?* I gave her a place to stay and kept her safe! I didn't kidnap her!"

"Tell it to the judge."

"Nico, do something!"

"Shut up, Hoda! I helped you out, and this is the thanks I get?"

She seemed more upset by his harsh words than she did by the fact she was being arrested.

Freddie recited the Miranda warning, advising them to remain silent lest anything they said be used against them in court.

"Nico, please don't be mad at me. I can't handle that."

"Shut up," he growled.

"I love you! I never meant for any of this to happen."

"Hoda, I said to shut the fuck up before you make this worse for both of us."

"How could it be worse? They're taking me away from you. I need you!"

Sam let them air it out in the hope that they might say something incriminating. She sniffled and wiped at a pretend tear. "This is so heartbreaking, isn't it, Detective Cruz?"

"I'm positively decimated," Freddie said, making Sam smile and Hoda cry harder, if that was possible. "Let's get Crime Scene here to go through the place to see what other secrets our friend Nico has been keeping besides his teenage lover," Sam said.

"I'll make the call," one of the patrolmen said. "And we'll wait for them."

"Appreciate that," Sam said. "Make sure they get the bullet she aimed at me."

"You have no grounds to search my house," Nico said with growing agitation. "I didn't do anything. She did."

Hoda let out a wail that made Sam cringe. "*Nico!*"

"The minute she pulled a weapon on cops this became a crime scene, pal. Perhaps if you chose playmates your own age, none of this would be happening. Let's get them to HQ."

"Keep your fucking mouth shut, Hoda," Nico growled on the way out the door. "I mean it."

"Nico, please. I love you. Don't be this way."

"I see she has trouble with basic orders," Sam said with a wince. "That could be a problem when I get her into interrogation."

"You're enjoying this, aren't you?"

"Sure, it makes my day to nearly get my head shot off by an eighteen-year-old girl who's been allowed to run wild. Are we going to find evidence that you've been having all kinds of sex with her while she was holed up with you? Oh, holed up. What a great pun. Did you catch that, Nico? *Holed* up? Were you *holed* up in her?"

"You're a bitch," he growled.

"It *absolutely* makes my day when scumbags bring out the B word. Doesn't it, Detective Cruz."

"One of your favorite things, Lieutenant."

They stashed Nico in the back of the second Patrol car that had responded to the scene and sent him to be processed.

Hoda, still ugly crying, was put into the back of Sam's car. When they were on their way to HQ, Sam said, "I hate to see these teenage love affairs go bad."

"I do too," Freddie said, rolling with her as he always did. "You never forget your first love, especially when he gives you a gun and encourages you to shoot at cops."

"He didn't do that! You don't know what you're talk-

ing about! I know who you are. You're Brooke's aunt. I
saved her life! You could be a little more grateful!"

*Bingo,* Sam thought. Even though she was dying to
get into it with Hoda, she would wait until they were at
HQ and could record the conversation.

"She knows you gave her parents the money to send
her to that school, and she *hates* you for it."

While that news was hardly a surprise to Sam, it still
hurt to hear that Brooke had expressed hatred toward her.
Everything they'd done had been with her best interests
in mind, and that it had gone so very wrong…

Hoda sobbed and wailed all the way to HQ, and by
the time they got there, Sam felt a headache coming on.
"Let's put her through the paces on the gun charges,"
she said to Freddie before they got Hoda out of the car.
"Maybe that'll take some of the starch out of her before
we get her into interrogation."

"Good plan. I'll take her in."

While he marched Hoda in through the front door
and past the media that was still camped out waiting for
news about the case, Sam walked around the outside of
the building to the morgue entrance. The smell of snow
hung heavy in the damp air. Thick dark clouds hovered
over the District as daylight gave way to an early night.

Sam couldn't wait to get this case closed and hopefully salvage some time with Nick and Scotty during the
holiday. With that in mind, she headed straight for the
pit looking for an update from her team.

"Hey, LT." Gonzo took a measuring look at her. "Are
you okay?"

"I'm fine. She missed by a mile. Where are we with
our friend Brody?"

"He admits to videotaping the rape, but he flatly denies participating."

"Was he willing to name the fourth guy?"

"Nope. We're charging him with felony rape, video voyeurism and cyber-porn."

"Good. I guess the truth about his participation in the assault will be in the DNA. Any word on that?"

"Lindsey put a rush on it, but nothing yet."

"We got sidetracked in looking for Billy Springer when the shit hit the fan with Hoda and her boy toy."

"I figured as much. I've got his address in George-town. We can check it out after the four-thirty meeting." Sam would never admit to having forgotten about the meeting. "Sounds like a plan. I need a couple of minutes, and I'll be right there."

"Sounds good."

"Close the door, will you?" The minute she was alone, Sam popped a couple of pills, hoping to put a stop to her headache before it blew up into a migraine. She washed the pills down with an old bottle of water that sat on her desk and then reached for her cell phone to call Nick.

"Hey, babe. What's up?"

"Are you getting ready for your big meeting?"

"All showered and shaved and about to suit up."

"Wear the dark gray suit with the cranberry tie. I like that one. You'll look very vice presidential in it."

"I like how you can joke about this when I feel like I'm going to be sick."

"I don't want to add to your stress or anything, but because I'm far more evolved in the marital sharing de-partment than you are, I need to tell you I got shot at ear-lier. She missed by a mile, but I was the intended target."

His deep exhale was the only sound Sam heard on

the other end of the line for a long, long moment. "Who shot at you?"

"Brooke's BFF, Hoda."

"What the hell is a teenage girl doing shooting at a cop?"

"That's a very good question and one I fully intend to ask her as soon as we've broken her spirit a bit with processing, fingerprinting, strip-searching and other fun cop stuff."

"Here I am just going about my day, and you could've been killed."

"I was nowhere even close to being killed. She's a bad shot."

"Good thing she isn't a lucky shot."

"I didn't want you to hear it through the grapevine the way I heard about the VP thing."

"Your not-so-subtle digs are not so subtle."

That made her laugh. "I'm just pointing out how much better I am at the sharing stuff than you are lately."

"I gotcha, babe. Your point has been made over and over and *over* again."

"I'm just getting started. Call me the second you leave the White House."

"I will. Scotty is with Abby and Ethan at Angela's for dinner. When Spencer gets home, she's going to run to Tracy's to get more clothes for Abby and Ethan so they can stay there tonight. I'll pick up Scotty after my meeting."

"Thank you so much for helping out with the kids today. I know Tracy and Mike appreciate it, and so do I. In fact, when I get home, I'll show you how much I appreciate it."

"I think we need some loft time tonight."

"It's a date, Senator. Or should I call you Mr. Vice President?"

"Stop it," he said with a groan.

"I love you, and I'm so proud of you. To be wanted by the president to be his vice president is pretty damned cool no matter how it turns out."

"If you say so."

"I say so, and I'm always right."

"On that note, I'm outta here. I'll call you when it's over."

"Good luck."

"Oh and I love you too, and I'm very glad you're okay. Thanks for calling to let me know."

"It's just how I roll."

He was still laughing when she ended the call with a smile on her face.

# TWELVE

A KNOCK ON her office door put Sam right back to work. "Enter."

Jeannie McBride came in to update Sam on what she'd been working on, but it seemed like she had something else on her mind.

"Everything okay?" Sam asked her.

"Yeah, it's all good. I'll see you at the meeting." Jeannie turned to leave, but stopped in the doorway.

"You may as well tell me why you really came in." Wearing a small smile at Sam's persistence, Jeannie turned back to face Sam. "The trial."

"Come sit. Shut the door."

"It's okay. I know you're busy. We all are."

"Come in, shut the door and sit down. That's an order." This was said gently and with an affectionate grin for the woman who'd become a close friend after Jeannie's horrific attack.

Jeannie did as she was told, settling into Sam's visitor chair. "I had a meeting with Faith and Tom today," she said of the assistant U.S. attorney and her boss.

"It's coming up soon," Sam said.

"First week in January. It's all I can think about... Having to see him again." Jeannie shook her head. "I don't know if I can do it."

"I have no doubt you can do it, but it won't be easy. I feel sick when I think about having to face off with him in court, so I can only imagine how you must feel." Her own confrontation with Mitch Sanborn had resulted in a miscarriage that had broken her heart—and Nick's. "But the alternative…"

"Is letting him get away with it. That can't happen."

"No, it can't." Sam got up and went around the desk to sit in the other chair. She reached for Jeannie's hand. It was icy cold, so Sam held it between both of hers. "You're the toughest chick I know."

"Funny," Jeannie said with a small laugh, "that's what I say about you."

"Nah, I've got nothing on you. You make the rest of us look like wimps. Look what you endured and survived."

"Have I survived it? Truly?"

"As horrifying as it was, you didn't let it ruin your career or your relationship with Michael. You're back to work. You're planning a wedding. You're going on with your life. You're not letting him win. If that's not survival, I don't know what is."

"You and everyone here, the job… It gave me something to stay focused on when the darkness tried to tempt me. I wouldn't have survived without this to come back to."

"I've felt that way myself a few times, but you survived because of you. The job couldn't have saved you if you didn't want to be saved, Jeannie. How about giving yourself a little credit? And Michael deserves some too."

"Yes, he certainly does."

"One more hurdle to get through, and then you can really put it behind you."

"You're right. I know."

"I'll be right there with you the entire time you're in court. We'll get you through it."

Jeannie leaned into Sam's embrace. "Thank you. I can't tell you how much I appreciate all your support from the very beginning."

"That's what friends are for," Sam said, like Archie had said to her. The amazing brotherhood—and sisterhood—she'd found within the police department was second only to the bond she shared with her own sisters.

"We've got a meeting to get to," Jeannie said. "I'll be there in a minute."

After Jeannie walked out, Sam took a moment to get herself together. Thinking about Jeannie having to testify against that animal Mitch Sanborn made her want to vomit. Testifying against the perps they arrested was a necessary evil in their line of work, so they were all seasoned witnesses. But this one was personal. Not just for Jeannie but for everyone who had worked on the case against the former Democratic National Committee chairman and his cronies who'd been behind a prostitution ring that had been one of the District's best-kept secrets. Until the murders of two immigrant women unraveled the whole scheme.

Sam still couldn't think about the desperate day they'd spent looking for Jeannie in the midst of the murder investigation that had also brought down the Speaker of the House of Representatives, the senior senator from Virginia and Vice President Gooding's chief of staff.

Sam would rest a little easier when all four scumbags were put away for a good long time. But she'd never wanted vengeance quite the way she did in the case of Mitch Sanborn. When she thought about what that savage had done to Jeannie, all in the way of trying to intimidate the police that were hunting him down, she wanted his head on a platter so she could smash it with a sledge-hammer. That would make her feel a lot better.

She stood to gather her notes and file folders, ignoring the more insistent pounding that was coming from the base of her skull. Not a good sign, she thought, as she made her way to the conference room, trying to ignore the pings of light that were indicative of a migraine coming on.

Hopefully, the pills would kick in soon before the headache ruined what was left of her day.

NICK TOOK A cab to the West Wing entrance on Pennsylvania Avenue. Terry was waiting for him in the ground-floor lobby where they produced identification and went through security. The area was deserted late that Sunday, a day when the White House was closed to the public.

Terry looked almost as nervous as Nick felt. "Derek didn't say what this is about?" he asked in a low tone. "Well, I assume it's about the president making a last-ditch effort to talk me into a job I don't want, but no, Derek couldn't say anything more than come at four." A Secret Service agent escorted them to the West Wing Lobby. "Please have a seat, Senator. Mr. Kavanaugh will be right with you."

"Thank you."

Nick and Terry sat on a sofa beneath a painting of George Washington crossing the Potomac.

"That bookcase is from the seventeen hundreds," Terry said. "It's one of the oldest pieces in the White House collection."

"Where'd you get that random piece of trivia?"

"I was an intern here when I was in college. I paid attention. I once had rather lofty aspirations."

"Whereas I still feel like an imposter every time I walk in here with business to conduct. I felt that way even when I was only a staffer, and now it's even more surreal knowing what he wants to talk to me about."

"You've earned it, Senator. Look at what you've accomplished in the last year."

"What have I accomplished exactly? I stepped into a job that was handed to me when my best friend was murdered—"

"And you won reelection. Resoundingly. That's why they're so interested in you—that and the fact that you have national name recognition due to your amazing convention speech. Not to mention your connection to my dad and your high-profile marriage."

"Neither of which have anything to do with the *work.*"

"In politics, those things are everything. Come on, Nick," he added softly. "You've been around this game long enough to know that."

Terry was right, but that didn't make it any more palatable to Nick to be under consideration for the number-two job after only a year in the Senate. "It should be John."

Terry shook his head. "They wouldn't have asked him. Even though he'd been in the Senate five years when he died, he was still immature as a politician, and as a man. The stuff we've learned about his womanizing since he died would've derailed any higher ambitions he might've had. Besides, he never wanted what he had, let alone anything more than that."

"I didn't want it until it was thrust upon me," Nick reminded him.

"Despite his pedigree, you're actually better at it than he was. You care more than he did, for one thing. Not to speak poorly of my brother, but he was what he was, and he made no excuses."

Nick couldn't deny the accuracy of what Terry was saying about John. As much as Nick had loved him, as his top aide and best friend, he'd had a front-row seat to John's failings as well as his successes.

"I know you struggle with this issue," Terry said. "And as John's brother, I appreciate that you don't take for granted how you came to be here. But he's been gone a year, and you've more than stepped up to the plate in his absence. Anything that happens now is because you've *earned* it."

"That's nice of you to say, and I appreciate you saying it, but…"

Terry smiled. "I get it. Believe me. You'd give it all up to have him back, wouldn't you?"

"In a second."

"That, right there, is what the people love about you. You keep it real. They relate to that. You have every right to be sitting in the West Wing waiting for an audience with the president. He's no fool, and neither are the DNC leaders. They know what they've got in you, and they want to groom you."

The idea of being "groomed" to run for president made Nick feel slightly nauseated. Never in his wildest dreams, and he'd had some rather wild dreams for his life and his career, had he ever imagined things playing out this way.

Derek came into the room, wearing a navy sweater and khakis, which probably counted as dressing down on a Sunday in the West Wing. "Sorry to keep you waiting, Senator, Mr. O'Connor. The president will see you now."

Nick and Terry stood and shook hands with Derek. "Thanks for coming in on a Sunday," Derek said as he led them through the corridors of the most powerful office space on earth.

"No problem," Nick said with a grimace for Terry that nearly made his friend laugh.

"Sam and Scotty are well?" Derek asked.

"Scotty's great, but Sam has been sucked into the case on MacArthur."

Derek shook his head with dismay. "Nine kids dead. Horrifying."

"It really is. It's always tougher on the cops when kids are involved."

"I don't know how they do it day in and day out. I give them so much credit."

As Derek had one of the busiest jobs in Washington, that was saying something.

Nick had been to many a meeting at the White House, but he'd never before stepped foot in the Oval Office. The closer they got to their destination, the more the butterflies stormed around in his belly and the more surreal this entire thing became. *What was he doing here?* He recognized the outer office from having seen it on TV.

Derek approached the closed door, knocked and stepped inside, gesturing for them to follow him.

Looking for something to do with his hands, Nick reached up to make sure his tie was straight.

President Nelson was also casually dressed in jeans and a sweater. He was with White House Chief of Staff Tom Hanigan and Secret Service Director Ambrose Pierce in the sitting area in the middle of the Oval Office. All three men stood to greet the new arrivals.

"Senator," the president said, extending his hand. "Thanks so much for coming in on short notice."

"Of course," Nick said. "No problem. I believe you know Terry O'Connor, my deputy chief of staff."

"Yes." A longtime friend of Terry's father, Nelson shook Terry's hand. "Good to see you again, Terry."

"Likewise, Mr. President."

"I'm sure you both know Tom and Ambrose."

*More handshakes, more small talk, more bullshit,* Nick thought as they all took a seat. Nelson offered bourbon, and Nick gratefully accepted, hoping the liquor would calm his nerves. He also found it intriguing that Nelson recalled from their meeting on Air Force One that Nick enjoyed a good glass of bourbon. He couldn't deny it was flattering to have the president of the United States remember such an insignificant detail.

When everyone had drinks in hand, Nelson crossed his legs and looked extremely relaxed and comfortable. Nick figured anyone twice elected to the highest office in the land had the right to be comfortable and relaxed. "I'm sure you're wondering why we've summoned you today," Nelson said.

"I have a pretty good idea," Nick said dryly, making the others laugh.

"The last time we talked, you indicated this wasn't a good time for you or your family to make a big change.

I want you to know I truly respect that you put your family first. I honestly do. However, you're the one I want, Senator. You're the one the party wants. You're the one the people want, if our polling is to be trusted."

"Is that how the press caught wind of your offer?" Nick asked. "Because you polled on it?"

"Perhaps," Hanigan said. "We apologize if the leaks have caused you any discomfort."

"My wife wasn't too pleased to hear about it from a reporter."

Nelson winced. "Sorry about that."

"My own fault," Nick said with a shrug. "Since I'd turned down your gracious offer, I hadn't bothered to mention it to her."

"Ahh," Nelson said with a wry smile. "A rookie error."

Nick laughed at the witty comment. "Indeed. I've been soundly schooled on the error of my ways. Chalk it up to my newlywed status."

"You'll learn," Ambrose said with a grin.

Nelson propped his elbows on his knees and leaned forward to address Nick directly. "I like you, Senator. I like everything about you. I'd be deeply honored if you would reconsider my offer."

And there it was…

"I heard your concerns about your wife the last time we spoke," Nelson continued. "I appreciate and respect your desire not to disrupt her career or her life—or your son's life. I've asked Ambrose to be here to address those concerns." With a glance at the Secret Service director, Nelson passed the ball to him.

"You may not be aware that only the president, vice president, president-elect and vice president-elect are required to have Secret Service protection. Spouses and family members can opt out of protection, although we don't recommend it. I understand from the president you were concerned about your wife being required to have Secret Service protection, which would naturally impair her ability to perform her duties as a member of the Metropolitan Police Department. I'm here to tell you she can opt out of protection if she so chooses. We would recommend, however, that should you accept the president's offer, you provide protection for your son." Nick's head was spinning as he absorbed what Ambrose was saying. Sam wouldn't be required to have Secret Service protection. "Are you saying my wife would be permitted to keep her position with the MPD, go to work every day the way she does now and move freely around the city should I choose to accept the president's offer?"

"That's exactly what I'm saying," Ambrose replied.

To Nelson, Nick said, "And you'd be okay with that? You're aware of what she does and how often she makes headlines of her own?"

"I'm aware, and I'd be fine with it."

"She lives in constant fear of her work causing political trouble for me. That's always a possibility."

"I understand," Nelson said. "And since I'm not running for anything ever again—thank you, Jesus—that'd be your problem, not mine."

Nick felt his resistance weakening. "Her dad is a quadriplegic. He lives three doors up the street from us. She wouldn't want to move away from him, even if she was still in the District."

"We're aware of that," Ambrose said, "and we're prepared to make allowances to keep you in your current home. With some adjustments for security, of course."

"Well," Nick said, releasing the deep breath he'd been holding. "You've certainly given this a lot of thought and managed to allay my most pressing concerns."

"I'm still not hearing a 'Yes, Mr. President, I'd be delighted to accept your offer,'" Nelson said.

Nick felt the heat of all eyes on him. He wished now that he'd asked Graham O'Connor to come to the meeting too, although Graham would be jumping up and down by now, accepting on his behalf. The thought of that brought a smile to Nick's lips.

"You've given me a lot to consider," Nick said tentatively. "I'd like a little time to think it over, to speak to my family and my team."

"I understand," Nelson said. "However, time isn't on our side. Vice President Gooding's tumor is life threatening. He's been given three to six months to live."

"I'm so sorry to hear that." Nick liked the jovial vice president and was saddened to hear of his dire diagnosis.

"We're working with his office to keep his condition under wraps until we're ready to announce his resignation and our choice for his replacement at the same time. As you can imagine, he's anxious to resign so he can focus on his treatment and his family at this difficult time. In a best-case scenario, we'd like to make a move on Friday."

"*Of this week?*" Nick asked, incredulous.

"Yes."

"And if I decline? You have someone else in mind?"

"We have another candidate who's a very distant second to you. You're the one we want."

"I want you to know I'm incredibly flattered to be sitting in this room, in this building, talking to the president of the United States about something so far outside my reality I feel like I must be dreaming. No matter what I decide, please know how deeply honored I am to have been asked."

"I appreciate your candor, Senator. It's one of the things I most admire about you. We've certainly taken enough of your time when the Senate is in recess and you're probably wishing you were home with your family." Nelson stood and extended his hand.

Nick rose and shook his hand and Ambrose's too. "Thank you, Mr. President. I'll be in touch."

"I'll look forward to hearing from you. Tom, if you would, please give the senator my direct number."

"Of course, Mr. President," Hanigan said as he and Derek escorted Nick and Terry from the Oval Office. "I didn't want to say this in there," Hanigan said when they were in his office. "But Halliwell wanted to be here for the meeting, but the president said no. He didn't want to overwhelm you with DNC pressure on top of the pressure he was already exerting. But you should know the party leadership is incredibly jazzed about the idea of you as VP."

"That's good to know," Nick said, feeling like an elephant was sitting on his chest.

Hanigan handed him a business card with the president's direct line written on the back. "Thanks for coming in."

Nick shook hands with him. "Thanks for having me. I think."

Hanigan chuckled at the comment as he shook hands with Terry. "We'll be waiting to hear from you, so don't take too long to think it over."

"I understand the urgency."

Derek walked them out. "Pretty crazy, huh?"

"That's one word for it," Nick said to the man who'd been his friend for almost as long as Nick had worked in Washington. They'd come up through the ranks together as congressional staffers and had forged a close friendship in the process. "I'm really excited for you, Nick," he said in a low tone that couldn't be overheard. "Couldn't happen to a better guy."

Nick shook Derek's hand. "That means a lot coming

from you, my friend. Thank you. Hope to see you on Thanksgiving."

"I'll be by at some point."

"We'll be there."

Nick and Terry walked out of the White House into the November darkness that arrived earlier every day this time of year. The air was moist with drizzle, and the temperature had dropped with the sun. Nick buttoned his overcoat against the chill.

"Holy. Shit," Terry said when they'd cleared the White House gates.

"Tell me how you really feel," Nick said.

"This is freaking incredible! Are you going to do it?"

"I don't know. I need to talk to Sam, and right now, more than anything, I want to talk to your dad."

"Then let's go to the farm, Senator."

As SAM AND the others emerged from their meeting, Freddie was returning to the pit.

"How's our friend Hoda?" Sam asked him.

"As predicted, the intake process took some of the piss and vinegar out of her. She's in interrogation two with Officer Bailey keeping an eye on her until we're ready to talk."

"You ought to get in there and talk to her before she starts screaming about lawyers," Sam said.

"You're not coming?"

"As much as I'd love to rip that little bitch to shreds, she's tied to Brooke's case, and I don't want to do anything that would endanger that."

Freddie dabbed at his eyes dramatically. "I think our little lieutenant is finally growing up," he said to Gonzo, who busted up laughing.

"I'm not amused," Sam said, even though she had to admit it was pretty funny. She'd never give him the satisfaction of knowing that, however.

"I assume you'll be observing," Gonzo said.

"You assume correctly. Based on what we know about the timeline, she may have witnessed the homicide, so you'll want to get one of the Millers down here too."

"I'll call up there now," Freddie said.

Ten minutes later, the click of Assistant U.S. Attorney Faith Miller's stiletto heels preceded her into the pit. "What've we got?"

They brought her up to speed on Hoda's involvement in the case.

"It's possible she might've seen everything," Sam concluded. "Based on what she said to me about saving Brooke's life, I also believe she was the one who got Brooke out of there after the killings went down. Other than Brooke, Hoda is the only one we've been able to identify who might've been there when the killing happened and got out alive. I'm willing to deal on the malicious mischief charges associated with her busting Brooke out of school and the attempted murder charges in exchange for what she saw at the Springers' house." Sam paused before she added, "Despite her bluster, she's an eighteen-year-old kid who got in way over her head, so let's go at it with kindness until we have a reason to get tough with her."

"I want to hear what she has to say," Faith said, "but I tend to agree with the lieutenant about lesser charges in exchange for an eyewitness account to what happened in the Springers' basement."

"We'll see what we can do," Gonzo said. "Let's get to it, Cruz."

Freddie chased a bag of peanut M&M's with a bottle of cola and followed Gonzo into the hallway that led to the interrogation rooms.

"Is he always eating?" Faith asked. "Or is it only when I'm around?"

"Sadly, it's all the time," Sam replied as she followed Faith to the observation room. "I swear I gain weight just by working with him."

"He sure does wear it well."

"That he does. I tell him all the time that I hope I'm around to see his metabolism grind to a halt the way mine has." Sam clicked on the intercom so they could listen in to the interview with Hoda.

She was dressed in an orange jumpsuit. Her face was puffy and swollen from crying, and she slumped in her chair, showing much less bravado than she'd displayed earlier. Just as Sam had suspected, being booked on formal charges had taken the girl down a few pegs.

Gonzo introduced himself and reintroduced Cruz and went through the motions of getting her permission to record the interview.

"I'm going to be honest with you, Hoda," Gonzo said, diving right in. "You're in a shitload of trouble. Do you understand you're looking at attempted murder charges for firing at my lieutenant?"

"Yes," she muttered.

"I'm sorry. I didn't hear you."

"Yes! I know it was stupid, and it's a big deal."

"Do you know if you're convicted on the charges, you're looking at a long stay in prison, and that with four cops as witnesses to the shooting, the conviction would be a slam dunk?"

Hoda swiped angrily at the tears that ran down her

face. Sam had little doubt that Hoda was furious with herself for allowing her emotions to get the better of her. In some strange, odd way, Sam could identify with this kid with the chip on her shoulder. She hadn't been that different when she was eighteen. Only the fact that she hadn't been allowed to run wild had kept her from taking the path Hoda was on. "I know I'm in trouble. So what's the point of this conversation?"

"The point is, we believe you know what happened at the Springers' house the other night, and we're willing to consider lesser charges for you if you're able to help us get justice for the nine kids who were murdered."

She was shaking her head before he finished speaking. "I don't know anything about that."

"We think you do."

She continued to shake her head, but the tears pouring from her eyes told another story.

"Did you see who killed all those kids?"

"No," she said, wiping up the flood of tears.

"Hoda… I know this is really hard, but if you saw something and you don't tell us, it's possible they could get away with it. We haven't found a murder weapon. We have no sign of forced entry. We can't find anyone else, other than you and Brooke, who was drugged up and out of it, who were still there when the murders happened."

Hoda put her face in her hands as she continued to shake her head.

"Someone got Brooke out of there. We think that someone was you. Want to know how I think it went down?"

"No."

"Let me tell you anyway," Gonzo continued, speaking in a gentle, soothing tone. "I think Brooke went in the bedroom with Todd while you stayed out with the others, drinking, popping some pills, maybe fooling around with one of the guys. Perhaps you went into the bathroom and were in there when things went bad. Maybe they never saw you in there, but you saw them. You know who they were. You know what happened, don't you, Hoda?"

She laid her head down on her arms and sobbed. Freddie moved to the other side of the room and sat next to her, patting her back with the compassion Sam had come to expect from her kindhearted partner.

"The poor kid," Faith said. "Imagine witnessing that."

While Sam was empathetic to what Hoda had seen, she still wanted to hear the full story from her.

"Hoda," Freddie said. "I understand how upsetting this is for you and how horrifying the images have to be that are trapped in your mind forever. But if you tell us what you saw, maybe you'll feel better. Maybe you'll get some peace if you help us get justice for the kids who were killed."

"I can't say it," she said between sobs.

"What can't you say?" Freddie asked.

"I can't say what I saw because then he'll want to kill me too."

"We won't let that happen," Freddie said. "We'll take care of you, Hoda. You have my word on that."

"I shot at you and your partner. Why are you being so nice to me?"

"Because I believe you witnessed something no one should ever have to see, and that made you do something you wouldn't ordinarily do."

"I'm sorry I shot at your lieutenant. I was so scared, and I didn't want to have to go with you."

"I understand. Can you tell me what happened Friday night?"

She sat up, wiped her face and seemed resigned now to her fate, even as her chest continued to heave with sobs. "You know about me going to get Brooke at her school, right?"

"Yes."

"She wanted so badly to see Todd, and I wanted to help her. We weren't sure if it would work, but it did."

"What time did you arrive at Hugo's house?"

"Around nine thirty or so?"

"And what did you do once you got there?"

Hoda shrugged. "Had some drinks and stuff. Hung out, listened to music."

"You both took some of the pills Hugo had provided?"

She nodded. "It was Molly. We'd done it before."

Hearing Brooke had done Molly before, Sam closed her eyes and shook her head in dismay.

"What happened then?"

"Brooke went to hook up with Todd in the bedroom. I stayed in the other room. I was kind of hanging with Kevin, making out and stuff. After a while Todd came out and some of the other guys went in the back bedroom. I had to go to the bathroom, and I think I fell asleep or something while I was in there. I woke up when I heard someone screaming. The music was really loud, but I could hear screaming. So I opened the door a crack to see what was going on." Her voice broke on those words and new tears tumbled down her cheeks.

"It's okay, Hoda," Freddie said, offering her a drink of water. "Take your time."

She drank a couple of mouthfuls of water and wiped her face. "Hugo's brother, Billy, was there. They were right outside the bathroom door so I could hear them. Billy was screaming at Hugo about stealing from him, and how he was in deep shit because Hugo had taken stuff from his apartment. Billy said, 'You don't even know what you've done.' Hugo told him to fuck off and leave him alone. He went back to fooling around with the girl he was with. Billy went upstairs and came back down with a knife and just went sick. He started with Hugo, and he went around the room. The music was so loud, no one could really hear anything, and the lights were off except for some candles they had burning. I thought it was over and then a girl came out of the bedroom, and Billy saw her, so he went in there. I was so scared he was going to see me, so I stayed really quiet, even though I was crying and freaking out about Brooke cuz I knew she was in that bedroom. He came out of there, and was breathing really hard. I was still peeking through the crack in the bathroom door. I held my breath, and I was praying so hard he wouldn't see me.

"And then he went upstairs, and I heard the front door open. As soon as I knew he was gone, I ran for my phone and asked my friend Davey to come get me. I went into the bedroom to find Brooke." Hoda wiped her face and took another sip of water.

"There was blood everywhere, but someone had put a comforter over her, so he didn't see her. I could feel her chest moving so I grabbed a sheet and wrapped it around her and dragged her out of there. I went into the garage and waited for Davey to come. He showed up with one of his friends and he helped me get her out of there."

"Did Davey know what you'd seen in the Springers' house?"

Hoda shook her head. "I didn't tell anyone. Even Nico doesn't know why I was so upset."

"Why did you and Davey take Brooke to her aunt's house?"

"Because her aunt would know what to do. Brooke's mom tends to freak out over the slightest thing, but Brooke always said her aunt was kind of cool. Plus she's a cop, so it just seemed like the right thing to do. We watched for them to come home. If they didn't come soon, we were going to call nine-one-one."

Sam tucked her trembling hands under her arms so Faith wouldn't see how undone she was after hearing how close Brooke had come to being murdered. "What do you think?" Sam asked Faith.

"It's going to be tough to go on the testimony of an eighteen-year-old who admits she was high on Molly and had been drinking before she became the lone witness to mass murder. It'll be a stretch to sell her as a credible witness to a jury."

"But she had the wherewithal to get herself and Brooke out of there, to call for help, to take Brooke to my house, to wait to make sure we came home and found her. That shows capacity, even if it was diminished."

"Still… I'm not convinced it's enough to go after Bill Springer's son for murder."

"And now we get to the crux of the matter."

"He'd shred her in court, and you know it, Sam. Her story would be so full of holes we'd be able sail an aircraft carrier through it by the time he was finished with her."

Sam couldn't deny that Faith made a good point. "So what do we do?"

"Find Billy Springer, get him in here and ask him where he was when his brother was killed. He'll give you an alibi that won't hold up. You'll search his apartment, and maybe get lucky and find the murder weapon. You know what you have to do."

"Yeah, but it sure would make my life easier if I could arrest him due to an eyewitness putting him at the scene and identifying him as our killer."

"It might be easier, but it's not enough."

"I used to like you," Sam grumbled.

Faith laughed. "And you will again when we're able to put together an airtight case that holds up in court."

"Fine."

"Fine."

"Happy freaking Thanksgiving," Sam added.

"It will be if you get this sewn up before turkey day."

When she saw Gonzo and Freddie heading out of the interrogation room, Sam went to the door with Faith in tow.

"How'd we do?" Gonzo asked, wearing a big smile.

"It's a good start according to Faith."

Gonzo's smile faded. "Just a start? It's not enough?"

"It's not enough," Faith said, reiterating her concerns with Hoda's ability to successfully testify.

"Let's go pick up Billy Springer," Gonzo said.

"Wait just a minute," Chief Farnsworth said as he joined them. "What's this about Billy Springer?"

Sam glanced to Gonzo, letting him know this one was all his.

"We have an eyewitness who puts him at the scene and saw him wielding a knife as he methodically took out a room full of teens."

"Ah, Christ," the chief said as he sagged with visible exhaustion. "You're really building a murder case against Bill Springer's son?" he asked, looking directly at Sam.

She held up her hands. "Don't look at me. This case is all his." She pointed to Gonzo.

"Gee, thanks, Lieutenant," Gonzo said. "You're a pal."

"You gotta take the bad with the good."

"Tell me what you've got," Farnsworth said.

Gonzo filled him on what they'd learned from Hoda as well as the fact that Billy Springer's name had come up repeatedly during the investigation.

"We may have a bit of a problem," Farnsworth said tentatively.

"What kind of problem?" Sam asked.

He rubbed a hand over his face. "Vice has had eyes on him for months now. We've got undercover officers positioned near him, and they're close to an arrest. Apparently, the stash Hugo stole from his brother's apartment was going to seal the deal. They were waiting for him to come home to arrest him, but Hugo got there first and carted off the goods."

"And they just *let* him?" Sam asked, infuriated and incredulous.

"You've been undercover, Lieutenant. You know how you have to sometimes look the other way to maintain cover and keep the greater prize in mind."

"Why didn't you tell me at the beginning of all this that another of Springer's kids was under investigation by our department?"

"I couldn't risk compromising that investigation."

"It was *relevant*. You should've told me."

"I did what I thought was right."

Sam's frustration mounted as she propped her hands on her hips. "Did they look the other way while their subject committed murder?"

"Of course they didn't," Farnsworth snapped. "They

didn't think anything of a routine stop by his parents' house, and were unable to break their cover until about twenty minutes ago to report in that he was there the night of the murders."

"So let's go arrest him," Sam said.

"Not so fast. They're *this* close to having him nailed on the drug charges. They want tonight to get it done, and then he's all ours in the morning."

"Since when do drug charges trump murder?"

"Since we've spent six months and significant department resources on this operation that's not only targeting him, but two other major dealers in the city. Our people are on him. He's not going to kill anyone else overnight with them watching him—"

"He managed to kill nine teens while our people were watching him," Sam reminded the chief.

"He told them he needed to run into his parents' house to talk to Hugo. He told them to wait outside for him, and he'd be right back. They didn't know yet that Hugo had made off with Billy's stash, so they had no reason to believe he was going to go ballistic with a knife. In six months undercover with him, they've never seen anything that indicated he had that in him. They're as surprised as anyone."

"How's that going to look for us when it gets out that we had undercover people on him when he committed mass murder?"

"I'm working with Public Affairs now to manage the spin on that."

"So you're the one who needs the time, not the narcs?"

Farnsworth glared at her. "Lieutenant Holland, I'm telling you as the chief of police that Vice will be allowed to complete their investigation of Mr. Springer and his associates tonight, and in the morning, your team will be permitted to proceed with your homicide investigation. Twelve hours isn't going to make a difference here."

"I hope you're right, sir, because I wouldn't want to have to explain why we allowed a murderer to run free overnight, especially if he manages to kill again."

"He's not going to kill again. We've got eyes on him, and we're watching much more closely than we were before."

"That'll help me sleep better tonight," Sam said as her frustration reached a boiling point.

"You're all released until zero seven hundred," Farnsworth said. "We'll pick this up then." He walked away, and they watched him go.

"This is insanity," Gonzo said. "Why do I feel like there's something else going on here that everyone knows but us?"

"It's seriously fucked up," Sam said. "Since when does narc stuff take precedence over homicide investigations?" She ran her hands over her hair and re-clipped it. "We've been handed our orders, so go home. See you back here in the morning."

"That's it?" Gonzo said.

"That's it," Sam said. "He's the chief. We do what he says."

"What about Hoda and Nico?" Freddie asked.

"Let's hold them overnight for arraignment in the morning," Sam said. "I want her in a safe house until we sort things out with Billy. I'll let her mother know what's going on as a courtesy she hardly deserves."

"And Brody?"

"I'm waiting on the DNA results to determine whether he's the fourth guy in Brooke's attack," Gonzo said. "Ei-

ther way, we've got him nailed for videotaping and posting the attack. So he can spend the night ahead of the
arraignment too."

"Enjoy the unexpected night off," Sam said as they
returned to the pit.

"Oh, I plan to," Freddie said, waggling his brows as
he flashed an adorable grin.

"Yuck," Sam said disdainfully.

He walked away laughing, a jaunty spring in his step
as he headed home to his hot-to-trot girlfriend for a night
of debauchery. Speaking of debauchery, Sam wondered
where Nick was and what had transpired at his meeting.
If she had to take a night off, she planned to spend it with
her husband and son.

# THIRTEEN

WHEN NICK CALLED SCOTTY to let him know he was going to Leesburg, Scotty asked if he could come along, so they swung by Angela's to pick him up. Now Nick and Terry were seated in Graham's cozy study while Scotty helped Laine, who was baking Thanksgiving pies in the kitchen.

"Scotty has gotten taller since I saw him last," Graham said.

"He's growing like a weed," Nick said. "I have to take him to get some new jeans this weekend. He's already outgrowing the ones we got him to start school."

"Just wait," Graham said. "Boys grow the most in their teens. It's about to get crazy."

"I wish we'd had more time with him when he was younger. I feel like we missed so much."

"You'll have plenty of time with him—all the time that matters as he becomes a man."

"True."

"Enough with the small talk," Terry said. "Cut to the chase, Nick. Tell him why we're here."

Terry's impatience made Nick and Graham laugh. "Ease up, son," Graham said. "That's no way to talk to your boss."

"He's not my boss right now. He's my friend, and he's got the biggest decision of his life to make."

"What decision?" Graham asked.

Nick appreciated hearing Terry refer to him as a

friend. Because Terry was so impatient, Nick gestured at him, giving him the go-ahead to bring his dad up to speed on what was going on.

"I thought you'd said no to him," Graham said when Terry had finished.

"So did I."

"Well... This is quite something, isn't it?"

"I guess you could say that."

"Nick..."

"I know what you're going to say."

"If that's the case, why'd you come all the way out here to talk to me?"

Nick laughed at the older man's comeback, thrilled by the sparkle of excitement he saw in his eyes. That sparkle had been dimmed over the last year since he lost his beloved son, so it was always a relief to see it return. His snow-white hair was disheveled, probably from a day spent riding horses. "Because I wanted to give you the chance to say it. I wouldn't dream of denying you that."

Graham's smile lit up his weathered face. "You know me far too well, my friend. Is there anything I can tell you that you don't already know? Such as the fact that my good friend David Nelson is handing you the nomination in four years on an engraved silver platter?"

"That thought may have crossed my mind." Nick put down the drink Graham had poured for him and propped his elbows on his knees. "But that's what I need to decide before I agree to anything. Is it what I really want?"

"Only you know the answer to that question, Nick. I certainly can't tell you what's in your heart. I can tell you what's in mine..." Graham said with a cheeky grin.

Nick laughed and shook his head. "This I've got to hear."

"I look at you and I see a man in his prime. I see a man of principle. I see a man who leads with his heart. I see a man who's one of the people, who came up the hard way with nothing handed to him."

"Except his most recent job," Nick said, though he was humbled by Graham's observations.

"I hate that you think that."

"See?" Terry said. "That's what I say too."

"Nothing was handed to you, Nick. The Virginia Democrats chose the very best man for the job, and nothing that's happened in the last year has changed our opinion of the man we chose. If anything, you've proven to us over and over again how spot-on we were choosing you to finish out John's term."

"That's very nice to hear."

"We've had this conversation often in the last year, and it really does my heart good to know you still mourn for John. I speak for my entire family when I say we have no doubt whatsoever you'd give it all up to have John back."

"I would," Nick said softly. "Of course I would."

"That's not going to happen, as much as we wish it was. All we can do is play the hand we're dealt in this life, and right now, my friend, you're holding *all* the cards—the royal flush most politicians would sell their souls to the devil to be dealt. And you didn't have to sell anything to get the hand of a lifetime, which makes you different from most right out of the gate."

"What about Sam and Scotty? What about what this would do to their lives?"

"How does Sam feel about it?"

"She says she'd work around it, but we all know that's easier said than done sometimes. And what if things go really well, and I have the chance to run in four years?

What then? She won't be ready to retire then, and the First Lady can't be out chasing down killers."

"Who says?" Graham asked. "Maybe she becomes a pioneer in a new age of first ladies who keep their lives separate from their husbands'. Just because it's never been done doesn't mean it couldn't *be* done."

"Why do you gotta make this look so damned possible?" Nick asked.

Graham grunted out a laugh. "Because it is. Nelson wants you bad enough to let you set your own terms, which means Sam can too. He's made it so you can stay in your home, Scotty can stay in his school, Sam can keep her job. The only thing that would really change is Secret Service protection for you and Scotty, a different office and probably a bit more travel, additional social obligations…"

"All of which my wife would hate."

"So don't take her. You've made her optional in all of this from the beginning. Nelson will respect that."

"What about the people of Virginia, who just elected me to be their senator for the next seven years? What do I say to them?"

"You tell them you were presented with an opportunity too good to pass up, that your heart will always be with the commonwealth and that you'll continue to focus on the issues that matter to you—and to them—in your new role."

"Damn, you're good. Are you sure you weren't a politician in your previous life?"

Graham's low chuckle made Nick laugh too. "What's your gut telling you, son?"

Nick would never be able to articulate what it meant to him when Graham called him that. He had a father of his own whom he loved, but he loved Graham as a sec-

ond father and a dear friend. "It's too busy being nauseated to tell me much of anything. And I've got no time
at all to really think about it because they want to make
the announcement on Friday. Gooding is really sick."

"I really hate to hear that," Graham said sincerely.
"Joe's a good guy. He and I are old friends."

"And here again I'd be benefitting from someone else's
misfortune."

"That's life, Nick. When someone gets sick or dies,
someone else takes their place. Life goes on. It's not like
you're going around killing people or infecting them with
deadly diseases so you can get ahead in your career."

"Yeah, look at Arnie," Terry said, "and the stuff he
did to get where he wanted to be. There's no comparison
between that kind of pol and your kind."

Arnie Patterson's greed for power had been the reason
Derek Kavanaugh's wife was murdered, and Nick appreciated the reminder that he was nothing like Patterson.

"You've given me a lot to think about," Nick said.
"The next step is to talk it over with Sam and see what
she has to say."

Graham stood. "You know where I am if I can be of
any help in the next few days."

Nick rose and gave Graham a hug. "You've already
been a tremendous help. Thanks for letting me air it out
with you."

"Any time. It's always my pleasure."

"Let's go see if Laine is ready to part with her assistant," Nick said as he headed for the kitchen to collect
his boy. He was eager to speak to his wife.

SAM ARRIVED HOME and was bummed to see no sign of
Nick's car on the street. He'd texted her to say the White

House meeting had been "interesting," and that it was too much to talk about via text. Scotty, Terry and I are running out to Leesburg to see Graham and Laine. Will be back in a couple of hours.

Since that had been a couple of hours ago, she'd hoped they'd be back by now. No such luck. Tossing her coat over the back of the sofa, she headed for the kitchen in need of something to eat. She stopped short in the doorway when she discovered their personal assistant, Shelby Faircloth, sitting at the table with a pad, pen and cup of tea. She wore a fluffy pink sweater with a matching headband.

"What're you doing here, Tinkerbell? I thought you went home for Thanksgiving."

"I did go home, but then I heard you'd caught another big case and that Brooke was in the hospital, so I decided to come back."

"You didn't have to do that. You have a right to a vacation like anyone else."

"I know I didn't have to, but my brother and his family were there. My sister-in-law is a whiner who does nothing but pick fights with my brother, their kids are brats, and I decided I'd much rather be here with you guys than there with them. Then I got a text from Avery about how his plans to go home to Charleston had changed…" She blushed as she shrugged. "I told my parents there'd been an emergency at work, and I needed to get back."

"So now you're using us to get away from the bitchy sister-in-law?"

"Sam… Now, did I say that?"

"Not in so many words," Sam said with a laugh. She couldn't deny she enjoyed her conversations—also known as sparring matches—with the woman who'd planned their magical wedding and then became their essential right hand in the last few months. Sam pointed to the pad and paper. "What're you up to?"

"Making a shopping list for the Thanksgiving dinner you promised your relatives and friends, which I bet you've done exactly nothing to prepare for since your vacation got canceled."

She also couldn't deny that Shelby knew her a little too well.

Shelby's laughter echoed through the kitchen. "I knew it! Where's my favorite twelve-year-old?"

"Off with his dad at Graham and Laine's. They should be home soon." Sam sent a text to both of them to find out where they were.

Scotty wrote right back. On the 14th Street Bridge. Where are you?

Home, waiting for you guys.

Terry is bringing us.

Sam wondered why Terry was bringing them, but she figured she could ask when she saw them. Ok, see you soon. Xoxo.

Gross.

Sam laughed at his last text and then showed the exchange to Shelby.

"You know he doesn't really think your hugs and kisses are gross at all. He adores you."

"And vice versa."

"And you wonder why I'd rather be with you guys than home with the Bickersons?"

"You're always welcome with us. You know that."

"That's very sweet of you. So what're you doing here when you've got a murderer to catch?"

"We've caught our murderer, but because of some departmental BS we're not allowed to arrest him until the morning." She shook her head in dismay. "Don't ask."

"Okay, I won't. But I will ask if you're okay. It's been a rough week around here, huh?"

"I'm better than I was. Things were pretty dicey for a while there with Brooke."

"But she's…"

"On the mend. Physically. Emotionally? That's going to take a while."

"Do you want to talk about it?"

"Not really, but thanks for asking. I'm kind of talked out on that topic."

"I'm here if you need an impartial friend."

"I appreciate that. Since I've got this unexpected night off, I'd much rather talk about turkey and stuffing."

"You've got it."

Fifteen minutes later, Sam and Shelby had a plan for dinner and dessert as well as a shopping list that Shelby would tackle in the morning. "Won't Nick be impressed by the way I've got this all figured out?" Sam asked with a teasing grin.

Shelby rolled her eyes. "If left up to you, your guests would've been served pressed turkey from the deli—if they were lucky."

"I'm offended by that statement."

"No, you're not."

Nick and Scotty came home a few minutes later, and

Scotty came dashing into the kitchen. He lit up at the sight of Shelby, one of his favorite people.

"What're you doing back?" he asked as he hugged Sam and then Shelby.

Shelby wrapped her arms around the boy who was taller than her, but it didn't take much to be taller than Shelby. Her diminutive stature was one of several reasons Sam called her Tinkerbell. "Home was way more boring than it is here."

"It's never boring here," Scotty said. "Wait till you hear the latest. Tell them, Nick! It's unbelievable!"

"I told you not to get too excited, buddy. It might not happen."

"Still… You gotta tell them!"

Sam noticed her usually unflappable husband looked more than a little flapped and maybe a tad bit drunk, which would explain why Terry had driven them. "I take it your meeting at the White House went well?"

Shelby let out a squeak of excitement as she kept an arm looped casually around Scotty's shoulders. "*White House?* What's that all about?"

"Between us, meaning you can't tell anyone," he said with his gaze fixed on Scotty in particular. "Vice President Gooding is ill and will be resigning on Friday. I've been asked to take his place."

"*Holy sh—*"

"Don't swear, Shelby," Scotty said.

"This might actually be a time for swears," Sam said.

"With you it's always time for swears," Scotty said, earning him a poke to the belly that made him laugh.

"I take it your plan to say 'thanks but no thanks' didn't go as planned?" Sam said with growing anxiety over what had transpired with the president.

"Not exactly. I really need to talk to you."

"Go talk," Shelby said. "Scotty and I are going to the movies."

"We are?" the boy asked with delight dancing in his brown eyes. He glanced at Sam and Nick. "On a school night?"

"This one time, and only because it's a short week," Sam said.

"And only if I can treat." Nick removed two twenties from his wallet and handed them to Shelby, who tried to protest. "I insist."

"Thank you," Shelby said to Nick before returning her attention to Scotty. "I've been dying to see that new superhero movie. What do you think?"

"Excellent!" Scotty ran off to get his coat.

"Thanks, Shelby," Sam said.

"Not a problem. You know I love hanging out with him."

"I thought you were off this week," Nick said.

"I thought you were too, and then I hear you're having meetings with the president."

"Touché," Nick said with a chuckle.

Shelby wrapped a pink scarf around her neck and pulled on her coat. "I don't know anything about it, but for what it's worth, I think you'd be an excellent vice president, Nick."

"Thank you," he said in a hushed tone. "That means a lot."

"We'll be a while," Shelby said. "He'll need ice cream after the movie. Enjoy some time alone to figure things out. I'll take care of your boy."

Sam hugged her because she'd just realized that at some point in the last year, Shelby had become someone she loved. They saw Scotty and Shelby off on their "date" and returned to the kitchen.

"This is a conversation for the loft," Nick said. "Is it your plan to sex me into compliance?"

"If that's what it takes."

"I need food."

"I could use some too."

Sam went to him and pulled his tie the rest of the way off and released the first few buttons on his dress shirt. "Why is Terry driving you around?"

"Because I had a few drinks."

"Why are you drinking?"

"Because the president had an answer for every concern I have about accepting his offer, and then I went to hash it out with Graham, and there was more bourbon. I figured being given a few days to make one of the biggest decisions of my life called for booze."

"*Days?*"

He put his hands on her hips and tugged her in closer to him, resting his forehead on hers. "Days. Gooding's in a bad way. They need to make a move, and they want to make it by Friday."

"As in *this* Friday?"

"This Friday."

"They don't call it Black Friday for nothing, huh?"

His soft laughter and appealing scent surrounded her as he held her. "True. Of course Congress has to approve the appointment, so it wouldn't be official for a couple of weeks. Let's order some food and take it upstairs. I desperately need some time with you."

"I'm all yours until seven tomorrow morning."

"I thought you were hot on the trail of a killer."

"So did I." After they called in an order to their favorite local Italian place, she filled him in on the latest with the case.

"That's very odd."

"We think so too. I just hope my colleagues in Vice don't let that scumbag slip through their fingers overnight."

"Is it okay to be secretly glad you got sprung for the night?"

"Hell yes, it's okay. I'm thrilled to have gotten sprung and to have a night alone with the hottest politician in town."

Predictably, he scowled and shook his head.

"In this case I wasn't necessarily referring to your physical hotness, which is as hot as ever. I meant your political hotness."

"I'm glad you're able to make light of it. I was afraid you'd be packing my bags and shipping me out by now."

"Never," she said softly, curling her arms around his neck. "Never, ever, *ever*."

"Samantha, don't be nice to me right now. I can't handle it."

Rather than tell him how she felt about him with words, she went up on tiptoes and kissed him. The instant her lips connected with his, everything else faded away—the case, the troubles with Brooke, her worries about her dad's upcoming surgery, the turkey dinner she was expected to produce on Thursday and the huge decision they had to make about his career. Right now, right here, there was only him.

"You're being nice," he whispered against her lips.

"I'm feeling *really* nice."

His sexy smile stretched across his face. "I need to get this suit off. It's hardly vacation attire."

"I'd be happy to help with that."

"We are going to talk about this, aren't we?"

She took him by the hand and led him upstairs to their bedroom. "Eventually. First, we're going to enjoy a rare moment alone before we ruin it with business."

"I do so love the way you think."

"Can I have that in writing for the next time you're accusing me of being off the rails?"

"Absolutely not."

The silly banter and sexy innuendo with her favorite person in the world were exactly what she needed right then, and exactly what he seemed to need too. Hovering in the back of her mind was the enormity of what he'd been asked to do and how it would affect them and their family. A tiny spike of panic gripped her when she wondered if he'd expect her to give up her job.

As she helped him out of the suit, she pushed that thought and every other one that didn't involve him and his pleasure right out of her mind.

"What're you doing, Samantha?" he asked as she dropped to her knees in front of him.

"Helping you out of your suit."

"You could've done that standing up."

"Yes," she said as she unbuckled his belt and freed him from the suit pants and boxers that slid down muscular legs. "But I couldn't have done this standing up." He sucked in a sharp deep breath as she took him into her mouth while stroking him with her hand. "*Samantha...*"

"Mmm." She purposely let her lips vibrate against his shaft as she continued to work him over with lips, tongue and a hint of teeth.

His fingers fisted in her hair, holding on tight as she

continued to tease and torment. "*Babe*... Oh my God, that's good. Don't stop."

She loved the desire she heard in his voice and felt in the tight grip he had on her hair. The slight bite of pain only fired her desire to give him more, to give him everything.

"*Sam*."

She recognized the sense of urgency in the way he said her name and intensified her efforts to finish him off. Taking him deep into her throat was all it took. With a shout, he came hard, clinging to her hair as he thrust into her mouth. She stayed with him until his legs began to quiver and he released his tight hold on her hair.

"Holy. *Shit*."

"This is a no swearing zone," Sam said as she ran her tongue around the tip.

"The boy isn't here, and that deserved a holy *fucking* shit. What brought that on?"

"I've told you before. Power turns me on."

He reached for her, helped her up and put his arms around her. "You never, ever cease to amaze me."

She smiled as she breathed in the scent of home: starch and soap and the slightest hint of citrusy cologne.

"My goal in life, Senator. Or should I call you Mr. Vice President now?"

"Nothing has been decided yet, and since you've completely scrambled my brain, I'm not sure anything will be decided tonight."

The doorbell rang downstairs.

Sam patted his chest. "Get changed and relax. I'll be right back."

Downstairs, Sam paid the delivery guy, set up the food on a tray, grabbed a bottle of red and headed back upstairs to find the bedroom light off but the hallway light on. Smiling, she headed for the second set of stairs that led to their hideaway in the loft.

Nick had changed into sweats and his favorite ratty Harvard T-shirt. He'd lit the beach-scented candles that took her right back to the best week of her life, the honeymoon she'd spent with him in Bora Bora.

She put the tray on the foot of the double lounge chair he'd bought to mimic the one they'd so enjoyed there. Corkscrew in hand, she set out to open the wine. "Let me do that, babe. You know you're no good at it."

Because he was absolutely right about that, she gladly handed the bottle to him. "I'm awfully good at drinking it, however."

"That you are." He deftly pulled the cork from the bottle and poured them each a glass.

They sat at the foot of the lounge chair and dove into the pasta and salad they'd ordered.

"Are we going to talk about it?" she asked after most of the pasta was gone.

He paused, put down his fork, wiped his mouth and looked directly at her. "You know I love you more than anything, right? I mean *anything*."

She did know, but it always made her heart race a little faster when he looked at her in just that way and said those particular words. "Yes," she replied, because what else needed to be said?

"It's an incredible opportunity. I won't deny that, but I don't need it to be happy. I don't need it to be fulfilled. I don't need it if it's not what we both want."

Sam swallowed hard and asked the one question that was foremost on her mind. "Would I have to quit my job?"

"No, babe. I'd never ask you to do that." He spelled out the concessions the Secret Service was willing to make in order to accommodate her job. "Only the president, vice president, president-elect and vice president-elect are required to have protection. Family members can decline it."

Hearing that, Sam released the breath she'd been holding. "That was my second question."

"What's your third one?"

"Would we have to move? Doesn't the VP live at the Naval Observatory?"

"Yes, but I explained about our close proximity to your dad, and they're willing to make it so we could stay here."

"Wow, it sounds like they really want you."

"It seems like they do. But there's one other thing we need to talk about right now before this goes any further."

"What's that?"

Since they were both done eating, he put the tray on the floor along with their glasses and reached for her. As there was nowhere she'd rather be, she willingly curled into his embrace. "What happens four years from now. If I say yes to this, I'm saying yes to a whole lot more than being VP for the next four years. I also become the heir apparent for the nomination."

Though she'd suspected that's what he would say, hearing the words brought home the stark reality of what they were considering.

"If that were to come to pass, I can't promise you'd be able to keep your job and everything would stay the same. I'd like to think we could forge a new path and do our own thing, but we both know it's not just about what we want. And because of the nature of your job..."

"It could be a liability."

"I don't care about that, Sam, and I never will. I've told you that before. But at that level it's not just about what I want."

"What do you want? In your heart of hearts, and thinking only of your career and not of me or Scotty, what do *you* want?"

"It's very hard for me to think about what I want without factoring you and Scotty into the equation," he said as he ran his fingers through his hair. "On the one hand, it's an incredible opportunity, but it's also a life-changing opportunity. I kind of like my life the way it is. And our life together is chaotic enough without adding an even higher-profile job to the mix. I also worry about what it would really mean for you. Sure, they'd let you keep your job, but yours is not exactly a low-profile job either. Would you actually be able to perform your duties effectively? I just don't know." He turned his head so he could see her face. "What do you think? And tell me the truth."

"I, um… I don't know what to think."

"Surely you must have some thoughts on the matter."

"This feels like déjà vu. Didn't we have a similar conversation a year ago when you promised me one year and done in the Senate?"

The left side of his face lifted into the half grin she loved so much. "So what you're telling me is I have zero credibility on these things."

"I'm reminding you that nothing has gone as planned in the last year."

"One thing did. March twenty-sixth went exactly as planned."

"Yes, it did," Sam said, smiling at the reminder of their wedding day. "At least this time you're coming to me with a potential twelve-year plan."

"I like to think I've learned to give you more information at times like this."

She cupped his face and turned him so she could see his eyes. "I think you'd be really, really, *really* good at it."

"Really?"

"Yes," she said, laughing. "Really, really."

"It could totally suck for you."

"I'd deal with it. I've already spent a year dealing with a high-profile politician significant other, and my career has survived just fine. I sort of like the idea of being a trailblazer by keeping my job and going on like I was before you ascended to the number-two spot in the country."

"Other second ladies have worked outside their official duties, but none of them in jobs like yours."

"Wait, back up. Official duties? What official duties?"

"As second lady, you'd be expected to make some appearances with me and on your own. You'd be able to take on some causes that are close to your heart, such as adoption, paralysis support, public safety, fertility, learning disabilities. Those kinds of things—and only if you were interested in bringing attention to those issues."

"You know how to hit a girl where she lives, Senator."

"I'm just saying, it's an opportunity for you in that regard."

"I suppose I could give up sleep to run these additional programs."

"You'd have a staff devoted to working on your causes. You'd show up for the big moments. And you'd have to get tricked out in fancy dresses once in a while." He raised himself up on one elbow to look down at her. "I'd buy you a new pair of designer shoes for every formal event."

Sam's eyes narrowed. "That's blackmail."

"Call it what you will, my love. I know the way to your heart is through your heels."

"That's not the only way," Sam said, fisting a handful of his shirt and tugging him down for a kiss. "Oh, sorry. I forgot about the ribs. Are they better?"

"Much better today. Feel free to bend me to your will."

She put her arms around his neck and looked up at him, still amazed after nearly a year that he was hers to keep forever.

"What?" He propped his forehead on hers and gazed into her eyes.

"Sometimes I still can't believe I get to keep you."

"Samantha," he whispered against her lips. "I feel that way every minute of every day. How can something so incredible even be real?"

"It's real," she said, combing her fingers into his soft hair. "It's as real as real gets, and if we do this great big huge thing, we have to promise not to let anything get in the way of what's most important to us."

"Nothing will ever be more important to me than you are. You and Scotty. The two of you are all I need to be happy. The rest is just gravy."

She drew him down to her, losing herself in the sensual strokes of his tongue, the sweetness of his lips, the rightness of their undeniable connection.

He gathered her up, surrounding her with his love and filling her with an overwhelming desire to feel his skin against hers.

She tugged at the hem of his T-shirt and helped him take it off before running her fingertips lightly over the bruises that marred his otherwise flawless chest. "My favorite man chest," she said as she eased him onto his back and kissed the well-defined pectorals, grazing his nipples with her tongue, before working her way down to kiss the purpling bruises.

He pulled on her top and removed it without unbuttoning it, tossing it to the floor. Next came her bra, and then they were chest to chest, and Sam exhaled a happy little sigh at the thrill she always experienced when she was close to him this way. Suddenly, she was in a big rush for more. She pushed his sweats down to discover he wore nothing under them, and then went to work on her own jeans, wiggling out of them while he watched her with hazel eyes gone hot with desire.

Sam loved when he looked at her that way, as if he wanted to devour her. His desire for her was a huge turn-on. No one had ever wanted her with the same desperation he showed her on a regular basis. She often wondered if or when their need for each other would settle into something more staid or predictable, but if anything, it only got wilder all the time.

Especially when they were here, in the escape he'd created to take them back to the blissful days and nights of their honeymoon, it seemed that anything was possible. Before him, she'd always thought her breasts were too big, but watching him worship each one with his tongue and hands and teeth, she knew they were perfect in his eyes. He drove her crazy with the insistent tugging on her nipple that sent a live current all the way through her, settling into an insistent throb between her legs.

"Nick…"

"What, baby?"

"I need you."

"I'm right here." His lips were soft as they moved over her belly.

"Come up here."

"In a minute. Or two."

When she realized his intention, Sam's arms dropped to the cushion in surrender. "You shouldn't be doing that. You're injured."

"I'm fine." His lips skimmed the sensitive skin on her inner thigh as her legs fell open to accommodate his broad shoulders. "We're all alone, so make some noise for me, babe," he said as dabbed at her with his tongue.

Sam moaned and arched into him, trying to hurry things along, but he wouldn't be rushed.

Using his fingers to open her to his tongue, he focused on the pulsing heart of her desire as he slid two fingers deep inside her.

She cried out from the dual sensations that rocked her and had her climbing quickly toward release.

He knew just how to touch her, just where to kiss her. His fingers curled inside her, sending shock waves through her entire body. "Come for me, Samantha." He sucked hard on her clit, pressed his fingers deeper into her and drove her to a scorching release that had her screaming from the sheer pleasure. And then he was poised between her legs, pressing into her insistently, sending her into a second wave of release that seemed to go on forever as he pounded into her.

She curled her legs around his hips and grasped his ass, which she knew made him nuts.

A low growl preceded a shout of pleasure as he came deep inside her. Every time she felt the heat of his release, she wondered if this might be the time their love created a new life. She clung to him, holding him as close as she could while she said a silent prayer that maybe this time... Maybe, just maybe...

"I love you," he whispered against her ear, his breath harsh and choppy from exertion.

"I love you too."

"We didn't decide anything."

"No, we didn't, but we had awesome sex, so the night wasn't a total loss." She felt his laughter deep inside her where he remained, still hard and thick and pulsing with aftershocks. Combing her fingers through his hair, she caressed his back with her other hand and reveled in the sweetness of their love, the completeness he brought to her life and the utter perfection they created together.

"You should do it," she said softly, so softly she wondered for a second if she'd said the words out loud or merely thought them.

When he raised his head to meet her gaze, she knew she'd actually said them. "What're you saying?"

"You should accept the president's offer. We'll figure it out the way we always do."

"Sam… You should be really sure before you say that."

"I'll never be really sure. What I am sure of is my faith in you. I've always said you were destined for great things. This just proves that, as always, I was right."

He smiled and shook his head at her cheekiness. "Remember when they asked you to run for your seat in the election?" she asked. "We talked about what kind of people we wanted to be and whether we were willing to settle for 'good enough' or whether we wanted to strive to be more."

"I remember."

"If you don't do this, we'll always wonder what might've been. I'd rather not spend the rest of my life wondering."

"This is all your fault, you know."

Her mouth fell open in shock. "How in the hell have you managed to convince yourself of that?"

"If I hadn't fallen for the sexy, bad-ass homicide cop, no one would've cared about a lowly senator from Virginia."

"Is that what you think?"

"That's what I *know*. Ninety percent of the attention I've gotten in office has been because of you."

"All the attention you've gotten in office has been because of *you*. You have no idea how amazing and smart and dynamic and stunningly gorgeous you are, do you?"

"Samantha," he said with a scowl. "Shut up."

"You don't even notice when all the moms at hockey are drooling over you! You're the whole package, Nick. You're smart and dedicated, and the fact that you're movie-star good-looking certainly doesn't hurt."

"I can't listen to this or my head will swell."

She tilted her hips against his. "I love when your head swells."

He laughed as he attacked her neck with kisses and nibbles that had her squirming under him. "If we do this, you have to promise you won't hate me when it totally sucks for you and gives you a huge pain in the ass."

"I promise I won't hate you. I may withhold sex, but I'll never actively hate you."

"Wait a minute. Withholding sex is a deal breaker."

Laughing at the horrified face he made, she kissed his cheeks and then his lips. "I'd only be hurting myself with that punishment. I'll have to think of some other way to exact my revenge."

And then he was moving inside her again, and Sam couldn't think of anything other than how amazing he always made her feel.

# FOURTEEN

THEY'D MOVED DOWNSTAIRS by the time Scotty and Shelby returned. Cuddled up to Nick and dozing in front of the fireplace in the living room, Sam heard Shelby say good-night and remind Scotty to go straight to bed so she didn't get in trouble for keeping him out late on a school night.

"I will. Thanks again, Shelby. I had a really good time."

"So did I, pal."

"Thanks, Shelby," Nick called to her.

"My pleasure. I'll see you all tomorrow."

"That movie was so awesome!" Scotty said when he joined them on the sofa. "Is Sam asleep?"

"Just resting my eyes," Sam said. "Glad you enjoyed it."

"It was so cool, and Agent Hill said he'd take me on a tour of FBI headquarters during Christmas vacation. I can go, right?"

Sam felt Nick's muscles tighten under her. "Sure, you can. So he went to the movies with you?"

"Uh-huh. I'm going to take a shower. I promised Shelby I'd get right to bed so we didn't get in trouble." He gave Nick a hug and kissed Sam's forehead. "Night, guys."

"Love you, buddy," Nick said.

"Love you too!"

"I adore that you guys are so free with the L word,"

Sam said as she watched the flames dance in the fireplace.

"I never heard that word growing up. I'm determined he'll hear it every day for as long as he lives with us."

"And I just fell in love with you all over again."

He pressed a kiss to the top of her head. "Let's go to bed."

"Thanks for tonight. I needed this time with you."

"So did I." He got up to bank the fire and closed the glass doors that would contain any stray embers. "What are you going to tell the president?" Sam asked when he took her hand and led her upstairs, where they heard the shower running at the other end of the hallway.

In the doorway to their bedroom, he turned to her. "You tell me what I'm going to say."

"You're going to call him tomorrow and say, 'Mr. President, I'd be honored to accept your kind offer to become your new vice president.'"

"Am I really? You're sure."

"Hell, no. I'm not sure of anything other than you'd be crazy to turn down such an amazing opportunity. I'll do everything in my power to make it work for you. That's all I can do."

"It's way more than I deserve in light of what I'm asking you to take on."

"Didn't you promise me a rose garden?" she asked with a saucy grin, referring to his proposal in the White House rose garden.

"I guess I did, didn't I?"

"You'd better get busy delivering."

"You promise we'll be okay?"

"I promise."

Sliding his arms around her waist, he leaned in to kiss her. "I'm going to hold you to it."

"Oh, jeez. Are you guys back to kissing again?" Scotty asked when he emerged from the bathroom with a towel wrapped around his waist. "I think I liked the fighting better."

"Go to bed, brat," Sam said.

He laughed all the way into his room, where the door shut with a thud.

Nick smiled and shook his head. "I can't wait until he falls for some girl and wants to be kissing her all the time. Payback will be a bitch."

"We so owe him some major abuse." Sam brushed her teeth and slid into bed, meeting him in the middle where they slept wrapped up in each other every night. "Hey there."

"How's it going?"

"Did you hear my adorable husband is going to be the next vice president of the United States?"

"I hadn't gotten that memo. Is he nuts?"

"No," she said with a sigh as she kissed him. "He's perfect."

NICK WAS STILL asleep when Sam slid out of bed just after six the next morning, feeling energized by the evening they'd spent together. As long as they could have a night like that every so often they'd be able to stay on track no matter how crazy their lives became.

She couldn't deny the flutter of nerves that attacked her always-sensitive stomach at the thought of him being vice president. But he'd assured her that very little would change for her, and she'd decided to take him at his word. She was so ridiculously proud of him. After his austere upbringing with a grandmother who hadn't wanted him around and two absent, teenage parents, he deserved every good thing that came his way.

What he'd said about growing up without the word "love" in his home had broken her heart and furthered her resolve to make sure he heard it every day in their home. That wouldn't be a hard promise to keep. Her love for him seemed to grow bigger and stronger with every day they spent together, every challenge they confronted and every new hurdle they faced.

That was why she felt so strongly that they'd find a way to deal with his new role. Their foundation was strong enough to bear the weight of more responsibility.

After a shower, she crossed the hall to the closet he'd had built to accommodate her vast wardrobe and pulled on jeans and a sweater. She pushed her feet into running shoes and grabbed a knit scarf to wrap around her neck, which bore a few marks from her husband's teeth.

While she knew she ought to be appalled that he'd marked her, she was secretly thrilled by the proof of how totally he lost himself in her. When she was dressed, she went into the bedroom to get her gun, badge and cuffs from the locked drawer in the bedside table, then leaned over to kiss him.

He never stirred as she brushed her lips over the rough whiskers on his jaw. "Love you," she whispered. She left him sleeping and went down the hall to wake Scotty. "Hey, buddy."

"Hey. What time is it?"

"Just after six. Time to get moving." He required a lot of time in the morning to get himself in gear, so they'd learned to wake him more than an hour before they had to leave for school.

"Okay."

"Nick is still out cold, and I don't think he set an alarm. Can I trust you not to go back to sleep?"

"Yeah, I'm up."

"Give me a hug."

He complied with one of her favorite kinds of full-body hugs.

"Sam?"

"Hmm?"

"What do you think of this vice president thing?"

"I think it's kind of cool. What do you think?"

"It's way cool. He'd be so awesome at it."

"Even if it means Secret Service guys trailing you around again?" Nick and Scotty had been under protection during Nick's recent campaign after Arnie Patterson made threats against Sam's family when she helped to arrest him for murder and other charges.

"I didn't mind that too much. The other guys at school thought it was pretty dope. Maybe I'll get a girl agent again."

Sam laughed at that and mussed his hair. "Maybe we can request one."

"So he's going to do it? He was worried about what you'd say."

"I think he is going to do it. He hasn't decided for sure, but he knows I have no objection."

"It's pretty crazy when you think about it."

"What is?"

"A year ago I hadn't even met you guys yet, and now I'm living with you, you're adopting me and my new dad might be vice president of the whole country. That's insane!"

"It is pretty insane, but you know you're the best thing

to happen to us in our whole lives, right? Nothing else matters as much as you do."

"That's pretty insane too," he said softly. He sat up suddenly and gave her another hug.

At times like this, Sam couldn't imagine loving a child she'd given birth to any more than she loved this boy who had so thoroughly stolen her heart—and Nick's.

"I've got to get to work to hopefully sew up this case so I can get busy making pies."

"You're going to actually make pies?" he asked with a skeptical look on his adorable face.

"For your information, I'm an excellent baker."

"Um, okay. If you say so. I learned a few tricks with Laine last night. You'll probably need my help."

She tickled him and made him squeal with laughter. "I don't *need* your help, mister, but I'd love to have it anyway." She kissed his forehead. "Have a fantastic, fantabulous day."

"You too. I hope you catch the person who killed those kids."

"Oh, I will, pal. You can count on that. See you later." Sam pulled on her coat and stepped out the front door into a sea of photographers, a street lined with satellite trucks and reporters screaming questions about Nick.

She turned right around, went back inside and straight upstairs to wake her husband.

"Mmm, hey, babe. Are you leaving?"

"I was leaving, but the entire DC press corps is camped out in the street, and they're full of questions about you."

"Shit. What the hell?"

"Does the White House have a leaker?"

He sat up and ran his hand over the scruff on his chin. "Seems like it."

"I need to get out of here."

"I'll walk you to your car."

"Normally, I'd scoff at such an offer, but there're a lot of them."

He pulled on sweats. "I'm sorry to have brought them here."

"Not your fault."

"What's going on?" Scotty asked from the doorway. "I thought you'd left."

"I tried to leave, but we've been taken over by reporters looking for the scoop on old what's his name." She used her thumb to point at Nick.

"So you said yes to the president?" Scotty asked, his eyes widening with excitement.

"Not officially."

"Then what're the reporters doing here?"

"That's a very good question. Let me get Sam out of here, and then we'll figure it out."

"This is way cool," Scotty declared.

"Glad you think so," Nick replied.

Sam could tell he wasn't happy about the press encamping outside their house when he hadn't even officially decided anything. They both knew from the last year in the spotlight how intrusive the media could be at times. That was certainly not going to get better if he took on an even higher-profile position.

Downstairs, he put on his coat and turned to her. "Ready?"

"Let's do it."

"Stay here, Scotty," Nick said before he opened the door to mayhem.

"Senator! Is it true you're in line for a high-ranking position in the Nelson administration?"

"What was your meeting about with the president?"

"Why was the Secret Service director there?"

"What does Nelson want you to do for him?"

"Is it true Gooding is stepping down, and you've been tapped to take his place?"

"Lieutenant, when do you expect an arrest in the Mac-Arthur murders?"

Nick shouldered his way through the crush and got Sam into her car. She waited until he was safely back inside before she drove away, creeping along so she wouldn't hit anyone, as much as she'd love to mow down the whole lot of them.

If this was what they were in for, Sam wasn't so sure she was ready for a whole new wave of attention when the initial wave had only begun to die down. But she'd do it for him. Of course she would. Their entire relationship had revolved around her crazy job and her crazier cases. How could she not step up for him when he'd been given such a golden opportunity?

Sam wasn't surprised to find another crush of reporters gathered outside the main doors at HQ, so she drove around to the morgue entrance. She lived in mortal fear of the day they discovered her "secret" way into the building.

"Oh my God, Sam." Lindsey pounced the second Sam walked through the door and dragged her into the morgue office. "Terry told me what's going on. Are you freaking out?"

"Um, no," Sam said, amused by her friend's reaction. "Not as much as you are."

"It's *vice president*," Lindsey whispered. "*Of the United States.*"

"Oh jeez, is that right? He told me it was vice president of the local Elks lodge. I feel deceived."

"How can you joke about this?"

"How can I not? It's surreal."

"Terry said it was all going to come down to what you thought of it. So… What do you think?"

"I told him he should do it," she said with a shrug that she hoped indicated she had no plans to overreact. "I don't have to move or quit my job or have suits following me around, so as far as I'm concerned, it's business as usual."

"Are you out of your freaking mind?"

"I very well could be. I've been accused of that before. Lots of times, in fact."

"This is some sort of coping mechanism, right? You play it down so you don't lose your shit?"

"Perhaps."

"So he's going to do it?"

"I think he might."

"Oh my God, oh my God, *oh my God*. That's amazing. Totally amazing."

"Glad you think so. Can I go to work now?"

"I know you'll hate me for it, but I've got to hug you first."

Sam didn't hate her for it. In fact, she was touched by Lindsey's show of affection and friendship.

"There," Lindsey said when she pulled back from Sam. "Now you can go to work."

"You got anything for me?"

"In fact, I do. Our friend Mr. Mitchell is a stone-cold liar."

"Is he now?" Sam said through gritted teeth.

"He's our fourth guy. Not only did he videotape the whole thing, his semen was found on her belly and between her legs. It was not found in her vagina, however."

"So he videotaped the whole thing and then got off on her?"

"It appears that way."

"So disgusting."

"I couldn't agree more."

"Thanks, Lindsey. Appreciate your help with this one." As Sam walked toward the pit, her heart was heavy over what had happened to Brooke. "At least she's alive," she whispered to herself. It had been so very close... The pit was deserted when she arrived so she continued on to the lobby area, anxious to speak to the chief. Raised voices had her moving a little faster as she approached the lobby.

There she found Bill Springer screaming in Chief Farnsworth's face.

"There's no way you're going to pin this on my son!"

"Bill, you need to calm down and listen to me."

"Don't tell me to calm down!" Springer's face was bright red, his hair wild and his normally polished attire in disarray. And then, with Sam and other cops all around them, Springer whipped his arm back.

With his intention obvious to her, Sam acted before he could deliver the punch to her chief's face. She took him down hard and had him pinned to the floor with a knee to his back before he knew what hit him. As she cuffed him, she looked up at the chief, who seemed shell-shocked by what'd taken place in front of him.

"Are you okay?" Sam asked him.

"I'm fine. You?"

"All good."

"As always, Lieutenant, your timing is excellent."

Sam smiled up at him and cranked the cuffs a little tighter. That's what Springer got for trying to take a swing at *her* chief.

"You're going to be very sorry you did that," Springer said through gritted teeth.

"Guess what? I'm not afraid of you."

"If you think you're going to come after my son and try to pin mass murder on him, you're going to find out what I'm capable of."

"Was that a threat, Chief?" Sam asked.

"Sounded like one to me."

Sam gestured for one of the wide-eyed patrolmen to come over to them. "Book him on attempted assault of a police officer and threatening a police officer."

"Yes, ma'am."

"I'll write it up for you," Sam said.

"Thank you." The patrolman hauled Springer off the floor and dragged him away, kicking and screaming the whole time that someone was going to pay for this.

"The guy is unhinged," Sam said as she and the chief watched him go.

"I feel bad for him losing his youngest son the way he did, but he's got to accept that he can't protect Billy from what's coming."

"And how does he know what's coming?"

"I'm still trying to sort that out. Captain Roback is waiting in my office to discuss what happened overnight. Would you care to join us?"

Sam had a sinking feeling as she nodded and followed him to his office. "I should ask Sergeant Gonzales to join us too."

"Of course," the chief said, still seemingly shaken by what'd just transpired.

"Could we get him a glass of ice water?" Sam asked the chief's admin as she walked past the reception desk.

"Coming right up."

"And please ask Detective Sergeant Gonzales to join us."

"I'm fine, Sam," the chief said when they were in his office. "Don't fret over me."

"You're not fine. You're pale and weird-looking in the eyes."

"He took me by surprise. That's all. I'm not used to people coming at me the way they used to when I was in the field. I'm out of practice."

"What's wrong?" Captain Roback asked.

"He had an altercation with Bill Springer in the lobby," Sam said, her tone accusatory, as was the glare she directed at the captain. "What I'd like to know is how he could possibly know we were looking at his son Billy for the MacArthur murders. It's not like we issued a press release about our intention to arrest him this morning."

"I'm trying to find out what happened last night. All I know is Springer made my guys, and he's in the wind. We're trying to track him down now."

Sam stared at him, shocked but not surprised it had transpired exactly as she'd feared it would. "So you let him get away." She nodded to Gonzo when he came into the room and shut the door behind him.

"We didn't *let* him get away. It didn't happen like that."

"How did it happen then?"

"I told you. I'm awaiting a report from my team, but their priority at the moment is finding Springer."

"This is exactly what I was afraid of," Sam said to the

chief, who was seated now behind his desk. "Based on what his father said, he knows we're looking at him for the murders. How would he know that?"

"I don't know," Farnsworth said in a weary tone. "Jack, you promised me if I gave you one more night to complete your operation that we'd have this sewn up. Now our number-one suspect in a mass murder is in the wind, and you can't even tell me how that happened."

"I'm working on getting more information from my people," Roback said, chastened by the chief's dressing-down.

Farnsworth waved his hand in Roback's direction. "Go. Don't come back until you have some answers."

The captain took his leave, and Sam dropped into a chair. "So we didn't get him for either set of charges."

"We haven't gotten him *yet*."

"The fact that he's tipped off to our intentions makes him a hundred times more dangerous," Gonzo said as he, too, took a seat.

"I realize that, and I also realize I made a huge mistake yesterday by putting the vice investigation ahead of the homicide investigation."

"I'm still trying to understand why you did that."

"Because! I have to fight for every dime this department gets from the city, and not allowing Vice to complete what had been six months' of expensive and time-consuming undercover work would've come back to bite me in the ass at budget time."

"This was about *money?*"

"Sam, everything is about money. You know that by now."

"What's going to happen when the press catches wind of the fact that we fucked this up so royally?"

"I'm hoping it'll get un-fucked before they find out." He looked at her with those steely eyes that could be both intimidating and compassionate. "I'm putting you in charge of finding him. Get your whole squad on the job and find him, Sam, before I find myself out of a job."

Because the thought of anyone but him in that chair struck fear in her heart, Sam and Gonzo were on their feet and heading for the door before he finished speaking. She went straight to Roback's office. "The chief has put me in charge of figuring out where Springer is. I want every member of your team that worked on his case in the main conference room in thirty minutes."

"Where do you get off giving me orders? Need I remind you I'm a captain and you are not?"

"I don't need any reminders. Get your people here in thirty minutes." With Gonzo in tow, she walked out before he could reply and headed for the pit. Freddie, Jeannie and Tyrone were gathered around Freddie's cubicle sharing a box of doughnuts and discussing the plan for the day.

"New plan, people," Sam said, eying the doughnuts with lust and longing. She brought her squad up to date with what had happened overnight.

"Unreal," Jeannie muttered. "How did I know this was going to happen?"

"Right?" Freddie said. "I told Elin last night this was going to go bad on us."

"It's not going bad on *us*," Sam said, "but it will go bad on the department and the chief. So we're not going to let that happen, are we?"

"No, we're not," Gonzo said. "What's the plan?"

"We're going to hunt him down and arrest him the way we should've yesterday," Sam said. "I've given the Vice detectives thirty minutes to get here to explain to us how they managed to fuck this up so royally. After we know more, we'll talk to Springer's father, who's in custody for attempting to assault the chief and threatening me."

"Damn," Freddie said. "When did that happen?"

"About twenty minutes ago. I want everyone on this," she said as Dominguez and Carlucci joined them. "Do you have a few more hours left in the tank, ladies?"

Both third-shift detectives nodded. "Absolutely, LT," Carlucci said.

"All right, I want every single word we can find on William Springer Jr. He's known as Billy, and clearly he's been involved in drug trafficking. I want to know about any involvement we've had with him, no matter how insignificant it might be. Carlucci and Dominguez, you focus on the internal. Tyrone and Arnold, get me external—school, work, known associates. Anything and everything. One hour, people." The four detectives took off to follow orders.

"McBride and Gonzales, I want you to talk to Brody, Hoda and Nico before their arraignments this morning and find out anything they know about Billy Springer. They were friends with his brother—at least Hoda and Brody were. Nico might know something too. Get me anything you can."

"On it," Gonzo said as he and Jeannie headed for lockup.

"We're going to talk to Brooke," Sam said to her partner. Because she hadn't gotten around to eating breakfast, she said, "Bring me one of those circles of fat and don't you dare say a word about the fact that I'm eating it. Am I clear?"

"Yes, ma'am."

They got their coats and walked out to Sam's car. When they were buckled in, Freddie silently handed her the doughnut wrapped up in a napkin.

Sam took the first bite and nearly moaned from the pleasure of the sugar and grease exploding on her tongue. Aware of the half hour she'd given the Vice commander to rally his troops, Sam drove faster than she should have through the city's congested streets.

"Can you even believe this crap?" Freddie asked. "Farnsworth told me it was because of the huge investment they've made in the undercover operation."

"He let this guy get away because of *money?*"

"It's more complicated than either of us can possibly understand. The chief is under a lot of pressure to justify the city's investment in the department, and if they didn't get a successful prosecution out of all the hours that went into that investigation, it could affect what we get next year."

"Still, the guy killed nine kids. How is money more important than that?"

"They asked for one night to finish their investigation."

"I'd really like to know how they managed to lose him."

"So would I. You gotta figure they're not having the best day of their careers."

"Yeah. True. Is this going to turn into a big scandal?"

"Not if I can help it." Sam figured she had about twelve hours before it would blow up into a scandal. Too many people knew they'd let Billy Springer get away. Someone who was looking to get Farnsworth fired, who had an ax to grind, who was looking to get ahead in their careers could blow the lid off the whole mess. As much as she liked to think the department was one big happy family, it was also a very dysfunctional family full of hidden agendas and ulterior motives.

At the hospital, they hustled into the ICU where they learned that Brooke had been moved to a regular room. By the time they found it, they'd used twenty-five of the thirty minutes she'd given the Vice commander.

Sam knocked on the door and tucked her head inside to gauge the situation before she brought Freddie in with her. Brooke was awake and staring at the ceiling. Tracy sat next to the bed, staring out the window. *Uh-oh.* "You'd better wait out here," Sam said to Freddie.

She pushed the door open all the way. "Morning," Sam said, going for cheerful in a room thick with tension. "How's everyone today?"

"Fabulous," Tracy said flatly.

"Great," Brooke said with an equal lack of animation.

"Something wrong?" Sam asked. "Um, other than the obvious?"

"Nothing new," Tracy said. "Same old attitude, same old song and dance. I'm sitting here wondering what has to happen for someone to get the message that she needs to make some changes in her life."

"And I'm sitting here wondering if someone could get me a knife so I can stab myself in the neck so I won't have to listen to *her* lectures anymore."

"You might want to watch your mouth," Tracy said, "or you'll find yourself locked up in the psych ward where you probably belong."

"As much as I'm enjoying this conversation," Sam said, "I'm on a bit of a schedule. I need to talk to Brooke. About the case."

"What about it?" Brooke asked.

Sam propped herself on the foot of the bed. "What do you know about Billy Springer?"

"He's Hugo's brother. Or he was Hugo's brother. I still can't believe he's dead."

"I know, honey, but if you can tell me anything you might've heard about him, like who his friends are or where he hangs out. Something that seems trivial to you might be huge to us."

"Is he... Is he in trouble?"

"He might be."

"Hugo said he's got some scary friends."

"Scary how?"

"They were into drugs and guns and stuff. Hugo said Billy was out of control, but he didn't care because their dad could get him out of anything."

"If Hugo knew that about him, why would he steal drugs from him?"

"Because his parents were away, and he wanted the party to be epic."

"He wasn't afraid Billy would come after him?"

"He said Billy wouldn't dare touch him or their parents would kill him."

"Sounds like a charming family."

"Hugo liked to say he was the spoiled rotten baby. He was used to doing whatever he wanted."

"Quite a few of your friends seem to have that in common, Brooke. Their parents let them run wild, and now two of them are dead, another is in jail. You're in here. I don't know what you and your mom are fighting about, but you might want to remember what became of your friends. No one wants to see that happen to you. This is bad enough." She leaned over to kiss Brooke's cheek. "I've got to get back to work, but I'll check on you later."

Tracy walked out with her. "I keep telling myself to be grateful she survived, but I'm wondering what it's going to take for her to get a clue."

"What's the problem?"

"She's being bitchy and contrary and acting like all of this is someone else's fault. The usual shit."

"Um, Mrs. Hogan?"

Tracy turned to a dark-haired boy holding a bouquet of flowers with a balloon attached. "Hi, Justin." Tracy hugged him. "This is Brooke's Aunt Sam. Sam, her good friend Justin from all the way back to elementary school."

"Nice to meet you," Sam said.

"You too. I'd like to see Brooke if that's okay."

"I'm sure she'd love a visit with an old friend. Let me check with her to make sure she feels up to it."

"I'll see you later, Trace," Sam said.

"Bye, Sam."

"Anything?" Freddie asked when she rejoined him at the elevators.

"Nothing specific, but apparently it was common knowledge in the Springer family that Billy was bad news. Into drugs and guns. He was convinced he was untouchable because of who his dad is."

"He sounds like a typical sociopath."

"And not-so-shockingly he turned out to be one." On the way back to HQ, Sam called the chief to brief him on what was being done. "I assume we've got people at his place?"

"Crime Scene is there as we speak."

"And we're trying to locate his car and cell?"

"We've had an APB out for the car since last night, and Archie is trying to get a read on the phone."

"Airports, bus stations, train station?"

"All being checked."

"I ordered Vice back to the house to air out what went down."

"So I heard."

"Roback is pissed."

"Just a little. Most captains don't appreciate being pushed around by lieutenants."

"It's not my fault that his people screwed this up."

"If you could attempt to be diplomatic, I'd appreciate it."

Freddie's snort indicated that he could hear the chief's end of the conversation.

"I'll try."

"Do that."

"We'll be back in five to meet with Vice. It would help if you could be there in case we get push-back."

"In case?"

"*When* we get push-back."

"I'll be there."

"Now that you've disposed of Stahl," Freddie said, "it's probably time to start making some new enemies."

"We wouldn't want to get bored."

"God forbid."

"What're you hearing about Stahl?" she asked. "Things have been oddly quiet on that front."

"I haven't heard a word. The quiet has me worried though. It's not like him to go down with a whimper rather than a bang."

Sam wouldn't confess to having had the same thought because she didn't want him to worry about her. And he would. If there was one thing Sam knew for sure, it was that she hadn't seen the last of her nemesis. But she had bigger concerns right now, and she wouldn't give that scumbag any of her precious brain cells.

The reporters outside HQ were clamoring to know when they could expect an arrest in the MacArthur murders. They screamed questions about that and about Nick as Sam and Freddie walked by them, keeping their heads down and their mouths shut.

Sam headed straight for the main conference room, which was a steaming cauldron of seething testosterone at the moment. Chief Farnsworth, Deputy Chief Conklin and Detective Captain Malone were the only friendly faces in the room.

Twenty men glared at her with unfettered hatred, no one more so than their commander.

"Gentlemen," Sam said. "Still no women in Vice?"

"You're wasting time we could be spending looking for Billy Springer," Roback said.

"Ahhh, speak of the devil," Sam said. "How about you tell us how you managed to lose track of our prime suspect in a mass homicide."

"Allow me, Captain," a muscle-bound officer said as he strode forward to meet Sam's steely gaze with one of his own. He had close-cropped blond hair and ice-blue eyes. "I've just spent the last six months of my life deep undercover with Billy Springer, who is the most arrogant, self-involved, narcissistic *douchebag* I've ever met in my life. I'll never get back those six months, and you'll have to pardon me if I wanted twelve hours to make sure all that time counted for something."

"And you are?"

"Cole McDonald. Lieutenant Cole McDonald."

"Lieutenant."

"It was my call. No one else's."

"You still haven't mentioned how he got away."

Frosty blue eyes met icy blue eyes in a standoff for the ages. McDonald made Sam's day by blinking first.

"He said he was going upstairs to take a shower. We think he went out through a bathroom window."

"Did he make you?"

"I'm not sure."

"Did someone tip him off?"

"I don't know that either."

"Where was the rest of your team when he escaped through a window?"

"They were preparing to take down several of his associates who were due to accept a big delivery of Molly last night."

"Did the delivery happen?"

"It did not."

"So he got away and his associates are still running free?"

"For the moment."

"And the operation you spent six months orchestrating?"

"Has been compromised."

"And you don't know how?"

"Not yet I don't, but you can bet I'm going to find out."

In a way, Sam felt for the guy. He'd put a lot of work into the case to have it blow up in his face. She'd once been exactly where he was. She'd gotten her guy, but not before a barrage of gunfire had left her subject's young son dead. Memories of Quentin Johnson lying bloody and dead in his screaming father's arms still had the power to reduce Sam to a quivering disaster area. She shook off those disturbing thoughts to focus on the task at hand.

"You've spent the most time with him recently," Sam said. "Where would he go?"

"We've already looked in all the usual places." Frustration and exhaustion clung to him.

A knock on the door cut into their tense exchange. Lieutenant Archelotta walked into the room. "Sorry to interrupt," Archie said. "I thought you might like to know we were able to get a ping from Springer's cell phone." He handed a sheet of paper to Sam, who scanned it quickly and was grateful to be able to clearly read the words that often appeared jumbled to her. "Who does he know who lives in Manor Park?" Sam asked McDonald.

"His maternal grandmother."

"I assume you haven't checked there yet?"

"No, it didn't occur to me that he'd be there because he never visited her in all the time I spent with him."

"I want SWAT on this," Sam said to the chief as she handed over the address she'd already committed to memory.

"Done."

"He's not getting away this time." She turned and walked out of the room with Freddie in tow. In the pit, she said, "Listen up, everyone. We've got a lead on Billy Springer. I want everyone in full armor to support SWAT. Suit up and let's get moving."

# FIFTEEN

WHILE THE OTHERS scurried around gathering their belongings and body armor, Sam did the same in her office.

Located to the east of Rock Creek Park, the Manor Park neighborhood was in the city's north end, next to Tacoma. The working-class neighborhood boasted many older homes, built in the early 1900s. Sam hadn't been up there in ages as it tended to be a quiet part of the city.

Gonzo and Jeannie rode with Sam and Freddie, the four of them quiet with their own thoughts as they headed north until Sam said, "I still don't know how Springer found out we were eying him for the murders."

"You think one of our people told him?"

"I really hope not," she said. "But I can't wait to get Springer into interrogation to find out."

While Freddie drove, Sam read over the information her team had gathered on Billy Springer, who was twenty-four, a graduate of Wilson High and a dropout from Catholic University. He'd worked as a plumber's apprentice, a store clerk and a bartender since leaving college three years ago. He had a sealed juvenile record along with several drug possession arrests that had been adjudicated with probation. Clearly, he'd been escalating since he dropped out of college.

They arrived to find the SWAT team already assembled, with Farnsworth, Conklin and Malone on the scene, as well. The house was an older stand-alone brick-front structure with two stories and a wide front porch.

"Everyone ready, Lieutenant?" Farnsworth asked when her team was in place.

"Yes, sir."

He had raised his radio to give the order to go in when shots rang out from the house. They dove for cover behind their cars. Sam took a head count on her team and noted with horror that Gonzo had been hit. She was gripped by fear as she crawled on her belly to get to him with Freddie right behind her. Jeannie and Arnold were with Gonzo, applying pressure to a wound on his neck.

"Is he breathing?" Sam asked.

"Rapidly," Arnold said, his face devoid of color as he held a hand to Gonzo's neck.

"Call for a bus," Sam said to Jeannie, whose hands trembled as she fumbled with her radio.

The cackle of "officer down" over the radio sent a bolt of fear through Sam's body as she watched Gonzo struggle for every breath. Around them, Sam was aware of the SWAT team receiving orders to go in and take the bastard, but her gaze was riveted to Gonzo and the pool of blood forming under him.

"Alex," Gonzo said haltingly. "Tell her to take care of him."

"Don't talk that way," Jeannie said as she blinked back tears.

"Christina," Gonzo said between ragged breaths. "Tell her…"

"You can tell her yourself," Arnold said, his voice tinged with hysteria he was trying hard to hide from his partner. "You're going to be fine."

"He's got an arsenal in there," the SWAT team commander said on the radio. "We believe he's holding at least one civilian hostage as well, and we can't confirm he's the only shooter. We need to regroup."

"Where's that ambulance?" Sam asked as her anxiety level peaked in the red zone.

"The paramedics won't come in here with an active shooter," Malone said.

"We can't move him with a neck wound," Sam said. "We need a backboard."

"I'll go get it," Freddie said.

"No way," Sam said, grabbing his arm. "You're not exposing yourself with Springer shooting at cops."

Freddie shook her off. "If someone doesn't go, he's going to die. I'll be right back."

Fear beat a steady cadence through Sam's bloodstream as she watched her partner move in a crouch behind the cars until there were no more cars to provide cover. All they could do at that point was hope the shooter was too preoccupied to pay attention to the officer sprinting down the street toward the waiting ambulance.

"Let's establish a connection," Farnsworth said. "Call his cell phone."

Reading from the same page Archie had provided with the GPS information, Conklin placed the call and kept his phone on speaker so they could all hear.

Someone answered the call, but didn't speak. "Billy, this is Deputy Chief Conklin with the Metro PD. The house is surrounded, and we'd like to get you out of there without anyone else getting hurt."

"I want to talk to that chick cop who's always in the news."

"Lieutenant Holland?"

"Yeah. Her."

Conklin looked at Sam, who shrugged as she reached for the phone, all the while keeping an eye out for Freddie's return. Maybe if she kept Billy busy, he wouldn't notice them getting Gonzo out of there.

"This is Lieutenant Holland."

His total silence had her on edge as she saw Freddie returning with the backboard tucked under his arm. She held her breath until he ducked behind the row of cars.

"Billy? Are you there?"

"Everyone lied to me. Cole pretended to be my friend, and he was a cop. The whole time, he was a fucking *cop!* And now my real friends want me dead because I let a cop get close to us."

"I understand this has been a difficult time for you. Can you tell me who else is in there with you?" As she continued to talk to him she kept an eye on her team as they loaded Gonzo on the board and began to move him toward the waiting ambulance. Arnold's right hand was still pressed against Gonzo's wound. Sam had never been a religious person, but she said a prayer right then for Gonzo and the others who were risking themselves to get him the help he desperately needed.

She leaned in closer to Conklin. "Tell them to stay put after they get him to the bus. They're not to come back."

Conklin nodded in agreement and conveyed her orders via radio.

"My grandma is here and two of my cousins," Billy said.

Sam pushed at the knot of pain that pulsated between her eyes. "How old are your cousins?"

"Six and nine."

Sam closed her eyes and blew out a deep breath. "I'm

sure you love them all very much and would hate to see them get hurt."

"I never wanted anyone to get hurt! It's all Hugo's fault! He screwed up everything."

Watching her team clear the row of cars and break into a run for the ambulance, Sam held her breath until they had safely delivered Gonzo. Arnold and Cruz climbed in the back with him while the others took cover in a parking lot at a nearby apartment complex.

"What did Hugo do?"

"He stole some stuff from me. Important stuff."

"Is that why you had to kill him and his friends?"

"I didn't want to hurt him, but when I got there... It was all gone. They'd taken almost all of it, and I needed it. I owe people money."

"I understand how things can spin out of control. I really do. But there's no sense in letting it get any worse by allowing your grandma and cousins to get hurt. Would you mind letting them leave?"

"No. They can't leave. If they do, you'll kill me."

"You have my word that we won't kill you. If you hold your fire, so will we."

Farnsworth nodded at her with obvious approval. Hostage negotiation wasn't her forte, and she was trying to remember lessons learned more than thirteen years ago in the police academy.

"I want my dad."

"He can't come right now. I saw him a little while ago, and he's busy." Telling Billy his dad was locked up wouldn't help anything, so she kept that detail to herself. "I really want to help you, Billy. Do we have a deal? Will you let the others go so we can get everyone out of there safely?"

"No. No deal."

"Why not, Billy?" She remembered it was important to keep using his name so he'd know she thought of him as a person. It showed compassion and a sense of connection. At least that was the goal.

"It's not going to matter. I still owe those guys money, and they're going to come after me to get it."

"We can help you with that too, but you have to help us. Let the others go, and we'll figure out what we can do for you."

"The grandmother and cousins are in a bedroom in the back of the house," the SWAT commander reported over the secure frequency they used during incidents. "Springer is pacing in the front room. Do you want us to go in?"

Sam looked at Farnsworth, who weighed the decision silently.

"Are you still there?" Billy asked, sounding like a frightened young boy rather than a full-grown man who'd made all the wrong choices that led to this moment.

"I'm here. I want to help you, Billy. Will you let me?"

They all waited breathlessly to see what he would say. "I can't," he said softly.

"Take him," Farnsworth said into the radio.

SWAT officers burst into the house through every door and window. A hail of gunfire greeted them, but they were ready for him.

"Hostages are secure."

"Suspect is deceased."

Sam sighed deeply at the thought of poor Mrs. Springer having to bury yet another son. She reached for her cell and placed a call to Freddie. "How is he?"

"I don't know. It's bad, Sam. He's lost a lot of blood,

and he's not conscious." Her partner sounded like he was on the verge of an emotional breakdown so she didn't push him for additional details other than to ask where they were taking him. "GW Trauma. You should call Christina."

"I'm doing that right now. I'll be there in a few." She didn't bother to update him about the case, because there'd be time for that when their friend and colleague was out of the woods. Her heart beat fast, and her entire body broke out in a cold sweat as she placed the call to Christina.

"Hey, Sam, what's up?"

"Christina... I'm sorry to have to tell you that Tommy's been shot."

The other woman's scream ripped through Sam's heart. "Listen to me. He's alive. It's serious, but he's alive. They're taking him to GW. Where are you?"

"I'm... I'm at home. With Alex."

"I'm sending someone to pick you up. Bring the baby with you, and I'll meet you there. Okay?"

Conklin heard what she'd said and called in the request to Patrol.

"Sam... Is he going to die?"

"I don't know. I really hope not."

"Oh, please God... *No*."

"Get ready, Christina. Patrol will be there in a few minutes to pick you up, and I'll be at the hospital shortly after you arrive."

"Okay. Okay."

Sam's next call was to Nick. "Gonzo's been shot," she said. "It's bad."

"Oh my God. Does Christina know?"

"I just talked to her. She's on her way to GW with Patrol and so am I. I thought you might want to be there with her."

"I do. I'll be there in a few. Is he…"

"I don't know. I don't know anything other than he was hit in the neck and has lost a lot of blood."

"Jesus. I'm coming, babe. Hang in there."

"Love you," Sam said as she wiped away tears that couldn't be thwarted despite her intense desire to hold it together for all the people who'd be looking to her for leadership and guidance. The last thing she wanted was to break down in front of her brass or other colleagues, but this was Gonzo they were talking about.

"I love you too, baby. I'm on my way."

His softly spoken words wrapped around her like the hug she needed so badly right then.

"Go, Lieutenant," the chief said when she ended the call. "See to your squad. We'll clean things up here."

Paramedics were tending to Springer's distraught grandmother and cousins. The medical examiner had been called, Crime Scene was coming, and there was nothing left to do for the Homicide commander, so she heeded the chief's orders and took her leave.

"Sam?"

She turned back to face the chief's weary gaze. "You did good work here. You did all you could."

"Will Bill Springer care that we did good work when he hears another of his kids is dead?"

"I think he knew almost from the beginning who had killed Hugo and the others, and that's why he was so unglued earlier. This isn't going to come as a total surprise to him."

"Perhaps not, but his sons are still dead, and I wouldn't wish that on anyone."

"This is one of those cases where we don't get a satisfying ending. We did our jobs, we did our best and no amount of justice was ever going to bring back those nine kids or undo what happened to Brooke."

"I know."

"Keep me posted on Sergeant Gonzales's condition. I'll come to the hospital when we're done here."

"We need to bring the families in and tell them what happened to their kids."

"I'll get that set up for tomorrow, and Captain Malone will handle updating the media on what went down here."

"Thank you."

"I don't have to tell you that these are the toughest times to be the commander. I have no doubt in your ability to get your folks through this."

Because she didn't trust herself to speak, she nodded, squeezed his arm and headed for her car, acknowledging the calls from colleagues to give Gonzo their best. She could only hope she got the chance to.

ON THE WAY to the hospital, Sam called her dad's house to update them on the shooting and the finale of the MacArthur case, before they heard about a cop being shot on the news and had time to think the worst.

"We'll pray for Tommy," Celia said simply. "And for you."

"Thanks, Celia."

Her stepmother's sweet compassion broke the dam on Sam's emotions, and she sobbed all the way to the hospital in the comfort and privacy of her own car. She had to pull herself together before she got there, but for now, for this moment, she was finally able to indulge in the torrent of tears that'd been threatening for days.

It was all too much—her assaulted niece, the murder of nine kids, the twists and turns of the case, the job offer for Nick and now one of her closest friends shot in the line of duty. She couldn't imagine life without Tommy Gonzales right at the center of it. His charming smile, his easygoing manner, his shrewd mind, his loyal and loving heart of gold...

Sam parked in the lot outside the emergency entrance but couldn't seem to bring herself to go in there. What if the worst had happened? How would any of them cope with that? Sure, it was always a risk with their jobs, but no one ever expected it to actually happen. Besides, hadn't they used up their squad's share of bad mojo for the next decade after Cruz was shot last winter?

Leaning her head on the steering wheel, Sam summoned the wherewithal to go in there and face this thing head-on the way she always did. Her team needed her, and this was no time to lose her shit.

A light rap on the window had her looking into the hazel eyes she loved more than any other. He opened the door and crouched next to her. "Come here, babe."

Sam took off her seat belt and practically flung herself into his arms.

"It's okay. No matter what happens, I'll be right there with you."

She held on tight to him and let him shoulder the load for a few minutes until she could breathe normally again.

"Are you ready?"

"I think so." Sam wiped her eyes. "Do I look like I've been freaking out?"

"You look like you've been out in the cold."

That earned him a small smile full of gratitude for the

fact that he almost always said exactly what she needed to hear.

He stood and held out his hand to her.

Wrapping her hand around his, she locked her car and walked with him into the Emergency Department. Her squad had taken over the waiting room, and they were rallying around Christina and baby Alex.

Nick went straight to Christina.

She flew into his arms and held on tight as her body shook with sobs.

"What's the latest?" Sam asked Freddie. She was almost afraid of what he would say.

"He's in surgery. The bullet nicked his carotid artery. The doctors said the pressure Arnold put on the wound is the only thing that gave him a chance, but he's in critical condition."

Sam glanced at Gonzo's partner, who sat alone in the corner, covered with blood and looking shell-shocked. She gave Freddie a hug and went over to sit next to Arnold. "You did good out there, Detective."

He released an unsteady deep breath. "A lot of blood. So much blood."

"He's going to be okay because of what you did for him."

"What if it wasn't enough? What if he dies? He can't die."

Sam reached for the young detective and held him as he broke down. "He's not going to die. He's at the best trauma center in the area, and they're taking good care of him."

Arnold seemed to realize all at once that he was crying all over his lieutenant. He drew back from her, and that's when she noticed his hands were stained with blood.

"Why don't you take a few minutes and get cleaned up?"

"Come on, Arnold," Freddie said. "I'll go with you." Arnold seemed incapable of resisting their suggestion as he let Freddie lead him out of the seating area.

"The poor guy is traumatized," Jeannie said as she sat next to Sam.

Her partner, Will Tyrone, took the seat Arnold had vacated. "Gonzo is going to be okay, isn't he?" Tyrone asked Sam, as if she had some sort of magical ability to make everything turn out the way they wanted it to.

"If you believe in any kind of higher power, this would be the time to appeal to him or her," Sam said. It wasn't what they wanted to hear, but it was all she had at her disposal. Taking her own advice, she closed her eyes and said a prayer for her friend.

HOURS LATER, GONZO's parents and sisters had arrived from out of town, the media had released the name of the officer shot in the line of duty—as well as the conclusion to the MacArthur case—and they were still waiting to hear that Gonzo was safely out of surgery.

Scotty had called to find out how Gonzo was doing, and Shelby had offered to stay with him as long as necessary. Sam's head occupied one of Nick's shoulders while Christina had claimed the other one. Alex had fallen asleep in his grandmother's arms, which had given Gonzo's mother some comfort while she waited for news about her son.

The rest of the squad was still there, and Sam knew that no one would leave until they knew Gonzo was out of immediate danger. Elin had come to be with Freddie, and Jeannie's fiancé, Michael, was there too. Lindsey and Terry had come as soon as they heard the news, and Farnsworth, Conklin and Malone were waiting with them, as well. Between them, Sam and Nick had taken calls from her dad, her sisters, the O'Connors, Nick's dad and Agent Hill, all of them filled with concern for Gonzo. She hoped he somehow knew how many people were pulling for him.

Sam was comforted by the fact that the surgery was taking a long time. That meant whatever was wrong could be fixed and was being fixed. He hadn't lost so much blood that he couldn't survive the surgery. He was surviving. She prayed fervently that he would get through this and still be the ace detective, loving father, friend and partner he'd been before.

And then a woman came into the surgical waiting room and went right over to Mrs. Gonzales. "Please give me my son."

"Excuse me?" Mrs. Gonzales asked, startled by the woman's sudden appearance.

"That is my son, and with his father incapacitated, I'll be taking him home."

Christina shot out of her chair. "No, you won't. You have no right to be here, Lori."

"I have every right! He's *my* son, and his father is unable to care for him, which means he rightfully belongs with me."

Nick stood and put his arm around Christina's shoulders. "Are you really going to do this now?" he asked Lori. "Do you care so little about the man who fathered your child that you would come here and upset people who already have enough to be upset about?"

Lori had the good grace to at least seem ashamed of herself but not enough to go away. "I want my son, and none of you has the right to keep me from him."

Nick withdrew his cell phone from his pocket. "We'll see about that. In the meantime, you're in a room full of cops, and I'd recommend you refrain from doing anything you'll regret."

Sam assumed he was calling his friend Andy, who had represented Gonzo in the custody case. She watched him with a sense of pride and awe as he stepped up for Christina—and Gonzo. He walked away from the group to talk to Andy.

Lori hovered awkwardly in their midst, watching her sleeping son with barely restrained agitation.

Sam watched her closely. She wouldn't put it past the woman to pull a gun on them to get what she wanted. The fact that most of the people surrounding Mr. and Mrs. Gonzales were cops might not deter her.

Nick returned a few minutes later and took a seat next to Sam. "Andy is on his way with everything we need to get rid of her. Apparently Gonzo anticipated this very scenario and took steps to ensure it couldn't happen."

"Thank goodness," Sam said with a sigh of relief. The tension in the waiting room was amped up by Lori's presence as everyone tried to pretend she wasn't there while they waited for word about Gonzo. Sam had no doubt that every one of her colleagues was prepared to do battle to keep Gonzo's son where he belonged. No one moved or said a word, but they all had eyes on Lori.

Sam smiled to herself. The poor woman had no clue what she was up against with Gonzo's squad watching out for him. Sam didn't think cutting Alex's mother out of his life was in the child's best interest, but Lori had lost major points with all of them by barging in there to take advantage of the fact that Gonzo had been grievously wounded.

Andy arrived a short time later, as did the social worker who'd overseen the custody case on behalf of the court. When Andy produced documents outlining the legal arrangements Gonzo had made should he ever be injured or unable to care for Alex himself, Lori read them as everyone else watched and waited for her reaction.

"As you can see, Sergeant Gonzales was very clear about who he wanted caring for his son if the need should ever arise."

"He can't just decide that! I'm Alex's mother!"

"Yes, but he has full custody so he *can* decide. He has directed that Ms. Billings and his parents care for Alex in his stead. I'm sorry, Ms. Miller, but you have no standing here."

Lori looked to the social worker. "Will you tell him that's not true? Tell him I'm the mother. I have rights!"

"Lori, the court gave full custody to Alex's father. He does have the right to decide who cares for Alex in his absence."

"This isn't fair," Lori said as she broke down.

"You really need to go now," Andy said.

"Come on, Lori," the social worker said, curling her hand around Lori's arm. "Let's go."

Thankfully, Lori went quietly, and Sam breathed a sigh of relief.

Andy sat with her and Nick. "Unreal," he muttered.

"No kidding," Nick said. "To come here and try to take advantage of the fact that he's injured..."

"Takes a special kind of person to do that," Sam said.

"Tommy was very concerned about something like this happening, so he had me draft documents right away that spelled out his wishes," Andy said. "I had no idea we'd need them so soon. What are they saying? He's going to be okay, right?"

"We don't know," Sam said. The not knowing was starting to get to her.

"Before things got so crazy this week, I was planning to call you for an update on Scotty's adoption," Nick said. "Have you heard any more?"

"As you know, the P.I. is trying to track down his birth father. We have to make every effort to find him, and once we've done that, the rest should be a formality."

"What if we can't find him?" Sam asked.

"Then we can move forward without him. We just have to show an effort was made to locate him. I wouldn't worry. Even if we find him, his father never had anything to do with him, so I can't imagine he'll discover a sudden interest in him."

The thought of that was enough to send Sam's anxiety further into the red zone, so she decided not to think about it.

After what felt like an endless wait, the surgeon finally appeared to speak to Gonzo's parents and Christina.

"It's okay," Mrs. Gonzales said as the entire squad stood behind her and her husband. "These people are his family too. They can hear whatever you have to say."

"We were able to repair the wound to his carotid artery, and he's in recovery. He lost a lot of blood, and he's still in critical condition, but we expect him to make a full recovery."

Sam sagged against Nick, the relief coursing through her and making her legs go weak.

His strong arm around her was about the only thing that kept her from landing on the floor in a heap.

"When can we see him?" Christina asked.

"He'll be in recovery for the next couple of hours and then in ICU after that. We'll let you know when he's ready for company."

"Thank you so much for saving his life," Christina said tearfully. "He means an awful lot to all of us."

"He's a fighter," the surgeon said. "It was a very close call, but he hung in there. Whoever applied pressure to the wound in the field is the one who really saved his life."

The entire squad pointed to Arnold, who had tears on his cheeks as he heard his partner was going to survive. "Well done, Detective," the surgeon said before he left them to celebrate the good news.

Nick hugged Christina, who held on tight as her emotions got the best of her.

"You all should go home and get some sleep," Sam said to her team. "It's been a long week. I hope you'll all feel free to stop by at some point on Thanksgiving. We'll be home."

Every one of her detectives hugged her on the way out of the waiting room.

"I'm really proud of you," Sam said to Arnold. "You held up out there today, and you saved his life."

"Thank you, Lieutenant," Arnold said before he beat a hasty retreat.

Freddie was last in line.

"You did a very courageous thing today." Sam rested her hands on his arms and looked up at him. "Thanks for not getting killed while doing it."

Freddie's engaging grin couldn't hide the relief she saw in his eyes. Gonzo was one of his closest friends too. "I know how much you hate the paperwork, so I do what I can." He hugged her and held on for a good long time. "I'll see you on turkey day. Lots to be thankful for this year."

"Indeed. Bring your parents if they'd like to come."

"I'm sure they'd love to."

Elin surprised Sam by giving her a quick hug on the way by.

Christina had made arrangements to send Alex home with Gonzo's parents while she stayed at the hospital. Mr. and Mrs. Gonzales hugged Sam and thanked her for being such a good friend and boss to their son. They nearly reduced her to tears again with their effusiveness. "We love him very much," Sam somehow managed to say.

When it was down to just Sam, Nick and Christina, he turned to his longtime friend and colleague. "Are you sure you'll be okay by yourself? I don't mind staying."

"And I don't mind loaning him out for the night," Sam added.

Christina offered a faint smile. "I appreciate the offer, but there's no need to stay. I'm fine now that I know he's going to survive. I'll probably conk out in the ICU waiting room until I can see him."

"Will you call me if you change your mind?" Nick asked.

"Sure," she said as she hugged him. "Thanks so much for the shoulder tonight."

"Anytime."

Sam hugged her too. "Let us know what we can do for you and Alex. Anything."

"Thanks, Sam. I'm sure we'll be taking you up on that before all is said and done."

"The offer stands."

"I'll call you in the morning to let you know how he is," Christina said.

"I'll be waiting to hear."

She left them to head for the ICU.

"Would you mind if we checked in on Brooke before we head home?" Sam asked Nick.

"Not at all. Let's go."

"We should let the family know that Gonzo is out of surgery and expected to be okay," Sam said as they waited for the elevator.

Nick pulled his phone out of his pocket. "Group text."

"I probably need to get one of those smartphones one of these days."

"You'd go into shock with this much technology in the palm of your hand. You probably ought to stick to your ancient flip phone."

"Are you making fun of me?" After the horrendous afternoon and evening they'd spent waiting for news of Gonzo, it was a relief to return to business as usual with her husband.

"Would I be so foolish as to make fun of you, my love?"

"I believe you would. Makeup sex is one of your favorite things."

Laughing, Nick put his arm around her and kept it there on the walk to Brooke's room, where they found the teenager up and walking around, wearing a robe from home and fuzzy bunny slippers.

"Looks like someone is feeling better," Sam said as she hugged her niece.

"Much better, and going home tomorrow."

"That's great news. I'm so glad you'll be home for Thanksgiving."

"Me too. It's my favorite holiday."

"Where're your mom and dad?"

"They went home for a bit to shower and change and see Abby and Ethan."

"Come sit with me," Sam said, taking her by the hand and leading her to the bed, where they sat side by side while Sam filled her in on the resolution of the case.

"So Billy is dead too?" Brooke asked in a small voice.

"I'm afraid so."

"That's really sad for his parents after they lost Hugo."

"It's very sad indeed. Billy had every advantage—a family that loved him, the resources to go to college and a life filled with promise. His poor choices led to today's outcome. You realize that, right?"

Brooke nodded. "And I get what you're saying."

"You've been through a terrible ordeal, and you've got a lot of work to do to come to terms with what took place in that basement. But at the end of it all, you're going to be okay. You were very, *very* lucky to get out of there alive, and I hope you'll make good use of your second chance."

"I will, Sam. I promise I'll make better choices in the future. I was wondering, though… Would it be possible for me to speak to Hoda at some point? I know my mom doesn't want me hanging around with her anymore, but I'd like to thank her for what she did for me."

"I'm sure we can arrange something once you're home and settled, but of course it's up to your parents."

"Is she in trouble with you guys?"

"She'll probably face charges for firing at us, but she helped us to hone in on Billy, so the U.S. attorney will probably file lesser charges because of that. It's not really up to me."

"What about her friend Nico? What's happening with him?"

"He's facing a misdemeanor gun charge, and he should be sent home today."

"And Brody?"

"We discovered he was the fourth guy with you, but his participation was somewhat limited."

"How do you mean?"

Sam explained what the DNA had indicated. Brooke made a disgusted face and shuddered with revulsion. "How could he do that to me? I've known him forever."

"I don't know, honey. You have to figure the drugs and booze were making them do things they might not ordinarily do."

"I guess. What will happen to him?"

"I hope he pleads guilty for what he did. Even if he pleads, he's looking at lengthy jail time for videotaping the assault and not offering assistance to you, not to mention his own contribution..."

Brooke seemed to be taking it all in, and Sam was glad she was asking questions that had clearly been on her mind. "Thanks for finding out what happened to me and the other kids."

"I'm glad we were able to get you the answers you need, but there's one thing I want you to do for me."

"What?"

"I want you to be nice to your mom. You don't always have to agree with her, but please be nice. You have absolutely no idea how much she's done for you."

"I do know—"

"You can't possibly know, sweetheart. You were too young to be aware of what it was like for her to bring you into this world without your birth father in the picture. It was a very difficult, lonely time for her, and everything she did, she did for you because she loved you before you were even born. Mike came along and fell in love with you as much as he did with your mom. He's given you everything he had to give and then some. He gave you his name, and he's been a dad to you in every sense of the word. Please, Brooke... Please. Be nice to them. Be respectful of the sacrifices they've both made to ensure you had everything you needed."

Brooke wiped away tears as she nodded. "I'll try harder to get along with them." She glanced at Sam. "Do I have to go back to the school in Virginia?"

"That's a question for your parents."

"I think I'd like to. I bet no one there knows what happened."

"Nothing has to be decided today. Focus on getting better for now."

"Thanks for asking your friend Jeannie to come talk to me. It helped."

"I'm glad. Jeannie is a survivor, and so are you." Sam hugged her again, tucked her back into bed and left her with a kiss to the forehead. "I'll see you tomorrow."

"Thanks for all you did to figure out what happened to Todd and the other kids."

"I wish I could say it was my pleasure, but..." Sam shrugged. "Love you, honey. Get some sleep."

"Love you too."

Nick, who'd remained by the door during Sam's visit with Brooke, held the door for her as they left the room. "Well done, babe."

"Let's hope she got the message."

"I think she gets it."

He kept his arm around her in the elevator and all the

way to the parking lot, where they decided to leave her car and pick it up the next day. When he held the passenger door to his car for her, Sam turned to him and slid her arms up his chest to curl them around his neck.

"I have to go in tomorrow to meet with the families to tell them how their kids died and what they were doing when it happened. After I deal with that happy task and a shit ton of paperwork on this whole thing, how do you feel about half a vacation?"

"With you, my love," he said, sealing his sweet words with an even sweeter kiss, "I'll take whatever I can get."

# EPILOGUE

SAM WAS OFFICIALLY sick of hospitals. In particular, she was sick of the George Washington University Hospital, where she'd spent far too much of her time lately. With Brooke now home and Gonzo getting stronger every day, Sam was ready to be done with the place. But that was not to be.

Her dad had just gone into surgery for the removal of the bullet that had left him a quadriplegic almost three years ago. At the time of his shooting, doctors had told them it was far too risky to attempt to remove the bullet. In the last few months, however, the bullet had begun to move. The doctors now said the bullet had to come out before it did even more damage. So here she was, back at the hospital where she felt like she lived lately, waiting on yet another surgery.

Because there was nothing to do but wait, Nick had gone to work at her insistence. Congress was back in session today and gearing up for a major budget battle that required all hands on deck. Vice President Gooding had resigned on Friday and speculation was running rampant as to who the president would tap to replace him, with much of it focused on Nick, who was waiting for Nelson to make it official.

Her husband was going to be vice president of the United States, pending congressional approval, which was supposedly all but guaranteed. While she'd been repeatedly reassured that her life wouldn't change all that dramatically, she had her doubts about that. But she'd decided to roll with it the way he always did for her and take the lumps as they came. What else could she do? As long as she didn't have to quit her job or change who she was, she could handle being the country's second lady. Right?

"Better not to think about it," she muttered to herself as she took the elevator to visit Gonzo while her dad was in surgery.

She knocked on the door to his room and tucked her head in. "You aren't getting a sponge bath or anything, are you?"

"Already done," he said, his voice weaker than usual but already stronger than it had been the day before. "And fully enjoyed."

"Ewww." Sam stepped into the room and closed the door behind her. "I see you're milking this for all it's worth."

"Hell, yes." Other than the bandage on his neck and the unusual pallor occupying his skin, he looked good as he raised the bed ever so slightly so he could see her better. "How else am I supposed to get any time off from that sweatshop you run?"

"This is true."

"Skip is in surgery?"

"As we speak."

"And you're freaking out."

"What? Me freak?"

"He's going to be okay, Sam. He's almost as tough as his daughter."

"If you say so." She sat in the visitor's chair and propped her feet on the frame under the bed. "Where's Christina?"

"I sent her home to get some sleep in a real bed. She's running on fumes."

"She's been a trouper. I think she might actually love you."

His smile lit up his entire face. "Looks that way, huh?" He winced as he tried to find a more comfortable position.

"Need me to fluff your pillow or something?"

"I'm not that desperate."

"Thank God."

"Your bedside manner sucks."

"That's not what Nick says." Sam waggled her brows for effect.

"TMI. Speaking of Nick… I might've heard a rumor or two about him."

"That baby is not his."

"Very funny. And while we're on the subject of funny, you as second lady… Now that's funny."

"Glad you think so. It's positively terrifying to me."

"So it's true?"

"Apparently. I'm officially in denial."

"That's incredible, Sam. The part about him getting the job. Not you being in denial, although that's incredibly funny."

"You're a real pal, you know that?"

"So I've been told. Do you have to leave the job?"

"Hell, no. They've got it all set up so I can keep the job without Secret Service protection."

"Wow. That's cool."

"They wanted him pretty badly. They knew what buttons to push."

"When's the big announcement?"

"Tomorrow. At the White House."

"Holy shit. Do you have to go?"

"Well, *yeah*. My husband is being tapped to be vice president of the United States. I think he sort of expects me to be there."

"Don't get all testy with me because you're feeling testy about that."

"I'm not *testy*."

He snorted with laughter and then seemed to regret the movement. "Don't make me laugh. Hurts."

"Don't say stupid shit, and I won't have to make you laugh."

"Most people who come to visit are nice to me."

"I'm not most people."

"No, you certainly aren't."

"Nelson's people are telling us the confirmation process could get ugly."

"How do you feel about that?"

"Exhausted and it hasn't even started yet. The scrutiny will be intense, and I haven't exactly led a quiet, low-key life."

He visibly bit his lip to keep from laughing, which made her smile.

"I'm really glad you didn't die on us, Gonzo. That would've truly sucked."

"Gee, thanks."

"I mean it, you know."

"I know. The doctors said another millimeter to the left, and I was a goner."

Sam shuddered at the thought of how close they'd come to losing him. "Too many close calls lately. I hope we haven't used up our quota of good luck in the last couple of weeks."

"We haven't. There's plenty left for your dad too."

"Let's hope so." She traded insults with him for another hour before Christina returned, and Sam left them to return to the surgical waiting room, hoping for an update on her dad.

"Nothing yet," Celia said when Sam walked in. Sam's stepmother was rigid with worry that made Sam even more nervous than she already was. Celia was a nurse, so if she was worried, the rest of them ought to be too. Right?

"Let's get some air," she said to Angela and Tracy. To Celia, Sam said, "We'll be back in a few."

"I'll be here."

The sisters took the elevator to the lobby and walked into the frigid late November chill.

"This is unbearable," Angela said for all of them.

"I need a smoke," Tracy said. "Anyone got one?"

Angela and Sam shook their heads.

"Why did we ever give up smoking?" Tracy asked. "Whose big idea was that?"

"Um, I think it was the surgeon general's," Angela replied.

"Well, it was a stupid idea."

"Extremely stupid," Sam said. She'd quit smoking years ago, and other than an occasional shared puff with her sisters, hadn't had one since and didn't miss it. Most of the time. Right now she had to agree with Tracy—a cigarette would be most welcome.

"He's going to be okay, isn't he?" Angela asked.

"I don't know," Tracy said. "I just don't know."

"I'm so glad we had such a nice Thanksgiving with him," Sam said. "No matter what happens today, he went in there knowing how much everyone loves him." Throughout the entire day at her house, members of the

MPD—past and present—had stopped by to say hello to Skip and wish him well with the surgery.

"I just wish it hadn't felt like a wake," Angela said.

"It was *not* a wake," Sam snapped at her sister and then instantly regretted it. "It wasn't a wake, Ang. It was a bunch of friends stopping by to say good luck. That's all."

"Sorry," Angela said softly. "I'm just really stressed out, and I know you guys are too."

Tracy hugged Angela and then reached for Sam.

"It's going to be okay," Sam said. "It has to be." The alternative was something she wasn't ready to confront and probably never would be.

THE DAY CREPT by slowly, so slowly Sam wondered if the clock was actually working backward.

Nick came straight from work to check on them, bringing four tall coffees that Sam, her sisters and stepmother accepted happily, grateful to have something to do for five minutes besides worry about what was taking so long.

They'd been told to expect the surgery to last about five hours and had been given an update after two hours. Now in hour seven, their nerves were beginning to shred.

Nick took Sam by the hand, put her coffee on a table and led her around the corner from the waiting room, where he put his arms around her.

She slid her hands inside his suit coat and held on. "This was exactly what I needed."

"I had a feeling."

Breathing in the scent of starch and cologne and Nick, Sam tried to let go of some of the tension. No matter what happened with her dad, she would find a way to cope with it, and Nick would be right there with her. That was the only thing she knew for certain today.

"Sam." One word from Tracy conveyed a world of meaning.

Holding Nick's hand, Sam followed her sister to the waiting room, determined to face whatever happened next with the grace and courage her father had instilled in her.

The neurosurgeon had waited until they were all there to give his report. "It went as well as we could've hoped, but it was a complicated surgery and we have no way to really know right now what to expect in the way of recovery."

"From the surgery or the paralysis?" Sam asked.

"Both."

"So he could still die?" Angela asked.

"He came through the surgery, which is part one. The rest is out of my hands."

"Thank you, doctor," Celia said. "We appreciate that you gave him a chance."

"We'll let you know when we've got him settled in a room."

Sam left her family to follow the doctor. "Doc, about the bullet."

"Yes, we've got it bagged as evidence. What would you like us to do with it?"

"I'll have someone come to pick it up shortly. I'd consider it a personal favor if you could make sure nothing happens to it until we're able to arrange for pickup."

"I'll keep it in my possession." He handed her his card. "Call me when you're ready."

"Thank you." He walked away, and Sam made the call to Agent Hill, who answered on the first ring. She told herself that didn't necessarily mean he'd been waiting for her call. "My dad is out of surgery."

"I'll be right over."

"Thank you."

Avery arrived a short time later and found them in the waiting room. As soon as Sam saw him, she called the doctor, who promised to be down shortly.

"Thanks for coming," Sam said to Avery.

"No problem. How is he?"

"He survived the surgery. We're told that's part one."

"Glad to hear it went well." To Nick he said, "Senator, I understand congratulations are in order."

"Thank you. I think."

Everyone laughed at Nick's reply, which was a much-needed relief from the tension.

The doctor came into the room a few minutes later with a plastic evidence bag containing the chunk of metal that had changed all their lives so profoundly three years ago. Sam eyed the bullet with barely restrained interest, but made no move to touch the bag. Chain of custody would matter at some point, and she wasn't about to do anything to mess up the most substantial clue they'd had yet in her dad's unsolved case.

"This is Special Agent-in-Charge Avery Hill with the FBI," Sam said to the doctor. "He'll be taking custody of the bullet."

"I have a couple of forms I need you to sign, Doc," Hill said.

"Of course."

Avery produced the forms, which the doctor signed, and then he handed the paperwork and the bag containing the bullet to Hill.

"I'll get this to the lab and put a rush on it," Hill said. "But it's apt to be a few weeks this time of year."

"I understand. Thanks again."

"Sure thing. Give your dad my best wishes."

"I will."

As he walked away, Sam put her faith in him—and the FBI crime lab—to hopefully get them the answers they'd waited three long years for.

"What now?" Nick asked as he put his arm around Sam.

"Now, we wait."

* * * * *

*Turn the page to read MR. VICE PRESIDENT,*
*a bonus story from New York Times*
*bestselling author Marie Force!*

# MR. VICE PRESIDENT

THE ALARM WENT OFF at six, but Sam pretended she couldn't hear it. She burrowed deeper under the covers, wishing for a magic wand that would transport her and Nick and Scotty to a deserted island where the three of them could have uninterrupted time together. Her husband's lips on her shoulder were a reminder that she had no such magic wand, and their plan for this day had nothing to do with deserted islands or time alone together. Today, he belonged to more than three hundred million other people.

The thought of that made her want to cry. And then his hands were cupping her breasts, letting her know that for now anyway, he was hers and hers alone. Sam turned over to face him.

His arms banded around her as his lips went to town on her neck, making her shiver with desire. The slide of his tongue, the scrape of his whiskers and the urgent press of his erection against her belly made her forget everything other than the exquisite pleasure she found in his arms.

Over the last four chaotic weeks, they'd clung to each other as a storm raged around them. President Nelson had received tremendous pushback from the Republicans for his choice of a vice president who was "too young and too inexperienced" to step in should the president die or become incapacitated.

The media had gone into full feeding-frenzy mode as

they examined the issue from all possible angles while dredging up every detail of Nick's life—and Sam's. She'd learned of women from his past whom she'd never heard of before, and had her first disastrous marriage paraded before the world while she tried to carry on with her work and help to care for her dad as he recovered from surgery, all the while pretending the storm wasn't happening.

In short, it had been a nightmare, compounded by the ongoing wait for results from the lab analyzing the bullet that had been removed from her dad's spine, which seemed to be taking forever.

Sam hadn't breathed a word to Nick about how awful the storm had been for her. She didn't have to. He was fully aware and terribly contrite. More than once he'd contemplated removing himself from consideration so they could get back the lives that had already been hectic and complicated before they became more so. But she'd refused to allow him to give up without seeing the fight through to the finish, whatever that finish turned out to be.

And then late last night the word had come from the White House: They had the votes. Nick had informed her that under the twenty-fifth amendment, a majority of the House and Senate had to vote in favor of the measure. The Senate had never been in question. Nick had endeared himself to colleagues on both sides of the aisle during his year in office, and seventy-five of the Senate's one hundred members had pledged their support of his nomination.

The House had been another matter altogether, controlled as it was by Republicans who refused to give the Democratic president an easy victory. It had been nothing short of a dogfight, managed by the White House and the president himself, who'd been resolute in his effort to win confirmation for his candidate.

Nick had tried to stay out of the fray as much as he could, but with cameras thrust in his face every five minutes and his phone ringing off the hook around the clock, it was all he could do to keep his head down and his mouth shut until the political machinations worked themselves out.

It had all come down to today. The nine o'clock vote would be the lame-duck Congress's final act before they broke for the holidays. Nick would be sworn in right after to cover the month until Inauguration Day, when he'd be sworn in again. They'd stayed up late making calls to ensure everyone who mattered to him would be in the chamber for his history-making moment when he would officially become the nation's second-youngest vice president.

Nick moved so he was on top of her, looking down at her with those eyes she loved so much. "I'm so sorry for putting you through this. If I'd had any idea, I never would've—"

Sam pulled him into a kiss that she hoped would clear his mind of every thought except for how much she loved him. She angled her hips and took him in without giving way on the kiss.

"Samantha… You have to let me apologize."

"I'd much rather you made love to me."

"I can do both," he said, as he pressed deeper into her. "You've told me before I'm an excellent multi-tasker."

That he could make her laugh as he made her burn was proof that he was indeed a master multi-tasker.

He kissed her softly as he moved in her and above her. "I love you even more than I did a month ago, if that's possible, and I'm so sorry for putting you through this."

"Mmm." Carried away by his sweet words as much as the aching tension that grew and multiplied with every thrust, Sam dug her fingers into his back, holding on as he began to move faster. "Love you too. So much. You have no idea."

"Yes," he whispered, his breath on her neck giving her goose bumps. "Yes, I do. I've felt it every day for a year."

In the ultimate irony, he'd be sworn in on the one-year anniversary of the day John O'Connor was murdered—the same day they'd reconnected. But Sam couldn't focus on anything but the incredible heat of her husband's body on top of hers, the rough abrasion of her nipples against his chest, the bite of his whiskers on her skin, the rush of love and desire that had her crying out when she reached the peak suddenly and almost without warning.

"Christ," he said as he went with her, pushing into her and then falling into her embrace.

Sam buried her fingers in his hair and held him tight to her chest, wanting him all to herself for one more minute. Just one more…

"We were loud," he said after a long moment of silence.

"He's still asleep."

"Or so you hope."

"Or so I hope. He's going to be scarred for life living with us."

"No, he won't. He'll see what true love is, and he'll know what to look for in his own life."

"You've still got a way with words, Senator." She took a bite of his shoulder because it was right there and it looked good to her. "What'll I call you now?"

He startled from the bite, which reminded her he was still lodged inside her, as if she could ever forget. "Um, how about Nick?"

"I was thinking Mr. Vice President or maybe just sir."

He raised his head off her chest and met her gaze, lifting a rakish brow. "*Sir?* Now that sounds intriguing."

Laughing, she said, "You'd better get off me and let me start the beauty program, unless you want a hag holding the Bible for you today. And P.S., if I'm going to have to do this Bible-holding business twice a year, I ought to get paid a special stipend."

"I just made a deposit."

Snorting with laughter, she pushed at his shoulders until he relented, withdrew from her and let her up. With a glance over her shoulder, she noticed he was still as hard as he'd been before they made love. "You ought to do something about that before you get tagged as the randy VP or something equally unsavory."

He looked at her with intent and purpose as he came after her. In the shower he enticed her into helping him solve the "problem."

THEY GOT SCOTTY up and pointed him in the direction of his "work" clothes, which was what he called the navy blazer, khaki pants, dress shirts, ties and boat shoes they'd bought him to wear when he accompanied Nick on the stump during his reelection campaign.

Sam had bought a new red suit for the occasion, and she'd made sure this time that her substantial cleavage was well covered, unlike the day Nick was sworn in to finish out the last year of John O'Connor's term and she'd worried about flashing the chief justice with her sexier-than-intended outfit.

Today she was all about being conservative. She wrapped her hair up in an elegant twist, which she secured with several small clips. Next, she fastened the diamond key necklace Nick had given her as a wedding gift. Checking the full-length mirror behind the bedroom door, she decided she wouldn't embarrass him on national television.

He came into the room fully dressed except for the suit coat he'd left on the foot of the bed when he went down to get coffee for both of them. "Wowza," he said when he took in her outfit. "Hot, hot, *hot*."

"Not too hot, right?"

He put the mugs on the bedside table and went to her. "No such thing, but if I had my wish, the hair would be down."

"Really? It'll look awful on TV."

"No," he said, releasing the clips she'd strategically placed, "it won't." Her hair fell down around her shoulders and he nodded with approval. "Perfect."

"I'll let you get away with that, but only because it's your big day and you get anything you want."

Once again he raised that rakish brow. "*Anything?*"

"You've already gotten that—twice—and made us late in the process."

"We're not late. We're right on schedule, and *anything* presents a wide variety of options for our private celebration later."

"Don't you ever get enough?"

"Never." He laid his lips on hers and dug his fingers into her hips, tugging her closer as he kissed her.

"Oh my God, you guys," Scotty said as he came to the doorway and covered his eyes. "There's a child in the house."

They broke apart, laughing at the disgust they heard in their newly minted teenager's tone. He'd turned thirteen four days before Nick turned thirty-seven, and their combined birthday celebration had given them something to focus on while the media storm swirled around them.

"That 'child' is a teenager now, and he needs to grow up and knock on the door," Nick said.

"The door was open. There ought to be rules!"

"Speaking of rules, did you brush your teeth?" Sam asked him.

"I'm going to do it because I forgot to, but don't start that again. I'll be right back."

"How does he forget to brush his teeth?" Sam asked. "That's so gross."

"He's thirteen. He can't help it. Gross is in his DNA."

"Is it a circus outside?" she asked with trepidation as she pictured a street lined with satellite trucks and cameras trying to catch a glimpse of them leaving for the capitol.

"The Secret Service is handling it."

"My dad would like to see us before we go. How do we do that?"

"I figured you'd want to stop by there, so I've got a plan. Are you ready?"

Sam downed the last of the coffee he'd brought her. "As ready as I'll ever be."

NICK RELIED ON the help of several of the Secret Service agents who'd been assigned to his detail to exit their townhouse through the back door and head to Skip's via the alley they shared behind the houses. He ushered Sam and Scotty in ahead of him.

Celia, who was reading the paper at the table, looked up with surprise when they came in. "Oh, don't you all look so nice! I want a picture!"

Though they were short on time, they removed their

coats and posed for Celia. "I'm so excited. I can't believe this is happening in our family."

"Neither can we," Sam said dryly, making the others laugh. "Is Dad awake?"

"He is. He's watching the news, so go on in." They'd managed to bring Skip home after his surgery with the help of round-the-clock nurses who were assisting Celia as he recovered.

"What's this I see?" Skip asked as they went into his bedroom in what had once been the dining room. "Could it be our nation's second family? You're all they're talking about this morning, Nick. Or should I say, Mr. Vice President?"

"Nick is fine."

The right side of Skip's face lifted into a big smile. Sam couldn't deny that the surgery had left him diminished. He seemed smaller and grayer and older in the aftermath. She told herself he'd rebound the way he had before, after the initial injury, but she also wondered how much trauma one body could take before it ran out of gas altogether. Worst of all, he was in pain. Nerves that had been dormant for three long years while compressed by the bullet were coming alive again. Not enough to allow him to move the way he once had. No, just enough to cause him relentless pain in his extremities.

Doctors told them the pain should be temporary, but they really weren't sure as his case was somewhat unprecedented. Despite the pain, Sam saw some of his old sparkle as he took in his son-in-law, who would soon be sworn in as vice president.

"We're so proud of you, Nick," Skip said. "I sure hope you know how much I'd love to be there."

"I do know," Nick said as he squeezed Skip's right

hand out of habit. "Of course I know." Nick stepped aside so Sam could lean over the bed and kiss her dad.

"Take lots of pictures for me," Skip said to Scotty.

"I will. I'll come show them to you when we get home."

"I'll be waiting—and watching."

"We'd better get going," Nick said. "The vote is at nine. I think they sort of expect me to be there."

"Thanks for stopping by on the way out. Means a lot to me."

"We'll see you later, Skippy," Sam said as she left him with a smile. "Thank you for that," she said to Nick after they said goodbye to Celia and headed for the front door to meet the Secret Service.

"That was for me as much as it was for you," Nick said. "I love him too."

While they waited for the agents to get the black SUV in position, Sam curled her hands around Nick's arm and rested her head on his shoulder. This was a big day—a very, *very* big day. But at the end of that very big day, she'd get to sleep in his arms. She could endure whatever else came her way as long as she had that reward to look forward to.

IN THE END, the vote went as expected—seventy-five to twenty-five in the Senate and two-twenty to two-fifteen in the House, which was actually one vote more than they'd expected from the lower chamber. Nick would've preferred a more resounding mandate, but he was realistic enough to know that wasn't going to happen in the hotly charged political environment in which they worked. The simple majority was enough, and they had that.

It took an hour after the vote for the Speaker of the House of Representatives to convene a joint session of

Congress for the validation of the votes and the swearing in ceremony.

"Congratulations," President Nelson said as they waited for the signal to take the stage.

Nick shook the president's hand. "Thank you, sir, for your faith in me and for going to bat on my behalf these last few weeks. I appreciate it."

"What's a little political warfare between friends?" Nelson said with a lighthearted smile that belied the ground war he'd waged to get the vice president he wanted. "I hope you know the reason the GOP leadership fought this as hard as they did is because they know their job four years from now just got a lot more complicated. You shouldn't take it personally."

"I understand. Even though I've only held office for a year, I've been in this business a long time, so I know it's not personal. Well, most of the time it isn't. I heard from a friend who works for Stenhouse that the RNC went into full meltdown mode when they heard you'd chosen me."

"I bet they did," Nelson said with a laugh. "And that's why we fought so hard to make it happen. They're petrified of you. You're that rare politician who comes to the game with a clean slate. No baggage of any kind, and believe me, they looked for it in the last four weeks. You scare the living hell out of them, and that's why we love you so much."

When Speaker of the House Richard Claiborne convened the joint session, Nick, Sam and Scotty joined the president on the stage below the speaker's seat. Claiborne went through the motions of announcing the vote taken under the auspices of the twenty-fifth amendment to the Constitution. He noted that under the law of the Com-

monwealth of Virginia, Nick had offered his resignation
from the Senate to Governor Zorn.

"The chair requests that the chief justice of the United
States administer the oath of office to the vice president,"
Claiborne concluded.

With Sam and Scotty holding the O'Connor family
Bible and President Nelson standing next to Nick, Chief
Justice Byron Riley said, "Raise your right hand, Mr.
Cappuano, place your left hand on the Bible and repeat
after me. I, Nicholas Cappuano, do solemnly swear that
I will support and defend the Constitution of the United
States against all enemies, foreign and domestic; that I
will bear true faith and allegiance to the same; that I take
this obligation freely, without any mental reservation or
purpose of evasion; and that I will well and faithfully
discharge the duties of the office on which I am about to
enter: So help me God."

With a growing sense of the surreal, Nick repeated Riley's words and became the nation's forty-ninth vice president. A roar of applause from the joint session drowned
out the congratulations offered by the president and chief
justice.

The roar got louder when Nick kissed Sam and hugged
Scotty and then faced the joint session of Congress as
well as his invited guests as they applauded and cheered.
For him. For Nick Cappuano from Lowell, Massachu-
setts, who was now the vice president of the United
States. He looked up to the gallery, where Graham and
Laine O'Connor were cheering him on.

Graham caught Nick's eye and pumped his fist in support. On what was an otherwise sad and tragic day for
their family, Nick had given them something to celebrate.
Also on their feet in the gallery were Nick's father and

stepmother, Sam's sisters, their spouses and children, Shelby, Freddie, Elin, Christina, Gonzo, Terry, Lindsey, Derek, Andy, Harry and the rest of Nick and Sam's friends and colleagues.

When the applause finally began to die down, he released his tight hold on Sam's hand and waited until she and Scotty and the president had taken seats that had been arranged for them off to the side of the podium.

Speaker of the House Claiborne said, "Mr. President, members of the Congress and distinguished guests, I present to you the vice president of the United States."

During another round of resounding applause, Nick stepped up to the microphone and waited until a hush fell over the crowded room. Here he was, standing in the very spot where the president delivered the annual State of the Union address. Speaking of surreal…

"Mr. President, Mr. Speaker, Mr. Chief Justice, Mr. President Pro Tempore, members of Congress and friends, today we have seen our constitution in action, and it is a proud day for me and my family as well as all of America as we once again show the world why we are the greatest nation on earth."

During another deafening round of applause, Nick tried to forget how the eyes of the nation—and the world—were on him. "And P.S., Mr. Chief Justice, we really need to stop meeting this way."

That set off an uproar of laughter and more applause.

"Thank you for administering today's oath as well as the one last year. To the other justices, thank you for honoring me with your presence here today. To my former colleagues in the Congress, whether you voted for or against my appointment, whether you are a Democrat or a Republican, today we are all Americans, and our nation and our government continues on the path that was set by our founding fathers more than two hundred thirty years ago. Mr. President, please accept my profound thanks and appreciation for the trust you have placed in me. I am humbled by your kindness and hope to emulate the example of leadership you've set for our country.

"I'd be remiss if I didn't take a moment to honor the incredible contributions of my predecessor, Vice President Joe Gooding. I'd be hard-pressed to find a better example of the term 'public servant' than Vice President Gooding, who has faithfully served the people of Michigan and the people of America for more than forty years. Mr. Vice President, we wish you and your family Godspeed at this difficult time, and we'll keep you in our thoughts and prayers."

Everyone stood to applaud for Gooding, as Nick had hoped they would.

When the applause finally died down again, Nick continued. "I'd also be remiss if I didn't say publicly how lucky I am to have married so well."

The thunderous applause that greeted his statement indicated his colleagues agreed. How could they not? Look at her. She was stunning, and judging by the tight smile she directed his way, she was also fuming. He'd pay for the comment later, which was fine with him.

"Samantha, thank you for your unwavering support over the last year and for taking this incredible journey with me. To our son, Scotty, you made our family complete, and you bring us joy every day. And yes, you have to make up what you missed at school today."

More laughter and applause followed for Scotty, who beamed with pleasure at all the attention.

"I'd also like to note that this is not the first time my

life was permanently changed on this date. A year ago, we lost Senator John O'Connor, who was my best friend and boss."

A respectable round of applause was offered for John, which Nick appreciated.

"I never lose sight of the many ways in which John's death changed my life as well as the lives of his family and friends. We miss him, and we think of him every day as we move forward without him and try to make him proud with everything we do. I owe a debt of gratitude to John's parents, Senator and Mrs. O'Connor, who made me a part of their family from the first time I met them as a college freshman when John took me home to the farm and showed me the true meaning of family.

"A few weekends at Graham O'Connor's dinner table changed my life plan from finance to politics, and I've never looked back. As your vice president, I vow to continue to fight for American families, to assist President Nelson in any way I can and to be a voice for people who are still struggling to realize their American dreams. Thank you for your support, and let's join together to continue working to make this the greatest country in the history of the world."

During the standing ovation that followed his remarks, Sam joined him and put her arm around him, leaning into his embrace as they acknowledged the applause.

"I'm going to kill you," she said, her smile never wavering.

The roar of the crowd drowned out his laughter. "Bring it on, babe. I can't wait."

*Keep reading for a Fatal Series Q&A with Marie!*

# FATAL SERIES Q&A

**How many more books can we expect in the Fatal Series?**

As long as you continue to tell me you're enjoying Sam and Nick's story, I'll continue to write the series.

**Will Sam ever have a baby of her own?**

I don't know yet. If and that's a very big IF at this point, she does get pregnant again, I expect a pregnancy and baby would significantly change her life, and thus change the dynamic of the series. So I'm holding off—for now. That doesn't mean never. It just means not any time soon.

**Will Sam & Nick adopt again?**

We'll have to wait and see what life has in store for them.

**What is up with that pesky Agent Hill? He makes our wonderful Nick so mad, so why does he keep coming around?**

Because it's FUN to make Nick into a jealous fool! Let me be clear on one thing—there will never, ever, *EVER* be infidelity in Sam & Nick's marriage. I'm not interested in writing that, nor do I wish to destroy a relationship I've spent years developing. No one is going to cheat. **Read that again:** *No cheating.* However, a perfect relationship is a boring relationship, thus the need for characters and situations that allow Sam and Nick to grow as individuals and as a couple. One of my favorite lines in the entire series is when Sam tells Nick to resist the urge to lift his leg and pee on her when Hill is around. Without Hill, she never gets to say that. So let me have my fun, and don't worry about cheating. Are we good now?

**Who shot Skip?**

I still don't know, but won't it be awesome when Sam and I finally figure that out?

**Did you really just make Nick the vice president?**

I know, right?! Funny story about that too—I was about ten days from finishing *Fatal Jeopardy* and was out to lunch with my dad and husband. I told them what was happening in the book, about the White House seeming to leak the fact that Nick had been asked and putting some pressure on him to cede to Nelson's wishes. So my dad asks me, "Is he going to become the VP?" I said, "I don't know yet." To which my husband said, "Isn't the book due in two weeks? Shouldn't you know that by now?" Me: "That's just how I roll. Seat-o-the-pants, baby!" See? Sam and I have a lot in common! I was on the fence right up until the end of the book about which way it was going to go. Of course I look forward to hearing what you all think of Nick's promotion and whether he and Sam can really make it work...

Much more to come from Washington, D.C.! Thanks for taking this wild ride with me, Sam and Nick. If you have other questions, please contact me at marie@marie-force.com or pose them to the Fatal Series Reader Group <https://www.facebook.com/groups/FatalSeries/>. No spoilers in the main group please. Spoil to your heart's content in the Fatal Jeopardy Reader Group (AFTER you finish the book) and dish on the details: https://www.facebook.com/groups/FatalJeopardy/. Please make sure you join my newsletter mailing list at http://marieforce.com for regular updates about new books and other news!

# ACKNOWLEDGMENTS

A VERY SPECIAL thank you to Capt. Russ Hayes of the Newport, RI, Police Department who provided extra help with this book, including two hours of coffee shop time, which helped to jumpstart the story. I appreciate Russ's attention to detail and the finer points of police work he so willingly shares with me.

Thank you to everyone on "Jack's" team: Julie Cupp, Lisa Cafferty, Holly Sullivan, Isabel Sullivan, Nikki Colquhoun and Cheryl Serra. Years ago I had a vision of someday working with most of my favorite ladies. Now that vision is my daily reality, and I couldn't be happier. To my spectacular beta readers, Ronlyn Howe, Kara Conrad and Anne Woodall, thank you so much for all you do to help me out—usually at a moment's notice! My appreciation goes to Sarah Spate Morrison, Family Nurse Practitioner, who helps with the medical details.

Thanks to my editor Alissa Davis as well as Carina Press Editorial Director Angela James and everyone at Harlequin for their hard work on behalf of the Fatal Series. My wonderful agent Kevan Lyon is a fabulous partner on this journey, and I'm appreciative of her many contributions.

The most special thanks of all go to the readers who have embraced Sam and Nick's story from the start and to those who have joined the party along the way. Thanks to all of you, *Fatal Jeopardy* was a *New York Times* best-seller. I'm very grateful to all of you!

To discuss the Fatal Series with other avid readers, join the Fatal Series Reader Group on Facebook at www.facebook.com/groups/FatalSeries/. To dish about the details in Fatal Jeopardy, with spoilers allowed and encouraged, join the Fatal Jeopardy Reader Group at www.facebook.com/groups/FatalJeopardy/. I love to hear from readers! You can contact me at marie@marieforce.com. Thanks for reading!

xoxo

*Marie*

SPECIAL EXCERPT FROM

Read on for a sneak preview of
*FATAL SCANDAL:*
*BOOK EIGHT OF THE FATAL SERIES*
by New York Times *bestselling author*

# MARIE FORCE

The dual scandal ripped through the city with the power of a tsunami, flooding the airwaves with headlines that struck fear in Sam's heart. "Springer Alleges Farnsworth's Incompetence Caused Son's Death" and "Detective 'In Bed' with Judge on Custody Matter."

Sitting in front of the TV in the master bedroom, Sam hung on every word that was being said about her beloved chief of police, the man she'd known first as Uncle Joe. And her close friend, Detective Tommy "Gonzo" Gonzales, who'd been shot during the Springer investigation shortly after he'd been granted full and permanent custody of his young son Alex.

"Springer alleges that Farnsworth personally ordered the homicide investigation into the stabbing deaths of his younger son Hugo and eight of Hugo's friends be put on hold to allow for the conclusion of a six-month undercover narcotics investigation that had focused on Billy Springer and his associates." The talking head on CBC seemed to be taking great pleasure in reporting on the events that had led to Billy Springer's death at the hands of a Metro PD SWAT team.

CARMFEXP00273

"Are they going to mention how he shot at us?" Sam asked the TV. "Of course not. That won't be brought up."

"The department faces the secondary scandal surrounding Detective Sergeant Thomas Gonzales, who was shot in the neck by Springer during the confrontation at Springer's grandmother's house in Friendship Heights."

"Thank you!" Sam said. "Finally! Thanks for remembering Springer actually shot one of our people!"

"Gonzales's custody case was heard in the courtroom of Family Court Judge Leon Morton, the brother of Eva Morton, whose homicide case was investigated by none other than newly promoted Detective Thomas Gonzales. Neither the judge nor the detective disclosed their earlier connection, which is a conflict of interest, according to the attorney for the baby's mother, Lori Phillips."

"Oh my God, Gonzo," Sam whispered. She couldn't even think about what it would mean to Gonzo if he lost custody of the son he adored. "What a fucked-up mess."

*Don't miss*
***FATAL SCANDAL:***
***BOOK EIGHT OF THE FATAL SERIES***
*by Marie Force, available in print January 2016!*

www.CarinaPress.com

Copyright © 2015 by HTJB, Inc.

CARMFEXP00273

Fast-paced political ingrigue, gritty suspense and a romance that makes headlines.

**The Fatal Series** by *New York Times* bestselling author

# MARIE FORCE

Over one million books sold!

Add to your *Fatal Series* collection,
read exclusive online content and learn more at
TheFatalSeries.com

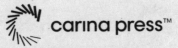

www.CarinaPress.com

CARMFFS2015

# MARIE FORCE

| | | | |
|---|---|---|---|
| 00257 | FATAL AFFAIR:<br>BOOK ONE OF THE FATAL SERIES | ___$5.99 U.S. | ___$6.99 CAN. |
| 00258 | FATAL JUSTICE:<br>BOOK TWO OF THE FATAL SERIES | ___$5.99 U.S. | ___$6.99 CAN. |
| 00259 | FATAL CONSEQUENCES:<br>BOOK THREE OF THE FATAL SERIES | ___$5.99 U.S. | ___$6.99 CAN. |
| 00269 | FATAL FLAW:<br>BOOK FOUR OF THE FATAL SERIES | ___$5.99 U.S. | ___$6.99 CAN. |
| 00270 | FATAL DECEPTION:<br>BOOK FIVE OF THE FATAL SERIES | ___$6.99 U.S. | ___$7.99 CAN. |
| 00271 | FATAL MISTAKE:<br>BOOK SIX OF THE FATAL SERIES | ___$6.99 U.S. | ___$7.99 CAN. |

*(limited quantities available)*

| | |
|---|---|
| TOTAL AMOUNT | $ _____ |
| POSTAGE & HANDLING | $ _____ |
| ($1.00 for 1 book, 50¢ for each additional) | |
| APPLICABLE TAXES* | $ _____ |
| TOTAL PAYABLE | $ _____ |

*(check or money order—please do not send cash)*

To order, complete this form and send it, along with a check or money order for the total amount, payable to Carina Press, to: **In the U.S.:** 3010 Walden Avenue, P.O. Box 9077, Buffalo, NY 14269-9077; **In Canada:** P.O. Box 636, Fort Erie, Ontario, L2A 5X3.

Name: _____

Address: _____ City: _____

State/Prov.: _____ Zip/Postal Code: _____

Account Number (if applicable): _____

075 CSAS

*New York residents remit applicable sales taxes.
*Canadian residents remit applicable GST and provincial taxes.

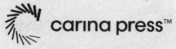

carina press™

www.CarinaPress.com

CARMF00272BL